Watch for the Morning

BY ELISABETH MACDONALD

Watch for the Morning

The House at Gray Eagle

Watch for the Morning

🙎 ELISABETH MACDONALD 🙎

CHARLES SCRIBNER'S SONS / New York

Library of Congress Cataloging in Publication Data

Macdonald, Elisabeth, 1926–
  Watch for the morning.

  I. Title.
PZ4.M134614Wat [PS3563.A2767] 813'.5'4 77-13662
ISBN 0-684-15358-0

1 3 5 7 9 11 13 15 17 19 V/C 20 18 16 14 12 10 8 6 4 2

PRINTED IN THE UNITED STATES OF AMERICA

ACKNOWLEDGMENTS

The author's gratitude to those who, in many different ways,
helped with the making of this book:

A. Karl Larson, historian, teacher, and cherished friend
Elnora King, unflagging critic, unfailing friend
L. G. Macdonald
Mary and G. D. Macdonald
Verlynn Bradshaw
Ruth McLeod
And, of course, Patricia Myrer

For my mother and father,

IN LOVING MEMORY

*I wait for the Lord, my soul doth wait, and in his word
I do hope. My soul waiteth for the Lord more than they
that watch for the morning.*

Psalm 130:5–6

Watch for the Morning

Kate

Favour is deceitful and beauty is vain; but a woman that feareth the Lord, she shall be praised. Give her of the fruit of her hands; and let her own works praise her in the gates.

Proverbs 31:30–31

Chapter 1

The chatter of the kitchen servants ceased abruptly as the stairway door was flung open. Mistress Fitzhugh stood there, her ample bosom heaving from exertion. She so seldom came below stairs that they stared in frightened astonishment, immediately sensing trouble for one of their number. Her pale face mottled with rage, she advanced into the kitchen and bore down upon Kate, the scullery maid.

"You sneaky little bitch!" All Mistress Fitzhugh's pretensions to gentility vanished as her furious shriek rang through the cavernous, smoke-stained dungeon that was the Fitzhugh kitchen. The odors of a hundred years' meals clung to its walls, augmented now by a pot of mutton bubbling on the stove, filling the room with a scent reminiscent of the source of the meat. Candles on the rough, food-stained table flickered fitfully in the dank heat from the massive iron stove.

Past experience had taught her that the mistress was not above striking the help, and Kate shrank back against the wall, wondering what had aroused the lady's ire. Perhaps it would blow over like most of her tempers. If not . . . and Kate was suddenly filled with dread at the possible consequences. All she had in the world was her position as a maid. No funds, and no friends, only those other servants cowering now in the back of the room, their faces carefully blank. Not one of them would dare defend her, or they would all find themselves penniless on the streets of Liverpool.

Then she understood. Bridget had told, for she stood on the stairs behind Mistress Fitzhugh, ferret eyes gleaming in her fat face. Kate knew the mistress meant to make an example of her so that no one else would dare defy her tyranny. Almost sick with anger at the informer who had brought her to this dire situation, Kate stared back at Bridget, knowing she had learned a lesson for all her life. Never again would she confide in anyone, never again share her joy, even though it filled her to the bursting point. The need to share that joy had been so great it had poured forth this morning as she and Bridget worked in the pantry. Why had she never guessed that Bridget hated her? Didn't Bridget know she would gain nothing in this effort to curry favor with Mistress Fitzhugh, for that lady could turn on her as quickly and for less reason?

"The Church of England is the religion of this household," the mistress's harsh voice continued, her pug-dog face gleaming in the hot light of the candles. "I'll have no blasphemers here. And to think of all I've done for you . . . hired you with no letter . . . a mill hand's daughter with no training . . . let you learn the duties of a maid at my expense . . ." She paused long enough to remove a scented kerchief from her bosom and mop her damp face. "You were always arrogant, Kate. Your father was a fool to starve himself to send you to school. Learning only made you think you're above yourself. How dare you defy my rules . . . sneak out at night to attend meetings or God knows what. You . . . you . . ."

"Bitch." Bridget mouthed the word behind her mistress's back, grinning at Kate, all her jealousy vindicated.

"If I could have my wage . . ." Kate began timidly, staying well out of arm's reach. She was shamed and sickened by the scene, and the smell of boiling mutton made her stomach lurch.

"You'll get no wage from me." Mistress Fitzhugh's lips parted in a snarl. "And no letter, you may be sure of that. Now get out of my house!" A fat, bejeweled finger pointed toward the door, and the butler moved to unbolt it.

With bitter certainty, Kate knew what lay beyond that door. The dirty streets of Liverpool in 1850, swarming with beggars and thieves, harlots and the starving poor. At seventeen, with no money and no family, to step beyond that door meant descent into a nightmare. "Please." Her voice took on an edge of desperation. "I have no money . . . nowhere to go . . ."

"You should have thought of that," Mistress Fitzhugh sneered. "Leave this house now . . . this instant!" and she advanced on Kate.

KATE

The butler opened the door, sympathy and fear warring in his averted eyes. A blast of cold autumn air came through the stifling kitchen and Kate shivered, moving quickly to avoid the mistress's blow.

"Go with those infidel Mormons and be damned!" Mistress Fitzhugh shouted, and the oaken door slammed shut.

Cold drizzle stained the streets, the foul weather turning afternoon quickly into evening. For a moment Kate stood uncertainly in the courtyard. A glimpse of the groom grinning at her from the shelter of the stables made her shudder and move toward the streets of the city. Hugging her thin shawl about her slender shoulders she moved slowly in spite of the dampness. Tears welled in her eyes and her mouth trembled. Droplets of mist gathered on the dark brown hair dressed in a neat pompadour knot. In all the cold and dismal city before her there seemed no place to turn. If her poor mill hand father had given her nothing else he had given her pride. Mistress Fitzhugh had another name for it . . . arrogance. By either name it would not add to the lone halfpenny in her pocket. Yesterday the world had seemed to open before her like a flower opening to spring sunlight. She had been baptized and confirmed a member of the Church of Jesus Christ of Latter Day Saints, the Mormons, a word Mistress Fitzhugh used as an epithet. The spirit had seemed to soar out of her as Elder Hamilton lifted her from the water and smiled into her eyes. In this moment of despair, that glorious event seemed part of a lovely dream. Only a month now she had been attending the Mormon meetings, and she did not know any of the members well, except her mentor, Elder Hamilton. If only the Mormons had a church she knew she could go there, but they were too poor a congregation and met in the homes of members. Of course! Brother Spencer's house on Charles Street! Immediately her head lifted, her eyes glowing with hope. It was a long walk, but if she hurried she could be there before dark. Perhaps they would direct her to Elder Hamilton, for she had no idea where his lodgings were located. "Please, God," she whispered and hurried, almost running down the gloomy street.

The door where she had first been welcomed to the Mormon Church was closed and locked. No lights gleamed inside Brother Spencer's shabby house. Someone had to be there! They had to!

"Brother Spencer," she called, pounding desperately at the unresponsive door. "Please, God . . . let them hear me . . . let someone be home!" Tears poured down her icy face. Her hands, stiff with cold, ached from beating at the door. Sobbing, she stumbled down the stone steps and looked about at the unfamiliar neighborhood. A lamplighter made his plodding way along, and gas lamps flared in the growing darkness. The drizzle had turned into a steady, freezing rain. Even the beggars who inhabited all Liverpool's streets had disappeared into whatever shelter they could find.

Shivering with cold and fear, Kate huddled in a wide doorway down the street. Surely the Spencers would return soon. She had no choice but to stay and watch for them.

"What's yer price?" A burly seaman peered at her in the dim light of the street lamps.

"God! Help me!" she cried out, shrinking back from the huge hands reaching for her. Taken aback, the seaman dropped his arms and stared in astonishment. Then he shrugged his massive shoulders and walked on down the street. Within half a block he had found the harlot he sought.

Sick with revulsion and despair, Kate slid down in the doorway, bent her head on her knees, and wept. Had God deserted her so quickly? Was this all that was left to her . . . to join the nameless, faceless creatures who sold their bodies to survive? Maybe Elder Hamilton had been wrong in urging her to join his Church, she thought, overwhelmed by an anguished sense of loss. Maybe she had not been chosen to live the Gospel after all. He had proudly said the Mormons would suffer for their beliefs, but they would prevail at last through all the earth and Heaven. She had only half understood his meaning, never guessing that she would immediately pay a price for her new religion. How could it end this way, when she had believed with all her heart that God, in His goodness, had guided her to Burns Hamilton.

That day, a month ago, wan September sunlight lay on the dirty streets and grimy buildings. The package containing her lady's fine silk gloves clutched to her, Kate had walked slowly, reluctant to return to the household where she was not even allowed to weep. The message had come that morning from Bolton: Papa was dead and buried. Mistress Fitzhugh allowed no time for grieving. Ignoring Kate's tear-stained face, she had sent her on an errand to the glover's, something she often did, taking advantage of Kate's ability to read and write. Grief was a great sore spot, aching somewhere inside Kate, but her eyes were at last burned dry of tears. The dearest being in her life lay dead, worn and old before his time by the unending poverty and the years of grinding labor in the mills.

"I'm really alone now," she said to herself . . . said it aloud, walking down the soot-stained streets of Liverpool. A ragged beggar stared at her.

Her brothers and her sister, Charity, so much older than she, were scattered to the mills and mines as though they had never been a family. The youngest by many years, Kate had been her father's darling. Mama, dead since Kate was three, had been "queer" after Kate's birth, a strange, alien creature she never really knew.

Papa's pride in his youngest child had been the bright spot in his work-burdened life. Even while he coughed himself toward death and dragged through the long hours at the mill, he had refused to let Kate work there. She was a lady, he told her, as good as any of the gentry, and made her believe it. When he scraped together the few farthings to send her to school, she found reason to rebel against the life she had been born into. The world opened to her by books beckoned with vistas glorious beyond dreaming. There was a life where one was never cold and one's stomach never ached with hunger. Two years ago, when Papa was once more out of work, she knew the time had come for her to help. Dressed in her shabby Sunday best, she presented herself at the mansion of the rich merchant Fitzhugh and found herself fortunate to arrive on a day the housekeeper needed a new scullery maid. Delighted that his daughter had risen in the world and found herself a safe place of employment, Papa had gone off to Bolton and now would never return.

Alone, she thought now, and the sense of desolation left her so chilled she might have stood naked in the street.

"Penny, Miss?" A pitiful child beggar, grimy and stinking, held out a hand.

"I have nothing," she said. The hard-eyed child shrugged and turned away.

Watching him, Kate lifted her chin and drew her mouth tight. Immediately she remembered how Mistress Fitzhugh disliked that posture. Well, at least she had the Fitzhugh roof to go to and food and clothing. But tears pricked at her eyes once more. A roof was all, no one who loved or cared. The tears were not for her dead father, but for herself. The future seemed gray and empty, consisting only of the cold, bare attic she shared with the other maids, Mistress Fitzhugh's continual scolding, and the footman pinching her each time she passed him. Life took on the aspect of a nightmare in which one runs and runs, yet never progresses.

Nearing a public square, she saw a young man addressing a group of people, many of whom were obviously heckling him. The speaker answered his tormentors with dignity and composure. A motley crowd, they were mainly the poverty-stricken with coarse, ill-fitting clothes, their pale faces meek and resigned. Among them moved the hideous beggars with which Liverpool abounded. Curious, her painful thoughts pushed aside, Kate paused at the edge of the crowd to watch, attracted by the young man's bearing and his handsome face. He was fine-looking, tall, deep-chested, and broad-shouldered, his brown hair thick and neat. Beneath the luxuriant, dark brown moustache his mouth was firm and strong.

"What proof do you Mormons have that people should be baptized by dunking?" a heckler shouted.

"Christ himself was baptized by immersion," the young man replied, his brown eyes blazing. "Only the pagan Church of Rome introduced the sprinkling of babes to baptize."

"Do you believe an infant who dies before baptism is damned?" a woman near the front asked tremulously.

"Madam," the speaker said kindly, leaning toward the sad-eyed woman. "A babe who dies in its innocence will be raised up into the glory of God and His Kingdom."

The woman began to weep, and Kate felt sudden tears hot on her own face. Bending toward the weeping mother, the young man spoke softly and handed her a tract from the package bulging his coat pocket.

Scarcely aware of what she was doing, Kate pushed forward in the crowd until she stood near the speaker. Her tear-stained face lifted toward him, she longed to reach out and ask comfort for her own bereavement, longed to touch the weeping woman and share their grief. The pale sunlight seemed brighter when it touched the young man's face, as though the glow was intensified by the radiant faith within. She had overheard talk about this new religion at the Fitzhughs'. Rumor had it that all Mormons were dreadful, scurrilous creatures, of the lowest class. Yet here stood a young man of commanding presence, obvious intelligence, and kindness. Forgetting she was due at the Fitzhughs', she stood caught in the golden net of his words.

"I am Elder Burns Hamilton," he told his audience. "Born and raised in Wiltshire, where the Gospel of Jesus Christ was brought to me by Franklin Richards, an Apostle of God in the Church of the Latter Day Saints. I bear you my testimony that this Gospel is the true Church returned to earth through God's Prophet Joseph Smith."

I bear you my testimony . . . the words rang like church bells in Kate's head. Grief forgotten, she listened spellbound, for Elder Hamilton was a fiery and persuasive speaker. He told the story of God's visits to Joseph Smith the American Prophet, of the translation of the Book of Mormon, and of the restoration of the true priesthood. Then he spoke at length of the persecutions the Saints had endured in Illinois, Missouri, and Ohio, of their hazardous trek across the American prairies to the valley of the Great Salt Lake; of the new Zion being built there in the valleys of the mountains, where one day in the fullness of time, Christ would reign in His glory. While the Elder spoke, there were no interruptions, for he held his listeners. At the end he began passing out his tracts, and Kate, half-mesmerized, moved forward to take one. The young Elder's hand touched hers as he handed her the paper, their eyes met, and it seemed her very soul flew from her.

"There will be a meeting at the home of Brother Spencer on Charles Street tomorrow night," Elder Hamilton said. "Will you come if I give you directions?"

"Yes," she answered breathlessly, not knowing how she would get away from the Fitzhugh mansion, but certain that nothing on earth could keep her from that meeting.

The other maids thought she was sneaking out at night to meet a man. It made a common bond among them, and they snickered coarsely when they let her in the back door. In a way they were right, for it was the man who drew her to the meetings where she sat in silent adoration of his fiery faith. He offered a religion with a clear path laid out to glory in the Hereafter. Along with guidance into Heaven, the Mormon faith also offered hope for a better life here on earth, an escape from poverty, and a new beginning for all the poor and dispossessed. His God was a loving Father, in her mind much like the one she had just lost. Peace and comfort would be hers if she embraced this Gospel.

She had scarcely heard Elder Hamilton's admonitions that God would surely try the faith of the Saints, that the road to Eternity was rocky, strewn with temptations and trials.

Now, huddled in this doorway, homeless and penniless, it seemed she should have heard those words, for within a day her new faith had cost her what little security she had in the world, her position at the Fitzhughs'.

Where could she go now, except to the hell that was the streets of Liverpool? Fresh tears dampened the icy hands covering her face. At the sound of footsteps she cringed back into the doorway. Another man would come and, unlike the sailor, refuse to be rejected. "Dear God," she whispered into her wet palms, "help me. Be with me now and I will serve You all my life."

"Sister Kate?"

Lifting her tear-wet face, she looked into Burns Hamilton's inquiring eyes. In that moment she had her testimony. God loved her. She was of His true Church and He would forever guard her from harm.

"What are you doing here?" he asked, regarding her with a puzzled frown. Taking her hands he lifted her up from the filthy doorway. Without quite knowing how it happened, she was in his arms, weeping out the story of her misfortunes.

Anger darkened his wonderful golden brown eyes. "God will curse the vile rich who would turn such a girl into the streets." Producing a kerchief, he wiped the tears from her eyes, gently dabbing at her grimy face. "Blessed are the righteous, Sister Kate," he said, his handsome face stern. "They shall endure all things and one day dwell in Paradise with our Heavenly Father." Faint with relief, Kate stood in his embrace, sure that a miracle of God had sent this man to provide her sanctuary. "No more tears now," he commanded. Kate struggled to obey, still leaning against him, exquisitely conscious of the strength of his arms holding her. "The Church takes care of its own," he told her, as he turned to lead her down the street. "I'm going to take you to the Allenbys. Brother Spencer is out of town. It's lucky I came by to check on his house."

A glow, brighter than the gas flame of the street lamps, spread all about them until the cold drizzly evening seemed to melt away. The strength of his hand on her arm was sheer joy, and Kate was suddenly as giddy as though she had taken too much wine. Looking up at his strong, confident face, Kate knew in that instant she loved this man with all her being. Nothing was hopeless or impossible. Shining to-morrows stretched before her. Surely God had lifted her into the light and set her feet on a path forever upward.

Stout, affectionate, and childless, Sister Allenby took Kate to her heart at once. She and her husband were excessively fond of Elder Hamilton, since he was responsible for their conversion to Mormonism. Brother Allenby was a shoemaker by trade, and his business was such that he employed a number of people and was able to live in a substantial manner. Although their home could not be compared with that of the Fitzhughs, it was large and comfortable and, as Elder Hamilton said, "filled with the spirit of God." Hired as a maid on his glowing recommendation and, Kate was sure, because of her pitiful story, she was soon more of a companion to bustling, kindly Sister Allenby.

To Kate's joy Elder Hamilton often came to conduct meetings in the household. He was always so correct and gentlemanly she could not guess whether he returned the love she had felt for him almost from the beginning. He was still a missionary, and spreading the Gospel required his full time and attention. Trying to conceal her feelings, she knew how inadequately she succeeded by the sly looks between the Allenbys when Burns was present and by their constant contriving to leave the young couple by themselves.

On a cold spring evening the four of them shared supper and afterward sat before the blazing hearth in the drawing room. Any pretense that Kate was a maid in the household had long since been dropped. Bertha Allenby had the daughter she had always longed for. She delighted in buying clothes for her and teaching her the ways and manners of a lady. As Kate sat working at the embroidery Sister Allenby had taught her, she surreptitiously caressed the heavy green bombazine skirt of her gown, letting its richness flow through her fingers, knowing this, too, was part of the miracle wrought in her life by Burns Hamilton. The V-shaped neckline of the dress, trimmed with Alençon lace, accentuated her heart-shaped face, Sister Allenby said. "I don't wish to make you vain," she would comment and once more voice her admiration of Kate's wide blue eyes with their heavy dark lashes, her full pink mouth, and fine skin.

"I've been called to fulfill a new position for the Church," Burns said abruptly.

Startled, Kate looked up, flooded with anguish at the thought of his going away. She loved him so. Whether or not he loved her, as long as he was in Liverpool she had the comfort of his occasional presence.

"President Richards told me you would be in charge of the Liverpool Mission." Brother Allenby smiled, puffing on his pipe, as proud as though Burns were his own son. "He thinks highly of you, Burns."

"With God's help, I'm sure I can handle the job." Burns's eyes rested reflectively on Kate. Feeling her face grow warm, she lowered her eyes, drenched with relief that he would not be going away. An awkward silence fell.

Clearing his throat, Brother Allenby said he must work on some accounts, if they would excuse him. His coat tail had hardly disappeared through the doorway when Sister Allenby announced that she must consult with Cook this minute about tomorrow's menu.

The low murmur of the coal fire was accompanied by the hiss of rain against the windows. Kate's needle darted in and out of the embroidery, her hands clumsy, cold as ice. She dared not look up, knowing her heart was in her eyes, wishing the Allenbys had not been so obvious in their desire to leave the two of them alone.

"A mission president needs a wife, Kate," Burns began. "A man alone can't run the Conference House, with missionaries from England and the Continent coming and going all the time."

He was waiting for an answer, and she hardly dared trust her voice. Fear and hope fought a painful battle inside her head. "There are many good ladies in the Church who are still unwed."

"There is only one I love," he said softly.

Standing before her, he took her hands in his. The embroidery fell to the floor unnoticed. Enraptured, Kate gazed up at him, almost drowning in the warmth of those golden eyes. *My love . . . my love . . .* the words sang inside her head. Speechless, she watched as he kissed the palm of her hand. Slowly he lifted her up and tilted her pointed chin to kiss her lips. In his embrace was all the urgent passion of a young man who has long restrained his feelings. Dizzy with joy, Kate returned that embrace with a warmth that was not at all proper.

"Dear girl," he said, sighing as he drew away and looked into her eyes. "You will be my wife?"

"With all my heart," she answered, pressing close to him. The words sounded like a prayer of thanksgiving. "With all my soul, for all my life."

Delighted at the outcome of the love affair they had so shamelessly promoted, the Allenbys served a wedding supper, well attended by members of the Church. They made up the bridal chamber in their own house and presented the young couple with a Lowestoft tea set, an item Kate had never dared hope to own.

Now Kate lay in the bed, wearing the tucked and lace-flounced nightdress Sister Allenby had made, a little flown with wine, listening to the sounds of her husband preparing for bed in the dressing room. Tomorrow they would go to their home at the Church-owned Conference House. But tonight . . . this was her wedding night, and she still only half-believed she was not living out a dream.

The guttering candle on the bedside table was the only light in the room, but it was enough for her to see the passion in her husband's eyes. Response surged through her, so urgent she could scarcely contain herself.

"Sweet Kate," he murmured. Tenderly he took her hand and kissed the palm. The warm, moist touch of his mouth, the scratchy moustache, tingled along her nerves. An ache grew in her body, intense, unfamiliar, yet somehow eternally remembered.

With one quick breath the candle was extinguished and he lay beside her. The pain was quickly over and what followed was surprisingly pleasurable. The act she had thought so uncouth in others seemed natural and good between them. It would bring them children, she thought, love for him rising hot and fierce so that she could have wished he would begin again. With a sigh, he moved to lie beside her, pillowing her head on his shoulder.

"My dearest wife," he murmured and fell asleep.

Lying awake, listening to his deep, even breathing, Kate pondered this new miracle. Man and wife forever now, with all life stretching before them under God's good auspices. This was the man she had dreamed of and prayed for. She would love him all their life together and care for him and give him children to build up his own Kingdom in the Hereafter. Now she would be forever safe and forever loved, never again alone and afraid. Contented sleep took her until she awakened in the darkness to find Burns reaching for her. She gave herself to him totally. At dawn, Kate lay beside her sleeping husband, sated with love. If this side of Eternity held such joy she could not begin to imagine what lay in store in the Hereafter.

Chapter 2

꿈꿈 Standing alone on the deck of the *John M. Wood*, her hand on the grimy, paint-scabbed railing, Kate stared out across the dirty gray water toward the spires and smokestacks of squalid old Liverpool. Seagulls swooped and banked, weaving intricate patterns beneath the windswept March sky, their melancholy cries echoing over the dull face of the harbor.

Once more her eyes turned to the copy of the Church weekly, *The Millennial Star*, in her hand. The item pleased her, indicating as it did the importance of her husband. She knew it by heart: "Brother Burns Hamilton has been released as president of the Liverpool Mission. He and his wife, Sister Kate Hamilton, will sail from Liverpool within the week bound for Utah via New Orleans. While President Hamilton's firm and kindly guidance will be missed in this mission, we wish him and his wife safe journey to Zion."

The dateline was March 2, 1854.

Wind plucked at the furled sails of the *John M. Wood*, whistling through the creaking ropes. Choppy waves broke rhythmically against the sides of the ship. Even the stench of the River Mersey was whisked away in the brisk breeze. Shouts of the seamen punctuated the low, anxious murmur of the passengers pacing the deck, settling down below, awaiting the moment of departure. Screaming children ran gleefully about exploring their unfamiliar surroundings.

A familiar hand touched her shoulder. Even after almost three years of marriage a delicious weakness ached in her limbs as she turned to meet the eyes of her husband. Wonderful eyes, she thought, light brown with flecks of gold and depths both warm and cool, glowing now with anticipation.

(15)

"I've settled our baggage down below," he said.

Kate leaned into the touch of his arm. On a deck crowded with emigrants one could not say "I love you" and embrace, so she merely looked up with the eyes of love and asked, "Do you think we'll ever see England again, Burns?"

For a moment his face sobered as his eyes turned toward the soot-stained city beyond the water. His big, square hand lay on the railing and Kate covered it with hers. When he turned to look down at her his smile was confident, without regret. "We will be in Zion among the Saints."

"I will be with you, Burns," she said softly, knowing that above all else his presence was essential to her happiness.

Smiling, Burns took her hand tightly in his. A familiar catch in her throat, filled with love and pride, Kate regarded her handsome husband. Burns's carriage was that of a man used to command, the total impression one of vigorous, driving ambition. But the beloved brown eyes were soft now, regarding her in a way that made her long to have his arms about her. Her eyes lingered on his firm mouth, remembering how that mouth felt pressed against her own.

Cupping her chin in one hand, Burns smiled tenderly at her. "Zion will bring all we have prayed for, my dear."

Tears pricked at her eyelids. "Burns . . . do you think . . . a child?"

The brown eyes clouded and he glanced away. He knew how desperately she longed for a child, and she saw that he had no wish to burden her with his own disappointment. After three years, still no child had come to bless their marriage. Surely God, having granted them such happiness in each other, would not temper that blessing by letting her be barren.

"All things are possible with the Lord," he assured her, and his arm tightened about her shoulders.

Sighing, Kate laid her head against his shoulder. All day he had been so busy helping the brethren board and make ready for the sea journey she had hardly seen him. Burns was a high priest, a leader among these people. Earthly desire and earthly gain, he told her, must be suppressed in the service of the Lord. If one were faithful, followed counsel, all things would be added; one would prosper here on earth and move onward to glory in the Celestial Kingdom of God.

KATE

All things are possible, she echoed the words inside her head. Sadness welled within her so that she wished to be held and comforted. She had longed for a child, prayed God would give her one, loved her husband as though her passion could force conception. Perhaps in Zion the dreams would be fulfilled.

"Brother Hamilton," the agent called. "Need your help here. This man says they're one of your families, but they seem to have lost a ticket."

Nodding, Burns patted Kate's arm and walked toward the terrified family of mill hands who had just come aboard from the lighter boat.

Disappointed by the interruption, Kate's eyes followed the tall, self-assured figure of her husband as he competently took charge of the frightened family. Hope began to light the pale, weary faces as Burns spoke to them and led them toward the agent's office.

Alone, Kate turned back to the rail. On her slender figure, the dark gray traveling dress appeared of finer quality than it was, just as Kate herself appeared to be of finer quality than the other women aboard. Her grace and bearing were that of an aristocrat, the pointed chin lifted in a kind of arrogance. That bearing put people off, so that she had never been truly close to anyone of her own sex. She stood alone while the other passengers lined the railing for their last look at England.

The lighter boat moved away. Sailors shouted to each other and began to cast off. The anchor rose, creaking, grating, dripping seaweed. Sails unfurled to catch the evening wind, the *John M. Wood* moved out with the tide to where the dirty River Mersey stained the sea. In the spanking breeze the land slipped away swiftly behind them. England was gone forever. Kate wiped the unexpected tears and turned her eyes to the open sea. Beyond that ocean awaited Zion where the Saints had made the desert blossom as the rose. The beautiful phrase filled her head with visions of a green and verdant land where all were equal and lived in harmony. Surely in Zion the child would come. Obey my word, God had said, and all things shall be added unto you.

The primitive log huddle that was Fort Supply stood on Smith's Fork of the Green River in a high sweeping valley. Only two years old, it had been built by the Mormons after they fell out with old Jim

Bridger and refused to patronize his fort twelve miles away. All Mormon wagon trains stopped here to rest their oxen and repair wagons for the tortuous journey through the Wasatch Mountains into Salt Lake Valley. A current of excitement ran through the emigrant train now that they were so near the end of the journey. Behind them were the long months spent crossing the American prairies. Memories of the crowded misery of shipboard and the shabby encampments on the banks of the Mississippi River seemed of small moment when Zion lay just beyond the mountains.

"Burns, wait. We could get lost. What if there are Indians out here?" Clutching her skirt, Kate held out a hand to her husband as he reached to help her across one of the many creeks flowing through the valley toward the Green River. His warm eyes met hers and love flowed through her, as moving and inexorable as the water flowing in the creek at her feet. The network of winding streams surrounding the fort was lined with grassy meadows, cottonwood trees, and thickets of willow. In the shimmering distance lay the flat-topped hills over which they had traveled from South Pass. To the west the snow-capped Uinta Mountains, blue as sapphires, gleamed against a cloudless sky.

Cottonwood trees, already turned color here in this high valley, rustled and shone in the exhilarating September breeze. The grass about the fort had been cropped short by the many animals on the emigrant trail this season, yet here and there a few late summer flowers had survived, tiny and pale. Hundreds of birds called from the frost-colored willow thickets and, overhead, honking geese fled southward. The pole walls of the fort were out of sight now behind the trees. Only the sounds followed: ringing hammers, bellowing oxen, and shouting children.

As Burns reached to help her, Kate's eyes fastened on the strong forearm revealed by his rolled-up sleeves. It was brown and hard, the tendons leaping out as he lifted her. A rush of heat filled her body, and a familiar ache.

"I won't let the Indians get you," he said with a grin, drawing her close, his mouth eager against hers.

Kate's body arched against his and her kiss carried all the pent-up longing of the past three weeks. It seemed forever since they had had a chance to love each other. Captain Curtis, the wagon master, had asked them to take Sister Lawrence into their wagon. She was an old lady, emigrating with her daughter's family, and she was ill. The daughter had five small children and was far along in pregnancy. The old woman needed quiet. There were only the two of them in their wagon. It was the Christian thing to do, yet when the three of them lay in the wagon bed at night, they listened to the old lady's stertorous breathing and could not bring themselves to the act of love.

"Come on . . ." Burns took her hand. The sounds of industry at the fort faded behind them as they wound through a maze of willows, grass, and low brush.

"Do you know where you're going?" she asked, stumbling over a fallen branch hidden in the brush.

"No," he said, and they laughed together. Kate's heart soared with delight at this carefree mood she so seldom saw in her earnest husband. How little she had really known him at the time of their marriage. She scarcely guessed at the intensity of his zealous commitment to his religion. Every new responsibility laid upon him by his Church was accepted eagerly and discharged with fervor. Driven by ambition to better himself, Burns had left behind all semblance of the miller's son from Wiltshire. How many times had he told her how he hated being poor, hated being kicked aside by the squire's sons, for it was the squire who owned the mill where Burns's father toiled for a meager living. In the Mormon doctrine he had found the promise of a better life here on earth and a path laid out for him to follow to eternal exaltation in the Hereafter. When he was baptized his father had turned him out, even as Mistress Fitzhugh had turned her out on the streets. But the Mormons had made him a missionary. While he traveled about England preaching the Gospel, he studied constantly and now boasted that he felt he was better educated than most gentlemen.

As a young bride it had been a joy to study with him, awed by his quick mind and his strength of purpose. She knew that she pleased him, although he sometimes forgot to tell her so. She had become the kind of wife he wanted. His pride in her accomplishments reminded her of her beloved father. If he was quick to point out her mistakes, she was just as quick to correct them.

He had a temper, too, although it was most often under control and seldom turned on her. When he found the dealer in St. Louis had sold them untrained oxen he had flown into a dreadful rage, asking God's curse on the dishonest man with such vehemence Kate felt sure the dealer must have fallen dead that instant. Under Burns's firm guidance the oxen had become docile pets, even eating grass from Kate's hand.

Breathless now, with trying to keep his pace, Kate found herself drawn into a thick clump of willows, held in his demanding embrace. Aglow with her own longing, she looked up into his passion-darkened eyes. His hand fumbled with the bodice of her dress.

"I can't love you with old lady Lawrence listening," he murmured, his lips caressing her throat. "And I can't not love you for this long. Please, Kate."

"Please?" Kate laughed softly. Was it possible he didn't know how much she wanted him too? She sank down to sit on the grass beneath the willows. As he sat beside her, Burns took her hand and kissed the palm, a caress that ever since her wedding night had signified for her the miracle of love.

"Dearest," she whispered, "are you sure no one will see us?" In his urgency he seemed not to have heard the question. Gently he pushed her back onto the grass and his body covered hers. The pungent odor of mint crushed beneath her filled her nostrils. Wind brushed across the grass, stirred the ocher willow leaves on their russet branches. Above them those leaves formed a canopy of golden lace, almost translucent in the lowering sun. Water murmured softly over the stones of the creek bed.

"Kate . . . Kate . . . my little wife . . ." Burns's mouth was warm on her throat, moving to search out her breasts. Smoothing his hair with her hand, she thought how good he smelled, always neat and clean, not like most other men who stank of sour sweat. "Kate!" His voice was urgent and she reached to help him with her clothing.

Never before had it been like this. They were so completely one her spirit seemed to flow out of her body and blend with his. The golden canopy wheeled against the blue sky. She heard her voice cry out with joy. As surely as though the heavens opened and God smiled down upon her, she knew they had this moment begun a child. On the brink of their new life, the prayers had been answered.

Burns lay beside her, cradling her head on his shoulder. "Did I hurt you?" he asked, his eyes concerned.

With a sigh she caressed the bare forearm that had aroused her first. "Dearest, you never hurt me . . . my gentle lover."

The golden brown eyes darkened. "I never will . . . never. Kate, I love you so."

Palm against his cheek, she turned his face to kiss his mouth. Did he know? Did he guess what they had accomplished here in this golden bower hidden in the hills of their new land?

"Darling," she whispered, "something wonderful happened. Would you believe me? I know it. We'll have our baby now."

"Yes . . . I knew it, too . . . a son. Oh, my dearest wife." Burns drew her into a fierce and joyful embrace. Like a benediction, he added, "God keeps His promises."

The glow of the campfire that evening concealed all the ugliness of the primitive fort. Its flames cast shadows on the pole walls like a ghostly assembly dancing beyond the firelight. Dust and dirt were gilded or hidden in shadow, the worn clothing and weary faces magically renewed. Most of the company gathered after supper for preaching, counseling, and praying, for singing and sometimes for dancing.

Kate loved the song they were singing now, the sound lifting into the starry night sky:

> Come, come ye Saints, no toil or labor fear,
> but with joy wend your way.
> Though hard to you this journey may appear,
> grace shall be as your day.
> 'Tis better far for us to strive
> our useless cares from us to drive.
> Do this and joy your hearts will swell . . .
> All is well! . . . All is well!

All is well, she thought, and her heart filled with exultation. Within her lay her husband's child. Beyond those mountains lay their eternal home. The man who loved her, whom she loved with all her being, stood just there across the campfire. *Darling* . . .

darling . . . she almost said the word aloud. With pride she watched his handsome head bent, intent on his conversation with Captain Curtis, his face ruddy in the firelight, his tall, well-muscled body leaning negligently against the wagon. Memory of the afternoon in their bower of willows flooded through her and desire rose, hot and aching. Perhaps tonight . . . if they waited until Sister Lawrence was sound asleep. Her thoughts were interrupted by the creak of the wagon tongue as Melissa Gunther sat down beside her.

"Those wild Indians of mine are finally asleep," Melissa said, settling her calico skirts about her.

Kate smiled. She had grown fond of Melissa in the months they had traveled together. The outgoing Melissa had taken the initiative in their relationship, for that was the only way Kate had ever been able to make friends. The lonely, motherless childhood had made her shy of women. Her first confidence betrayed by a maid named Bridget, she had learned to hold herself aloof. Arrogant, Mistress Fitzhugh had said. Queenly, said Sister Allenby, weeping her goodbyes. Once more her eyes fastened on the man across the fire. She had Burns, lover and confidant; she really needed no one else.

Melissa's husband, Henry, was a great ox of a man who had pioneered in Kentucky before joining the Church. The Gunther family had three wagons carrying their goods, their four children, and two grown nieces of Henry's. There were snide whisperings about the nieces. The girls were really Henry's plural wives, one of the women had told Kate. With a cold stare, Kate cut off the coarse creature's prurient gossip and walked away filled with the sick dread the mention of polygamy always brought. What was still only a rumor in England and Europe had been presented to them at the camp in Missouri as a revelation and commandment of God. Apostle Parley Pratt had been there to welcome the emigrants, a speaker of fire, passion, and persuasion. It was he who took Burns aside and explained the principles of the Everlasting Covenant of Celestial Marriage.

"It's only for the worthy," Burns had told her afterward. "Only for the leaders of men who must multiply their seed if they are to achieve their own Godhood."

What did the words mean? So much of the Gospel, the words of the Book of Mormon, the many revelations, twisted and turned inside her head just beyond understanding. Burns, with his superior mind and education, would always simplify what seemed garble into meaningful maxims for her.

"Does that mean you?" she asked, ice-cold with fear.

A flash of horror passed across his face. "No!" he said abruptly. "Not for me." The expression on his face told her the subject was closed. They had not spoken of it again.

Now Kate drew her shawl closer about her shoulders, for the campfire could not dispel the chill of the autumn night. "We'll soon be home in Salt Lake," she told Melissa. "It'll be easier for you to handle the children there."

Melissa did not reply. Her face was a pale oval in the firelight, eyes glittering damply. Kate turned to follow her gaze. Hannah, one of Henry's nieces, stood silhouetted against the fire. There was no mistaking that the girl was pregnant. Kate heard her own breath go out sharply. Sickness clutched at her throat. It's true, she thought. Oh God, the rumors were true. Poor Meliss. She doted on that great oaf so, surely this would break her heart.

Melissa must have caught Kate's horror-stricken look, for she rearranged her features to blankness, shrugged her shoulders, and said in a low, bitter voice, "Well, now you know. You and everyone else."

"Hannah is Henry's plural wife?" Kate whispered, the words loathsome on her tongue.

When Melissa merely nodded, Kate could not restrain herself. "Oh, Meliss, how can you bear it?"

After a long moment's silence, Melissa began a set little speech, obviously memorized. "Celestial Marriage is God's law. It was revealed to Joseph Smith that we must do the works of Abraham and enter into this holy order so that we may multiply and replenish the earth; to bear the souls of men into this dispensation that our husbands may be exalted in the Hereafter and we along with them."

Meaningless words again, Kate thought, but the repugnance searing her throat was real. Memory of the glorious lovemaking she had shared that afternoon reassured her. It was not for them, she told herself confidently. She and Burns loved each other so completely she could not imagine he would even entertain the thought of taking another wife. "But how can you stand it?" she asked, staring at her friend in disbelief.

Melissa turned away, and Kate, hearing the half-choked sob, reached out to embrace her friend. "Sometimes I can't," Melissa muttered, trying to suppress her tears. "Sometimes even God can't stop me from wanting Henry all to myself."

Sister Lawrence's breathing diminished to a rhythmic snore. Beyond the opening in the back of the wagon cover, stars wheeled in the dark night sky, brilliant as jewels. A faint breeze rippled the canvas. Frost tinged the September night, and beneath the quilts Kate snuggled close to her husband, the warmth of his body comforting and arousing.

Whispering, she told him about Henry's wives. Burns nodded. Yes, he knew. It was one of the reasons the Saints had been driven west, one of the reasons for their continuing persecution. Henry had to keep it secret because there were non-Mormons with the wagon train.

"It isn't a requirement of the Gospel, is it, Burns?" she asked and a great pain filled her chest as she waited for his answer.

"No." His hands were gentle on her body. He was not interested in theological discussions tonight, she thought, responding to his touch. Tonight he did not even care about Sister Lawrence. Nor did she, for when they were joined there was no world existing beyond the two of them, nothing but the wild consuming joy of loving.

Surfeited, they lay still in the darkness. Sister Lawrence's snoring continued its braying rhythm. Scalded with love for him, Kate held her husband fiercely to her.

"Burns," she whispered, "I couldn't bear it if you married another wife."

Relaxed and drowsy from loving, Burns kissed her and smoothed her hair. "Not ever, sweetheart," he assured her in low tones. "Plural marriage is only for those who have the call and the means to live it. You will always be my one and only love . . . my dearest wife."

Chapter 3

That day she had stood on the ship's deck watching England fade on the horizon she had known God would give her a child if she kept the faith. He was a year and a half old now, born their first spring in Zion, just nine months from that golden afternoon in the autumn wilderness. Gently Kate laid her hand on the baby's chest so that she could feel the rise and fall of his breathing, the faint thud of his tiny heart. A hundred times a day she did such things to make sure he was still there, still alive, still hers. The boy lay lost in sleep, his dark hair tousled, dark lashes against his round cheeks, thumb barely slipped from his pink, half-open mouth. Such a surge of love filled her she could hardly restrain herself from lifting him up into her arms, to hold him, feel his warmth and life against her breast. Burns was right, of course; she held the boy too much. He didn't want his firstborn to grow into a spoiled Mama's boy.

The log-walled bedroom was furnished with the spool bed Burns had traded work for, the trundle bed he had built, their trunks . . . and the cradle. As she turned away from the trundle bed where little Brigham slept, her eyes fell on the empty cradle, and she fought down the sob rising in her throat.

Her breasts ached. It was time to pump the milk from them . . . wasted milk, meant for the baby who lay now two weeks in his grave. She was glad Burns was at the mill and Brigham asleep, for she had determined she must not cry in front of them again. Baby Joseph had been in her arms less than a week. He hadn't even been ill or fussy. When she wondered why he hadn't awakened crying for his dinner, she had gone to the cradle to find her baby cold and dead.

Joseph had come early, almost a month. If God should see fit to give her another child, she would know better than to make soap when her time was so near. The awful fumes of cottonwood lye and grease had been staggering, although it was fall and she made the soap in an open kettle in the back yard. Even when the pains started, she knew she must finish. Nothing could be wasted. The soap had to be stirred until it would solidify, then poured into molds. Only then could she walk painfully across the yard to the mill and tell Burns to go for Sister Reed, the midwife.

When the baby died Burns had said that Joseph was a choice spirit of God, translated from mortal to immortal in the twinkling of an eye.

"Then why did God send him at all?" Kate sobbed.

"To try our faith," Burns told her. "His mysterious ways work for our betterment."

Silent, Kate stared at him, knowing he could never understand. He was not a woman who had lost her baby. When you have lost a part of your own flesh it is difficult to accept God as wise. Still, she had little Brigham, and she reached to smooth the child's hair. She was always touching him, holding him, watching him, forever haunted by the fear that she might lose him, too. Looking at him now, Kate remembered Burns's exalted face when he came to her in the rooms they had rented on Emigration Street in Salt Lake City. The hours of wracking agony were over at last. Her husband knelt beside the bed, eyes filled with love. Taking her hand, he kissed her palm.

"We have a son, Kate," he said. "A son!" Turning back the blanket he gazed upon the wizened, red face of his child, visibly swelling with pride.

"We'll name him for President Brigham Young," Burns told her. "I've just seen him and he's asked me to run his grist mill out on Cottonwood Creek. Franklin Richards recommended me. There's a two-room cabin there. We'll have a home for our boy."

"Oh, Burns," she whispered. "God has been so good to us."

"Pray with me, Kate." Their hands joined across their tiny son. Burns bowed his head and began. "We thank Thee, dear Lord . . ."

Exhaustion fell over her like a smothering blanket, and before he finished Kate was asleep.

It was said of Brigham Young that he was a superb judge of men. He took a fancy to the hard-working, devout young Elder Hamilton and occasionally drove by the mill, walking about with Burns, discussing its operation. One day last spring he had even stayed for dinner. Shaken by the honor of serving the Prophet in her modest home, Kate apologized for the inadequate food and the mismatched dishes. The Lowestoft tea set, its one broken cup carefully mended, had been brought down for the occasion. How proud Sister Allenby would be when Kate wrote her about using the tea set to serve the head of the Church. Brigham Young ate with gusto, brushing aside her apologies, complimenting her on the cooking, on her handsome son who was his namesake, smiling with approval at the evidence of a child growing inside her.

As Kate watched the Prophet of God sitting in her house, earthy as any man except for the sense of power in his strong face and piercing gray eyes, she thought that the dreams of Zion she carried in her head from England had been the visions of a child. But the infinite vastness of the American prairies had half-prepared her for the reality. Salt Lake Valley stretched away toward the Oquirrh Mountains on the western horizon, where the Great Salt Lake reflected the setting sun. To the northeast of the city, light brown foothills, splotched by dark patches of scrub oak, rose steeply toward the Wasatch Mountains rimming the city on the east and south. After Liverpool, the city seemed so small, its houses widely scattered. No great factory smokestacks belched filth into the skies here. Although Salt Lake City was only seven years old, already there were rows of young trees lining the wide, brook-edged streets and everywhere evidence that Zion was growing. The town centered on Temple Square, a walled-in block where the Temple to the Lord would stand. Now it was a confusion of construction: granite blocks from the quarry east of the city, stacks of lumber, and shouting workers. East of the Temple site, on South Temple Street, stood Brigham Young's beautiful home, the Beehive House. Behind its stone fence one could glimpse ornate balconies and cornices. Next door another home was being built for President

Young's enormous family, a long, gabled building to be called the Lion House, after the affectionate title applied to him: the Lion of the Lord.

Salt Lake City was a constant bustle of business, crowded with wagon trains of gold seekers on their way to the strike in California. Trading with these Gentiles, as the Mormons called those not of their faith, had brought prosperity to some of the settlers. Still, far too many converts arrived to be absorbed into Salt Lake City's economy, and they were soon called to colonize other parts of the territory.

Burns had been fortunate to find employment near Salt Lake. Often, as they lay in bed after loving, talking over the day's events, he would confide his hopes for the future . . . for a farm and perhaps a grist mill of his own. In England he would never have dared hope for such things, but in Zion all things were possible.

The pain in her breasts grew urgent. With a lingering look at the sleeping child, Kate hurried out of the bedroom.

The kitchen was small and snug with the luxury of an iron stove rather than a fireplace for cooking. The table and chairs had been acquired by trading, and Burns had built the neat cupboard standing against the wall. From the cupboard she took a breast pump and began working the milk from her engorged breasts. She hated the mechanical thing. A baby's mouth drew the milk out so easily, so gently, the sucking sending warm rays of pleasure through her body. Tears burned her face again.

A loud knock at the door shook Kate from her melancholy thoughts. Wiping the breast pump she quickly laid it back in the cupboard and buttoned her bodice. Sister Reed said the milk would soon dry up and Kate prayed it would, for it was a constant reminder of her loss.

The plank door shook beneath the fist beating on it. As she flung it open, cold fear blew in with the icy November wind. An enormous Indian stood glowering at her, the rank odor of his buckskins heavy and sickening in her nostrils. Behind him in the doorway a straggly group of Indians huddled together: bucks, women, and children, some on horseback. The year's first thin, patchy snow lay beneath the cottonwood trees and the wind whistled through the bare gray branches. Below the wind, the grumbling noise of the mill was almost lost.

"Food!" His hard thin mouth seemed not to have even opened, the broad dark face impassive. Then his hands came up in an impatient gesture. "Food!"

Terror clutched at her throat, her limbs seemed to have turned to water. Somehow Kate found strength to nod assent. Brigham Young always counseled the Saints to feed the Indians. It was cheaper and easier than fighting them, he said. The neighbors had many wild tales to tell of begging Indians, but never before had they come to her house. With shaking hands, she took a clean sack and put in the light bread, fresh-baked yesterday. What else, she wondered? Oh dear God, help me! The man had stalked into the kitchen behind her and stood looking around. He mustn't go in the other room, mustn't get near her baby. Jerking the lid from the pot of pork boiling on the stove, he grunted. His gesture seemed to indicate that he wished to take the meat.

"It's hot," she protested and could have bitten her tongue when his black eyes stabbed her. Another sack . . . the half-cooked steaming pork shank lifted from the pot and dumped into it.

The Indian grunted again. "Good!" With a sack in either hand he went out the door. A clatter of hooves on the frozen ground and they were gone. Kate slammed the door and threw the bolt, her knees trembling so she could hardly stand.

"Brig," she murmured to herself and almost ran into the bedroom. The child protested mildly at being lifted up from sleep. Sitting down in the rocking chair she held him close against her. He was warmth and comfort and life . . . and he was hers. After a moment his thumb found his mouth and he slept once more.

Burns must have been busy inside the mill and did not even hear the Indians, she thought, wishing there were windows in the cabin so she could see where they had gone. Their horses had been moving fast. She hoped Burns would think she had handled the terrifying situation well. One did not resist savages. This frontier was a whole different world from England. Self-sufficiency was important. States goods were high and hard to come by, for money was short, most business being done by barter. Yet everywhere in Zion they had found someone to help, to teach and advise.

Kate bent to kiss the sleeping boy's head. She could be happy in Zion, and content. In spite of her grief for Joseph, she knew there would be another child. And yet it was always there, in the hidden recesses of her mind, like a gnawing canker . . . polygamy. Here in Salt Lake Valley it was all around them, the principle for which the Mormons had been most persecuted. Some of the families seemed happy enough, although others were like a houseful of quarreling cats. Most of their close neighbors and their friends in the city had entered into plural marriages. Brigham Young had many wives, no one knew how many. Some of them were much older than he and surely not real wives. Whenever she thought of it, a sense of disquietude played along the edges of her mind. The Gospel, that beautiful plan for life and Eternity, was true and real as the breath in her lungs, but this . . . How could a woman who loved her husband so passionately and possessively ever accept this doctrine?

"You need a sister-wife for company," Bishop Adams often told her at Church meetings or parties, as though he had singled her out. "A man in Burns's position . . . a high priest . . . a Bishop's Counselor . . . it's his duty to help care for the lonely sisters."

Women converts had always outnumbered the men, widows and spinsters constantly arriving in Salt Lake and places having to be found for them. Sometimes the Bishop brought his two wives and six children to visit, as though to demonstrate the blessings of plural marriage. The first wife was overbearing and overproud of her husband's position, while the second wife was a mousy creature. Their children were wild and quarrelsome. The Bishop's conversation was salted with innuendos about the joys of entering the Everlasting Covenant. Kate had no answer for him, fear eating at her heart. Burns was her life, her love, and he had promised. He always looked embarrassed by the Bishop's urgings and changed the subject as quickly as possible.

"Kate!" It was Burns and the kitchen door was bolted. Hurriedly she laid the sleeping Brigham back in his bed. Burns would not be pleased to find her sitting holding her son in the middle of the day.

Cold wind sucked heat from the kitchen as she opened the door. Clutching his hat in one hand, Burns held a small Indian boy by the other. The child might have been two years old, frightened and half-naked. The terror in his black eyes touched her heart. Although his skin was dark, his hair long and black, he was little more than a baby . . . cold, hungry, and afraid. The demanding arrogance of the Indian who had been in her kitchen so recently had nothing to do with this small being.

"He was hiding in the mill," Burns said, looking down at the silent boy with dismay. "Now what will we do with him?"

"God sent him, Burns," she answered, pity for the boy and the memory of her lost Joseph filling her eyes. Kate held her arms out to the shivering child.

Burns jerked him back away from her. "You'd better give him a bath first off. He's probably crawling with lice. Most Indians are."

While he stripped the shivering boy of his meager clothing, Kate filled the washtub with hot water. Burns frowned at her description of the Indians who had stopped that morning.

"I suspect they're slave traders," he said, "or the boy wouldn't have tried to run away from them."

"They took our dinner," Kate told him as he lifted the rigid body of the boy into the washtub.

"Well, fix some salt pork and biscuits." He took his rifle from the wall rack. "I'll be in when I finish Brother Reed's grain." Pausing at the door, he turned to her. "If the Indians come back for the boy, let them have him."

Shocked, Kate looked up from scrubbing the child with lye soap. "But if they're slavers, they'll take him to Mexico and sell him."

"We can't start an Indian war over that," Burns replied curtly and closed the door behind him.

Obviously too terrified to resist, the child sat like a statue while she scrubbed him. Little Brig's clothes were small for the boy, but a flannel nightshirt covered him adequately. When she sat him at the table with a dish of salt pork and gravy, he ate like a starved animal, with both hands, black eyes watching her warily.

"What's your name?" she asked in a gentle voice. Would a child that small know his own name or remember his home? Brig did, but he was a white boy and a superior one at that. The boy mumbled something between mouthfuls of biscuit and butter that Kate thought sounded like "Tom." "Tom?" she asked. When he nodded, she smiled at him, patting the stubble of black hair she had cut close to his head so the lye soap could kill any lice lurking there.

"That will be your name," she told him. "Thomas Hamilton." She had already decided he would live with them if the Indians did not come for him. Pray God they would not miss such a small child among those they must have stolen from a weaker tribe to sell as slaves. Back in Liverpool she had seen too many orphans starving in the streets. Such things must not happen here in Zion.

When he began to nod over his plate, Kate carried him to the rocking chair. Gently rocking, she smiled at Brig stirring in his trundle bed, murmuring his awakening babble. After a moment Tom's tense little body relaxed against her, and he fell into exhausted sleep.

The Book of Mormon said the Lamanites were our brothers, and surely God had sent this small Lamanite to replace her lost Joseph. Looking down at the dark little face lying against her bosom she thought she would try to love him as she might have loved Joseph and raise him up in the ways of God.

Chapter 4

"Before I will again suffer, as I have in times gone by, there shall not be one building, nor one foot of lumber, nor a fence, nor a tree, nor a particle of grass or hay, that will burn left in reach of our enemies. I am sworn, if driven to extremity, to utterly lay waste this land in the name of Israel's God, and our enemies shall find it as barren as when we came here." Brigham Young's fist slammed against the pulpit. His bearded jaw jutted fiercely, the piercing gray eyes staring defiantly at his listeners. The Prophet was of medium height, barrel-chested, and growing stout, yet there was nothing average in the sense of absolute power exuding from the man.

Kate shivered, instinctively reaching out to draw the two small boys, Brigham and Tom, close to her side. Surely there would not be war, surely the United States would not send troops against the Mormons, their own people? She had thought to find peace and contentment and plenty in Zion. It was not so. The harvests of 1855 and 1856 had been poor. Every family in the territory was on short rations. There was little grain for Burns to grind at the mill, and it was portioned out carefully by the authorities. Last winter had been so severe there was no mail for months. Then, with spring came the news that the United States planned to send troops against the seditious Mormons who refused to accept any territorial governor other than Brigham Young.

President Young ended his speech in the usual manner, testifying to the truth of the Gospel and adding, "In the name of Jesus Christ, Amen."

A great sigh swept through the congregation crowded into the little frame meeting house of Cottonwood Ward. Brigham Young had come out from the city to speak at meeting, and the room was jammed with members seeking reassurance from the rumors of war spreading through the territory.

Sometimes Kate thought the Mormons delighted in persecution. Certainly they never had enough of telling tales of the atrocities they had suffered in Missouri and Illinois.

"Papa." Brig pointed a small finger at his father who had taken the stand.

"Shhh!" Kate touched a finger to the child's mouth, embarrassed by the smiling glances of those sitting nearby.

Burns took charge of a meeting with great authority, his deep voice rolling across the audience. There was a certain arrogance in the way he stood now, adding his words to those of Brother Brigham. Kate knew he enjoyed the prestige he had attained from such humble beginnings, just as she knew her husband was a born leader. Such opportunities would certainly have been denied him in the rigid society of England. Perhaps without the Latter Day Saints Church he would never have found what he sought here on earth, let alone in Heaven.

Little Brig leaned his head against her arm, looking up with the golden brown eyes of his father. Beloved child. Her arm tightened about him. Tom sat on the other side, silent, straight-backed. He had picked up English quickly, he and Brig were fond playmates, but he was such a self-contained creature for a child. She put her other arm about him and drew him close, receiving a shy smile in return. Lifting her eyes to her tall husband standing in the pulpit, she found she had missed an announcement . . . something about the militia, and Burns was giving the number of the next hymn.

"I love hearing Brother Brigham speak," the second Sister Adams said to Kate as they stood in the warm spring sunshine in front of the meeting house. She was trying not to look ill at ease. Her husband's first wife had asserted her position and captured Sister Lucy Young in deep conversation, glancing about to make sure her neighbors saw her consorting with the president's wife.

"Yes, we all do," Kate answered absently, turning to caution the two small boys to stay nearby. The Richardses had driven out from the city for the meeting and were coming home with them for dinner. Brigham Young would be taking Sunday dinner with the Adamses. Where was Burns? She had told him she must hurry home from meeting to set dinner on the table.

She saw that the Richardses had been detained by various members wanting to shake hands and talk with them. Her eyes quickly sorting through the crowd, Kate at last spotted her husband. He stood with Brigham Young, a little apart as though they spoke confidentially. Shade from the big cottonwood trees beside the dusty road mottled his face which was turned toward her, unseeing, intent on whatever Brother Brigham was saying. As she watched, that face was filled with shock, then pain. Burns bowed his head, shaking it slowly in a negative way. She could see only Brigham Young's broad back as his hand came to rest authoritatively on Burns's shoulder. After a moment she saw that Burns had acquiesced in whatever his leader was asking of him. Dear God, she thought, don't call him on a mission, don't take him away to serve in the militia and be shot at . . . please, God. I can't bear to have him away any more than he is now. And I want another child. I need him with me.

"Do you think there'll really be a war?" Sister Adams was asking.

Apostle and Sister Richards had interrupted Burns and Brigham Young. Kate turned back to the woman beside her, suddenly cold and uneasy in spite of the warmth of the spring day.

"A war . . . ," she began, and the talkative little woman continued as though she had not heard.

"My husband"—with proud emphasis on the words—"Bishop Adams says that President Young intends to ask all the Latter Day Saints in Salt Lake Valley to prepare to move south if the Army comes. We'll leave nothing but scorched earth behind us." She nodded her head for emphasis.

"War," Kate repeated with half-understood dread. Reaching out, she drew the two small boys close against her skirts.

"We do not seek war," Brother Richards said in his strident voice, helping himself to the last of the salt pork. Kate, watching the meat slide onto his plate and seeing the two small boys' eyes following it, repressed a sigh. That was the last of their meat. Now there would be nothing but cornmeal mush and milk, unless Burns shot some game.

"We have never sought violence," Brother Richards continued. "President Buchanan is in the hands of the contractors who will make a fortune from this expedition. No doubt he will make a fortune too. Vile and cursed man." His mouth full, he lapsed into silence.

"Every able-bodied man will be mustered into the militia," Burns said. "The Army will regret this decision to march against the Saints."

"Every able-bodied man?" Kate asked faintly.

"Brother Brigham has asked me to act as quartermaster to the militia," Burns said, a faint glow of self-pride lighting his eyes as he looked at Kate. "After the corn and grain are harvested and ground, every family must be prepared to move south. The militia will stay behind and make a stand in Big Cottonwood Canyon."

Kate stared down at the gravy congealing on her plate, unable to swallow, her hands two blocks of ice on her lap. Was this what Burns had been discussing with Brigham Young? War plans? The talk turned to the logistics of the move south, and Kate listened, watching Burns covertly. He seemed so uneasy, in spite of the bold statements he exchanged with his friend Brother Richards. He had left the house very early this morning. Perhaps he was still angry with her about last night.

Visiting the members of his ward had kept him very late. A catechism had been sent out by the Authorities of the Church. Each and every member must be examined by the priesthood, must memorize and live by those rules, be rebaptized and rededicated to the Gospel of the Lord. It was Burns's duty to take this Reformation into the homes of his congregation. Almost every night he was away, working for the Church.

Although it was spring, the nights were cool and wind creaked through the cottonwood branches. Tiny animal feet scrabbled across the roof. In the far distance a coyote howled. As he often did when awakened in the night, Brig crept out of the trundle bed he shared with Tom and crawled in beside her. How she loved this child, Kate thought sleepily, curling close to his small, warm body, her arm about him as she dozed off.

"This has to stop!" Burns shouted, startling everyone awake. Setting down the candle he carried, he seized Brig's arm and dragged the child from the warmth of the feather bed. Brig stood shivering in his nightshirt, small and pitiful, staring fearfully at his father. Kate sat up, looking at Burns in astonishment. He had seen Brig sharing her bed before and only carried him back, sound asleep, to his own bed.

"Burns, for Heaven's sake. We heard the coyotes howling and he was afraid."

"You're making a sissy of him." Burns's voice was ragged, his eyes dark with anger. "Get back in your own bed and stay there," he said with a threatening gesture toward the baby. Brig scampered back to the trundle bed where that taciturn little child, Tom, looked on in silence.

Watching as Burns bent to remove his boots, Kate felt her heart burn with resentment. "You had no need to treat him like that. He's only a baby."

"And he'll always be one," Burns answered in a bitter voice, "if you don't leave him alone." Blowing out the candle, he lay in silence beside her. She waited for him to reach for her, afraid to approach him. But there was only silence, and at last he slept.

Dear God, she thought, lying stiff and cold beside him, tears seeping from the corners of her eyes. What kind of man is jealous of his own son—and would fly into a rage over such a small thing? Or had some other unknown turmoil brought on this tantrum?

Now she watched the dust rolling up from the wheels of the Richardses' buggy until it was obscured from sight. A lowering sun glittered on the dusty road, turning it into a ribbon of dull gold. Their visit would have been more enjoyable without last night's constraint still separating her and her husband. She wondered whether Brigham Young had said more to him than he had been able to confide in the presence of their friends. With a sigh she returned to the house.

Burns had already changed from his Sunday clothes. Without a word to her he took the milk bucket and headed for the barn. When

the boys were asleep, he might feel free to talk with her about his
militia duties and the move south. If not, there was always woman's
eternal way of reconciling with her man.

She had never seen him so morose, Kate thought, when she came
into the kitchen after tucking the boys in bed. Burns sat beside the
stove where a fire still burned against the chill of the spring evening,
his head in his hands. Perhaps he was so troubled he could not bring
himself to speak to her. She went to him, smoothing his dark hair
with a gentle hand.

"Burns, dearest, what is it?"

"Oh my God, Kate!" He seized her about the waist, pressing his
head against her breasts. "I can't do it," he muttered. "But Brother
Brigham says I must."

"What?" Kate trembled.

His eyes were desolate as he looked up at her. "I'm to take another
wife."

The blood seemed to drain out of her, carrying her life away. For a
moment she feared she might faint. That which she dreaded most
had come to pass.

Burns drew her down to sit on his lap. Pressing her face against
his, she waited, too weak to move, too shaken to speak.

"Her name is Nelly Armstrong," he said in a dull voice, "a widow
from England with a three-year-old son. Her husband and baby died
of the cholera in Missouri. She's in dire need."

"Oh, Burns!" Tears swam in her aching eyes. "Can't you refuse?
Can't you say no, you don't want another wife?"

Some sort of struggle took place inside him. When he spoke she
knew there was no escape. "Brigham Young has said I must. He said
I can never rise in the Authority of the Church unless I accept the
Everlasting Covenant of Plural Marriage. He's the Prophet of God on
earth. I can't refuse."

Kate sensed then some sort of ambivalence in her husband. He
loved her, of course he loved her. But if he entered plural marriage
he would be among the elite of Mormondom, to be exalted in this
life and the Hereafter. In spite of his unhappy face, there was in his
eyes a faint glow of pride. He had been invited to join the aristocracy.

Tears burned her face. When he saw them, Burns tried to kiss them away. "Kate, dearest Kate," he said in a distracted way. "Please help me. I love you more than life. Help me bear this burden God has laid on us."

"I can't," she sobbed. "I can't bear it. I haven't the strength."

"Pray with me then," he whispered.

They knelt beside the kitchen chair, Burns's arm about her. Fire snapped in the stove, the wind scraped cottonwood branches mournfully against the roof. Her knees cold on the bare, scrubbed floor, Kate listened to Burns pray God to give them strength and courage to accept this charge He had sent them. Her own agony was eased only a little by the knowledge that her husband fully shared it. Acceptance was no easier for him than for her. Brigham Young thought Burns a worthy man to live the Celestial Law. Whatever came, she must discipline her jealous and possessive nature, reconcile herself to sharing him, for plurality was a path to exaltation in the next world. One did not question the counsel of the Authorities.

Their lovemaking that night had something of desperation in it, as though they knew nothing would ever be the same again.

A grim-faced Kate watched the buggy approaching the house. All the time she had cooked supper for Burns and his new wife she had wanted to scream aloud, to weep, to protest this awful thing that had happened to her. Brig and Tom were playing in the kitchen. She mustn't upset them. They had been told that Aunt Nelly and her son Charley were coming to live with them, but had no way of comprehending what that meant. The clop of horses' hooves and the whir of buggy wheels passed the house. Kate turned to check the supper table set for six. Burns had gone this morning to the city where he and Nelly were to be married . . . a woman he had never met, chosen for him by Brigham Young.

Steeling herself, Kate watched the opening door and stared in amazement at the woman who stood there. Her shabby clothes hung loosely on her thin body. She was excessively plain, with protruding blue eyes, bad teeth, and a bony face, her skinny nose red and dripping. A small, chubby boy with straw-colored hair clung to her skirts. Ashamed of herself for being glad Burns's new wife was so unattractive, Kate held out her hand.

"You are welcome, Nelly."

To her surprise the woman began to weep, her haunted eyes staring at Kate like those of a wounded animal. What suffering must lie behind that plain, sad face. Poor, pathetic creature. Pity filled Kate's heart so that her own eyes grew damp. Stepping forward, she took the weeping woman into her arms, patting her back. "Come, now," she said. "You mustn't cry. You're home."

Chapter 5

Summer haze lay across the green fields of Utah Valley. To the east the great blue-green shoulders of the Wasatch Mountains rose abruptly toward the sky. Iced with snow, Mount Timpanogos guarded the northern edge of the valley, swimming in the gauzy light. The patch of corn near the house on Burns Hamilton's farm stood in soldierly rows, leaves wilting in the hot, windless day. They had bought the farm five years ago, in 1858, at the end of the Mormon War. President Brigham Young had called Burns to move to Provo then, and just as he promised they had prospered. The square, two-story frame house was plain and comfortable. Inside that house the warm, sweet odor of fresh-baked bread filled the kitchen. Neatly uniform in size and color, the loaves of bread lay cooling on the kitchen sideboard, the fire dying now that midday dinner was finished. The room was silent except for a faint thump as the burned-out wood fell into coals inside the grate. In the distance Kate could hear eight-year-old Brigham calling Tom to help him turn the water on the garden. Her hands grasped the round back of the kitchen chair so tightly her knuckles stood out white as bare bones.

"I'll never forgive you if you do this, Burns." Her voice wavered as she met the angry eyes of her husband staring at her across the kitchen table. Resolutely she stared back at him, although her whole body seemed to have dissolved into internal tears. Wincing as the child inside her kicked, she looked down at her swollen body. Since dawn she had been on her feet, doing the baking for their household of ten before the heat of the day. Her feet and legs were as swollen as her belly. It was not pregnancy causing the sickness washing over her now, wave after wave of nausea. Struggling to control her emotions, she whispered hoarsely, "Please, Burns, don't do this to me."

Her husband's mouth, beneath the luxuriant dark brown moustache, grew thin and hard. At the age of thirty-six Burns Hamilton was a fine-looking man who carried himself with total self-assurance. That fiery young Elder she had married was a man of consequence now.

Brigham Young had been impressed by Burns's efficiency as quartermaster to the Mormon militia during the winter of 1857 and the spring of 1858. President Buchanan's ill-advised expedition against the Mormons had brought humiliation to the United States Army. Lot Smith's Mormon raiders burned Fort Bridger and Fort Supply, destroyed three Army wagon trains, and drove off over a thousand Army oxen and mules. Without supplies and equipment the Army dug in for the winter at the remains of Fort Bridger awaiting reinforcements. With spring they prepared to march into Salt Lake Valley. Thirty thousand Latter Day Saints left their homes ready for the torch and encamped on the barren flats west of Provo awaiting further orders.

In that miserable camp with its dirt and flies and short rations, Kate's third son had been born dead. Weeping as she lay in the wagon bed she shared with Nelly and their three boys, she thought that dead baby was one more sacrifice demanded by the Church. She had been too far along to make the rough drive from Salt Lake with Bishop Adams's company. Burns was away with the militia, and the Bishop had sent his fifteen-year-old son to drive the Hamilton wagon. The Church takes care of its own . . . she remembered Burns's young voice saying those words long ago.

Clothes were worn out, food and tempers short in the huge camp, so two months later when news came that a compromise had been worked out, it was with relief that the people began their homeward trek. The governor appointed by President Buchanan would be accepted, although everyone knew Brigham Young would still rule Utah through the Church. The Army would establish a camp in the barren valley west of Utah Lake leaving the Mormons strictly alone.

Readying the wagon for the trip back to Cottonwood, Kate was interrupted by a rider with a message from Burns. She and Nelly were to proceed to Provo and lodge with Bishop Smoot until Burns came for them.

The day he had arrived at the Bishop's home flashed into her mind now: She saw him as he was then, standing in the Bishop's lace-curtained parlor. A new wagon filled with goods stood outside in the yard. The spoils of war? she wondered, but dared not ask. The clothes Burns wore were a curious mixture of army and civilian, yet he managed somehow to look commanding. There was a new air to him, she had thought, pompous, almost arrogant. He had gone as a man doing his duty, defending his home and his people against an enemy bent on their destruction. Now he returned like a conquering hero, surely not the same sad-eyed man who had kissed her good-bye three months ago and sent her, eight months pregnant, with the fleeing Saints he meant to help defend. Burns was a man of duty, and above all things, above home and family and life itself, came his duty to the Church.

"We'll be staying in Provo permanently," he announced. "Brother Brigham has placed me in charge of the Tithing Office here. I'll also be overseeing the construction of a new meeting house." Kate saw that he was trying to look properly modest, though to her it seemed he was filled with the sin of pride. "When the mail situation is straightened out," he continued, "I'll probably be the new postmaster."

Nelly gasped, properly impressed, holding her hands over her burgeoning belly. Kate watched her bleakly. She had taken that poor, lost creature into her house, thinking she would never be truly a wife to Burns. But when Burns took a duty upon himself he did not shirk. That duty extended to giving Nelly children. She must not think of that now, Kate told herself. The miserable farce of a war had ended. Burns was home again, and whatever his faults, he would take care of her and love her.

To be in Brigham Young's favor was to prosper. Everyone knew that. In the past five years Burns's prestige had grown. People deferred to him. He managed the employment and lives of numbers of men. He enjoyed his position; he had worked hard and he was ambitious; he had come a long way from the mill in Wiltshire.

Inexplicably, in this tense moment, Kate thought how she had always loved his eyes. Now there were tight, angry lines gathered around those eyes glaring at her. In twelve years of marriage she had never openly opposed him on anything. A woman should know her place and keep it, as President Young often counseled the members of his flock. She should respect her husband's priesthood and love him so completely that his will was her law.

"Kate!" The deep voice could still shake her just as it had that first day she heard him preach so long ago in Liverpool. "You're forgetting yourself. Celestial Marriage is the law of God. It's a man's duty to multiply and replenish the earth. There are unborn souls awaiting bodies to come to this earth." He paused and the beloved eyes bored fiercely into hers. "You accepted the doctrine of plurality when Nelly was given to me."

Yes . . . Nelly, Kate thought bitterly . . . Nelly, upstairs now nursing her third baby. Nelly, with a five-year-old son named Burns Hamilton, Junior. But Kate had called that wound "duty" and suffered it as such. Staring defiantly at her husband, she thought she had shared him all she wished to share. Two wives were enough. They were not rich like Brigham Young who had more than twenty wives, or Heber C. Kimball who had said he thought no more of taking a wife than of buying a cow. How could one man, even one as hard-working and ambitious as Burns, support three families in comfort, or even in poverty? Nelly was his duty to God and the Church, she knew that. Until this moment she had found consolation in the knowledge that she was Burns's true and only love.

"I accepted Nelly because President Young asked you to take her and she was in dire need," Kate said, controlling her voice with an effort. "But this Alice . . . this ripe young thing . . . she's neither God's idea nor the president's."

"You're talking like an apostate, my dear." In spite of the endearment, Burns's voice was harsh. He drew himself up until it seemed to her he was seven feet tall. The smooth back of the chair grew slick with the sweat of her hands. His voice fell into the cold, measured tones he sometimes used in chastising the children. "I counseled with Brother Brigham when he was here last week. He said it's my duty. Now I tell you before God and the Prophet Joseph, this marriage between Alice and myself is ordained by the Lord."

Trembling, Kate clung to the chair, fearful her aching legs might give way. Sick and weak, stripped of pride in herself as a wife, stripped of the love she had thought he felt for her alone, she stared back at him, dry-eyed. She must not weep. Burns had only contempt for weeping women. Should she have guessed? He was always so busy, with little time for her these days. Their lives were filled to each hour of the day. No longer did they talk over the day's happenings as they lay in bed at night. The old, sweet closeness was gone. So many men stray after twelve years of marriage, but she had never believed it could happen to her.

How could he do this to her when he knew Nelly almost drove her wild every day? He had no need of another wife. She and Nelly kept the house and garden and entertained his guests in good style, even when they had to stay up half the night cooking for the brethren visiting from Salt Lake. And this Alice Swanson . . . seventeen years old, maybe . . . ripe, ready for the picking, but not, dear God, by a man of Burns's age. Hurt pride lashed out of her. "Ordained by God?" she asked, looking straight into his eyes. "You mean ordained by the lust of Burns Hamilton."

The astonishment in his face was quickly replaced by rage, and she was immediately sorry she had been so bold. Burns's temper was well known in this household. It sometimes took the victim weeks to get back into his good graces. Deferred to in public, he had come to expect nothing less at home.

"Go to your bedroom," he told her, obviously holding his anger in tight rein. "Fall down on your knees and pray God to forgive you. Tonight at family prayers we will all pray for you to bow before the will of the Lord." With one last furious glare he stalked from the kitchen.

On her knees beside the bed, she found she could not pray. God seemed to have deserted her in this moment of trial. Vaguely, through the whirlwind of pain consuming her, she could hear Nelly nagging at the little girls to take their afternoon naps, Nelly's three-year-old Jane sharing a bed with Kate's Mary Ann and Drusilla. The sound faded and Kate's mind drifted back . . . back to the long, dreary ocean voyage from Liverpool to New Orleans . . . back to the journey up the Mississippi to St. Louis where they had joined a Mormon wagon train heading for Salt Lake Valley . . . back to a bower of golden willows in Wyoming where her beloved son had been conceived. She remembered Burns's words the night he had wept and told her he must accept Nelly: "I love you more than life." And the promise, broken now and forgotten, he had made in the darkness of a wagon bed at Fort Supply: "Always my one and only love . . ."

Recalling those words now as she knelt alone in her bedroom, Kate thought she might die with anguish. She looked down at her ungainly figure, miserably comparing it with Alice's girlish curves. How could Burns choose so giddy a girl, almost twenty years younger than he? She had been chastised more than once for flirting with the boys at meeting and should have been called down for wearing her blonde hair in curls and dressing in so bold a manner. President Young was forever counseling the women against being overly concerned with adornment. I was a fool not to have known this was coming, Kate thought. She had seen Burns talking to Alice after meeting, smiling, bending over her, swinging her in a quadrille at the Church dances, his eyes blazing with a light she had not seen there in a long time.

"Oh, dear God," she moaned aloud. "How can I stand it?" How could a marriage begun with such devotion, such joy and passion, come to this? Naive as any bride, she had thought love would last forever. All her work for the Church of the new Israel, all the years of hardship and faithfulness had been in vain if she could not control the anguished jealousy she felt toward this young girl Burns intended to marry. Her heart must surely break at this loss of her husband's love. She had cherished him so, her whole life bound up in him, believing in him as she believed in God. She had even convinced herself he would never ask her to accept a younger wife. Other men might . . . all the Authorities had done so, but not her beloved Burns. Surely this was a trial of faith beyond her strength to endure.

No words of prayer rose to her lips, and she sank to sit on the bright rag rug, leaning her head against the side of the spool bed. Her hand ran along the coverlet she had pieced with such painstaking care. How many nights had she lain in that bed in Burns's arms . . . loving him, sometimes in such transports of joy Burns had seemed embarrassed by her passion. Never again, she thought bitterly, never again. No, that was a lie. It was her duty to be wife to him as it was his duty to give her children. But never again with love. Such a pain of loss stabbed through her that she nearly cried out. Her hands seized the coverlet violently as though to tear it into shreds.

"Damn you, Burns," she said aloud. "Oh . . . damn your whoring soul!"

Bishop Smoot and his wife gave Kate and Nelly a ride home from the wedding.

"Are you feeling all right, Sister Hamilton?" he asked. Kate wore a voluminous Mother Hubbard gown to conceal her pregnant figure, but the Bishop was aware of her condition.

"I'm fine," she lied. "Leave us off at the lane gate. I'll feel better for the walk to the house."

The rattle of his buggy faded in the distance. Silence lay over the moonlight-silvered fields and trees.

"It was a nice wedding," Nelly said in her tentative way, and Kate wanted to scream.

Of course it was a nice wedding. Burns was an important man and Alice's parents were well-to-do. There had been hired fiddlers for the dancing and tables spread with food and drink. Too far gone with child for the dancing, Kate sat in a straight chair and watched. Her face felt like plaster of Paris with the fixed smile she had pasted there early in the evening. Why had Burns insisted she attend and endure this torture? Her condition was excuse enough to stay at home. It was the custom, he said when Kate objected. It wouldn't look right if his other wives weren't present, and appearances were important to Burns. Appearances might be important, she thought wryly, watching him dance with Alice, but he could not disguise his infatuation. His eager eyes scarcely left the girl who was now his wife. Oh, she was a pretty dish all right, her smooth, almost childish face lifted adoringly to Burns. One hand lay on Burns's shoulder, white, unworn, and Kate looked down at the hands twisting in her lap, red and rough in spite of the tallow she rubbed into them. As she watched, Burns bent to whisper in Alice's ear, holding her so that her young breasts crushed against his chest. Like a bull after a cow in heat, Kate thought, sick and angry at once. Shocked at herself, she glanced quickly at the people around her as though they might have heard her thoughts.

Brigham Young had come down from Salt Lake with the wedding party after the ceremonies in the Endowment House. The Prophet enjoyed a party and had danced with every lady present who was able to dance . . . twice with Alice. Watching them, Kate thought that Brother Brigham liked the feel of a young girl's waist beneath his hand, too. Presently he singled her out, drawing a chair up close beside her.

"Fine party," he said jovially, smiling and nodding at the dancers moving in the figures of a quadrille.

"Fine," she answered, almost choking on the word.

The strong face sobered, the piercing gray eyes turned on her. "Your husband regrets you've had so much difficulty accepting this marriage," he began.

Kate folded her cold hands tight together, steeling herself against whatever pronouncement he was about to make. Now she felt the full force of that powerful personality.

"You're the first, Sister Kate," he continued, "the bride of Brother Burns's youth. No one can take that from you. But the first wife must set the tone of the household . . . keep harmony. Plurality isn't easy for young wives like Sister Alice either. If you help your husband's wives and children you will reap great blessings and help bring Brother Hamilton into the highest positions here on earth and to eternal exaltation in the Hereafter."

With the hypnotic eyes of that powerful man staring at her, Kate nodded weakly. He was the Prophet of God on earth and the final authority of the Latter Day Saints Church. She had no choice.

"Brother Hamilton looked very nice, I thought," Nelly said now as they walked down the dew-drenched lane toward the farmhouse. Said it as though she could not bear Kate's silence.

Fool . . . fool, Kate thought, grinding her teeth to hold back the words. Nelly would not feel this desolation. She had suffered no loss, for Burns was her protector, not her lover. But he was mine, Kate cried inwardly, and I loved him and he promised. Now he has eyes only for another woman. I am nothing to him . . . nothing. Her fingernails pierced the palms of her hands. With relief, she saw the lights of their farmhouse gleaming in the half dark. Now Nelly could go to bed, she would be rid of her infernal chattering.

Lying in the bed she had shared with her husband, there was no sleep for Kate. Tonight he shared another woman's bed, loving her as he had once loved . . . Oh, dear God! She sat up, almost stunned with pain at the picture in her mind. Burns . . . Burns . . . The tears were like acid on her face as she stumbled down the dark stairs. She made her way across the dooryard, moving ponderously, heavy with child, and stood by the pasture fence. Moonlight shimmered through her tears. Burns with Alice. Another woman where she should always be. The image would not die. An agonizing pain twisted through her as though a giant hand gripped her insides and tore at them. Leaning across the pasture fence, she vomited again and again.

The labor pains began just before dawn. It was a month too soon. Filled with fear at the memory of the two dead sons who had come too early, Kate counted the time between pains before calling Nelly.

"What'll I do?" Nelly asked, wringing her hands helplessly. Caught in the throes of pain, Kate wanted to scream in frustration at the woman's eternal indecision.

When the pain subsided, she swallowed her bitterness. "Wake Tom and send him to bring Sister Barker. He'll have to take the wagon since . . ." She stifled a scream that was as much anger as pain. ". . . since Papa has the buggy."

Within minutes Kate heard the horses driving out of the yard. That was Tom, whip-quick and always dependable. Sister Barker was a competent midwife, and everything would be fine once she arrived. But Nelly . . . she could never seem to retain what must be done. Between pains, Kate gave her instructions.

Mid-morning. She could tell by the way the light lay on the bedroom window. Sister Barker wiped the sweat from Kate's face with a damp rag. "Won't be long now," she said, her heavy, almost masculine face staring down at Kate.

Somewhere beyond the wall of pain, Kate heard a rig drive into the yard below, then a commotion downstairs. She had told Nelly to have Tom and Brig take the other children with them, away from the house, to the fields or the barn. Presently the rig drove away again and Nelly fluttered into the bedroom like a nervous sparrow.

"It was Brother Hamilton," she said.

"Well, where is he?" boomed Sister Barker, looking up from examining Kate.

Nelly's eyes darted about the room. "He took Alice home again. Said it was no time for her to be here." Nelly began to sob. "She could have helped . . . she could have . . ."

"Shut up and help me," said Sister Barker. "This baby's comin'."

Drowned in pain, Kate clung to the smooth wooden turnings of the spool bed and pushed her son Isaac into the world. Somewhere beneath the pain of birth another pain seared her, one she knew might never end until the long-awaited morning of the Resurrection when all love would be returned a thousandfold.

Chapter 6

Beyond the kitchen window in the early spring dusk, cotton drifted from the burst buds of the cottonwood trees, like an unseasonable snowstorm. Absently, Kate wiped the dishpan dry, her eyes on the white puffballs floating earthward. Never in England had she felt the change of season as she did here . . . this sudden lifting of heart as spring came on, the melancholy of autumn, the long hush of winter. In this beautiful valley she had found a rhythm that matched her own, a place where she belonged.

Tangled in the cottonwood branches, the ghost of a full moon hung in the darkening sky. The moon had been full that night nine years ago, she thought, stabbed by a pain that would never ease. Nine years ago . . . when her husband took himself a young wife. Kate knew now that the pattern had been set immediately. Alice was lady of the house. She had become pregnant almost at once, then miscarried at three months. Now she kept her own room and helped a little in the kitchen. Burns would always say, "Alice is fragile . . . Alice isn't well . . . she mustn't do heavy work." Kate learned to curb the sharp tongue she sometimes laid so scathingly on Nelly, for Alice would scurry to Burns in tears. He would then descend furiously on Kate. Alice had his doting ear now, and Kate was the outsider.

Nine years . . . or nine eternities? she wondered, thinking of the changes in their household since that day. Alice had been almost constantly pregnant, although she managed to carry to term only two babies, Burns Swanson and David. Kate's own family had grown, with Elizabeth coming two years after Isaac, and then the two little boys, Hyrum and Franklin. Almost three years now since that terrible day, with diphtheria ravaging the countryside, when those two little boys had died in her arms, one after the other. Had Robert not been born a few months later she might have gone out of her mind with grief. Robbie was an extraordinary child, everyone said . . . her joy, her own personal gift from God.

"She looks like the cat that swallowed the canary," Nelly's voice brought Kate back to the present.

Her brief pleasure in the spring evening suddenly gone, Kate hung up the dishpan and did not reply. Nelly's penchant for inconsequential chatter was often irritating, but she knew very well whom Nelly meant. Alice had gone to the April General Conference of 1872 in Salt Lake City with Burns. He took his wives, turn about, to Conference, always a great social occasion as well as the most important of Church gatherings. Whatever happened in Salt Lake, Alice knew about it and they did not. With that irritating air of self-importance she liked to assume, Alice had announced after supper that she must lie down and rest.

Nelly's speculations as to the reasons for Alice's smug behavior began to wear. "Never mind!" Kate's voice had an edge to it. "She can't keep a secret long and, anyway, he will certainly tell us about Conference this evening."

The entire family gathered in the front room for family prayers. Burns stood before the fireplace, feet apart, hands behind his back, surveying his wives and offspring. Kate, sitting in the Congress armchair with Robbie on her lap, hoped her husband wouldn't deliver one of his long sermons. Even she became restive when he went on at too much length. She looked about at the nicely furnished room. Everything had been acquired by dint of much sacrifice and hard work . . . making soap for Sister Watson to have the rag carpet woven, and the many pounds of dried apples gone to purchase the plush-covered sofa. Kate frowned. Alice lay on the sofa now, with a knitted afghan covering her. Burns Swanson and David, her two small sons, sat on the floor beside her.

"My dear family," Burns began after clearing his throat loudly to quiet the chattering little girls. "We have been called to fulfill a great and glorious mission for the Lord." A terrible sinking sensation drained through Kate. A mission. That meant they would have to move again, just when they had the house nice and the farm running so well. It meant leaving this valley she loved, this first earthly place where she had been truly at home. By 1872 all the beautiful northern valleys had been occupied. There remained only the southern settlements . . . barren desert and poverty.

"Where, Papa?" one of the children asked, and Kate sat too dazed to know who had spoken.

"We will help build a Temple to the Lord!" Burns's voice rose, his eyes burning zealously. "President Young has called me to be in charge of gathering in the tithing to build a Temple in St. George."

St. George. The sinking feeling rolled into a ball of lead in the pit of her stomach. All the stories of the difficulties of that mission came to mind: the poverty, the desperate struggle to raise cotton in that desert land. Brigham Young had envisioned the warm southern country as a new Dixie. A company of colonizers had been sent in 1861 to plant cotton and later build a cotton factory for the weaving of cloth, their mission made more urgent by the oncoming War between the States. It was one more step in President Young's dream of self-sufficiency for Zion. But no one had reckoned the price the desert exacts for every drop of water and every inch of mineral-impregnated earth. The people struggled and grew cotton, then starved because there was no market for it, and they had grown little in the way of food crops. Now the Civil War was over and the market for their cotton even more limited. No member, however devout, rejoiced at being called to Dixie. The children would have to leave their friends and their school; the crops were barely in and it looked like a good season.

"Since our crops are in," Burns continued, as though reading her mind, "some of us must stay, dispose of the property, and gather the harvest. Foodstuffs are scarce in southern Utah, and we will need to bring our own supplies."

Alice made no attempt to suppress the smug little smile she had worn all evening. With rising anger, Kate guessed Burns's next words before he spoke.

"My good Kate," he said, smiling benignly at her. "Ever a thrifty and efficient manager. Since your children are older, they can manage the harvest with a little help from the neighbors. Alice will go with me to prepare a place for you in St. George."

Kate stared at the top of Robbie's head, struggling to contain her indignation. The only place Alice would ever prepare would be for herself. Even after nine years, and in spite of his disappointment at her not being able to raise a big family, Burns still doted on Alice, still favored her, still gave in to her coaxing for frills and special presents. No matter how much Kate hated leaving Utah Valley, she would have liked to be first, to be the one at her husband's side.

"We'll leave for St. George immediately," Burns continued. "Excavation work has already begun. The people of St. George badly need this work." He turned a severe look on Kate. "Not one of you must feel resentful at doing the labor of the Lord. Men will be called from all the southern settlements to work on the Temple . . . artisans, carpenters, masons. It is God's will."

Kneeling beside a chair, he signaled that family prayers were to begin. The prayer was long, importuning God's blessing on this mission they were about to undertake, asking Him to fill every heart with joy at being called to do the work of the Lord.

Kneeling beside Robbie, her hands resting on the scratchy woolen seat of the armchair, Kate did not feel thankful to God as Burns had just said they all did, nor did she wish to be tested any further. Enough, God! she wanted to cry out. But she knelt in silence, looking down at the child kneeling beside her, his curly head resting on his small folded hands. Not yet two, but so quick and bright. Love for him flowed out of her like water from an overfull cup. She half-reached to embrace him. No. Kate bowed her head and said the words under her breath. "Thank you, God. Thank you for the comfort and joy of this wonderful child."

After prayers, the children were sent to bed. Alice went upstairs pleading fatigue from her trip. Nelly followed, her pale face blank and frightened, for Burns had not once mentioned what she was to do.

Kate knelt at Robbie's bedside prompting his halting prayer, trying not to let her inner distress come between her and this beloved child. Tucking the covers about him, she bent for his good night kiss. Soft baby hands clung to her neck, his wide brown eyes adoring.

"I love you, Mama," Robbie whispered.

Eyes damp, Kate held him fiercely close to her. "You make up for everything, Robbie," she murmured, kissing him again.

The round childish face was puzzled. "Everything?"

Almost everything, she thought, but she smiled reassuringly, and said, "I love you more than everything."

Content with that, Robbie reached to pat her cheek. "G'night, Mama."

One small child could ease your heartaches, Kate told herself as she walked down the stairs, but he could not make them go away. Oh dear God, am I always to be shunted aside, left behind, always second best to a younger wife? Pride is hard to subdue. Be not prideful before the Lord. But why could not Burns leave her something, some token of caring, some feeling of devotion? When she walked into the front room to see Burns banking the fire for the night, the hurt had grown into simmering anger.

"Why Alice?" she asked, her voice harsh in the dim, quiet room. Only one lamp still burned, the one Burns would carry to light his way to Nelly's bedroom.

"What?" He turned to look at her, uncomprehending. The fire banked, the room had already begun to grow cool, and Kate felt a shiver run along her arms.

"Shall I quote Brother Brigham, Burns?" she went on. "I'm your first wife . . . the bride of your youth. Or have you forgotten that? Why should Alice have all the privileges, always be in your company?"

"You mean why am I taking Alice and Nelly to St. George instead of you?" He seemed surprised she should even ask the question.

"Yes!" She bit off the word.

"Why, my dear Kate," he began in a soothing way, "I could never leave Alice in charge here . . . feather-headed Alice to dispose of our property, to oversee the harvest . . ." He smiled indulgently. "Believe me, I'd as soon leave one of the children to do the job." Giving her a perplexed look, he continued, "You have a good head for business, Kate. You're a good manager and I trust your judgment. Alice couldn't take care of such things. Why, she always needs someone to take care of her."

A sour taste rose in Kate's mouth. Was that all she meant to this man she had loved . . . she was a good manager? "Alice is smart, isn't she?" she asked, her voice deceptively soft. "I wish I had the opportunity to learn her wiles. If you're weak, if you need to be cared for, someone will always care for you. But if you're strong and carry the load, someone is always willing to add to that load."

Burns stared blankly at her. He didn't even understand, Kate thought, a painful stinging behind her eyes. He had no conception of what she meant. This strong and brilliant man had no intuition as to what lay behind her words. He saw only his road directly ahead, his duty to the Church and his progression into the Celestial Kingdom in the Hereafter. All else fell by the wayside, including this first wife who had loved him with all her heart.

Turning, she walked heavily up the stairs, his "Good night, my dear" echoing after her. She was a shell, empty and drained of love, thankful he would not be spending the night with her.

Chapter 7

The last rays of light glinted off the silvery surface of Utah Lake. Shadows of the leafless Lombardy poplars stretched across the empty garden. The mountains had been so beautiful this fall, a giant patchwork of scarlet and gold, the oak and maple trees bare and gray now against the evergreens. Standing at the kitchen window, Kate looked up at the encircling arms of those lofty mountains, not gentle and rolling like the hills of England, but strong, tall, and protective. Utah Valley had been her promised land, green, fertile, safe. Now she must leave it.

That low October sun turned the snows of Timpanogos red as blood. Timpanogos, the Indian maiden who had died for love. The sorrowing gods, so the legend went, laid her upon a bier and turned her into a mountain to sleep forever along the northern edge of the Utah Valley. Something painful caught at her throat and Kate turned away. Utah women no longer died for love, she thought bitterly, they died for lack of it.

The months since April Conference seemed interminable. She and her children had been left to harvest the last crop from the farm which had been their home for so long. It had been sold to Brigham Young, although they received no cash for the sale, only credit to their account at the Tithing Office. They would be able to draw food and goods as needed against that credit. Half the business in Utah was conducted through the Tithing Office where people paid their tithe to the Church however they could, in produce, goods, or money.

Looking out the window at the bare cottonwoods, their leaves lying in dusty piles in the dooryard, she saw Brig and Tom coming toward the house, carrying the night's milking in tin buckets. How tall those two boys had grown, and what a help and support they had been this summer. Her firstborn, Brigham, long prayed for and dearly loved, was now a manly, solemn sixteen-year-old. They had always counted Tom a year older than Brig, although they could not be sure of his real age. He had grown into a handsome boy, tall and strongly built, his skin the color of burnished copper, prominent nose and high cheekbones, black eyes that often spilled with laughter as he teased the girls or chided Brig for being so solemn.

A chilling sweep of autumn air came into the kitchen with the two boys. Mary Ann, her dark brown hair tied back with a ribbon, took the milk buckets and began pouring milk through the strainer into the wide, flat pans where it would set until morning for the cream to rise.

"Will Papa be back from Salt Lake tonight?" Brig asked, going to the basin to wash his hands.

"Be careful, Mary Ann!" Kate's voice was sharp as the girl carelessly slopped milk onto the table. Tom reached to take the heavy bucket. "I don't know." Kate turned to check supper cooking on the stove. "He has to meet with President Young."

Burns had returned from St. George to attend the October General Conference, report on the progress of the new Temple, and finish disposing of his property in Provo. The move south would be a permanent one, and this time Kate and her children would go along.

Brig took an empty milk bucket to the stove and splashed hot water from the tea kettle into it. "Papa should have taken you to Conference with him," he said, an odd undertone to the mild words.

Wishing he hadn't voiced such an opinion, Kate replied quickly, "Isaac and Elizabeth were sick."

Mary Ann gave her a strange look. "They're all right . . . besides, I could have taken care of them." At twelve, Mary Ann could be responsible when she wanted to, even though she would rather ride horses with Tom and Isaac than help in the house.

"Finish with the milk, so we can get supper on," Kate told them, ending the conversation. Turning away, she busied herself at the stove so the children couldn't see her face. She had expected to go to

Conference with Burns. It would be lovely to shop in the Salt Lake stores and be entertained by their friends, the Richardses and the Spencers. But Burns had said no. She must stay and prepare for the return journey. It was important to leave immediately to avoid the autumn storms. Even this early in the winter there was often snow on the passes. Hurt and angry, she had watched him drive away in the fine new Ahlander buggy. Five months she had been here alone with her children, caring for his property, wishing for his company. If he had never come back she could have learned to be content without him, but the affection he rationed out kept a tiny flame alive. Burns was her husband, and she was bound to him by the vows they had taken at the Endowment House for time and all eternity; bound to him by their children, by her duty to live the Gospel of the Lord. He had never been deliberately unkind, but it hurt that she seemed to matter so little to him. Perhaps one never stopped wanting to be first with one's husband.

"Robbie doesn't feel good," Drusilla announced, coming into the kitchen. "He's hot as hell and he threw up."

"Drusilla! Watch your language," Kate snapped, glaring at Mary Ann who had giggled.

"But he's hotter than fire, Mama . . ." Drusilla looked up with innocent blue eyes. ". . . so he must be hot as hell."

"Little girls don't say hell," Kate told her firmly. "Here, Mary Ann, stir the gravy. Tom can finish the milk." Hurrying to follow Drusilla into the front room she saw Robbie sitting on the floor, his face against the sofa, moaning softly. "Get a rag and clean up the mess," she told Drusilla. Lifting Robbie, she kissed his burning forehead. How she loved the feel of a baby in her arms, and this one was most precious of all.

The hour grew late and Kate knew Burns would not return that night. He was among friends in Salt Lake, eating heartily at their tables, being regaled with the latest gossip. Thank God she hadn't gone. Perhaps it was meant to be, for Robbie was deathly ill. Whatever ailed Isaac and Elizabeth, the older children had thrown it off, but it seemed too much for the baby. Nothing she gave him stopped the vomiting or the diarrhea. After each attack he lay moaning and exhausted, small hands clutching at his stomach. If only she had some laudanum, but Burns would not allow such medicines in his house, believing only in the efficacy of prayer and the power of the priesthood to heal. There were few doctors in this country, anyway, and none would ever be allowed in Burns's home.

Tom built a fire in the front room where Kate spread quilts on the sofa to make a bed for Robbie. The children, who usually gathered in the kitchen after supper, came to sit there. Mary Ann took out her school books and made Tom sit beside her and read aloud.

Tom had been sent off to school with Brig when he was seven, coming home that first day with torn clothing, his face swollen and bleeding. Grim and slightly battered himself, Brig had told her how Tom was forced to spend most of the day fighting his tormentors. No matter that Tom was well spoken and had learned his manners, he was still an Indian in a white man's school. Those children had heard too many stories of Indian atrocities and seen too many Indian beggars to be tolerant.

"Do you want to go back to school?" Burns had asked at the supper table, staring at Tom's swollen lip. With downcast eyes, Tom shook his head. Charley snickered and Kate clenched her fists to keep from getting up and slapping him. Under Burns's furious eyes, Charley shrank into silence. "Perhaps it's for the best," Burns said with a heavy sigh. "The hired man can use your help, and Mama can teach you your letters."

Tom had seemed not to mind, even seemed happy to stay at home working on the farm. Now that he was seventeen they no longer needed a hired man. With Brig and Isaac to help this fall and a crew for the harvesting, everything had gone smoothly under Tom's discreet guidance. Burns was proud of "my Indian boy" as he called Tom when he was pointing out to others in the Church how the Lamanites could be saved and civilized.

In spite of her concern for the sick baby, Kate had to smile at the two heads bent near the pool of light from the coal-oil lamp. Mary Ann took charge of Tom as though he were her child, teaching him the lessons she learned in school, correcting his manners. Tom obeyed in docile adoration, even though he was a grown boy and Mary Ann still a bossy little girl.

How she had managed to bear a girl as unruly as Mary Ann, Kate could not imagine. "She should have been a boy," Burns had said a hundred times, shaking his head over his oldest daughter's latest escapade. Schooling was too easy for her, and the teacher often complained that she was impudent and sassy. Just now Mary Ann was in a coltish stage, neither child nor young girl, but one could see the promise of a handsome woman with her father's dark hair and eyes.

Across the table, Drusilla's golden head was bent over the sampler she was embroidering. At eleven Drusilla was a young lady already, completely feminine, sweet and compliant, never causing trouble.

Then there was Isaac, who might have been Mary Ann's twin, he was so unmanageable. Kate sighed, remembering her agony of mind before Isaac's birth, wondering if that had made him so rebellious and difficult. He was a good worker, when forced to it. Between them, he and Mary Ann could keep an uproar going. Isaac sat now staring into the fire, his blue eyes intent on something only he could see, his dark hair awry as always. Kate could not have said where his looks came from, for his features were somehow awry too, not fine and regular like those of the other children. Once when she had mentioned it to Burns, he frowned and turned away abruptly, saying Isaac resembled his father. Poor Isaac, Kate had thought, for Burns had no love for the father who had turned him out when he joined the Church.

Seven-year-old Elizabeth sat at the table, her towhead lying on folded arms, blue eyes intent on Tom's face as he read, frowning when he stumbled over a word.

Her brief joy in the children vanished as her eyes fell on the restlessly sleeping Robbie. Fear went through her like a winter wind. Dear God, she thought, don't take him. I can't bear to lose another of my children and he's my baby—my special love . . . to make up for my other lost boys.

Family prayers that night were for Robbie alone. When they were finished, Kate sent the children to bed. Papa would surely be back from Salt Lake tomorrow, she told them, and there would be much to do before they started their journey to the south.

Brigham lingered after the others had gone, his gold-brown eyes dark with concern. "Do you think he'll be all right, Mama?"

"I don't know," she answered, suddenly near tears. Reaching out, she grasped Brig's hand tightly. As she looked up into his handsome, somber face, so like her young husband of long ago, she thought that she loved all her children, but this tall boy was dearer than life to her. "Stay with me," she said, eyes swimming. "Stay and help me with Robbie."

Through the long night, he was beside her, bringing cold water to sponge Robbie's small, feverish body, helping change the sweat-soaked sheets and the diapers. Robbie woke, crying with pain, and fell again into exhausted sleep. Toward dawn, Kate dozed in her chair, awakening to find Brig kneeling beside Robbie, his earnest young face lifted beseechingly to heaven in silent prayer. Standing up, she went to him and laid her hand on his shoulder. Brig seized her hand, kissing it, and she felt his hot tears burn her skin.

"Come, dear," she said wearily. "It's almost morning. After breakfast you can go for Bishop Smoot, and we'll have the Elders administer to Robbie." Turning away, her mouth trembling, she fought down the sob rising in her throat. "Oh . . . surely God won't take Robbie from me."

Still dizzy with sleep, Kate looked up into Burns's frowning face. The disapproval there, the desolation of afternoon light in the half-empty bedroom brought an ache to her throat. She had left Robbie with the girls after dinner and lain down for a short rest. He had seemed better after the Elders came, anointed his head with the consecrated oil, and prayed God to heal this child.

"I have strict orders from Brother Brigham to leave tomorrow," Burns said sternly. "I don't see how it can be done now, since nothing at all seems to have been accomplished while I was gone."

Rising on her elbow, Kate stared at him, so exhausted she felt she could not even sit up. "Robbie took so sick yesterday. I was up all night with him."

"The girls could have looked after him," he snapped, obviously upset that he would not be able to follow Brother Brigham's orders.

Brother Brigham, first, last, and always, Kate thought, feeling resentful tears sting her eyes. "I couldn't bear to lose Robbie," she said, her lips trembling. "I couldn't bear it."

"We can bear what the Lord sends us." Burns's voice was suddenly gentle. "Robbie was awake when I came in. Mary Ann says he's better."

"Oh, thank God!" Kate stood up, anxious to go to her baby.

Burns took her in his arms, patting her back, holding her close against him. "I missed you, Kate. Wished I'd taken you with me. All our friends asked after you."

Burns seldom admitted he wished he'd done anything differently. Touched by his words, thinking of the long, lonely summer with only Robbie to share her bed, Kate yielded to his embrace. The roughness of his moustache, the touch of his strong masculine mouth filled her with suppressed and denied longing. Whether she could ever again love him as she once had, his regard was important to her and she was pleased that he had missed her.

"Well," he said, holding her away from him. "We'd best get on with our packing. We'll load beds and stove last. Are your trunks ready?"

The brief moment of closeness vanished as though it had never been. Sighing, Kate smoothed her hair and straightened the rumpled dress about her slender figure. "The trunks in the front room are ready."

As soon as they arose next morning the beds were dismantled and loaded. Robbie was worse again. Kate sat beside the fireplace holding her feverish baby, no longer interested in pleasing Burns or Brother Brigham, or being ready to leave for St. George. A child as sick as this one could not travel, no matter what Burns said. They would have to stay until Robbie was better.

Coming in from loading the wagons, Burns looked at the boy, touched his forehead, and, frowning, went into the kitchen to speak to Brig. After a moment Kate heard the sound of a horse being ridden away. Brig returned with Bishop Smoot and Brother Webster. Once more Robbie's burning forehead was anointed with oil. Now three Elders laid hands on the child's head and Burns acted as mouth, saying the prayer asking God to keep and heal this child.

Robbie sighed, turning to pillow his face against Kate's breast. His glazed eyes closed and the child slept.

Burns's face glowed. "God will spare him," he said confidently. "He will be well again." Kate, seeing the triumph in Burns's eyes, was drenched with relief. The power of the priesthood, in the person of her husband, had surely saved her beloved baby.

Yet, within the hour, the teams hitched and the wagons ready to roll, Robbie lay slack and feverish once more. "We can't go, Burns," Kate said. "I won't go until Robbie's better. I won't chance losing him."

Burns took a familiar considering stance, feet apart, hands behind his back, and stared out at the loaded wagons. The rasp of the broom Tom was using to sweep soot from the empty kitchen echoed through the bare front room.

"We're called to go, Kate," Burns said at last, his measured tones falling like hammer blows on her heart. "God will care for Robbie. The trip may be just what he needs . . . the fresh air and sunshine." He smiled into her incredulous face. "Come, my dear, bundle up the child and we'll start. It's a beautiful day to begin our journey."

"For the love of God, Burns," Kate cried hoarsely. "Can't you see this child is too ill to travel? You've asked much of me in the past . . . but don't ask this."

"I'm already a day late starting. I'm carrying orders for President Snow. I'm needed in St. George and I intend to take you with me. Come." He started for the door.

"I will never forgive you if anything happens to Robbie," Kate whispered to his retreating back, and he seemed not to hear.

Chapter 8

The child in her arms moaned softly with every jolt of the buggy. For two days she had held him, seeking to ease him from the roughness of the road. Her arms were numb now and beyond pain. Beside her on the seat a silent Burns concentrated on driving the horses. Their two wagons and those of the Benson and McAlpine families, also heading for St. George, were strung out behind them. The wagons driven by Brig and Tom were loaded to the canvas with furniture, food, and tools. Isaac, on horseback, kept track of the horses and milk cows. The three girls sat in the buggy behind their parents. Now and then they would walk to rest themselves. They could always catch up with the wagons at nooning or evening camp.

Across the rolling valley, the little settlement of Salt Creek had been in sight for hours. Burns had made arrangements for Kate and the girls to stay there for the night with their old friends, the Gunthers. The boys would camp outside of town with the stock and the other wagons. When at last the buggy rolled into the Gunther home yard, Kate felt the tears rise at the sight of Melissa's welcoming face. How huge Melissa had grown, broad as a barn, with great, sagging, uncorseted breasts.

Henry Gunther came to meet them, bareheaded in the evening cold; picking his teeth for they had interrupted his supper; his blue bib overalls stained with manure around the cuffs. He had grown nearly as broad as his wife. "Sick baby, huh?" he said, peering at Robbie. "Let Meliss take him. She has a way with sickness."

Melissa took the child from Kate's aching arms, cooing softly to him. She soon had a bed made for him near the sitting room fire.

(65)

While Melissa devoted herself to Robbie, Henry's three other wives scurried about the kitchen, making supper for their guests.

"If that baby isn't better by morning, you'd better not move him," Melissa told Burns in positive tones. Burns looked shaken, but did not reply, pausing to stare down at the limp child on the couch before going outside with Henry.

With Robbie sleeping and the girls bedded down with the Gunther girls, the women gave themselves over to reminiscing about their long-ago trip across the plains. It amused Kate, the way Melissa ordered Henry and the other wives about. The loving, heartbroken Melissa she remembered was all matriarch now. Although Alice and Nelly sometimes complained at Kate's exacting demands, she could never treat Burns in that manner.

"You're plumb wore out," Melissa told Kate. "Get on to bed. I'll sit up with Robbie." She touched the sleeping child's forehead. "Fever's down."

Kate leaned to kiss the baby's forehead and smooth his damp hair. "I guess you're right, Meliss. He does seem better and I am surely worn out." She squeezed her friend's hand. "Call me if he gets bad in the night. He always wants his Mama."

"Kate." Disoriented, lost, Kate opened her eyes into the gray dawn of an unfamiliar bedroom. She looked up into Melissa's broad, tear-streaked face. "Oh . . . Kate!" Next to her Burns stirred uneasily and groaned in his sleep. Flinging back the quilts, Kate sat up, the cold air painful as a sharp knife.

"Robbie?" she asked.

"Kate . . . I'm sorry," Melissa sobbed. "I dozed off . . . and he . . . he just slipped away."

By noon Henry Gunther had fashioned a small pine coffin. It was a craft he knew well, having buried several of his own children. The Gunther families and the Hamiltons gathered in the parlor for a short funeral service. Henry's neighbor, Brother Lang, was leaving for Salt Lake in the morning with a load of freight. He agreed to take Robbie's body to Bishop Smoot in Provo so that the child might be buried there beside his brothers as Kate wished.

Burns bowed his head, his strong, resonant voice loud in the crowded room. "Oh Lord, our God. Thou hast seen fit to call this boy home." His voice broke and there was a brief struggling silence before he continued. "Surely this child was a choice spirit which You had need of in Heaven. We know that he dwells with Thee this day in everlasting glory. Give us strength, oh God, to bear and understand our loss. Help us to so live that in the great Hereafter Robert may be restored to us once more and we shall have the privilege of raising him up to manhood. We thank Thee for the true Gospel of Jesus Christ restored to this earth through Thy Prophet Joseph Smith. Bless us in Thy infinite wisdom that we may understand and accept Thy Gospel plan . . . that we may be worthy to dwell with Thee and be reunited with Robert once more. We ask these blessings in the name of Thy son, Jesus Christ. Amen."

She must stop crying, Kate told herelf, the silent tears hot on her cheeks. It upset the children so. Tom and Brig stood quiet and grim-faced, Mary Ann embraced Drusilla and Elizabeth, and Isaac wept against his mother's sleeve. As Burns prayed she stared at his bowed head through blurred eyes. This man was her husband, the love of her youth, and she thought she would choke on the bitterness she felt toward him. Robbie would be alive if they had stayed in Provo until he was well . . . the trip was too hard on him. Yet there was no evidence that Burns felt any guilt for insisting they go. A man who was law in his household came first, he would have no time for regrets. Death was no stranger to her. She had buried four sons already, but Robbie had seemed God's gift to make up for those lost boys. She was forty-one. There might never be another baby now, and there would certainly never be another Robbie. Burns cared more for the Church and Brigham Young than he did for his son. He had brushed aside her pleas and sacrificed Robbie to his zeal for the Church. How many times before had he hurt and ignored her, and when the wound scarred over she learned to care for him again simply because he was her husband and her only refuge? This time the wound was too deep ever to heal. She would never live long enough to forgive him.

As Brother Gunther dedicated the coffin to the Lord, Burns came to place his arm about Kate's shoulders. She stood cold and still, unyielding to the pressure of his hand. God forgive me, she thought, I hate you for what you've done. She could not look at him.

When suppertime came, she could not eat. Melissa insisted that she go to bed. The bedroom was too cold and she was too exhausted to kneel to pray. Lying on her back, staring into the darkness, she whispered into the silent room.

"Dear Lord, help me accept the loss of my baby. Help me to know he dwells in Paradise with Thee now . . . and oh, my God, help me to cleanse the bitterness toward my husband from my heart that I may once more be a wife and mother in the new Israel."

Saying the words seemed to ease the pain a little, though it occurred to her that God was sometimes cruel and His purposes obscure. Sleep did not come.

When Burns came to bed and embraced her as though ready to perform his conjugal duties, she pushed him away and turned her back to him. In all the years together it was the first time she had denied him.

"Kate?" he said in a surprised voice. "Kate?" She did not reply. After a moment he leaned over to kiss her cheek, then turned on his pillow, yawned, and fell asleep.

She curled up tight on herself as one does to ease an inner pain, and the tears squeezed endlessly from beneath her closed eyelids.

Kate stood on the Gunther porch, hugging her shawl against the cold, and watched Brother Lang's wagon move off down the road. The pleasant weather in which they began this journey had given way to the leaden skies of an approaching autumn storm.

The pine-clad slopes of Mount Nebo rose abruptly from the valley floor to the east. Timpanogos was a faint blue line on the northern horizon, framed by rolling brown foothills. Along the road squares of golden wheat stubble and brown plowed earth cut straight lines through the undulating sagebrush.

Each time the wagon hit a bump in the road, the small coffin lifted and jolted between the grain sacks. Kate wished they had put some straw in the wagon bed to cushion her baby. Don't hurt him, she wanted to cry, drive slowly . . . he's been hurt so much for such a little boy.

Burns's arm was around her and he patted her shoulder. "Come inside, Mother," he said. "You'll take a chill standing here in the cold."

Staring straight ahead, she ignored him, and only with an effort fought down the bitter words rising to her tongue. Burns sighed, patted her again, turning to herd the red-eyed children into the house. Only Brigham remained on the porch with his mother.

Desolate with grief, Kate stood, her eyes still straining after the wagon growing smaller and smaller across the rolling plain. After a moment she felt Brig's hand take hers. Grasping it tightly, she pressed it against her wet cheek. A blast of icy air rattled the leafless vines hanging from the porch. Black crows roosting in the bare cottonwoods shifted about, cawing dolorously into the wind.

Chapter 9

꧁꧂ The heat was smothering . . . inescapable. You could even smell it, as though the air were filled with the essence of living things drawn from them by the blazing desert sun. The red dust of the streets was like fire, so that barefoot children scampered across to cool their feet in the irrigation ditch before proceeding on their errands.

Hell couldn't be hotter than St. George in the summertime, Kate thought, lifting her apron to wipe the sweat from her face. With the stove going constantly in this kitchen, it was enough to make you think hell might be preferable. Not yet noon, and already her clothes were stained with perspiration.

"Nelly," she snapped. "Why isn't the floor swept? You know it has to be done after breakfast. Some of those men have the manners of pigs." Nelly sniffed, wiped her nose on her sleeve, and went to find the broom. She had grown skinny as a crone since coming to St. George and moved slower every day. It was enough to drive a person wild.

Sighing, Kate turned to watch the girls putting away the last of the breakfast dishes. The kitchen was huge and well equipped, with an enormous nickel-plated iron stove, plenty of work tables and cupboards. President Erastus Snow, head of the Dixie mission, had built this great four-story house, with its twenty rooms, not only for his large family, but to accommodate travelers from Salt Lake and those passing through on the old trail to California. Now he had leased the house to the Church as a boardinghouse for the men from all parts of the territory called on work missions to build the Temple.

The Hamilton family had been in St. George only two months

when President Snow's third wife, who had always run the Big House, fell ill and Brigham Young asked them to take over the boardinghouse. Burns had been pleased, Kate remembered, trying to smother her resentment. The day was hot and she was tired. She must not forget Burns's admonition that his family was in this way helping to build a Temple to the Lord. All but Alice, she thought grimly, lifting a basket of string beans to the table. Her fingers snapped and strung the beans violently, as though they represented Alice.

Brigham Young had ordered that there be no further private building in St. George until the Temple was completed. While there were some who did not comply, Burns was ever a man of duty. On his arrival he had bought a small house from a Brother who had left the mission. When Kate and her family arrived, he told her they would all live there until the Temple to the Lord had been built. Only then would he provide a better home for them.

The little house had been in chaos. Alice had just delivered another stillborn child, and Nelly was the usual slovenly self to which she alway reverted when not supervised. Within a week Kate had the place organized, the parlor turned into a bedroom so that each wife had her own room. The covered wagon boxes were set up in the yard with beds inside for the older children, the younger ones sharing their mothers' bedrooms. Alice remained in the house now, not well enough to help in the boardinghouse, Burns claimed. Nelly's youngest, Josie, lived with Alice to help with her work.

The beans snip-snapping quickly through her fingers, Kate called to Nelly's oldest daughter, a younger edition of her mother, "Jane, you and Elizabeth set the table for dinner. Mary Ann, bring in the potatoes, and Drusilla can help you peel them."

Orders . . . orders, she thought as everyone flew to do her bidding. It wasn't fair that her girls never had time to laze away the hot summer afternoons, or even to sit on the porch in the warm evenings. At least she had the meat going, having put the beef to boil before breakfast was started. She hoped Brother Winsor would send another supply of beef and cheese in from the Church herd at Pipe Springs before Sunday or she would have to call on President Snow to request more contributions from St. George residents. The women did laundry and cleaning for the Temple workers. That was enough, they were getting tired of donating their chickens to feed them. Brother Oxborrow would be by soon to deliver the bread and cakes. At least they had no baking to do.

It seemed to her she was always yelling at the girls and Nelly nowadays, always sharp and irritable with them. As soon as dinner was on the stove she would brew a little tea for all of them. They deserved at least that comfort.

Burns would be here tonight to begin his two weeks in the Big House . . . a week with Kate and a week with Nelly. If he came for supper late, the two of them might eat alone and she would tell him she was pregnant again. Another child . . . so perhaps God had answered her prayers. Burns would be pleased, she knew. She also knew that the difficulties of pregnancy seemed to increase with age. Every morning she was so dizzy and light-headed, with a vague nauseous feeling and aches in her pelvis all day. No wonder she was irritable.

His position in St. George satisfied Burns. People deferred to him here even more than they had in Provo . . . Brother Hamilton this, and Brother Hamilton that . . . He was Brigham Young's personal representative and a member of the Bishop's Court. Two of his families were housed and fed at the expense of the Church, although they worked hard for it. The boys—Charley, Brig, Tom, and Burnie—were helping haul rock for the Temple. Isaac did his part, too, chopping and carrying armload after armload of wood for the cook stove.

Under her guidance the boardinghouse ran as efficiently as she had run Burns's household all these years. He never had to give it a thought, except when Nelly or Alice complained that Kate was too demanding. The Gospel said that a woman's exaltation in this life and the next was no more or less than that of her husband. She had to believe that, and believe, too, that she was a fortunate woman to be the wife of a leader like Burns Hamilton. Oh, it had been hard not to nurse her bitterness over Robbie's death, not to blame Burns for putting duty first. It had taken many months and many prayers before she could feel affection for her husband again, and pride in his position had been a cold comfort. Long ago she had thought they would go down through the years, surrounded by their children, their love growing stronger, ever closer in mind and spirit. Did it happen like this with other women, or did they not mind that there was no real touching of spirit with their mates . . . that life boiled down to a series of daily tasks?

The pile driver started work . . . echoing through the valley . . . over and over, monotonously pounding. Would they never be through beating rock into that unlikely site Brigham Young had chosen to build the Temple? Even after they stopped work for the night Kate could hear it thumping inside her head. There were some who criticized Brother Brigham's choice, since it was necessary to tamp tons of volcanic rock into the soft earth so that it would support the great Temple building. Kate's head began to throb. The Mormons would build a temple in hell if Brigham Young said so . . . and the Devil himself could not stop them.

The potatoes were boiling and the green beans Brother Dodge had brought were simmering on the stove. The men would eat well today, all sixty of them. How heavenly that tea smelled. Even Burns could not live the Word of Wisdom to the extent of giving up his tea. A little ashamed of how hard she was on the girls, for they never talked back—except Mary Ann, of course—she set cups out for all of them and called, "Come have a little tea, girls."

Nelly sighed heavily as she sat down, her eyes sunken and haggard in her thin face. Poor Nelly, this country was enough to kill anyone. The water would likely rot your kidneys. It was so tainted with mineral, one could hardly bear to drink it straight. The river water was even worse. Virgin Bloat, the locals called it, "too thin to plow, too thick to drink."

The girls took their places around the oilcloth-covered table in the big, dim kitchen. Outside the pile driver relentlessly drowned out all other sounds. Kate began pouring tea, wondering whether she could ever learn to be content in this country. The winter hadn't been so bad. She had even enjoyed the mild weather and the early spring, although there were cold rains and sometimes an icy wind sweeping down from the snows of Pine Valley Mountain. The site for St. George had been chosen between two volcanic ridges, strewn with black lava boulders in some long-ago upheaval of the earth. The country to the south fell away toward the Virgin River, with brown and barren foothills beyond. The river was deceptively placid, flowing along between banks lined with cottonwood and willow. Its flash floods repeatedly destroyed the irrigation dams, and the Virgin Ditch had to be rebuilt over and over to bring water to the fields below the town. To the north a red sandstone ridge towered directly above the town. It was topped by a huge, eroded rock almost circular in shape known locally as the Sugar Loaf. Where water seeped from them, the red cliffs were patched with green. From this sandstone formation flowed the brackish springs providing the village with water. It was a favorite place for picnics and celebrations, and for young lovers walking out in the evenings after the burning sun had gone down behind the barren western mountains.

"Whew!" The screen door slammed behind Burns. "Hot enough for you?" His smile took in all of them. Immediately the atmosphere of the room changed. The girls were fond of their father and proud of him. They seemed to take on a glow in his presence. Certainly his company was so rare they valued every moment. Burns was still a handsome man although he had put on a little weight, his moustache was streaked with gray, and the hair was thinning at the back of his head.

"You're just in time for tea, Papa," Mary Ann said, jumping up to find a cup for him.

"I could use it," he replied, drawing up a chair and sitting down at the table. "It might help me through the day." Kate smiled. The girls and Nelly burst into appreciative laughter. It was a family joke, and they never sat down to tea without someone repeating that phrase for the amusement of all.

How long ago it seemed . . . back in Provo. All the children had chicken pox, not really ill, just itching, irritable, and bickering. Alice was in bed after another miscarriage. Kate had come downstairs from caring for her to find Nelly had all the children sitting at the kitchen table. Some of them were still in nightclothes, all of them pocked and peeling. Each child had a cup in front of him and Nelly was pouring tea. She brushed back her graying hair with one hand and looked at Kate apologetically. In her heavy Cockney accent she said wearily, "I thought we'd have a cuppa tea." She sighed as though at the end of her rope. "It might help me make it through the day." As tired and distracted as Nelly herself, Kate looked at the ridiculous group and began to laugh. The children joined, and Nelly, too, the miseries and bickering of the past week forgotten.

Because of Burns's position, the fact that they occasionally broke the Word of Wisdom and partook of tea was not bandied about. Anyway, it was usually saved for some special or especially trying occasion.

"President Snow tells me you girls are doing a wonderful job here," Burns said, his eyes warm as he looked around at his daughters. They smiled in modest appreciation, each one trying to catch her father's attention with some anecdote about their trials in running a boardinghouse.

His smile faded at last and he turned to Kate. The girls fell silent, knowing their turn was over.

"Can you spare one of the girls?" he asked. "Josie's sick and Alice isn't able to take care of her."

What was Alice able to do, Kate thought resentfully. Nelly started and leaned forward, her hands gripping the table edge.

"Let Nelly go," Kate told him.

"Shall I go now?" Nelly asked, for she never made a decision without Kate's approval.

"Yes, get your things and go ahead." With sympathy, she watched Nelly's trembling hand set the teacup down.

Kate and Burns lingered at the table after Nelly had gone and the girls were busy with their duties. It was so seldom now they had a chance to sit and talk like this, she clung to the moment.

"I'm leaving for Pine Valley this afternoon," he said, draining his teacup. Kate drew in her breath with disappointment. She had been looking forward to having him here tonight. Although it was not a thing to be discussed, or hardly thought about, she still found their physical relationship rewarding. She had never been like Sister Morgan who said, "Thank God for polygamy, it means Sam only sleeps with me a few times a month instead of every night." Kate wondered whether she dared ask to go with him. It would be like heaven to be in the mountains again. No, of course not, she was needed here.

"Why?" she asked.

"You knew I'd taken up those timber rights," he said. "I'm planning to buy a sawmill up there. The Temple will require a lot of lumber, and Brother Brigham has asked me to get it ready now."

Carefully pouring the last of the tea into her cup, Kate considered what a good businessman her husband had become. He had turned part of his cattle in for stock in the Winsor Cattle Company, and the dividends had made that venture profitable. His own cattle had increased gratifyingly. The salary he received from the Church enabled him to purchase property throughout the town from those who had been called to other missions, or who had simply given up and left Dixie.

"I rode out to Mount Trumbull with Bob Gardner last week and found a location for the Church sawmill out there. The machinery has been ordered for it."

"How long will you be gone?" she asked, wondering if he would skip her week completely.

"Not long . . . a few days . . ." He seemed distracted, drumming his fingers on the oilcloth. After a moment he cleared his throat and assumed that familiar didactic pose she disliked most. "Kate . . . I'm sure you know that Alice's female problems have been a heavy load for me. As they have for her, of course," he added quickly. "I'd hoped to follow God's commandment to multiply and replenish the earth . . . to build up a kingdom for the Hereafter."

He sighed and Kate's mouth tightened. Did he expect her to feel sorry for him? She hadn't wanted him to marry Alice in the first place.

"I'm thinking of taking another wife," he said, avoiding her eyes.

A weight seemed to settle on her shoulders. What did it matter now that she was with child? What would he care if he had already chosen a young wife to give him children?

"Who?" she asked in a strained voice. She had no forewarning as she had with Alice, for it seemed to her she was a virtual prisoner to this boardinghouse. Sundays had to be carefully planned so that she had time to go to church.

"Lovinia Crandall."

Oh yes, she thought, Lovinia Crandall, young and buxom . . . she even looked fertile, like a good milk cow. Her father was the

Bishop's Counselor . . . a prominent family. It surprised her how little it hurt. Perhaps she had passed some sort of milestone beyond which it was impossible for anything Burns did to hurt her.

"Her father has given his consent, as well as President Young."

"And you asked me last?" Her voice was resigned.

"You've always supported me in living the Gospel, Kate. I knew you wouldn't object."

"No." She shrugged, without emotion. "I don't object." She looked up to see Mary Ann watching them, her eyes hot and resentful on her father's back.

When Alice arrived later that afternoon her eyes were red and swollen from crying. Alice was still a pretty woman, although she had grown a little plump with the years and all those incomplete pregnancies. She wanted to speak to Kate alone, she said, and they climbed the stairs to Kate's bedroom, hot and still under the eaves.

Alice sat on the bed, sighing and smoothing her skirts. She wore a dove gray delaine dress with knife pleats and tuck-ups. Even though time and the desert mineral water had turned her blonde hair drab, Alice was still vain about her appearance. Much of her share of Burns's income went for clothes and frills for herself. In contrast, Kate looked at herself in the mirror above the dresser. Her skin was still good, although the lines of forty-two years were all there. She wore her hair, graying now, in the pompadour knot she had worn as a girl. The blue eyes looked piercingly back at her, the pointed chin lifted in what Sister Allenby had long ago called "that regal way." Without vanity, she thought herself a handsome woman, but she was not soft or pretty or compliant, and her dress was plain blue cotton.

"I guess you know Burns is going to marry Lovinia Crandall," Alice said, her pink mouth trembling.

"He told me," Kate replied briskly. She had no time to sit up here and gossip with Alice. There was work to be done.

"Can't you do anything to stop him?" Alice began to cry, producing a handkerchief from the bosom of her dress.

"You know I can't." Kate's voice was cold.

"Oh, it's my fault," Alice sobbed. "It's because I can't carry my babies. Burns wants more children, and I can't seem to give him any." She paused to blow her nose daintily. "And you and Nelly are too old."

Kate's mouth twisted. Alice always managed to stick that knife into her. Too old or not, her babies had survived. It would be cruel to tell Alice she was pregnant, and, after a moment's hesitation, Kate decided against it.

"You'll have to accept it, Alice," she told her. "Sometimes we have to concentrate on the glories of the next world in order to endure the pains of this one."

When Alice only wept louder, Kate continued, "Burns is determined to build up his kingdom for the Hereafter. The Gospel is the most important thing in his life, not his wives. If you didn't know that before, you do now."

She had thought when this moment came she would be filled with triumph, glad that at last Alice felt the pain she had felt when Burns took Alice for his wife. Instead she felt sorry for her . . . sorry for this woman whose babies never grew to term. Burns had catered to Alice for years, always hoping her health would improve. He had defended his choice for a long time, but in the end she had failed him. Now Alice would have to grow callouses on her feelings and a shell around her heart, just as Kate had. She had no comfort to give her, and Alice went home looking miserable and defeated.

The air began to cool a little after sundown, although some nights it never cooled off at all. They even sprinkled water on the sheets before they went to bed when it was so hot, for the cotton actually seemed to burn the skin. Nelly, tired and worried, walked back to help with supper, saying she was sure Josie had the ague. She should never have let her go over to the Cotton Factory at Washington with Burns and Alice. All those people over there had the ague from the swamps. This damned country, Kate thought bitterly, half the people here lived with chills and fever, those who didn't have big-neck or kidney trouble from the drinking water.

"You girls get ready for the Retrenchment Society party tonight," Kate told them when the supper dishes were finished and the men had departed for their rooms or the town. "Brig and Burnie can take you."

KATE

"Don't we need to get things ready for breakfast?" Jane looked at her with dutiful eyes.

"I can do what needs to be done," Kate said. "You don't have many chances for parties. Now scoot!"

How sweet they all looked when they came downstairs dressed in their sprigged muslin summer dresses, giggling and chattering. Even skinny Jane was glowing, Mary Ann trying to act nonchalant, Drusilla excited and bubbling. Three young girls on the brink of womanhood, and for one brief, sad moment Kate wondered what life had in store for them.

The boys came down, dressed in their Sunday pants and clean white shirts, Brigham tall and dignified, the heedless Burnie capering about and making jokes. Both of them were so tanned from their days hauling rock in the broiling sun that they were almost as dark as Tom. Charley had already left with a group of boys, and Kate thought she must talk to Burns about the company Charley was keeping. Nelly could never believe Charley did anything wrong.

Speculating about who would be on the program before the dance, the girls hurried off.

"You sure you won't want me to stay and help?" Brig asked, pausing at the door.

Kate forced a smile, hoping he couldn't tell how weary she was, how terribly her head hurt. "Go have a good time, son. Take care of your sisters."

"All right, Mama." With a doubtful frown he turned to go.

The kitchen was suddenly silent and empty. On the back steps in the warm darkness, she could hear Tom telling stories to Isaac and Elizabeth. They were too young for this party, and Tom never seemed to want to go. More than anything on earth Kate wanted to go upstairs and lie down. She had felt so miserable all day, even worse since Burns and Alice had been here. Sighing, she looked at the bushel basket of peaches a Brother had delivered this afternoon. They would be fine stewed for breakfast. That meant peeling, pitting, and cooking them tonight. She put another stick of wood in the stove. Tom and the children would help with the peaches, but Tom, who never asked for anything, needed to rest after all day in the hot sun.

Breakfast had to be started at night. Kate measured cornmeal for mush and began slicing the salt pork. Her back hurt so . . . her whole pelvis . . . it was almost like labor pains. Then she felt the warm blood running down her legs and knew it didn't matter that she hadn't told Burns she was pregnant. She was going to miscarry. Better get to the bedroom quickly.

The whole thing came out in one great gush . . . a hideous, bloody mess on the kitchen floor. Swaying, near to fainting, she looked down at it and reached out for support, laying her hand on the hot stove. Too stunned to cry out, she jerked it away, smelling burned flesh.

The screen door slammed and she looked up into Brigham's horrified face. "You're home early," she said stupidly, and he caught her as she crumpled.

Chapter 10

The mellow chiming of the Tabernacle clock wafted through the quiet morning air. Beyond the bedroom window, framed by thin muslin curtains, the sky echoed the red cliffs below. Awakening in the half light, pain rising into consciousness, Kate lost track of the notes . . . five o'clock . . . six? The clock in the steeple of the Tabernacle announced Church meetings, timed the changing of water turns, called one to duty . . . I must get breakfast started, she thought, and gasped with pain as she tried to sit up. Trembling, she fell back against the pillow. A simple miscarriage shouldn't make her this weak and sick. She couldn't have been more than two months along. It was then she became aware of the bandaged hand resting on a pillow, throbbing painfully.

"Mama?" Brig's anxious face bent over her. "Are you all right?"

She nodded, too weak to frame the words, all the strength gone out of her. In the dim light she could make out the glisten of tears in Brig's eyes. Oh, my dearest son, she thought, I would give anything on earth to have spared you this. Reaching up with her left hand, she touched his cheek gently, wiping away the unheeded tears. "You came back to help me last night?"

"Thank God I did." His voice broke. "Thank God."

"What happened to my hand?" As she tried to lift it pain lanced along her arm, and she gasped.

"You burned it something awful. Tom went for Sister Meeks. She dressed your hand and . . . and took care of everything else."

Everything else . . . Kate looked at her son's stricken face. How terrible that he had to see her in such a condition. He was too young

. . . too dear. Remembrance of her responsibilities descended heavily. "I can't lie around here," she said, struggling to sit up. "There's breakfast to get for the men."

Taking her shoulders in his hands, Brig gently eased her back against the pillows. "Aunt Nelly came back when Isaac went after her. She sent for the Relief Society Sisters and they'll take turns helping until you're well. The girls are here too. You don't have to worry about anything."

Too weak to really care, she lay back with a sigh. "Have you been here all night?"

He nodded and, sitting down, held her hand tight against his mouth. Kate felt the hot tears splash on her knuckles. "Oh, Mama. You were so sick . . . and your poor hand. I prayed all night God wouldn't take you away from me."

Looking up into that desperate young face, Kate felt a great surge of love for her firstborn. Seventeen and nearly a man. There was even a faint stubble of whiskers on his chin this morning. He was so much like the young Burns Hamilton she had loved . . . the same thick dark brown hair, the same golden brown eyes. She hadn't known Burns at seventeen. Had he ever looked so vulnerable, so sensitive? When had the soft mouth hardened to a firm line, the jaw grown set with ambition? "Dearest boy," she whispered, "I will never leave you."

With a timid knock, Nelly entered looking even more wan than usual. "I wanted to bring this up before the men start coming for breakfast," she said, setting the tray of tea and hot biscuits on the bedside table. She looked down at Kate, her mouth working peculiarly.

"How's Josie?" Kate asked, seeing at once that Nelly was upset.

"Bad," Nelly replied. "It's the ague. I'll have Charley bring her up here today so's I can look after her." Pausing, she wrung her thin hands together, her face distracted.

"What is it, Nelly?" The tea Brig was pouring smelled so good. Kate wished she could close her eyes and have Nelly gone. Sometimes she got so tired of being the strong one and having all of them lean on her.

"It's Brother Hamilton," Nelly said, her pale blue eyes suddenly damp. "Mary Gardner came to help this morning and she said he took Lovinia to Pine Valley with him. Bishop Gardner married them."

"Dear God," Kate said softly, and turned her face away toward the hot light growing beyond the window, a heavy leaden feeling inside her chest. How little he cares! Didn't he know how it would look to everyone? Oh, it was wrong, wrong! He should have waited until October Conference and taken Lovinia to Salt Lake so they could be married there in the Endowment House. He must know the gossips' tongues would be busy over the abruptness of this marriage.

The crash of the teacup Brig had dropped to the floor startled her from her thoughts.

The boy's face was flushed with anger. "I could kill him. Leaving you here to work like a dog while he's off taking himself another wife. Oh . . . damn his soul!"

Shocked at such vehemence from her quiet son, Kate reached for his hand. "Don't, Brig . . . don't ever talk like that about your father. He's only doing his duty toward building up the Kingdom of God. He didn't know I was sick."

Embarrassment staining her thin face, Nelly knelt to clean up the broken teacup. Kate held her son's hand and tried vainly to smile at him. The words she said to Brig were true, and because he loved her he would accept them. But could she accept them, quell her bitterness, not feel like a used and torn rag doll cast aside by an uncaring child? It was a hard and bitter road God had set her on. A jealous and possessive woman could only suffer in Celestial Marriage. One must pray and learn to bear all things, even being relegated to the position of a used-up and worn-out wife. The Kingdom of God was foremost with Burns, his wives and children stepping-stones to his own Godhood. It was true . . . the Gospel was true! If it were not, her life had been wasted and she would go down to dust like a dead animal. It was true! Burns would call her up on the morning of the first Resurrection, and thereafter she would know only joy and happiness eternal. She could bear Lovinia as she had borne all her other trials, secure in the knowledge of what awaited her in Eternity.

But a week later when Burns returned from Pine Valley and brought Lovinia to the Big House to live, it was not so easy to be pleasant or to conceal the quiet hatred she felt for the buxom, simpering young woman. Lovinia was not especially pretty, her blue eyes a little too close together, her hair a plain light brown, but she had the freshness of youth. Strange how possession of a new and willing wife put a gleam in a man's eye and a spring in his step, Kate thought as she led Lovinia and Burns up the stairs to the fourth floor.

"I'm sure the four girls won't mind sharing a bedroom," Burns said. "Lovinia must have a room of her own." Kate could hear him patting Lovinia, and her mouth tightened resentfully. Burns never considered how he might be inconveniencing other people. The bedrooms were small and the girls would mind, but there was nothing to be done about it. Burns had wed his fourth wife. He would take her to October Conference in Salt Lake, he had said, where they would be sealed for time and eternity in the Endowment House. She would give him children, arrows for his quiver and stars for her crown—a multitude of descendants to build up his kingdom in the Hereafter.

"I'll send Mary Ann up to move the girls' things," Kate said curtly, as she led them into the room that would be Lovinia's. Burns set Lovinia's cases down, and the three of them stood looking at each other in awkward silence. At last Kate realized Burns was waiting for her to leave so he could be alone with his new wife.

The light was dim along the stairway, for the shades had been drawn early in an attempt to hold in the cool night air. As she slowly descended Kate knew this sickening ache inside was no longer caused by love. It was pride . . . the longing for some knowledge that she had meaning to Burns as a person, not just another chattel, another wife, another Mother in Israel. Why was it so hard, even at her age, to stop wanting to be cared about? Whom the Lord loveth, He chasteneth. Humble yourself, Kate. The Gospel is not for the prideful.

The Temple workers ate supper and departed. Lovinia was little enough help. Under Kate's hard and angry eye, she finally helped dry the dishes. When Burns returned, Lovinia scurried to serve him from the food waiting in the warming oven. Kate, sitting across the table from Burns, watched her wearily, wondering how long it would take to reshape all their lives because of this young woman.

At last they could bank the fire. A faint breeze brought its welcome coolness into the kitchen. The children had gone to bed. No need to ask where Burns would spend the night, she thought, seeing the doting smiles he bestowed on the suddenly helpful Lovinia. Kate was still ill from the miscarriage, the burned hand healing, but still painful. Nelly had a sick child in her room. Poor Nelly. Her children were her life, and Josie failed a little every day.

Lovinia looked smugly at her new husband and asked, "Will you be coming up to bed soon, Brother Hamilton?"

"Yes, my dear," Burns replied. "You go along. I'll be up shortly."

Silence fell in the kitchen, the only sound the sibilant whispering of the hot summer wind through the open door. Kate felt Burns's hand touch her arm gently. "You're feeling better, aren't you, Kate? The burn is healing?"

Too wound up inside herself to speak, she replied by nodding. The hand pained terribly after the day's work, and the flow of blood from her body was so heavy she was always conscious of it. But Burns had no desire to hear these things, so she kept silent and listened to her husband talk.

He told her of the timber rights he had been granted on Pine Valley Mountain, of the sawmill he had purchased there. "We need to have the sawmills in the right hands," he said. "Too much of the lumber has been sold off to the Gentiles at Pioche. Some of the brethren are so anxious to get their hands on the money from the mines, they don't care that the Tabernacle is unfinished for lack of lumber and refuse to even think of what will be needed for the Temple."

Kate listened to him in silence, her quick, well-ordered mind taking in the information about his business dealings. He had lent money to Brothers in financial distress. One or two of them were disaffected with their mission in this hard country and likely to leave, in which case Burns would own their houses and lots here in town. If a lot became available on Main Street where the new courthouse had been built and a business section was developing, he planned to buy it. Kate watched his earnest face, still handsome, but now so self-assured, so confident of his own importance. It seemed another life ago she had fallen in love with him back in England, another life ago they had been married for time and all eternity in the Endowment House when at last they reached Salt Lake City. This man she had taken as her husband, to love and cherish and obey for all eternity, sat across the table now talking to her as he would to a business partner.

A rustle of noise drew her eyes to the doorway where Brig stood taking off his gum boots. After the day's work at the Temple he had walked out to Burns's field to take their water turn.

Burns consulted his watch. "Water turn finished?"

Ignoring the question, Brig came into the room, stocking-footed, staring at his father in a hostile way. "Hasn't anyone told you Mama's been sick?" he asked abruptly.

"Why, yes." Burns reached across the table to pat Kate's hand. "Sister Meeks told me it was bad, but that you're healing up just fine. Too bad there'll be no more babies, but at your age I guess that's to be expected."

Kate closed her eyes, holding her lips stiff to stop their trembling. "Oh, Burns," she said in a shaky voice.

"Now, my dear." His voice was comforting. "You've given me a beautiful family and ever been my companion in living the Gospel. You must have no regrets."

"No!" Brig exploded. "She should have no regrets . . . but you should have plenty of them. Leaving her here to work like a slave while you're off taking yourself a new wife. What would you care if she died . . . you have Lovinia!"

"Brigham!" Burns rose from his chair, his face scarlet with rage.

"I'll have my say, Papa," Brig continued defiantly. "I'll say it because Mama won't. She'll live her religion and do your bidding if it kills her. I want you to get her a decent house and get her out of this backbreaking job. She deserves as much consideration as Aunt Alice for a change."

"Oh, Brig . . . don't," Kate begged, horrified at this defiance of Burns.

"Young man." Burns's furious voice rose above Brig's. "Fall on your knees and ask God to forgive you for such disrespect to your father and the priesthood."

"You aren't God!" Brig cried. "And my mother isn't your slave."

Angered beyond control, Burns struck Brig across the face with the flat of his hand. Blood spurted from the boy's nose and tears filled his eyes. Sick and scared, Kate grabbed a dish towel and rushed to stanch the blood.

"Oh yes, Mother. Dry his tears and wipe his nose," Burns said sarcastically. "He was always your son . . . always Mama's boy." He started for the door, ready to mount the stairs to where his new wife lay waiting. He turned a scathing look on his wife and son, and his harsh tones echoed through the dimly lit kitchen. "I pray God will send me one son I can be proud of."

Chapter 11

A cold November breeze skittered dead leaves along the dark street. Oblongs of yellow light marked the windows of the houses hidden by the darkness, and the pungent odor of wood smoke filled the autumn evening. It was only a short walk from the Big House to Brigham Young's new winter home, the White House. Burns carried a lantern to light their way, his other hand holding Kate's elbow.

It occurred to her now that marriage is one long series of emotional estrangements and reconciliations. For a moment she wished they were young again . . . young enough to pause here in the darkness beneath the leafless cottonwoods and exchange kisses. Her new silk dress rustled pleasantly and her hands were warm inside the fur muff Burns had brought her from Salt Lake. He had taken Lovinia with him to October Conference so they could be sealed in marriage at the Endowment House. On his return there were gifts of clothing for all his wives, but the fur muff had been something extra just for Kate. An extravagance for one so careful as Burns. Secretly pleased and avoiding Alice's jealous eyes, Kate had thought the muff a kind of peace offering, the apology Burns would never make . . . for all the hurts she had borne, and for Lovinia.

The long, blazing, miserable summer was behind them now. After the dreadful scene between Brig and his father the boy had been sent to Pine Valley to work at the sawmill. Kate had missed him, he was always so thoughtful and helpful, but his absence seemed to have healed over the wound his words must have caused Burns. If Brig's feelings had not changed, at least he hadn't voiced them since his return.

KATE

Burns was in a light-hearted mood tonight. Their invitation to the Prophet's home was indicative of Burns's position in the Church and of Brigham Young's personal regard for him.

"It's good to have 'Ras Snow back in St. George," he said. "This mission might never have succeeded without his leadership . . . and he's been a good friend to us."

"I'm glad Brother Brigham is giving 'Ras and Min a welcome-home party." Kate smiled at her husband.

"Few enough parties you get to, my dear." Burns squeezed her arm affectionately. "It should be a fine time. Brother Brigham doesn't stint when it comes to entertaining."

Kate's own heart grew lighter, as though the cold fall wind had swept away all the miseries of the summer. She was too thin, she knew. Her strength had never been the same since her miscarriage, and she bled too much and too often. The scarred hand sometimes bothered her terribly, though there was no use to complain of it.

An acquisitive man, Burns had found that with two of his families housed and fed at Church expense he was able to use his salary toward acquiring property of his own. In that respect he differed not at all from President Snow or any of the other Authorities. Glancing up at the strong face partially illumined by the flickering lantern light, Kate wondered whether he would ever adequately deal with the problem of Lovinia.

Even though she would never feel as bitter toward Lovinia as she did toward Alice, the girl was a trial. She simply did not keep her place as a fourth wife should. After Josie died, Nelly took to her bed for several weeks, overwhelmed by grief for her little daughter. There was no need to press the poor creature, for Lovinia could take over her duties. Kate knew, too well, the pain of losing a child, and Lovinia's lack of sympathy offended her.

Sister Crandall had brought her daughter up to be a good house-wife. It was simply that every woman had her own way of running a house, and Lovinia could never be convinced that hers was not the only way. Only yesterday there had been another scene, just when Kate had thought they'd reached an understanding.

Sitting in the study working at her accounts, Kate had heard the crash of crockery from the kitchen where the girls were doing dishes.

"You clumsy ox!" Lovinia seemed unable to speak softly.

"I couldn't help it." Drusilla sounded near tears. Hurrying into the kitchen, Kate saw Mary Ann fly to her sister's defense.

"She didn't do it on purpose, stupid." As tall as Lovinia, Mary Ann stared boldly into the woman's eyes.

Arms akimbo, ignoring Mary Ann, Lovinia confronted Drusilla. "Always mooning around . . . thinking about boys . . . never paying attention."

The swinging door to the kitchen vibrated behind Kate. The hostile little group turned toward her, and Lovinia rushed to defend herself. "If I'm to be in charge of this kitchen . . ."

"Shut up, Lovinia," Kate said in quiet fury. "You're not in charge of this kitchen. What happened?" she asked Mary Ann who had her arms about her sobbing sister and was sticking her tongue out at Lovinia.

"My hands were wet," came Drusilla's muffled reply.

"Well, clean up this mess," Kate snapped, determined to stare Lovinia down.

"So there!" Mary Ann flounced past Lovinia to take the broom and dustpan from behind the stove.

"None of that, Mary Ann," Kate ordered. "Now, Lovinia, for the last time . . . I'm in charge of this kitchen. Hard as my girls work, I won't have you treating them like slaves. Do you understand?"

Lovinia shrugged, her face bland as that of a cow. Kate had an almost irresistible urge to slap her. Sighing, she returned to the study, knowing that no matter what she said Lovinia would not change her ways. It had become almost impossible for her to work with Mary Ann without a quarrel. More than once Kate had chastised the quick-tempered girl, begged her to ignore Lovinia. Burns had even spanked his half-grown daughter after one particularly loud and silly quarrel over who should scrub the pots. God sends us trials, Kate thought now, and He had surely sent her one in the person of her unruly daughter. She had thought she would die with shame two months ago when Mary Ann was called before the Bishop. Kate cringed inwardly, remembering that day in meeting at the Tabernacle.

KATE

The St. George Tabernacle was one of the most beautiful buildings she had ever seen. Built of the local red sandstone, carefully cut and dressed, the rectangular building rose at the front to a white-painted steeple with a clock set in it. Stone steps on each side led to the double front doors, with above them a scrolled white slab inscribed "Holiness to the Lord," the All-Seeing Eye painted below. Inside, one passed through a foyer with an elegant curved staircase leading up to the galleries. Kate sat on the main floor that day, with Isaac and Elizabeth beside her. The girls had gone upstairs to sit with their friends in the gallery, a balcony supported by a row of smooth, white-painted pillars. Burns, in his position as stake president, sat with the other dignitaries on the ornately carved and painted stand at the end of the meeting hall. Brig and one of the Gardner boys stood at the table where the bread and wine were being prepared. They would bless the Sacrament.

September was warm in St. George, even warmer in the packed Tabernacle. Kate fanned herself and the two children beside her, as much to brush off the pesky flies as to cool the air. The congregation stood to sing, with Brother Macfarlane leading the singing, "We thank Thee O God for a Prophet . . . to guide us in these latter days. We thank Thee for sending the Gospel to lighten our minds with its rays . . ."

Mid-morning light fell softly through the tall windows . . . two thousand panes shipped around the Horn to San Francisco and laboriously hauled overland to St. George. It glanced off Brig's dark head bowed to say the sacramental blessing. A thrill of pride went through Kate, and she offered up a little prayer of thanks that her son was home to stay. The two-handled goblet of wine passed from hand to hand, each member taking a sip, as the prayer said, in remembrance of the blood the Son had shed for man. One or two of the brethren drank deeply and the goblet had to be refilled. It would not do to think of the other mouths that had touched the rim of that goblet. Kate took a quick sip and passed it to Elizabeth. To her amusement, fussy Elizabeth turned the goblet around and drank near the handle. Just then the hot, shuffling silence of the meeting house was broken by the giggling of girls upstairs. The Bishop raised his bowed head and darted a look of fury at the gallery. Kate looked up, shrinking with shame to see that the culprits were Mary Ann and that silly Ames girl from south of town. Mary Ann knew better than to associate with those people anyway.

The ceremony of the Sacrament completed, Bishop Gardner stood up, stared straight into the gallery at the now red-faced and silent girls. His voice was loud and stern. "We are in the house of the Lord. We are here to worship Him in silence and reverence. We are not here to make light of His Sacrament, nor is this the time for levity in God's house. The spirit of God seems to have deserted you young ladies, certainly you have offended Him and this company. I expect you to report to me immediately after this meeting." Turning his gimlet gaze, he looked out over the congregation. "Now, Brothers and Sisters, if you will take your hymn books we will sing something appropriate to the occasion . . . 'Do What Is Right, Let the Consequence Follow.' "

There was no help for it. Resigned and angry at once, Kate knew she would have to stay and see her daughter through this disgrace. Lovinia and Nelly and the other girls would have to handle Sunday dinner for the men. As the congregation departed to stand around in front of the Tabernacle, shaking hands and talking, Kate stayed in her place, staring straight ahead, ignoring the amused and inquiring glances of her neighbors. Finally Mary Ann and Jenny Ames came to sit on the bench beside her, white-faced and scared. Jenny's parents seldom bothered to attend church and were not highly thought of in the town.

Brigham came down the aisle and leaned across to whisper to Mary Ann. "You half-wit, you're a disgrace to the family."

"Oh shut up," Mary Ann snapped back, and stuck out her tongue. "Mr. Perfect."

Kate had to restrain herself to keep from slapping her daughter right there in church. "Go on home, Brig," she said. A look of understanding passed between them. "See if Aunt Nelly needs help. I'll be along as soon as this is over."

The two trembling girls stood scared and silent before the members of the High Council and the Bishopric, among them Burns, looking furious. The Tabernacle was empty now except for the Authorities waiting on the stand.

"Now, young women," the Bishop began. "Would you mind telling me what it was that you found so amusing about our meeting today?"

The girls exchanged frightened glances. The Ames girl seemed struck dumb, and at last Mary Ann replied, "We were reading the hymn book."

The Bishop's bushy eyebrows rose. "I know every song in that book and none of them are meant to be comic." When the girls hung their heads and made no response, he continued, "Well? What was it that caused you to disrupt our Sacrament with unseemly laughter. Surely not just the hymns?"

No reply from the shame-faced girls. "Well . . . what was it?" the Bishop demanded. "Mary Ann?"

"We were playing a game," she mumbled.

"What sort of game do you play with a hymn book?"

The Ames girl began to sob noisily. "I don't want to say," Mary Ann muttered.

"Confession is good for the soul," the Bishop told her. "Go on."

The words came out so fast Kate could hardly understand them, as though Mary Ann wanted to say them quickly and be rid of them. "Between the sheets," she said. "You add it to the song title, like, 'Abide with me . . . between the sheets.' We laughed when it was 'I need Thee every hour . . . between the sheets.' "

The Bishop stared at her in pious horror. Burns bowed his head in his hands, and Elder Cannon struggled to quell the twitching at the corners of his mouth. Kate closed her eyes in despair and sighed deeply. Everyone in town would know by this afternoon. Why couldn't Mary Ann be like her sisters, not forever embarrassing the family with her unladylike behavior?

"You realize such things are offensive to God, young women?" the Bishop asked harshly.

"Yes, sir," the reply came in low, chastened voices.

"And you are heartily sorry for your offense?"

"Yes, sir."

"You will both apologize to the congregation at Sacrament Meeting and ask their forgiveness for your behavior. Do you understand?"

"Yes, sir."

"Then I'll expect you here this afternoon to make things right with God and His people."

When Burns arrived at the Big House for Sunday dinner he gave Mary Ann a tongue-lashing that would have broken a lesser spirit. Mary Ann only retreated into silence.

Doggedly Kate returned to Sacrament Meeting and sat shamed and embarrassed as Mary Ann stood to ask forgiveness for her levity in church. That forgiveness was granted by a show of hands. Kate had hoped the incident was closed. More than one boy was later given a bloody nose by an indignant Mary Ann for shouting at her, "Hey, Mary Ann . . . wanna go between the sheets?" Kate counseled her to ignore the taunts, but it was not in Mary Ann to suffer in silence. The surprised and wounded young men soon left her alone.

Burns blew out the lantern and hung it on the picket fence near the gate. Brigham Young's new winter home was a large, handsome, two-story house of whitewashed stone and adobe. The veranda extending along the front and sides of the house rose to a balustraded balcony with access from the second floor. Brother Brigham often stood there when one or another of the local bands or choral groups came to serenade him. Like a king, Kate had thought once, seeing him stand there waving and bowing. The Lion of the Lord. The king of this far-off, isolated desert land, nevertheless a king whose every wish became a command. His visits to the settlements differed only in elegance from the processions the kings of England once made about the isle of Britain.

He had brought his favorite wife, Amelia Folsom, to spend the winter with him . . . he who counseled his brethren in plural marriage against favorites. His half-forgotten wife, Lucy B., lived in St. George most of the time now, but she had not moved into the big new house; that was for Amelia. It was said that Amelia put on airs. She did dress extravagantly and had made Brother Brigham build a mansion for her to live in alone in Salt Lake. If Kate envied her anything it was this ability to manipulate her husband, one all too lacking in herself.

At Burns's knock, the front door was opened by a typical English butler in his formal black and white, bowing and obsequious. Kate almost laughed. A butler in St. George! Amelia had outdone herself this year.

"Good evening." The butler took their coats. Kate longed to nudge Burns and smile, thinking how many times she had watched guests arrive at the Fitzhughs' door with the butler handing their wraps. Burns behaved as though having butlers take his coat had been part of his entire life.

They stood in a long entryway lighted by an exquisite hand-painted glass hanging lamp. A stairway to the second floor rose along one side of the entry, its banister beautifully turned from the local white pine lumber. Burns's hand on her arm, Kate entered the large drawing room where a jovial Brigham Young stood before the black marble fireplace with Amelia beside him.

The Prophet's wavy beard and hair were heavily streaked with gray, but his mouth under the hairless upper lip was still straight and firm. He had aged since she last saw him, grayed and weathered, yet he still exuded that aura of strength and power.

Amelia wore a wine-colored watered silk gown with pearls wound at her throat, and she carried herself with style. She was not the sort of woman Kate would have expected Brother Brigham to choose for his favorite. Her jaw was too prominent, her eyes too small, her teeth too large although she seldom smiled to show them.

This was the first time Kate had been in the house since its completion, and she looked around, awed by the elegance. A grand piano stood before the front windows; chairs and settees were covered with silk damask; and the rugs on the polished wood floor were fine States carpet. Blue velvet draperies hung over the windows recessed into the thick stone walls.

Immediately behind the Hamiltons, the Snows arrived. President Snow was noted for being late to any gathering he attended, even though it irritated Brigham Young no end. He and his second wife, Minerva, had been gone most of the year: he on a mission to Europe and she to her family in New England. Erastus Snow was stout and deceptively bland-looking, his gray hair thin, blue eyes deep-set and shadowed. Minerva, dressed in a fine blue cashmere with ruching at the neck, wore her hair skinned back tight from her face, accentuating her prominent nose.

Bishop Gardner was there, smiling and amiable, his chin whiskers neat and trim. With him was his wife Mary. Kate thought that Robert Gardner followed his leader, for his two older wives lived at isolated Pine Valley, while the handsome and society-loving Mary enjoyed the community living in St. George.

The butler moved among the chattering guests, serving wine. Of the wine turned into the Tithing Office, President Young's cellar was always stocked with that made by John Naegle, a master winemaker who lived in Toquerville. Some of the local inexperienced brethren vintners turned out a product nearer vinegar than wine. Brigham Young was sparing with the drink, for he had no use for any man who would drink enough of it to become addled.

Presently Brother Brigham urged his guests into the dining room where a fire blazed pleasantly in the fireplace. The candles in the huge glass chandelier gleamed on the mahogany sideboard and the fine china and silver, catching light from the cut crystal wineglasses. Kate found herself seated next to stern, handsome John McAllister. His first wife did not allow herself to be shunted aside. She sat, stout and homely and enjoying herself, across from Burns.

Brother Brigham led the table conversation with the men. Their wives contributed by listening, except when addressed directly by President Young. After questioning President Snow about his mission, he turned to the problems of the Dixie mission. He was, he said, unhappy that the cotton factory was not doing well; the people were planting food crops instead of cotton, and that must be dealt with. In the spring the local men must be released from the Temple building to rebuild the Virgin Ditch, which always went out with the spring floods. He was pleased with the progress on the Temple, but he would have to send a wagon train through all the southern settlements again to collect the tithes needed to provide for the Temple workers. New workers would soon be called on their two-month work missions.

KATE

After dinner, at Minerva's urging, Amelia played the piano. The men talked business and the ladies chatted quietly, uneasy in the presence of the regal Amelia.

It must be that the wine had made her a little giddy, Kate thought, when they had said good night and started home. Her feet seemed so light, the fatigue that overlay everything she did lately all gone. At the corner they called good night to the Gardners and proceeded toward the Big House. Kate leaned to press her face against the sleeve of Burns's coat. It had been a long time since she felt this close to him and her mind flew ahead to sharing his bed tonight.

"It was such a lovely party," she said. "Having President Young here does make the winter more enjoyable."

"Amelia doesn't really like to entertain in St. George," Burns growled. "She thinks she's above us, you know."

Kate laughed. "How did it feel, Burns, being waited on at dinner by a butler? Just think how far we've come . . . me a servant-maid and you a miller's son. It's as though we were being entertained in the house of a king."

"Don't talk nonsense." Burns voice was sharp. "Brother Brigham is the Prophet of God . . . not a king. As for how far we've come, that's the basis of our Church . . . eternal progression."

Chagrined, Kate fell silent. After a moment, Burns continued defensively, "I have nothing I haven't earned twice over."

"But I only thought it was amusing. That butler might have worked in the same house where I was a maid, long ago." Her voice was low and placating.

"Not amusing at all!" Burns sounded almost angry. "You're not a maid now. You're the wife of an important man. Try to remember that."

Silent, thoroughly chastised, Kate walked beside her husband, her scarred hand aching and hot inside the fur muff. Not a maid now, she thought, remembering the hour she would have to arise in the morning to cook and serve breakfast for sixty of God's chosen men come to build a Temple to the Lord.

Chapter 12

ᔕᔑ   "Oh, Mama, we're going to miss the parade," Jane wailed as she brought a stack of dirty dishes in from the big dining room. Her words were almost drowned by the noise like a giant thunderclap reverberating between the black ridge on the east and the one on the west. Dishes rattled in the cupboards and Kate frowned. They had been saluting the Twenty-fourth of July since sunrise with black powder blasts. There had been a time when they used the cannon Brother Crosby brought back from the Mexican War, but it had been converted into the pile driver used for the foundation of the Temple, its barrel filled with lead and encased in heavy timbers bound with iron straps. A device for hoisting and dropping the cannon had been constructed to pound rocks into the earth for a foundation. Although that foundation had been finished and the Temple cornerstone laid in April, the cannon still could not be fired. A dangerous business with this powder, Kate thought. She had warned Isaac and Burnie to stay well back while the older boys and men set off the blast. They had bolted their breakfast and rushed away with Charley and Brig and Tom.

"You won't miss the parade," she told Jane now. "Your Mama and Lovinia . . ." with a hard look at Lovinia ". . . will do the dishes." Since the arrival of her son, Erastus, three months ago, Lovinia more than ever thought herself the queen, bossing the girls about and Nelly, too.

"Hurry along, girls," Kate urged, refusing to acknowledge Lovinia's petulance. "Get your costumes on." Mary Ann and Jane were wearing pioneer costumes and sunbonnets, walking with a group

(98)

depicting the handcart companies. Drusilla and Elizabeth were to ride on the Co-op Store float, dressed as angels, with Steve Marshall playing the part of the Prophet Joseph Smith. "Quickly now! We'll be through here in time to see your parade end up at the Tabernacle."

Three weeks ago there had been a Fourth of July celebration with speeches, bands, and dancing, but the Twenty-fourth of July, Pioneer Day, the day the Mormons first entered Salt Lake Valley in 1847, was the holiday of the year in any Mormon community. The girls rushed upstairs to change. Kate, hurrying back and forth between the kitchen and the dining room, listened with pride to the beat of the drums, for Brigham was playing one of them. They would have to rush because the parade was to start at eight o'clock.

Drusilla appeared, nervously twisting her tinsel halo. "I have to come back and change before the program starts at ten. Do you think I can make it?"

Kate gave her a fond smile. "You mean they won't let an angel sing with the chorus?"

Dru laughed. "Oh, Mama!"

What a beautiful girl Drusilla was, Kate thought, as her daughter hurried away . . . sweet and compliant, an easy child, and Elizabeth growing up just like her. Then there was Mary Ann, and Kate sighed, hoping her oldest daughter would stay out of trouble today. Even at fifteen she was likely to run in the footraces against the boys and fight with them if they teased her.

In the brassy blue sky a lone cloud melted quickly away. The hot summer sunlight reflected off the buildings and the wide, dusty streets with eye-searing brilliance. Beyond the shimmering heat waves, the land below the town rolled away toward the Virgin River winding slowly to the southwest, toward the broken mesas and escarpments twisting and writhing into the barren mountains of Out South, Mount Trumbull visible in the distance. Far to the east rose the square-topped cliffs of Mukuntuweap, washed pale mauve and lavender in the strong light.

The crowd around the Tabernacle watching for the parade had already trampled the dry red earth into a fine, hot powder. People had come in from surrounding communities. Their horses and wagons stood along the sides of the street where the irrigation ditches flowed, in the shade of the mulberry and cottonwood trees. The band arrived first playing loud marching songs, followed by other marchers, horsemen, and floats. Brigham, pounding his drum in time, threw Kate a quick smile.

Nelly squeezed Kate's arm, pointing as Jane and Mary Ann marched up to the Tabernacle with the dusty, bedraggled, and sweat-stained handcart company. "Sweet girls." Nelly's thin face shone with pride.

Kate and Nelly. Nelly and Kate. Sometimes she grew so weary of having Nelly forever with her . . . like a faithful dog. Kate was instantly ashamed of herself for longing to be free of Nelly. Poor thing, she was nothing but skin and bones, always complaining how tired she felt. Losing Josie had been such a blow to her.

Alice, standing nearby with some women friends, nodded to Kate. Starting to show with another baby, Kate saw, and holding her two little boys by the hand. Eight and six years old now, but Alice never allowed them to run about wild as most little boys did. Maybe she had lost so many babies she had to cling to these two. It must be hard on the boys, being called sissy and Mama's boy, and never allowed to fight back.

When Brigham Young had established the United Order of Enoch in St. George early this year, Alice had stood her ground with Burns and refused to turn her house into the community-held property. All goods were to be held in common, the Authorities counseled, with each to give according to his ability and take according to his need. A man in Burns's position could not dissent, but Kate knew he had been secretly relieved when President Young said a man could pledge only a portion of his worldly goods if he wished. A part of Burns's cattle and his farm had constituted his pledge. Given the nature of human beings, Kate thought the plan unworkable. Already there were murmurings against its inequities.

Lovinia had walked down from the Big House by herself. Presently Kate saw her standing near Burns, proudly displaying her baby to their friends.

"Such a crowd," said Nelly, as they squeezed into the hot Tabernacle where some of the older boys and men had to stand along the wall. All those sweating bodies. Kate sniffed, moving her cardboard fan faster to waft away the odors. Elizabeth came to sit with them.

Reaching a scrawny hand to touch the child, Nelly whispered, "You look so pretty, darlin'." Tears stung Kate's eyes. Elizabeth looked at her mother inquiringly, too young to understand that for a moment she was surrogate for the lost Josie.

On the stand were the honored members of the original pioneer company of 1861 who first settled this desolate desert country. Burns offered the opening prayer, asking God to help this people remember the trials of the pioneers and not complain of their own troubles. Then the congregation stood to sing . . . "Come, come ye Saints, no toil or labor fear . . . but with joy wend your way . . ."

President Erastus Snow was speaker of the day. He stood in the pulpit, stout and bland, looking over the audience, smacking his lips in that peculiar way of his. The trials of the Saints were his subject, and he told of those he had shared . . . of Nauvoo and the Prophet Joseph's martyrdom, of crossing the plains and settling in Salt Lake Valley, and then the call to Dixie. He exhorted the people to keep faith with those pioneers who had come to settle in the valleys of the mountains and build up God's Kingdom. The Beloved Apostle, he was called, Kate thought, only half-listening to the stories she had heard so many times. A strong leader, yet still a good and kindly man.

"We've come a long way," she could hear the people whisper proudly to each other. Yes, a long way, she thought . . . a long way from the bare, cold attic of the Fitzhughs', a long way from the desperate poverty of the mill towns, and a long way from the young wife emigrant, so much in love and praying she might give her husband a child. A long way, the speaker said, and endured many trials. Oh, she was glad she hadn't been here to share those first ten years . . . the floods and starvation, the scorching heat, the plagues of black canker and diphtheria and ague, the Indian wars and the horrors of the Mountain Meadows Massacre. It was a peaceful town now, almost pleasant but for the heat and the water and the barren surroundings. These stories, like the stories of the persecutions in Missouri, the expulsion from Nauvoo in the dead of winter, the atrocities at

Haun's Mill, the dreadful dying trek across the plains, and the miracle of the seagulls eating the crop-destroying crickets . . . these stories, too, would pass into Mormon legend to be told and retold until they seemed to have been a part of your own life.

When the Girls' Chorus sang following President Snow's speech, Kate sat looking with pride at her beautiful daughter standing straight and slender, head erect. Drusilla's hair had turned to a dark blonde and hung in glossy ringlets down her back. Her face was a perfect oval with a fine English complexion, shining blue eyes, straight small nose, and full pink mouth. She was a beauty and already there were boys making eyes at her. Not that Dru discouraged them, for she loved the attention of men of all ages.

Brother Walker read one of his poems about the trials of pioneering in Dixie and reduced his audience to delighted merriment. The String Band played and Bishop Gardner spoke. Then the audience stood to sing the song that said everything about the Dixie mission: "Hard times come again no more . . ." The program ended with prayer.

Kate stood up, the back of her dress wet with sweat. Well, dinner would be ready. She had left baked beans in the oven and Tom had stayed to keep the fire going. He was ever a faithful help to her. With a faint twinge of guilt she thought how little of this part of life he shared. He went to church with her faithfully, but when it came to social functions he remained an outsider . . . always a spectator. Then she smiled to herself. Tom would enjoy the races this afternoon. On foot or horseback there wasn't anyone who could beat him. There would be races for the children, too, with candy prizes. Hop beer and lemonade would be served and tonight in the Tabernacle basement, a dance to crown the celebration.

Burns and Lovinia did not return for dinner, though all the Temple workers were there and waiting. Only fifty of them now, but that was more than enough when some of the Danishmen down from Sanpete country could not even speak English.

Brig appeared as they were serving the men. He came to stand close to Kate beside the stove. Shame-faced, he whispered, "Papa and Aunt Lovinia have been invited to eat at Gardners'."

"Lovinia knew she was needed to help," Kate said harshly, continuing to fill the serving bowls with beans.

"Let me help, then," Brig said, taking the ladle from her hand.

Biting her lip, Kate turned away so Brig could not see her face. It was always a bitter pill to be left out, shunted aside for a younger wife. She liked company, too, and being invited out, and all she had was cooking for these insatiable men. Well, perhaps at the dance tonight Burns would see fit to at least dance with all his wives.

Feet tapping spontaneously in time to the music, Kate sat with Nelly on one of the benches surrounding the dance floor, watching the laughing couples whirl in a quadrille. Round dances were prohibited, especially the scandalous waltz, but no one seemed to mind. A good exhilarating reel or quadrille should be enough dance for anyone. Brother Blake was floor manager, in charge of keeping order and making up the sets, for the floor was too small to accommodate all those present at one time. Burns had come with Lovinia and danced with her, then Alice, then Nelly. Working his way up to the first wife, Kate thought ironically when her turn came. But she enjoyed dancing and moved to the caller's droning voice, proud that she was still slender and graceful, certainly not a wife a man would be ashamed to own.

A sweep of air made the candles along the walls flicker briefly. Over the sound of the music she heard a commotion. Brother Blake was involved in an argument with a group of young men.

"Oh, Burns," she whispered as he do-si-doe'd around her. "It's Charley. I think he's drunk."

Burns frowned toward the door. He had never been fond of his stepson, and the boy's wild behavior lately had done nothing to enhance his affection.

"Aw . . . come on, Blake, old boy . . . give us a chance." Charley's voice was so loud it carried over the music. "You old bastards hog all the women."

Strains of melody trailed away as the orchestra stopped to stare. Every eye in the hall was turned toward the scene at the doorway. Charley and the three young men with him began shoving Brother

Blake. "No drunks allowed on the dance floor," Blake protested in his squeaky voice.

"The hell you say, old man!" One of the boys shoved him aside.

As though at a signal, Burns and several other men headed for the doorway. Tom already had Charley by the arm, scuffling with him. Overwhelmed by numbers, the four young men were summarily ejected from the dance hall, their boisterous voices fading into the night.

Burns returned to Kate, looking grim. "They'll be called before the Bishop's Court," he said. "I don't know what we're going to do with Charley . . . can't seem to make him toe the line. He's brainless enough without adding wine to it."

The fiddlers started the half-finished quadrille over again, the dancers took their places, and the interruption was temporarily forgotten, although it would supply gossip for several days to come. When the next set was made up, Burns's partner was Mary Gardner and Kate danced with the Bishop. Moving through the familiar figures, she glanced toward the door where Tom still stood. He never danced, but he liked to watch. What was he thinking behind that dark, unsmiling face? she wondered. Then she was whirled away in the dance, her concern forgotten.

"Goodness, I'm all out of breath," Kate said, sitting down by Nelly, nodding to Sister Miles beside her. Nelly's mouth was trembling as she struggled to keep back tears. Charley's behavior had shamed her. Patting her hand, Kate thought that surely now Nelly would have to pay attention to her admonitions about Charley's waywardness. She had denied the rumors for so long.

Some of the younger people were dancing now. Kate felt a glow of pleasure at the sight of her handsome son. Brig was a favorite with the girls, even more so with the parents for his reputation as a steady and sober young man. With dismay she saw that his partner was Nancy Carroll, daughter of the newspaper editor and a Gentile. Gentiles were generally not welcome at dances, but she supposed one of President Snow's daughters had invited the girl. Being the president's daughter had its privileges. The two young people seemed quite taken with each other, eyes intent, oblivious to others on the dance floor.

Kate looked to see whether Burns was observing this and met his frowning glance. He didn't approve of it any more than she did. It was a relief when the Gentile girl returned to her seat and Brig chose Lucy Gilbert. The Gilberts were trashy people, but Lucy was pretty and at least she was a Mormon. The girl obviously adored Brig, though he treated her as casually as the others.

Drusilla danced with Steve more than Kate thought seemly. She was too young to be that devoted to any young man and would have to be spoken to about it. Jane and Mary Ann were never as popular as Dru, for Jane was unpretty and Mary Ann's reputation as a tomboy put the boys off.

When the next set began Kate saw Mary Ann dancing a reel with Ben Morgan. Since he was inclined to be a rowdy, she hoped Mary Ann had sense enough to make him behave. Mary Ann was a good dancer, and her partner was enjoying himself.

"Swing your partner," Brother Primm called. Ben picked Mary Ann up and whirled her around so that her skirts flew wide. Everyone present had a glimpse of her bloomers and crinolines. Kate gasped. Would Mary Ann never learn how to behave properly? Brother Blake laid his hand on Ben's shoulder, shaking his head in warning. Mary Ann was laughing, for Heaven's sake! Ben grinned, half-shamed, half-pleased with himself, but he nodded soberly and began to dance with exaggerated caution.

Burns stood frowning down at Kate. "I think it's time we took our family and went home," he said. "I feel a need to ask God to chastise our children for their unseemly behavior this evening."

Obediently, Kate gathered the family together and they followed their grim-faced father up the dark street. The painful silence of the group contrasted sharply with the joyous lilt of music pouring from the Tabernacle.

"We will pray," Burns announced as they gathered in the kitchen of the Big House. Each of them knelt beside a chair or a bench, except Lovinia, who had hurried upstairs with her baby. Alice had gone to her own house. No one knew where Charley had disappeared to, but the rest of the family knelt before Burns's stern gaze. Tom, inscrutable as always; Brig, sober-faced; Mary Ann, stubborn and recalcitrant; Dru and Jane, resentful at being taken home early; Burnie, Elizabeth, and Isaac, wide-eyed, not understanding; and Nelly, giving way to tears now.

"Dear Lord," Burns began, "we gather before Thee at this time to ask forgiveness for our unseemly behavior this evening. Bless us, oh Lord, that our daughters may keep themselves pure in body and in mind; that they may be ever mindful of Thy commandments; that they may realize that even the appearance of evil is an abomination in Thy sight. Help them to understand their great calling to become Mothers of Israel, the Kingdom Everlasting; that they may cast out wickedness and be ever pure in heart."

Through half-closed lids, Kate saw Mary Ann's face red and burning with embarrassment, her eyes closed tight and a tear streaking each cheek. The other two girls were prim and bland, knowing very well at whom Burns's prayer was directed.

"And help our sons, oh Lord," Burns continued, "that Charles may cast out the vile curse of drunkenness and see fit to do the work of the Lord. Help our son Brigham to understand the danger of association with Gentiles, help him to walk in Thy ways, a companion of Latter Day Saints, that he may not be tempted to depart from the Gospel Plan."

Brig raised his head, staring at his father in astonishment. Over Burns's bowed head, Kate gave her son a sympathetic smile. Poor boy, he didn't even know he had done wrong, he had only been kind to a stranger. One dance, that was all, she thought, forgetting how dismayed she had been. Burns didn't need to chastise him in front of the whole family and pray so long over him.

Her knees hurt and she felt a sinking despair that this day that had started so happily had ended so miserably. Her own childhood was so different from that of the children kneeling here she could scarcely understand why all of them, except perhaps Brig, seemed not to appreciate how well they lived. Kate's eye fell on Mary Ann who was no longer weeping, her mouth tight with resentment. What caused the rebellious streak in a girl with such an appearance of quality? A flash of memory seemed to fill her eyes: the young Kate knocking at the Fitzhughs' door, resolutely rebelling and changing her life. But that girl had no mother. A sigh escaped her, lost in the hands held before her face. Children were a constant care, even when they were grown. One had a duty to guide them in the paths of righteousness, obedient to the Gospel, to teach them that appearances were important too. It was just that sometimes she didn't quite agree with Burns's methods.

Chapter 13

It was going to be a fine house. Kate drew her shawl closer against the chill February wind and looked up at the new two-story addition where Brig and Charley were helping Brother Pearce shingle the roof. The red sandstone ridge above the town glowed against a dull winter sky. Just a block down the street the white spire of the Tabernacle pointed heavenward, and below the town she could see the rock walls of the Temple rising against the dead brown hills of Out South. She had always admired Brother Elmo's gardens, annoyed now by the evidence of the builders' trampling feet in a flower bed. Brother Elmo had a love for green growing things and had made his home a garden oasis. Only when his wife died and he was old did he give up and return to Salt Lake to live with his daughter. Burns had bought the property, intending to rent it out or sell it at a profit. Silver had been discovered twenty miles to the northeast at Silver Reef, and a boom town was growing there, the overflow bringing prosperity to St. George.

President Snow himself had sent Burns's plans awry. Remembering, an ironic smile touched her lips. It came as no surprise to her, for she had already heard the gossip. The third Sister Snow was a woman of great energy; she was well again and she missed living in the Big House where she could entertain visiting dignitaries in style.

"How many Temple workers do you have boarding here now?" President Snow had asked that day, sitting behind his own desk in the study of the Big House.

"About thirty," Kate replied quickly, "more or less."

"It's not the heavy load it was at the beginning," Burns added, a puzzled line appearing between his brows. The two of them sat side by side facing Brother Snow.

"Ah, yes." The swivel chair squeaked and the bland face across the desk seemed to be studying the ceiling. Then he turned his pale blue gaze on Kate and smiled benignly. "You've performed a great service for the Lord, Sister Hamilton. I know your health hasn't been the best, nor that of your sister-wife, Nelly. I feel the Church should release you now from this mission of the boardinghouse."

Kate looked down at the hands lying in her lap and ran the fingers of her left hand along the smooth ridged scars of the right palm. It would certainly be unseemly to appear too jubilant at the news, but a great weight seemed to have been lifted from her as the yoke from the neck of a weary ox.

Sitting bolt upright, Burns stared at President Snow. " 'Ras, I want you to know that my family has never complained about running the boardinghouse. It's been an honor for them to help do the Lord's work in this way."

Kate saw that he was trying to conceal his agitation. Apparently he had not been consulted previous to this meeting, and he had undoubtedly not heard the gossip she had heard.

Burns's protestations were rewarded by a thin smile. With a sigh, 'Ras Snow straightened his heavy shoulders. "The honor as well as the burden must be shared by all," he replied. "My wife is improved in health and feels she could oversee the house if she has sufficient help."

Watching the two men, Kate knew this had upset some plan of Burns's of which she had no knowledge. She also guessed that wifely pressure had been brought to bear on President Snow. Relief flooding through her, she looked down at her hands again. Of course Sister Snow would have all the help she needed. As the wife of an Apostle she was nobility and she would have everything she demanded.

"I'll need time to make some arrangements for my families," Burns said, resentment faintly coloring his voice.

"Of course." President Snow rose and reached for his hat, giving Burns a knowing smile. "We'll discuss it further then."

Kate sat very still while Burns saw President Snow to the door. Staring at the multicolored rag carpet, she listened to Burns's footsteps returning. He closed the door of the study with unnecessary force.

"Damned inconvenient!" he said, beginning to pace back and forth on the carpet.

"We have no choice, Burns." Kate said the words carefully, her eyes following his nervous pacing. "It shouldn't be too difficult since you own some houses here in town."

"I had other . . ." he stopped short, giving her a piercing look. "They're all rented except the Elmo place, and it's only one room."

"Perhaps Brother Pearce could build an addition." Kate held her breath, almost praying he would accept her suggestion. She was so tired of feeding hungry men, and she needed her own place with her own things around her. No doubt Sister Snow felt the same.

With a sigh, Burns turned to stare out the window, hands behind his back, feet wide apart. "No choice . . . of course . . ." he muttered as though to himself. "Well, the Elmo place is in a fine location and already planted." Shrugging, he turned to her. "I'll make the arrangements today."

"Oh, Burns!" The words burst from her with joy unconcealed. "You don't know how happy I'll be to have my own home again."

Taking her hands in his, he smiled for the first time since the interview began. "Why, my dear, I had no idea it meant so much to you."

Tears spilled from her eyes as she stood up and moved into his embrace. "I had no idea," he repeated, holding her close, patting her shoulders. Lifting her damp face, she kissed him warmly and he responded as though surprised at her emotion.

Clearing his throat, Burns looked down at her questioningly. "Now, about Nelly . . ."

Brushing away tears with her hand, Kate smiled. "I'm so used to Nelly I'd miss her if she didn't live with me. Besides, she's not well and she needs someone to look after her."

Burns appeared relieved. "Then that's settled."

Before he could continue, Kate interrupted, fearful of what more he might ask of her. "I can't live with Alice, Burns, I just can't. God forgive me . . . or Lovinia either. She quarrels with the girls constantly."

"Yes," he replied, looking embarrassed. "She's young and has a lot to learn. I'll make arrangements for her to stay on here and help Sister Snow."

"Thank you, Burns," Kate whispered, her arms encircling his waist. "You don't know how happy this makes me."

Grasping her shoulders, he bent to give her a brief husbandly kiss. "I'd better get started," he said briskly. "I had a full day planned before this came up."

Burns was a good provider, Kate thought as the study door swung shut behind him. No member of his family had ever been hungry or cold. Only hungry for love . . . the thought came unbidden and she tried to put it away. She was too old now to worry about that kind of love. Life had a way of never being what one expected. Even the Gospel had somehow changed since she first accepted it so long ago. Oftentimes it seemed the true meaning of the Scriptures escaped her, as though their reality lay tantalizingly just beyond reach of her mind. Beneath his stern and proper exterior, she had to believe Burns still cared for her. Perhaps he, too, in the darkness of night, remembered how it had been with them in the beginning.

The weather was so mild in St. George that they had been able to work on the house all winter. A two-story addition of adobe had been built crosswise to the original house so that it formed a T. The new front door would open onto the old porch. She was so pleased with it . . . with the spacious front room and the big kitchen behind it, and the pantry. She would make the original one room into a parlor, and there were bedrooms upstairs for Nelly and the children with one downstairs for Burns and herself. It would have been nice to have a handsome entry and stairway like Brigham Young's house, but Burns had done the planning as economically as possible. There was no entryway, and the stairway was tucked between two closets off the front room. At least it was her home, her own place once again. She bent to touch a rose bush growing by the porch, its leaf buds already swelling pink.

"Hello, Sister Hamilton." Kate straightened up to see Lucy Gilbert simpering at her.

"Well, Lucy," she said. "Why aren't you in school?"

"Pa says I had enough learning," the girl replied, her eyes straying to Brig's figure on the roof. "Schooling ain't for girls anyhow, Pa says."

Your Pa would, Kate thought. The Gilberts lived south of town. Lucy was their only daughter, and her four brothers were considered wild. It was said of George Gilbert that he had only one wife because he was too lazy to support any more. Certainly he lived off the Tithing Office more than he had a right to.

Charley descended the ladder for another load of shingles. "Well, Lucy." He grinned. "Here you are again. Don't know how we'd get this house built without you stopping by every day."

Lucy turned a fiery red and ducked her head. "I was on my way to the T.O.," she said defensively. "I just stopped to say hello to Sister Hamilton."

At Charley's suggestive laugh, Lucy's color deepened. She stood staring at the ground until he had climbed back to the roof. "I have to be going," she muttered and hurried away.

Kate looked after her speculatively, not pleased at this girl hanging about Brig. He could do better . . . maybe even one of the Snow girls. Anyway, Brig was too young to be thinking of marriage; he needed to have a trade or a business. He should go on a mission before he even thought of settling down. She frowned, thinking she would have to tell Burns that the time to send Brig on a mission had arrived.

Dismissing Lucy from her thoughts, she strolled about the house, pleased at the full-grown trees surrounding it . . . the mulberry trees near the street, remains of the effort to establish a silk industry; the row of poplars along the ditch; the big cottonwoods near the house. Brother Elmo had planted one of the few lawns in town, though it was winter-brown now. In the upper lot there were bearing fruit trees, peaches and apples, plums and apricots; a lucerne patch to feed their milk cows and horses; and a big garden plot, plowed and fallowing. The barn was better built than the house, the boards of the two-story pitched roof building and the adjoining shed weathered gray in the harsh climate. There was a pole corral, a chicken run, and a pig pen. Best of all, a long grape arbor led from the outbuildings to the house, full-grown California grapevines covering it.

"Mama." Kate turned at the sound of Drusilla's voice. It was her girls on the way home from school: Drusilla and Mary Ann, with Elizabeth and Jane behind them. Mary Ann's hands were blue with cold; the careless girl must have lost her mittens again. Nancy Caroll was walking with them. She was a pretty girl, Kate admitted to herself, so slender and such lovely dark hair. Still it was too bad the children were forced to associate with Gentiles in school. She had heard the Presbyterians were trying to start a free school and hoped they succeeded. Nancy's father was still struggling to make a go of his newspaper, but his chances for success seemed poor since people paid their subscriptions reluctantly.

Giggling, Mary Ann nudged Drusilla and pointed at Brig hurrying down the ladder from the roof. He bent to fill his carpenter's apron with nails from the keg beside the house. "Hello there." His shy glance rested on Nancy, then slid away. Kate frowned at the tittering girls.

With all the aplomb of a girl who is much admired, Nancy gave Brig a dazzling smile. "We miss you at school, Brig."

Flushing, Brig gave his mother an embarrassed look and hurried back up the ladder. Charley laughed, making some remark that turned Brig's face red and furious. Thank God Charley wasn't her son. It was bad enough to have him living in the same house.

"Come on, girls," she said. "We'll have to stop at the T.O. on the way home."

The Tithing Office was a small, one-story building with a low porch across the front. Its dim interior was filled with vinegarish smells from the rows of molasses barrels, the sacks of dried fruit, and bins of grain. In the yard behind were haystacks and firewood turned in as tithing by the members of the Church. Mahonri Snow counted out the eggs Kate asked for, charging them off on his books to the Temple workers' account. Idly watching him, Kate wondered how much of the Hamilton account was left after Alice had lived off it for four years. She would find out soon enough when they moved into the new house next month. Burns wouldn't like a quarrel over the furniture, but Alice had to give back the spool bed and the rosewood desk. Maybe Burns would take her to April Conference in Salt Lake and let her buy some new furniture, there was so little available at the Church-sponsored Co-op Store across from the Big House.

When Nancy said good-bye and set off toward her father's office,

Kate's eyes followed her, speculating. Brig was eighteen, a young man, and the girl was very pretty. She must make time tonight to discuss Brig's future with Burns.

Lights in the Tabernacle basement gleamed through the sweet-smelling spring dusk . . . only a block from the new house where they had lived since March. Kate watched her laughing daughters walking ahead of her, carrying their fancy decorated box lunches. The boys had gone by themselves, except Brig, who carried his mother's box and Nelly's. Nelly moved so slowly they had to force their pace down to hers.

Kate looked up at her tall son, his handsome face barely visible in the oncoming darkness. Tears stung her eyes at the thought of his going away. The occasion tonight was Brig's missionary farewell party. There would be dancing and a program. Every lady had been asked to bring a box lunch which would be raffled off later in the evening to help raise money to finance Brig's mission. It was kind of the Bishop to have organized the fund-raising part of the farewell.

She and Burns had agreed there were too many young girls too interested in Brig, particularly Nancy. Two years spent preaching the Gospel of Jesus Christ would mature him. When he returned he would be better qualified to earn a living and far better able to choose the right wife. But now that it had come time for him to leave, she was filled with regret, imagining already the loneliness of two years without the daily presence of this beloved son.

Burns stood at the door of the Tabernacle basement with the Bishop, shaking hands with people as they came in. He frowned at Kate and Brig. "I was afraid you'd be late to your own party." Tempering the frown with a smile, he reached to shake Brig's hand.

"You can be mighty proud of this boy," the Bishop said to Kate.

"I've always been proud of him," Kate replied, the realization that Brig was truly going away sinking like a stone inside her chest.

"Yes, sir," Burns chimed in heartily. "It's a joy to a man to have a son who is faithful in the ways of the Lord . . . to know he'll go out into the world and spread the Gospel."

Taking her box lunch from Brig, Kate left him to greet the guests with his father and followed Nelly to the table where the lunches were arranged. She moved among the ladies, smiling and nodding at their compliments on her son, and wanting to cry. How was it, she wondered, that it was so hard to let him go? She had known this day would come, or one like it. Children always went away, it was the way of life. Still, it was not just because Brig was the first, he was also the dearest. Shocked at herself, she realized she would have given up any of her children rather than this one.

Presently the Bishop called the crowd to order and opened the meeting with prayer which included a long exhortation of God to guide Brother Brigham Hamilton that he might bring enlightenment to many souls and baptize them into the Gospel fold. The Girls' Chorus sang. Brother Walker gave a hilarious recitation on the trials of being a Mormon missionary. President Snow then spoke, cautioning Brig against falling prey to the wiles of evil while far from home and loved ones. Burns spoke, emotionally to Kate's surprise, expressing his pride that his son would be serving the Lord in this way. She thought then how strange that they had been married so long and knew each other so little.

Elizabeth's Sunday School class had prepared a song for the occasion. Some of the children were totally out of tune, but when the last notes of "God be with you till we meet again . . ." faded there was hardly a dry eye in the room.

Kate's heart leaped as her son stood up to speak. At eighteen Brigham Hamilton was taller than his father, though he resembled him in many ways . . . the brown-gold eyes, serious now; the dark brown hair, thick with a little wave in it. In spite of the resemblance there was a softness to his features that Burns had never had . . . a kind of gentleness. In deference to the seriousness of undertaking a mission for the Church, Brig had been growing a moustache.

He had always taken part in Church affairs and was at ease before an audience. But he looked so young, she thought, so vulnerable. If only we could shield our children somehow, never let them out to be hurt and tried by the cruel world. That was not the way of life, nor the way of God. The young must grow just as the old must die. The lump in her throat seemed about to choke her.

"My dear Brothers and Sisters," Brig said. "I feel inspired tonight by this outpouring of love and confidence you have shown. It is a great honor indeed to be chosen to spread the Gospel among the Gentiles. I shall labor diligently to bring the Word of God to all those with whom I come in contact. I feel that I take with me a trust from you that binds me to God and my Brothers and Sisters in the Gospel. I appreciate all you have done and I know your prayers go with me."

Someone was sobbing aloud. Kate looked around and saw it was Lucy Gilbert. Frowning at the knowing eyes looking at Lucy and then at Brig, she thought in disgust that the girl was nothing to Brig. How could she have the nerve to make such a spectacle of herself?

Brig appeared uncomfortable for a moment, then turned his eyes directly on Kate. "I thank God I have had such a wonderful mother," he said. Tears filled Kate's eyes. "She has ever guided me in the paths of righteousness, ever lived the Gospel and taught her children to do right. My mother is one of God's own angels, and it is with deepest regret that I part from her. Yet I feel God will care for her in my absence and watch over her. I thank her as I thank the presidency for this chance to go on a mission and do the work of the Lord.

"Brothers and Sisters, I bear you my testimony that this is the true Church of God, restored to earth through His Prophet Joseph Smith and that those who accept and live the Gospel shall know life everlasting. In the name of Jesus Christ. Amen."

Drawing a handkerchief from her sleeve, Kate wiped her moist eyes. Sister Primm leaned over, her eyes shining. "Oh, Kate, you must be so proud. I don't remember any missionary ever giving such a tribute to his mother."

Unable to speak, Kate nodded, patting Sister Primm's hand. Other women came to speak to her, and it was several minutes, while the audience milled about talking, waiting for the dancing to begin, before her eyes met Burns's across the room. He was upset, she saw immediately. Upset and hurt, and she guessed at once that he had not liked it that Brig saw fit to pay tribute to his mother only . . . not his parents as was the usual case. Well, she thought, resenting his cold glance, he could just not like it. He had seldom been home to guide his children . . . always busy with Church work, or his other families. Brig had expressed his true feelings. If Burns hadn't known before how things stood, he certainly did now.

When the dancing began, it was several sets before Burns asked her to dance. Lovinia and Alice came first, then Sister Snow and Sister

Gardner. It was ridiculous of him to try to punish her in this way. Brig chose her for his partner in the first set and she danced with head erect, smiling, not looking at Burns. Finally Burns did dance with her, in silence except to comment that there was a nice turnout.

He did not even bid on the box lunch he knew very well was hers and ended up buying Alice's. This was the first time Alice had been out since she had delivered a baby son, George. Kate supposed Burns felt he owed Alice some recognition. To Burns's delight, the baby seemed to be thriving.

When Brother Walker, acting as auctioneer, presented Kate's box lunch, Brig bid on it immediately. No one bid against him by what seemed common consent. As the two of them sat sharing the lunch, she caught Lucy's furtive, resentful glance. Lucy's lunch had gone to Charley and she looked unhappy and restive, ignoring her partner. Kate could not suppress the little surge of triumph she felt. Her handsome son preferred her company over all the young girls and had this night told the world how much he cared for her. Surely no mother had ever been so blessed.

"I'm glad Papa decided to let you go to Salt Lake with us," Brig told her, finishing off a leg of fried chicken.

"I need to buy some things for the new house." She gazed at him fondly. "Besides, if I go, we can be together another three weeks."

Brig nodded, serious-faced. "It's only right. You haven't been to Salt Lake since we moved south. Papa shouldn't go every time and not take you."

"I wasn't free to go until now," she answered, wondering why she continued to make excuses.

The orchestra began to tentatively tune their instruments, waiting for Brother Blake's signal to begin the dancing again. "I'll have this dance with you, Mama," Brig said. "You dance better than anyone I know."

Kate tried to hide her pleasure at his choice. "I guess you know all the young girls are furious with you for spending so much time dancing with me . . . and you must dance with your sisters."

"There's no one who means more to me, Mama." His eyes darkened and his young face was intense with repressed emotion. "No one in the world."

Chapter 14

I

My darling Mama,

By now you will have received the letter recounting my journey by train from Salt Lake City to New York. We were greeted at Albany by the mission president, Brother Jones, who seems to be a man firm in the faith and of strong, perhaps obstinate, mind. I think he would not bear crossing, as I have already heard tales of missionaries who have tried and been severely chastised. However, I am here to serve the Lord and carry the Gospel to the Gentiles that they may be saved. If Brother Jones is a difficult man, you well know that I am able to accommodate myself and get along with almost everyone.

Now I will tell you a little of my work since my arrival here in upper New York State. My companion is Brother James Carpenter, a married man of middle years. As Papa would say, a steadying influence. It may turn out, however, that I am the steadying influence, since Bro. Carpenter seems overfond of the sacramental wine. Still, he is a good man and a fiery speaker. He has two wives in Salt Lake and explains the doctrine of Celestial Marriage far better than I have ever heard. This is a great help, as we have found polygamy to be the bludgeon with which our enemies belabor us. There are many vicious rumors abroad about the Mormon harems. Their ignorance appalls me, as it has been my observance that plural marriage brings far more trials than joys. If God wishes to test His people, this doctrine is surely one to try their souls.

Bro. Carpenter and I find few in this countryside who are ready to listen or even to tolerate our preaching. Last week, Bro. Carpenter arranged for a hall where we might hold a meeting to explain the principles of the Gospel. But when the landlord found we were Mormons he refused permission for us to use the hall, although he had already been paid the hire. When we speak on street corners and public squares we are constantly beset by hecklers. It is a great trial to both of us to maintain the dignity of our calling and answer these infidels back calmly and persuasively. Bro. Carpenter says he feels I will make a good missionary, for I have an earnest and convincing manner. This is his second mission, so he is speaking from experience. I pray I may live up to his expectations and to yours.

I find this country a joy to the eye, everything is so green and grows entirely without irrigation, the rainfall being adequate for the needs of the crops. Each farm has its own copse of woods, and I often think of Joseph Smith praying to God for enlightenment in just such a woods.

Now I must tell you of a most remarkable experience. When Pres. Jones sent myself and Bro. Carpenter to this area we found the population to be sorely lacking in the spirit of God. We were both low on funds, as you know missionaries are supposed to travel without purse or script, and we were sore put to find lodgings, let alone a meeting place. We slept in a haystack near Brighton Falls after several days' preaching in which we failed to find any response. Then we felt we should journey to the next town. As we walked down the dusty country road I spied a stand of woods and thought immediately of the Prophet Joseph. Bro. Carpenter, I said, let us go into the woods and pray as Joseph Smith did. I feel God will inspire us and lead us to help and comfort if we do so. He was agreeable and we prayed earnestly.

A short way down the road we came to a small farm, with a comfortable farmhouse, well kept and thrifty-looking. I felt inspired to knock at the farmer's door. We were greeted by a stout gentleman in his sixties, still hale and hearty and farming his own land as he has no sons.

We immediately explained to him that we were Latter Day Saints missionaries trying to spread the Word of God and His everlasting Gospel. To our surprise and delight he seemed most agreeable. He said he had heard of the Mormons, but had never had their doctrine explained to him. He belongs to no church, but is a man of inquiring and intelligent mind, ever anxious to learn. In short, we were invited into his home where we were introduced to his fine wife and his daughter, Monica. The daughter is a lovely child of seventeen, born late in life to Bro. and Sister Barnes. They also have two married daughters living near New York City. I found Monica a rare spirit, a gentle creature, yet with a bright and inquiring mind. Her blue eyes are so large one almost feels he is looking into a pool of sparkling water, her hair dark and shiny as a blackbird's wing, her skin pale . . . in fact, altogether the loveliest young lady one could see anywhere.

But I digress. After Bro. Carpenter and I had explained some of the principles of the Gospel as revealed to Joseph Smith, and answered Bro. Barnes's sharp questions, we were invited to sup with the family and provided a bed in the loft of the barn. I feel God has surely guided us to this family. Bro. Barnes seems most interested and receptive. His wife is a domestic creature, devoted to his comforts and that of her beautiful daughter, apparently thinking of little else. During our discussions I noticed that Monica followed the talk with great interest. She is an accomplished musician and later played the organ for us. I was happy to have along the hymn book you gave me and to teach her some of the hymns that are peculiar to the Latter Day Saints. Oftentimes I feel much more can be conveyed in song rather than talk.

Dearest Mother, I am very uplifted tonight and thankful to God for guiding us to this family where the seed of His Word will surely be sown on fertile ground. My only sorrow is in being so far from you, knowing how much my presence means to you in your many trials and illnesses. Please do not fail to write. As much as I miss your presence I also miss your firm and righteous guidance. My love wings across the miles to you tonight as I kneel and pray God to care for you in my absence.

Your loving son,
Brigham

Kate smoothed the pages of the letter out on the round oak table beside the front room window, admiring Brig's fine handwriting. She had read it three times already since Isaac brought the mail from the post office. Pride swelled in her as she reread the words. It was the letter of an educated man, a sensitive man, strong in the faith. Perhaps he didn't write in the way he spoke, but what man of training did? For the first time in a long time the memory of her dead father flooded back. Oh, he would be so proud to know he had a grandson such as Brig . . . to know how far his daughter had come. He had wanted so much for his children to escape the miseries of the lower class in England. It seemed she was the only one who had done so, thanks to Burns Hamilton and the Mormon Church. Once every few years there was a letter from her sister, Charity, the only contact with her family in England. Poor Charity was illiterate and had to hire someone to write the letters. When Brother Wainwright went on a mission to England she had asked him to look up her family, then was mortified when they turned him away. But the Allenbys took him in, sending word that they had given up hope of emigration since Brother Allenby's stroke.

Rising, she walked to the window and looked at the stone walls of the Temple rising against the barren hills of Out South. A feeling of intense joy flooded through her. How could she have been so blind? There was a way to give to her father all the things she had gained. When the Temple was completed she would do her family's work there. Her father and mother would be married and sealed to their children, everyone of them would be baptized, by proxy. Then they could all be together in Paradise. This would be her mission: to bring her family up out of the darkness into eternal light.

II

My dearest Mama,

I feel inspired tonight to thank God for giving me a mother such as you. One who has ever guided my feet in the paths of righteousness, ever cared for me with tender love and understanding. I know what a sacrifice it is for you to send me on this mission for the Church. Not only have you given up the help I could render to you at home, but also the financial sacrifice. I thank you for the money you sent and shall spend it carefully that it may do the most to spread the Word of God.

Our work here has been most rewarding in the last weeks. Although Bro. Barnes continues interested in the Gospel and involves myself and Bro. Carpenter in discussion on points of religion, yet he refuses to accept and be baptized. Still, he has been of great help to us. In the small town of Ashton nearby he has made arrangements for us to hold meetings at the Odd Fellows Hall, of which he is a member. I do not understand why he holds back. Perhaps the time is not yet for him to see the Light. Because of his backing and because we have a meeting place we have been able to attract an audience. Some come to heckle and stay to listen. We have been greatly aided by Sister Monica's music. She comes to each meeting and plays the organ for the hymns. In fact, she has come to know our LDS music so well I now feel fully confident in letting her choose the music for our meetings. This girl is a rare and precious spirit. Oftentimes she will seek me out alone to discuss the Gospel and never tires of hearing me tell of the Angel Moroni's visit to Joseph Smith. Did I tell you that the two of us sang a duet at a cottage meeting last week? She has a fine soprano voice which blends well with my own baritone. As we walked home from the meeting I prayed God might guide me to bring this beautiful and wonderful girl into the Gospel fold. I think she would now be baptized if I asked her, yet I do not wish to have her go against her father's wishes. I will wait, and I know God will inspire her to request baptism herself, whether or not her stubborn father accepts the Gospel.

I must tell you that last Saturday, Bro. Carpenter and myself baptized a family of five, the parents and three children, in the pond at the Barnes's farm. Afterward Bro. Barnes and his wife kindly entertained the group, both members and investigators in their home. Monica had been up at daylight making cakes and other delicacies for the occasion. She is indeed a girl of unusual insight and goodness. I often feel when she is in the congregation where I am speaking that I am doubly inspired.

We are still sleeping in the loft at Bro. Barnes's, though when winter comes on we will surely have to find warmer quarters. As our congregation here is growing, slowly but steadily, I feel God will open the way for us in this matter.

As I mentioned in an earlier letter Bro. Carpenter is overfond of wine and has, of late, been a trial to me because of this. I find that I have to conceal the wine jug and must water the wine heavily when preparing it for the Sacrament. It disturbs me greatly, as all the progress we have made here could be lost if Bro. Carpenter descends into drunkenness. I have prevailed upon him to pray with me that God may help him overcome this weakness. He wept and swore he would imbibe no more, yet I live in constant fear that he may do something to embarrass the Church. If Pres. Jones were a man of more understanding I would seek his advice, but I feel sure that if it were brought to his attention Bro. Carpenter would be sent home in disgrace and perhaps cut off from the Church. I pray God will guide me to make the right decisions.

I must bring this letter to a close now and prepare for the cottage meeting in town tonight. Sister Monica will go with me to lead the music. I feel sure I shall soon have the privilege of baptizing her into the true Church of God. She is ever a help and inspiration to me. Every day I thank God for sending me here that this dear and beautiful girl may be led into everlasting salvation.

Now, my dear Mother, I fear from what Mary Ann writes that you are working too hard. You must remember that your

health is delicate and you must guard yourself, for you are infi-
nitely dear to me and to all your family. Our lives would be desolate without you. Please write to me quickly that I may know
you are in improved health. I pray for you constantly.

Your loving son in the Gospel,

Brigham

Kate sighed, wishing Mary Ann hadn't told Brig her mother was
ill. A young girl like Mary Ann couldn't understand all the problems
of going through the change. From now on she would be more
careful to conceal her misery from the hot flashes and the sudden
racking spells of fatigue. Certainly there was no need to worry Brig
about it.

Carefully she folded the letter, having read it several times already.
She had known he would do well, that God would be with him in
his mission. Even Burns would be proud when he read the letter.
Reaching up to lay the letter beside the clock on the kitchen shelf,
she looked out the open window into the dry, still air of late summer.
Mary Ann was sitting on the back porch step in the shade of the
trumpet vine that climbed the porch post, its orange blossoms cascading among glossy green leaves. Beside her, Burnie and Isaac stretched
out lazily, while Elizabeth rocked her doll in her miniature rocking
chair.

They all looked up to greet Tom who had just come in from turning the water on the lucerne patch. Tom paused for a dipperful of
water from the burlap-wrapped water barrel by the porch. It was
Isaac's job to fill it each morning from the town ditch before the stock
were turned out to graze along the streets.

"How do the bees make honey, Tom?" Isaac asked, reaching up to
brush the bees from the trumpet vine.

"Like this." Tom chose a blossom and carefully pulled it from its
calyx. "Open your mouth." He placed the bottom of the flower's
tube on Isaac's tongue.

Isaac smacked his lips. "Tastes like sugar water, only better."

"It's nectar," Tom explained. "The bees take it back to the hive
and make it into honey."

"I'd like to be a bee." Isaac laughed and plucked another blossom.
"Taste it, Burnie."

(124)

"Be a bee," Burnie crowed. He and Elizabeth tried it, sucking the nectar from one blossom after another.

Mary Ann, serious-faced, held the blossom against her lips long after the nectar was gone. "How did you know that, Tom?" she asked, looking at the smiling young man leaning against the porch post.

"Tom knows everything," Isaac said, picking blossoms with both hands.

Tom shrugged, smiling at Mary Ann. "It's just logical."

For a moment Kate forgot the letter in her hand, looking at the tall young man lounging beside the porch. She didn't know what she would have done without Tom in Brig's absence. Isaac and Burnie were good help, but Charley was so heedless and wild. Yet as she watched Tom now, his dark eyes smiling at Mary Ann, his thick, straight black hair fallen across his forehead, she realized for the first time that he was indeed a grown young man. What would become of him? she wondered, with a pang of guilt for taking him for granted for so long. He was a good and faithful boy, yet beyond their home there seemed to be no life waiting for him. Where could he find a wife or a home or a trade other than caring for Burns's cattle and farms? He should marry soon. The Hathaways had two adopted Indian girls. Surely one of them would suit Tom.

"You're making an awful mess," Mary Ann cried to the children. "Now clean up all those blossoms before Mama sees it. She'll tan your hides."

Kate smiled at Mary Ann's unnecessary threat, forgetting Tom and unfolding the letter to read it once more.

III

My dearly beloved Mama,

How I wish you were here tonight to share my joy. All your years of training and guidance in the Gospel of Jesus Christ have borne a fruit beyond compare. This day I had the privilege of baptizing into the Church of Jesus Christ of Latter Day Saints Sister Monica Barnes. This wonderful girl, this rare and beautiful spirit, rose from the water; her face suffused with a holy light so blinding one could hardly bear to look upon it. Then she placed her arms about me and wept with joy. I could not restrain my own tears, nor could the other members who were present. The autumn sun came from behind the clouds at that moment and seemed to bathe the scene in the Glory of God. The day was marred only by the fact that Monica's parents did not join her in accepting the Gospel. Since they dote on her excessively it was not difficult for her to obtain their permission. They seem unable to deny her anything.

Bro. Barnes remains a puzzle to me. He is ever tolerant and helpful to me and Bro. Carpenter, he studies the Book of Mormon and the *Doctrine and Covenants* daily, yet says he cannot accept the Gospel as a whole. There is a strangely cynical streak in him which perhaps keeps him from God's Word. If he does not eventually accept and be baptized I feel Monica would be better off in Utah among the Saints where she would be helped to follow always the paths of righteousness and live the Gospel. You would love this girl, Mother. She is so like you, ever understanding and gentle. I feel almost unworthy of the deep regard she seems to have for me. This winter I intend to labor diligently at my mission, hoping to bring many souls to the Light of God, and to make myself worthy of my beloved Mother, as well as this precious girl.

One of the new members who lives in Ashton has offered lodging for the winter to Bro. Carpenter and myself. It will be handier for us to be in town when the snow comes. We will be nearer the majority of our flock and it will be easier to arrange the meetings. Yet I depart from my hayloft with regret, for I shall be denied the daily presence of Sister Monica which has come to mean so much to me. Her father did not press me to stay on, and I feel perhaps he is not pleased at the growing affection between us.

You have, in the past, dear Mother, urged me to take care in the choice of a wife, for surely a wife is sunshine or shade to her husband. I will not say that I have made a choice. I pray earnestly to God that He may guide me in the ways of righteousness, that I may keep His commandments and live the Gospel that I may be one day raised up into His presence. My testimony grows stronger each day.

I pray my absence is not a trial to you. Tom and Charley can handle the heavy work and Isaac must be growing into a big boy now. I would counsel the girls to be faithful and helpful to their dear Mother and obey her words.

Dearest Mother, I hope you share in the happiness of this day with me. I love you more than all the world and your joy is mine also.

Your son,
Brigham

Kate folded the letter and slipped it back into the envelope. The affection Brig expressed for this young girl he had known such a short time depressed her. Every time she read the girl's name she felt a twinge of fear. Surely now that Brig would be away from daily contact with Monica he would see clearly that this girl was not for him. She pondered whether she should write and tell him so, then decided she mustn't . . . that she would pray God would guide her son to make the right decision. Brig might resent her directing his life from so far away, and her not even knowing Monica.

"Mama!"

"How many times do I have to tell you not to slam the screen door, Isaac?" Kate looked at her younger son in irritation as he flopped down on a chair beside her at the kitchen table. She liked to have this time to herself after the mail came, to read and reread Brig's letters.

"What did Brig say?" Isaac asked, his grubby hand reaching tentatively for the letter. "Can I read it?"

Kate handed over the letter, thinking maybe Isaac could learn something from his brother's words. Isaac and Brig were as unlike as two brothers could be. Isaac hated school, hated going to church, couldn't sit still. He was forever writing in the hymn books, carving his name on benches and desks, disturbing the class; and when he was dismissed he exploded out the door as though shot from a cannon. He adored Tom who seemed to know everything Isaac really wanted to know—about animals and the outdoors. He shadowed Tom just as Burnie shadowed him. Burnie was a good boy, but not as quick and bright as Isaac. Even though he was four years older he still looked to Isaac for leadership.

"I think he's sweet on that girl," Isaac grinned, dropping the letter on the table. At Kate's admonishing frown, he loped off, adroitly picking a cookie from the cookie jar as he headed for the door.

Kate smoothed the pages of the letter, which Isaac had managed to crumple in the few moments he held them, and shook her head. Well, perhaps when it came Isaac's turn to serve a mission he would be able to settle down. She knew Nelly had hopes of sending Burnie when Brig returned, but the boy simply wasn't that capable. He was fifteen years old, he should soon be learning a trade other than carrying hod at the Temple. Burns seemed reluctant to let him go, but the time was coming. Perhaps she should speak to Brother Mansfield about taking Burnie as an apprentice blacksmith. No doubt it would be left to her to handle the problem and soothe Nelly. Burns was gone again, helping set up the sawmill at Mount Trumbull to provide more lumber for the Temple. When he returned there would be another trip through the settlements to collect tithes to help pay for the Temple. Little by little she was learning she must run her life and that of her children by herself. She, who had once believed she would never again be alone and uncomforted . . . but Brig would be home again in a year.

IV

Dearest Mama,

I have written you often this winter of my feelings toward Sister Monica Barnes. With the exception of my beloved mother a more beautiful, wonderful woman never lived. We have been much together this winter, as she is the church organist and I lead the singing. We often sing duets at church programs and entertainments, requiring some hours of practice together. Her parents offered no objection to her spending so much time in my company, although Bro. Carpenter took it upon himself to chastise me for what he called "doing my courting instead of tending to my mission." I assure you, Mother, he was wrong. I have attended faithfully to my duties in seeking to spread the Gospel of Jesus Christ among the brethren here and have brought a number to accept the Gospel and be baptized.

Bro. Barnes still discusses religion with me and I still hope to convert him. At one point he asked me bluntly whether a single missionary, such as myself, was bound to a vow of celibacy for the term of his mission. I told him this was so, to help the missionary attain purity of heart by not being concerned with worldly and carnal things. He seemed much relieved, and it occurred to me he must have felt I had dishonorable intentions toward his daughter. I was much hurt by his attitude and felt constrained to absent myself from Monica's company for a number of days. Oh, dear Mother, I cannot tell you how I was tried during this time, for she has become as the breath of life to me.

The next week when I walked her home from a cottage meeting I could hold back no longer and told her of my love for her. She answered that her feelings for me were the same, and my heart overflowed. We pledged this secret between us until such time as I am free to speak to her father.

Dearest Mother, I live for the day I may bring home to you this daughter, so like you she might be your own, and take her for my wife. I pray God will bring this to pass. I shall work earnestly for Him and spread His Word and in all ways endeavor to make myself worthy of Monica's love. I know you will love her as I do. The happiest day of my life will be the day I am together with the two beings I love most on this earth, my wife-to-be and my dear mother.

Good night, sweet Mother. God bless and keep you.

Brigham

With trembling hands Kate slipped the letter into her apron pocket, glad Burns was away and would not need to read it, hoping Isaac and the girls would not ask. How could Brig be so reckless? Brother Carpenter was right, courting while on a mission was against all the rules. Brig knew it. He should have been more circumspect, spent less time in the girl's company. What kind of girl was this he had chosen, she wondered, her eyes suddenly filled with tears. A girl raised in a Gentile home, spoiled by her parents who had refused to accept the Gospel. Hurrying into the parlor, Kate sat down at her rosewood desk and drew out the writing paper. Brig must be cautioned to go more slowly, to take care. Perhaps she could even persuade Burns to let her go to New York and meet this family before any marriage took place.

V

My dearest Mama,

My heart is sorely troubled as I write this. The hour is late and the night birds come north with the spring are calling outside my window. Inside our narrow room Bro. Carpenter snores heavily, for I fear he tipped the wine jug too often this evening. Bro. Carpenter has been an increasing trial to me in this matter of strong drink, and there have been some whispers among the membership concerning his behavior. Yesterday (Sunday) he grew quite tipsy before Sacrament Meeting even began. I refused to let him take any part in conducting the meeting. In anger, he departed from the meeting house and took the train to Albany to see Pres. Jones. I had, at that time, no knowledge of his whereabouts and worried throughout the night for fear he had met with an accident. Today he returned with Pres. Jones who immediately called me on the carpet and chastised me severely for spending so much time in the company of an unmarried Sister (Monica). He said what I was doing was shameful in God's eyes, that I was not attending to my duties, which were to spread the Gospel, and further added that I would be transferred as soon as he could arrange it. I answered that nothing untoward had transpired between Sister Barnes and myself, that I hoped one day to make her my wife, and would do so immediately if he would consent to such an arrangement. I felt this was not asking more than could be accomplished; since Bro. Carpenter's wife intends to join him the last six months of his mission and commonly the more affluent missionaries take a wife with them. At this he flew into a rage, denied consent, and said Bro. Carpenter was to be in complete charge from this time on. I was to make arrangements to leave as soon as he sent me word.

I sought a few moments alone with him to tell him that I feared all our work here would be destroyed by Bro. Carpenter's weakness for wine. He refused to listen and departed immediately on the train. Bro. Carpenter went to the station with him and did not return, as I am sure he was ashamed to face me. Late this evening he did return in the condition he lies in now. I pray God will help me to not despise this Brother in the Gospel who has betrayed me so shamefully and unnecessarily.

Oh dear Mother, my heart is sore that I must part from my darling Monica. I have yet a year to serve on my mission, and the thought of being a year away from her fills my soul with pain. There remains only a day or two to say farewell to her and to the friends I have made here.

I will send you my new address as soon as I am able, and in the meantime you may write me in care of Pres. Jones. How I long for your comforting presence tonight, your voice, the gentle touch of your hand. I feel I have served God well here and could do much more had I not been betrayed by a man in the clutches of the Devil. I must not despair. God will be with me. Pray for me and all will be well.

Your loving son,
Brigham

That despicable man Joseph Carpenter! Kate thought as a tear splashed on the letter and blurred Brig's words. May he burn in eternal hell for what he has done. And that vengeful fool, President

Jones, how could he censure Brig this way, humiliate him before his followers. Wiping her eyes, she folded the letter away . . . another one Burns must not see. Perhaps, after all, it was best that Brig be transferred away from Monica. It would allow time for his feelings to cool, time to think things over. If only it hadn't been done in such a cruel way. Well, Brother Carpenter would not go scot free for his dastardly conduct. If Brig were too kind or too timid to report him to President Jones, she was not. She would write this very day and tell him of Brother Carpenter's drunken behavior.

VI

Beloved Mother,

I write this as I wait at the station in Chicago for a train to Salt Lake City. Sick in heart and soul as I am, there is no other to whom I can pour out my anguish. At times I think I cannot bear to continue living. When I lie down to sleep and cannot, I pray for the everlasting sleep to release me from the pain of this life. But the morning comes, and it is God's punishment that I must awaken and continue my suffering. Time has no meaning. It seems months since last I heard from you, and yet I know that cannot be true. It seems a million years since I wrote you that Pres. Jones had ordered me transferred to another mission post to part me from my darling Monica.

With aching heart I went about preparing for my departure, saying good-bye to the dear friends I had made, avoiding Bro. Carpenter for I could not look at him without feeling ungodly anger. At last I walked out to the Barnes farmstead to say my good-byes. Monica had been weeping, I saw at once, and I found that the news of my impending departure had spread already. Bro. Barnes invited me to stay for supper and tried to be jovial. I replied in kind, saying (for Monica's dear sake) that the year would soon pass and I would be back with them. Bro.

Barnes seemed surprised at this statement and looked sharply at Monica. She lowered her eyes and her beautiful face colored. I knew then that he guessed our secret and thought it best to speak now. I asked him if I might have permission to return when my mission ended and court his daughter, as I wished to make her my wife. Frowning, he demanded to know how many wives my father had. I answered four and tried once more to explain plural marriage, which has always been a stumbling block in his acceptance of the Gospel. I also answered that a majority of the LDS men had only one wife, that surely a man with a wife like Monica would never bring himself to take another. I also pledged him my word that I would never enter plural marriage, as I felt Monica would not wish me to do so, nor did I feel I had the calling. His manner became very cool and he said, "Well, a year is a long time and Monica is very young. We shall see. She may join several other religions by then." I was deeply hurt by his attitude toward his daughter's sincerity, as well as toward me. Monica was in tears, and my heart ached to comfort her. Her mother said nothing, as she is entirely submissive to her husband. Bro. Barnes stood up and offered me his hand, wishing me good luck and thereby dismissing me.

As she walked to the door with me Monica managed to whisper to me to wait in the woods nearby. I knew I could not part from her with only a handshake in front of her parents, and no promises made, so I repaired to the woods where I wept a few tears of my own. I could see the farmhouse from where I sat, and presently the lights went out as the family retired. After a short time Monica appeared clad only in her nightdress and wrapper against the cool spring night. I took my beloved into my arms and . . . Oh my God, dear Mother. How it happened I do not know. It was like being taken by a whirlwind. When I awakened my dearest Monica lay sleeping in my arms, and her father stood over us with his lantern lighting the dark woods.

I cannot recount to you what happened after that, the vile things that were said, the names I was called and perhaps deserved for my weakness in breaking a commandment of God. I think if he had held a gun at that moment, he would have killed me, and I would not have blamed him. My loved one could only weep while her angry father held her away from me. I begged him to let us marry, told him I would leave my mission immediately so that she could become my wife. He refused to listen and, dragging Monica with him, called out that I had better leave, for he would be back with his shotgun.

I could not return to town, nor could I sleep. I spent the night in a nearby haystack, praying to God for forgiveness and suffering such agonies of soul I could hardly bear it. I prayed that in the morning Bro. Barnes might be more reasonable, that he would not ruin my life and his daughter's for our one moment of weakness.

When I knocked at his door, he answered, and I knew he had slept no more than I. Immediately he began calling me names, saying, "You Mormons are as rotten as they say . . . debauching young girls." I protested that I loved Monica and wished to marry her. He replied cruelly that she and her mother had left for New York City on the morning train, that I would never see her again. He vowed he would kill me if I ever showed my face at his door. I replied that I would rather be dead than to lose my beloved Monica. At that, he cursed and slammed the door in my face.

Heartsick and burdened with guilt, I returned to my quarters, not knowing what else to do. Alas, I found Bro. Barnes had already sent a telegram to Pres. Jones who was waiting for me. He asked me the nature of Bro. Barnes's charge against me. I could not bring myself to reply except to say that I wished to marry Monica Barnes. Presently Bro. Barnes appeared and, in a scene so terrible I shall never erase it from my mind, accused me of seducing his daughter and all manner of other evil things. Dear God! I cannot tell you how tormented I felt to be forced to confess that I had taken that innocent girl who had given herself to me in love. Pres. Jones cursed me for a lecherous weakling, saying I would be sent home in disgrace and disfellowshipped from the Church. Pres. Jones is as good as his word. When I reach Salt Lake, I will be cut off from the Church until such time as I can seek and be given the forgiveness of my brethren and sisters and be rebaptized.

Dearest Mother, you read the words of a tormented soul, sick with guilt and tortured by the loss of my beloved. I return to you in disgrace, bringing shame to you and our family. I pray constantly for God's forgiveness. I pray, dear Mother, for your understanding and forgiveness. Yet I wonder shall I live long enough to forgive myself. In a moment of weakness and sin I lost the love I valued above all things. I have written to her every day since this happened. I would travel a million miles to have her with me once more, yet I know it will never be. This is God's punishment upon me. I broke my vows to Him, broke His commandment, and He has plunged me into a hell on earth for my own redemption.

Forgive me, dearest Mother. I love you.

Brigham

"God help us!" Burns's voice was so strange Kate looked up from the letter to meet his anguished eyes. When Burnie brought the mail from the post office the two of them had sat down at the round center table in the front room to go through it. Struggling to hold back the tears Brig's letter had brought, she quickly folded and slipped it into her apron pocket, hoping Burns would not think to ask to read it.

"It's from the mission president." Burns's voice shook. Dropping the letter on the table, he buried his face in his hands. "Dear Lord," he muttered. "What have I done to deserve this?" When he handed her the letter she saw there were tears in his eyes. The language was cold and formal, although the mission president was a friend of Burns's. It added nothing to what she had already learned from Brig's letter, except the postscript, obviously scribbled quickly at the bottom: "My heartfelt sympathies to you and your dear wife, Kate." As though their son were dead, she thought, losing the struggle to hold back her tears.

Burns's arm was about her shoulders. "I'll never forgive him for breaking his mother's heart like this," he said bitterly.

"Oh, Burns," she sobbed. "He's so young . . . so very young. We should never have let him go away from us."

"He can't be a child and a Mama's boy forever, Kate!" He withdrew his comforting arm, and she saw that he was working himself into one of his famous rages. "He's nineteen years old. Old enough to have some self-control. I tell you he's a weakling and a sinner."

"But, Burns, things like this do happen to young people," Kate protested through her tears. "If you think he hasn't suffered . . . here . . . read his letter." She thrust the envelope at him.

Wiping her tears, she watched Burns read Brig's letter. There was no sympathy in his face; it only settled into hard and angry lines. Shoving the letter back into its envelope, he said harshly, "Do you think I didn't desire you before we were married? A long time ago . . . but I remember still the struggle I had to restrain my carnal passions." He stood up and she knew he would never forgive Brigham. "I would ask no more of any man than I could do myself. I have sired a weakling. God help us all."

Holding out his hand to her, he said, "Come, Mother . . . pray with me. We'll need all the help God can offer to get through what lies before us."

Kate knelt beside him at the sofa, weeping painfully as Burns importuned God for strength that his family might bear this shame their wayward son had brought upon them.

Chapter 15

Everyone knew . . . everyone. Sick with anguish, Kate looked around the packed Tabernacle. In a small town there were no secrets. The whole congregation must know that Brig had appeared before the Bishop's Court last night . . . knew from past experience that he would have been given his instructions to confess his sins in Testimony Meeting today. What is it in human beings that makes them stop to stare at a suffering fellow man, seemingly to enjoy another's pain? Women who, one year ago, had congratulated her on having such a wonderful son bowed to her with smug smiles, eyes gloating, reveling in the scandal.

The meeting room was warm and heavy with the smell of human sweat. Fans moved everywhere, working against the heat and the ever present flies. Kate stole a glance at Brig, sitting stiffly beside her, staring straight ahead. His drawn face was a mask, hiding the almost unbearable agony of soul she had seen there the past few days. Dear God, she thought, don't let him break down in front of all these people. Let him keep some pride. Reaching to take his hand, she saw that those hands were clasped together so that the knuckles were white. No, she mustn't. A gesture of affection now might be too much for him. He knew she didn't blame or censure him and he would always know it. Of course it had been the girl's fault. No decent girl would go to a young man like that . . . alone in the darkness.

A grim-faced Burns sat with the other leaders on the stand. He spoke to no one, staring at the open Bible resting on his knees. She knew how sorely his pride had been injured, but he had no right to be so vindictive, blaming her for making a weakling of Brig . . . a Mama's boy. How many tears had she wept, wondering if it were true, if Brig's fall from grace had been her fault in some way?

Burns had refused to let her go to York with him to meet Brig's train from Salt Lake. "He's had too much Mother already" were the cruel words he left with her.

An unease settled over the family and they drew together, shutting out friends and neighbors. Only Charley remained an outsider. He had come in from the barn the night after Burns left, his nose spurting blood. To Nelly's crying and fussing he would only say, "That goddamn Injun."

Tom came in to supper, obviously having repaired the ravages of a fist fight by washing up at the ditch. The meal was silent and quickly finished. Afterward, when Kate went to carry the slops to the swill barrel that stood in the grape arbor, she saw Tom standing alone beside the corral.

"What happened, Tom?" she asked, trying to see his face in the gathering dusk.

The broad shoulders moved in a deprecating gesture. As though reluctant to answer, he muttered, "Charley said some things about Brig."

"You mustn't fight about it," she told him gently, wanting to cry when she remembered Brig defending Tom at school, and now Tom in his turn defending Brig.

"Charley's got a rotten mouth." Tom's voice was muffled with anger. "Other people are saying enough, without him . . ." He paused. "I'm sorry, Mama."

"I know what they're saying, Tom." Dear, faithful boy, he had always been Brig's champion. With a sad smile, she squeezed his arm affectionately. "Don't try to protect me. With God's help we'll make it through this. Now let me have that shirt to mend."

Since she had always found work an ease for mental suffering, Kate put on a quilt while Burns was gone. There were enough of them to do the quilting . . . she and Nelly and the girls. They wouldn't need to invite neighbor women to a quilting bee, didn't want them now. Leaves of the cottonwood trees beside the house cast moving shadows on the wall of the front room. Light flickered over the quilt stretched on the frame, shading and changing the multi-colored blocks. The stirring of those leaves was the only sound in the warm room. Kate and Nelly and the four girls stitched silently on the Attic Window pattern, pausing only to roll the frame when the outside edge was finished. Charley and Tom were working at the Temple. Isaac and Burnie were hoeing weeds in the garden, strangely solemn for two such active boys.

At the sound of the buggy driving into the back yard, six needles stopped stitching as of one accord. Kate looked up and straightened her shoulders, trembling inside, not knowing what she could say, only that there must be no recriminations, only love for Brig.

Nelly's skinny hands were making fluttering motions above the quilt top. Poor creature, she was at a total loss. Thank God, Alice and Lovinia had been told to stay home and keep their own counsel.

"Nelly," Kate said, clearing the lump from her throat. "Why don't you make a pot of tea for all of us?"

"Yes, Mama . . . do," Jane spoke up quickly. "It might help us make it through the day." For once those words brought no smiles. Kate carefully snipped her thread and stuck the needle in a pincush-ion. Then she smoothed her hair and rose to lead them into the kitchen.

Through the screen door she could see Burns striding across the bare back yard, the packed red earth mottled by the shade of the cot-tonwoods. That look of righteous anger still remained on his face. Oh Lord, she thought, the cruel things he must have said to that boy.

"Isaac . . . Burnie!" Burns called. "Go unhitch the horses."

The two boys responded, almost running into Brig as he emerged from the grape arbor carrying his canvas telescope. For a moment the three of them stared at each other. None of the children had been told why Brig was coming home, but they had all gathered that he was in disgrace. Certainly the older children knew. It was not a thing to be discussed openly. Brig set the telescope down, holding his hand tentatively to Isaac. Ignoring the hand, Isaac threw his arms about Brig's waist while Burnie danced up and down until he in turn had been embraced. Kate saw Brig's mouth tremble as he roughed the two boys' hair and sent them on their way. Then he picked up his bag, moving slowly toward the house.

She started toward him and felt Burns's firm hand on her arm. Nelly made so much noise fussing with heating water for tea that Burns turned to frown at her. Brig opened the screen door and looked at them standing in silence waiting for him. His face twisted as he fought to keep his composure.

Kate pushed Burns's hand away. "Welcome home, son," she said and held out her arms. Brig's self-possession shattered. Weeping, he stepped into her embrace. It was agony to see a young man cry like that, coals of fire added to her own sorrow. Behind them she could hear the girls sobbing.

"Oh, Mama . . . Mama . . ." Brig struggled to speak through the tears. "Forgive me, Mama."

"I'm your mother, Brig," she said, stepping back to look up at his tear-ravaged face. "You'll never have to ask my forgiveness." Turning to the others, her voice firm, she added, "You're with your family now. No matter what has happened or will happen, this is your home and we love you. Girls . . ." One after another the girls stepped forward to embrace Brig, weeping, stunned at seeing their brother in such a state. Burns watched in silence, stern and pale.

"The tea's ready," Nelly's trembling voice broke in.

Taking his handkerchief, Brig dried his eyes and blew his nose. "Thanks, Aunt Nelly," he said, trying to smile. "It might help me through the day."

The girls broke into nervous laughter and hurried to bring the teacups. Seated at the table, Burns said, "Let us pray."

Oh God, no, Kate thought. Don't torture this boy now with one of your prayers for his soul. But Burns sounded exhausted, his voice dull, and he merely asked God to bless their family and give them strength to endure all things.

A strange, sad homecoming. The children were as reluctant to ask Brig about his travels as he was to talk about them. He had thought to bring presents . . . shell necklaces for the girls and pocketknives for Isaac and Burnie, inexpensive trinkets from his meager funds. Kate had pictured so many times how he would come home in triumph, having baptized many Gentiles into the Church; how he would stand in meeting and report to the Ward on his mission; how honored and happy he would be then. But now . . .

Burns said he was worn out from the long trip and went to bed when the children did. Kate and Brig sat alone in the parlor, the coal-oil lamp flickering softly in the warm night breeze. On his knees, he wept in her lap just as he had done as a small boy when his small world went wrong. With an aching heart, Kate smoothed his hair, making the same comforting sounds she had made so long ago. Between fits of weeping Brig talked in incoherent snatches.

"I loved her so, Mama . . . she was so beautiful. Papa says there's no excuse . . . no excuse for what I did. Satan tempted me and I fell into his trap. I'll never forgive myself. Just like Papa said, I'm a sinner and a weakling . . . a sorrow to my family."

"Dearest son," Kate murmured, her throat swollen with pain for him. "You've always been my pride and joy. Nothing will ever change that . . . nothing. You mustn't let Papa make you believe you're the only one who ever broke a commandment. It happens all the time, right here in St. George. You know that." Anger at Burns almost choked her. How could he be so unfeeling as to add to his son's misery? He must have tortured this boy with his self-righteous preaching all the way home from York.

"But I was on a mission for God, Mama. I made my vows to Him . . . and God help me, I broke them. My life is ruined. I'll never be worthy to hold the priesthood again."

"No . . . no," Kate protested vehemently, holding his head close to her breast. "This will pass. God is forgiving. If we endure He will lead us into the light again. Believe that, darling . . . you must."

Racked with sobs again, Brig could not reply. "You're worn out," she said, smoothing the rumpled hair back from his damp forehead. "Please, son, go to bed. God will give you strength to face tomorrow."

Arm in arm they walked to the stairway where Brig bent to kiss her good night. "I thank God for you, Mama," he whispered brokenly. "Every day of my life, I thank God for you."

When, at last, the Bishop called on Brother Brigham Hamilton, a buzz of anticipation swept through the Tabernacle. Watching her tall son stand beside her, Kate thought for a moment she might faint in her anguish. If only she could bear this for him . . .

Brig's hands pressed against his sides as though to hold himself upright. The words came out slowly, forced out. "My dear Brothers and Sisters. I stand before you this day, a sinner in the sight of God and man. I was tempted by Satan and I fell. I broke a commandment of God . . ." His voice cracked and Kate closed her eyes tightly in pain, knowing he had to say the words. "I broke the vows of my mission . . . and I . . . I committed adultery." There was a short silence as he struggled for composure. God help him, please, Kate prayed, help him through this. It would fill some vindictive souls with joy if he broke down. Please God, help him make it without weeping.

"I ask your forgiveness." That awful, empty voice, not like Brig's at all. "I ask the forgiveness of my Brothers and Sisters in the Gospel. Jesus Christ forgave, saying go and sin no more. I wish to be rebaptized into the Church of Jesus Christ of Latter Day Saints . . . to be cleansed of my sins that I may once more live the Gospel and work for Life Everlasting. I bear you my testimony that this is the true Church of God; that Joseph Smith is His Prophet and the Book of Mormon is the Word of God. In the name of Jesus Christ. Amen."

Brig's sisters, sitting along the row, wept softly into their handkerchiefs. Beside his mother, Isaac scrubbed tears away with his fist, only half-understanding why he wept. In the row behind them Lucy Gilbert sobbed noisily. Kate sat, dry-eyed, staring at a spot on the wall just above Burns's head. As he sat down, Brig reached for her hand and she held on tightly, not daring to look at him.

The Bishop rose, clearing his throat. God, Kate prayed silently once more, don't let him give a speech. Just let him have it over with now . . . please God.

"My Brothers and Sisters," he said. "Youth is a time of trial. Some walk the straight and narrow path, and others fall from righteousness. I have talked with this Brother and I know he is truly repentant, desiring only to be purified in God's sight. As he said, Jesus Christ forgave all. Now, Brothers and Sisters, I ask that you signify by a show of hands your forgiveness and willingness to receive Brother Brigham Hamilton back as your Brother in the Gospel."

KATE

Hands went up all over the Tabernacle. It was the expected reaction. Never had forgiveness been withheld when it was asked. If anyone were mean enough not to raise his hand, he would suffer for it from the whispers of his neighbors.

It was over. Drained and weak, Kate clung to Brig's hand. He did not look up. The Bishop would arrange for Brig's baptism that afternoon. He was a good man, she was sure he would do it with as much privacy as possible. Brig had suffered enough.

The Bishop asked if anyone else cared to bear their testimony, and when no one stood up, Kate sighed with relief. Brig's confession had been the climax of the meeting, the reason a number of people had attended who seldom came otherwise. Sacrament was passed, and the meeting ended with prayer.

Kate, her head held high, her hand holding Brig's arm, walked slowly down the aisle, out the wide, hand-carved doors and down the steps of the Tabernacle. She spoke only to those who spoke first and did not pause in her stately progress. Taking their cue from their mother, her children followed with heads high. They must not give way now, she thought, although she could feel Brig's strength slowly disintegrating as they walked along the dusty street, picking their way around the fallen mulberries littering the roadside. Behind them the murmur of the visiting brethren followed through the warm, still air. Across the wooden bridge over the irrigation ditch, through the front gate, past bee-filled hollyhocks and Brother Elmo's blood-red roses and the lawn in need of mowing; safe at last behind their own front door. With quick commands to the girls about dinner, Kate led Brig into the parlor and closed the door, shutting out everyone else while he wept in her arms.

Chapter 16

The lights along the walls of the Tabernacle basement hall flickered every time someone opened the door and let the cold January wind whip through. The dancers, a multicolored whirl of calico and sober suits, seemed not to notice. Some of the men were even sweating profusely. Kate, sitting on a bench to watch, smiled as Dru and Steve skipped past her, moving in the figures of a reel. Arms folded, Burns sternly observed the dancers, for he was floor manager tonight. The Mormons were capable of dancing any time or place, but decorum must be preserved. This custom of forgetting their troubles in music and dance must have saved people's very sanity in the hard times. Suddenly Kate felt an elbow digging into her ribs and looked around into Brother Gilbert's homely, smiling face.

"Those two young folks of our'n," he said, nodding toward Brig and Lucy dancing together. "Startin' ta look like wedding bells."

Kate gave him a sparse smile and did not reply, turning to watch her tall, handsome son and his partner. How solemn Brig was, even in the midst of a dance. He had always been a serious boy, but it seemed to her he never smiled nowadays. After his baptism he never again discussed his mission or his fall from grace. It was as though he had closed a door forever. But he had changed, she thought, a pain catching at her throat . . . sadly changed. He went to church faithfully, blessed the Sacrament and offered prayer when he was asked, but he never stayed for the handshaking and visiting that inevitably followed every Mormon meeting. Walking home by himself, he would read the Bible or the Book of Mormon until the rest of the family arrived to begin Sunday dinner. The letters in which he had poured out his soul were carefully locked away in Kate's rosewood desk. Perhaps she should have burned them, destroyed the sad evidence of a young man's pain, but it seemed to her that some day, far in the future, those letters might come to have another meaning.

Lucy glowed as she looked into Brig's face, their hands locked as he whirled her about. She was young, Kate thought, and passably pretty. There was no doubt she had a compassionate heart or that she truly loved Brig. Since his return she had stopped by the house almost every day on one pretext or another . . . to bring a treat she had cooked, or to exchange books. It was she who had talked Brig into going to the dances and the winter socials, although in the beginning she had to call for him and take him with her. Throughout the winter Brig seemed to have fallen into the habit of waiting for Lucy to suggest their social life. He sought the company of no other girls. Nancy's father's newspaper had failed, and they had moved away while Brig was gone. Lucy was always available, eager and undemanding company. Kate sighed. It stung her pride that Lucy had been able to accomplish what she had not: to bring Brig out of the shell into which he had retreated. She supposed she should be thankful for anyone who could help Brig make peace with himself.

Sister Gardner came to sit beside Kate and Nelly, smiling and nodding toward Brig. "Those two seem to be getting mighty thick." Kate's mouth tightened. She felt as though she were on a runaway wagon. Lucy was not what she would have chosen for her son, nor would she have chosen a lot of other things in his life.

A grim-faced Mary Ann took her place in the quadrille set with Brother Hale smiling beside her. He was a head shorter than his partner, looking up at her with admiration. If Brother Hale had designs on Mary Ann for a plural wife, he was in for a disappointment. Whether Burns accepted it or not, Mary Ann would choose her own husband. He should have known that last fall when Brother Berger drove all the way from Santa Clara to ask for Mary Ann.

"I can't stand that man," Kate had said to Burns as the door closed behind Brother Berger's stout back. After conferring with Burns in the parlor, the man had paused in the front room to bid her good day. As he stood there, his small eyes darting busily about, she guessed he was looking for Mary Ann. His attention to her at Stake Conference last Sunday had been obvious to everyone, especially his two fat, frowning wives.

"He's a good Saint," Burns protested, "and a prosperous farmer."

"He beats his animals," Kate replied sharply. "I saw him whip a horse once. I wouldn't be surprised if he beats his wives."

"They certainly look healthy and happy enough," Burns answered. "I wish you wouldn't repeat silly gossip. Brother Berger is a fine man." He took that considering stance of his, hands behind his back, looking out the window at Brother Berger driving away in his fine new wagon. Berger was one of the Swiss immigrants who had settled Santa Clara, five miles away. Hard workers all, they had made that village one of the neatest and most prosperous in southern Utah.

"Come in here a minute," Burns said, leading the way into the parlor.

Kate sighed, already guessing the subject of their conversation.

"He wants to marry Mary Ann," Burns told her as he turned to face her across the lace-draped center table.

"I guessed as much from the way he hung around her at Conference. Of course you told him no."

Burns's eyebrows rose. "Certainly not! He's a good catch for a girl as unruly as Mary Ann. He'll keep her in line . . . make a good Mother of Israel out of her."

"Beat her, like as not," Kate snapped, deciding she would fight Burns on this, knowing very well Mary Ann would.

"Nonsense!" Burns began to look perturbed. "I've already given my consent. He has only to get the consent of the Authorities."

"What about Mary Ann's consent?" Kate asked, her voice deceptively quiet. For all Mary Ann's faults, she was her daughter, and no daughter of hers would be traded off like a cow to a man like Brother Berger. It seemed to her the worst of fates to marry without love. God knew, its passing was swift enough, but a life without ever knowing that kind of love would be empty beyond bearing.

"A daughter is expected to do her father's bidding," Burns said curtly. "I didn't expect you to question my judgment on this, but since you have, I must ask you to remember that I'm head of this household."

"Whatever household you're head of, Burns," she replied in a cold voice, "I insist that you tell Mary Ann immediately what you've done."

"Very well. Call her in." Burns's face was frosty. "But I expect you to back me up. A man is the Word of God in his household through the priesthood he holds."

Oh, damn! Kate thought. He looked such a pompous ass and she was so tired of having the everlasting priesthood thrown in her face. She had been making the household decisions for a long time . . . apparently without the aid of the Word of God.

Mary Ann's face was wary, as though she already guessed what was happening. Allowed to put her hair up when she was sixteen, she had tried a dozen different styles in the months since her birthday. Today she wore her thick brown hair in a braided coronet around her head. She had her father's gold-brown eyes, long-lashed, and her mother's firm, stubborn mouth and fine skin. A good-looking girl, though not a beauty like her younger sister. Yet she had a quality Drusilla lacked, a depth perhaps, and she almost vibrated with life. Kate frowned, thinking Brother Berger would consider her daughter good, healthy stock.

"Brother Berger wishes to marry you," Burns told her abruptly. "And I have given my consent."

Shock glazed Mary Ann's face. "I haven't given my consent," she said dazedly. "I haven't even been asked."

"Brother Berger asked me." Burns looked at her sternly. "I've consented, and I'm sure the Authorities will consent. He's a good Saint. He'll give you a home and children. What more could a woman want?"

A lot more, Kate thought, as she sighed and looked away. A woman could want to be cherished, to be cared about, to be loved always. Being a mother wasn't enough. Children helped fill the emptiness, but never completely.

As she recovered from her shock, Mary Ann's chin went up and the old defiant fire burned in her eyes. "I won't do it. You can't make me. I'll kill myself before I'll marry that old Dutch pig."

"You'll do as I tell you, young lady!" Burns's voice rose in anger.

"Never!" Mary Ann cried defiantly. "Never in a million years. I'll

run away from home. I'll go to Pioche and live in a whore house
. . . but I'll never marry him."

"Mary Ann Hamilton!" Burns was outraged.

"Your language, Mary Ann," Kate said, shocked that her daughter
even knew such a word, yet finding herself enjoying Burns's discomfort at his daughter's uncooperative attitude. He was such an over-
powering person it took courage to stand up to him. She knew that
all too well.

Mary Ann threw her a look of despair. "Don't let him do it, Mama
. . . please!"

"Your mother has nothing to say in this matter . . ." Burns
began.

"I have plenty to say." Kate cut him off, knowing Mary Ann could
not stand against him alone. "If Mary Ann doesn't want to marry
Brother Berger she doesn't have to. She's only sixteen . . . that's too
young. I won't allow it."

Totally at a loss, Burns's mouth opened and closed several times
like that of a helpless frog. Mary Ann began to cry. "I've given my
word," Burns said in disbelief.

"Then take it back," Kate said coldly and drew the weeping girl
into her arms.

Burns looked at her as though he had no idea what to do or say to
handle this rebellion in his household. "Well . . . it's damned embarrassing!" he shouted and stalked from the room.

Now here was another Brother casting his eye on Mary Ann and
doomed to disappointment. Although Kate admired her spunk, it was
the Gospel Plan to marry and bear children to the Lord. Oh, nonsense, Kate, she told herself, the girl is young, she has plenty of time
for the pains and trials marriage and children bring. Drusilla was
another story. She reveled in the admiration of the opposite sex and
was pretty enough to attract it. Too bad Steve was so young. He was
such a nice boy, and from a good family. Kate hoped Dru would wait
for him, but she had already decided her daughters would choose for
themselves, no matter how hard she had to fight Burns for that right.

The crochet hook caught the light of the coal-oil lamp as it flashed
back and forth looping the thread into a band of lace. Brig had gone

to walk Lucy home from the dance. Burns was spending the week with Alice. Everyone else had gone to bed. Nelly complaining how tired she was; Mary Ann making fun of Brother Hale; Dru and Steve lingering overlong on the porch. That would take watching. Kate wished Burns were here tonight so they could discuss the children. It seemed to her their whole life long he had been somewhere else when she needed him most. He had never been around when Brig was little . . . always off on Church business, and now the worst thing he could say to her was that she had made a Mama's boy of Brig.

"What are you doing still up, Mama?" Brig came into the kitchen and stood by the warm stove to remove his coat.

"Waiting for you." She smiled. "Would you like some hot tea?"

"Sounds good. Sure cold out tonight. Likely to freeze."

Sitting at the kitchen table, the Lowestoft teapot between them, Kate looked across at her son . . . at the premature lines in his young face, the subdued, forlorn expression in his eyes. If he could only learn to smile again.

"You've been seeing a lot of Lucy this winter," she said, her voice gentle, prompting.

"Yes." His eyes seemed to search the bottom of his teacup. "Lucy's been good to me. That's more than I can say for a lot of people in St. George."

"Some people are quick to cast stones whether they're spotless themselves or not," she told him, sick with anger at those who had hurt him.

Giving her a wry look, Brig stood up and began to pace back and forth, his tea forgotten. Beyond the kitchen window the icy wind whipped the trumpet vine into dark, moving shapes. Kate watched him moving between her and the window, his head bent, his whole attitude one of desperation.

"I don't know how long I can stand it, Mama. When I go to church . . . or the store . . . or to work on the Temple . . . it seems to me everyone is whispering . . . 'There's Brig Hamilton, did you hear what he did?' "

"Oh, Brig, they're not," she cried. "You were forgiven. It's over and done with."

He shook his head. "I wish it were, Mama. Wish people would

really forgive and forget . . . wish I could forget . . ." and his voice broke.

As he sat down again Kate reached to clasp his hand. "Do you want to go away, dear? Maybe to school at the academy in Provo?"

"No, not to school." His eyes slid away from hers. "Lucy thinks we should get married."

A sudden flush of heat drenched her body with sweat. "You mean she asked you?" In spite of herself, the words were sharp.

"No . . . no," he protested unconvincingly. "I told her we shouldn't decide until spring. I need more time to . . . to forget."

"Well then, nothing's settled, is it?" Kate sighed with relief. "Don't make any promises, dear . . . not until you're sure that's what you want." She squeezed his hand. "Just keep your faith in the Lord. He can turn the darkest night into a beautiful morning . . . the Bible says so."

Standing up, he gave her a vague smile and bent to kiss the top of her head. "Good night, Mama. God bless you."

Brig's footsteps receded up the stairs. Cold night wind rattled the window panes and whipped the bare trumpet vine against the porch. Kate looked at the full cup of tea cooling across the table from her, and a sense of foreboding enveloped her like the miasma from the Washington swamps.

Bells rang, pans clanged, and raucous voices filled the dark night. Kate jerked awake at the noise. Burns groaned, "Good Lord!" She should have known those uncouth Gilbert boys wouldn't let Lucy and Brig spend their wedding night without a shivaree. It was a custom she hated, a low-class custom.

"What shall we do, Burns?" she asked the dark figure mumbling and groaning beside her.

"Get dressed and give them some wine. Then maybe they'll go home and we can get some sleep." He groped in the darkness for his trousers. "Wish to hell they'd stayed at Lucy's folks' tonight."

Brother Gilbert had hired the Social Hall for the wedding dance, served wine and supper, and no doubt gone in debt for his next year's income. Kate had thought wryly that he and his wife were showing off. It was obvious they felt their only daughter was marrying above them and meant to give her a send-off in style.

KATE

The Temple was not yet ready for marriages, the sealing of vows for eternity, although the stone walls were being plastered now, and the roof rapidly going on. The basement was complete, ready for the great baptismal font which would rest on the backs of twelve bronze oxen, a gift of Brigham Young, now being freighted down from Salt Lake. Brig and Lucy had decided they would wait for the St. George Temple to be completed to receive their endowments rather than go to Salt Lake. They had been married in the parlor by Bishop Gardner. When the Temple was finished they would be married there for all eternity.

Lucy had been radiant and laughing, Brig solemn and quiet. Kate watched with a sinking heart, wishing she could have talked Brig out of making this commitment. She had tried to get Burns to hold him back. Lucy wasn't for Brig, she had told him, she just knew it would turn out badly. Burns replied in disgust that she would never find anyone she thought good enough for Brig. Besides, what happened in New York was proof enough that Brig needed to be married. They couldn't stand any more scandals in their family.

The girls were gathered at the head of the stairs, peering down. "Don't come down," Kate told them. "It's those Gilbert boys and their cronies and probably all drunk."

Charley was with the group, all of them reeking of wine. Burns brought out a jug of wine while Kate sliced the sorghum cake Nelly had made. Presently Brig and Lucy came down, fully dressed. Lucy's face was pink. Brig seemed merely irritated. Ribald innuendos and raucous laughter greeted them. The two of them struggled to take it all in good humor. Charley laughed and said to Lucy, "Well, you got an experienced man, Lucy." Kate wanted to slap his sloppy mouth. Charley was a trial, he had always been a trial. Brig pretended not to hear the words, and Lucy looked pained. When the jug of wine was emptied, Burns summoned his most authoritarian manner and sent the young men on their way. Lucy and Brig were leaving for their new home in Pine Valley in the morning, he said, and it was time to break up this shivaree.

Scrubbed clean of clouds, the blue skies shone like fine porcelain. The crisp air of early spring turned tingling cold with every vagrant breeze stirring the sagebrush. Kate sat, straight-backed, beside Tom on the wagon seat. She loved the colorful drive from St. George to Pine Valley, rough as it was. A dusty road led up through the black lava runs, with off to the west a fantastic jumble of white and red sandstone below the towering Vermilion Cliffs. As they reached a higher elevation, mesquite and chaparral gave way to sagebrush and dark green juniper trees.

The back of the wagon was loaded with wedding gifts, supplies, Lucy's well-filled hope chest, and the furniture Kate and Lucy's mother had managed to get together. Kate had ordered the chairs herself, six of Brother Cottam's mule-ear chairs with woven rawhide seats. He was to make a rocker for Brig's birthday. The horses and wagon were Burns's, lent for the trip. She and Tom would bring them home tomorrow. Brig's saddle horse trotted behind them, tied to the wagon.

Staring straight ahead, Kate was acutely aware of the young couple on the seat behind her silently holding hands. Well, they could thank her for having a nice home to go to and a way for Brig to make a living. Burns had refused to deed the house and sawmill over to Brig, but finally agreed that the boy would be better off away from St. George. The income from the sawmill could be split so that Brig could support a wife.

Twice before Kate had been to Pine Valley when Burns was invited to speak at church there as a visiting Elder. She had even approved the house he bought planning to move Lovinia up there. But Lovinia put her foot down on that. She wanted to stay in St. George near her mother where she had help with her growing brood . . . three of them now, two boys and a girl. When Alice refused to let Lovinia live with her, Burns had built a small house near the Crandalls for her.

Tom clucked to the horses, and they strained against their collars, the wagon rolling over a ridge above a deep lava canyon carved out by the creek. Involuntarily, Kate drew in her breath. It always made her gasp. You couldn't trust your memory that Pine Valley was really so beautiful. All that greenery met her desert-jaded eyes like the very Balm of Gilead. The small valley lay at the foot of the mountain's northern slope, a few houses nestled close to the mountainside on one street. Green fields and meadows to the north of the town followed the willow-lined winding creek. Deep pine forest grew to the east and south, the high slopes thick with the dark shapes of tall white pine and the light green of groves of quaking aspen. To the west the country fell away quickly into the sage-covered foothills. Beautiful grazing country, Burns said, and pastured his cattle there . . . those he had not turned in for stock in the Canaan Cattle Company after the United Order was disbanded.

The house was adobe brick . . . a nice house, though small and in need of some repair. The yard and garden plot had been neglected by the renters. There was a front room, a kitchen and bedroom downstairs and upstairs, two small bedrooms. Kate set to work at once, giving orders to the boys and Lucy, almost wishing she hadn't selfishly refused to let Lucy's mother come along now that she saw how much needed to be done. By supper time the house was in fairly good shape, the beds made up, the dishes and food put away. They were all weary and retired as soon as the supper Kate had brought was cleared up. Tom took his bedroll to the barn.

Lying in the upstairs bedroom with the tangy aroma of pine blowing in on the cold spring breeze, Kate could not sleep. Self-recrimination was a vain exercise, she knew, but perhaps she should have been stronger, insisted Brig go away to school at the academy in Provo, or the university in Salt Lake. It had been too hard to part with him. She had wanted him there with her, and in keeping him she had now truly lost him. But for her selfishness his life could have taken a different and better way. I'm so tired, she thought, her eyes burning, and yet can't sleep. The thick-ridged scars of her right hand felt slick beneath her fingers. Once she had a husband who kissed that palm, young and unsullied, and made her melt with love. Or was that another lifetime ago? Inside her head she began reciting verses from the Bible so that she would not think of her son and his bride in their bed downstairs.

Next morning she delayed their departure while Tom fussed impatiently with the horses he had hitched up and Brig repeatedly said he had to get out to the sawmill. She went through the house, rearranging furniture, straightening window curtains, while Lucy watched in lightly veiled resentment.

"Mama," Tom said at last, "we have to get started if we're going to get home before dark."

"Well, all right," she replied with a sigh. "Good-bye, Lucy dear," and she gave her new daughter-in-law a quick peck on the cheek. Turning to embrace her son, Kate felt tears mist her eyes. Holding him close, she kissed his mouth. "Good-bye, son," she said, her voice trembling. "Be happy."

Tom helped her into the wagon, seated himself, and clucked to the horses. Kate allowed herself only one look back at Brig and Lucy standing in front of their new home, arms about each other, waving good-bye. She had lost him now, she thought, and felt such an ache he might have been dead . . . lost him to another woman . . . the dearest being in her life, the only one who had always understood, always cared. And she turned her face away so Tom wouldn't see her tears.

BOOK TWO

Mary Ann

It was but a little that I passed from them, but
I found him whom my soul loveth; I held
him and would not let him go, until I
brought him into my mother's house, and
into the chamber of her that conceived me.

Song of Solomon 3:4

Chapter 17

The tiny octagonal blocks of material were sewn together in what was meant to be a quilt block of the Grandmother's Flower Garden design, but try as she might, it always came out looking more like a multicolored dish. Oh damn, Mary Ann thought, looking at Dru's Lone Star going together flat and neat, while Jane stitched the easy squares of her Nine-Patch. Once again Mary Ann ripped the stitches out, some of the tiny blocks fraying into uselessness as she did so. Outside the front room window she could see the tender young leaves of the cottonwoods, motionless in the warm spring air. The murmur of bees ransacking the honeysuckle vine drifted through the open window along with the sweet aroma. It was no day to be sitting inside, but Mama said there was sewing to be done. Each of the three older girls had begun a quilt for her hope chest and were to work on those while Kate and Nelly did the mending. Elizabeth sat beside her mother, laboriously learning to darn a sock. Sighing with frustration, her eyes wandering to the calm spring day outside the window, Mary Ann began once more, stitching the tiny octagons together.

"Mama told you that was the hardest pattern to make," Dru said.

"I thought it was pretty," Mary Ann retorted, biting her tongue as the pieces began to cup.

"You should have done an easier one, since you don't like sewing anyway," Jane said, spreading her Nine-Patch smoothly on her knee.

"Oh, leave me alone." Mary Ann's voice was sharp, her eyes stinging with angry tears as she saw this block would not come out right either.

Kate looked up from inspecting Elizabeth's darning, her piercing gaze on Mary Ann. She was always right, Mary Ann thought. Whenever you went against Mama you ended up finding she was always right. Viciously she jammed the needle into the last contrary octagon, missed, and stabbed her finger. Blood sprang out, staining the block in her hand. "Oh, damn this thing!" she cried in frustration and threw the blocks to the floor. Before she had time to think, her mother's strong hand was on her arm, raising her, propelling her toward the kitchen door while the others watched in stunned apprehension.

"No lady," Kate said in a harsh voice, "no daughter of mine will use that kind of language."

Jerking open the kitchen cupboard, she commanded, "Open your mouth." Mary Ann felt the sting of cayenne pepper on her tongue, so hot it brought moisture to her eyes. Her tear-filled eyes met Kate's furious blue ones on a level. Sick with humiliation, Mary Ann wanted to cry out that it was punishment for a child, not a grown girl. One did not dispute Mama.

"That might help you remember to watch your tongue, young lady!"

Mary Ann jerked away from her mother's grasp, beginning to gag as the burning pepper taste spread in her mouth. Damn you, she thought, I hate you. And she ran from the kitchen.

In the shade of the big cottonwood in the back yard, Mary Ann lifted the lid from the water barrel, rinsing her mouth again and again. Even if the tepid water could cleanse away the cayenne pepper it could not remove the bitter taste of her humiliation.

Brushing the tears from her eyes, she looked up and saw Tom in the upper lot, turning water on the garden. He was the only friend she had in the whole world. Skirting the grape arbor with its green fringe of leaves, she ran past the lilac hedge to the main ditch. Tom stood in the shade of the row of Lombardy poplars that marched down the ditch bank. Leaning on his shovel handle, he watched the water run down the neat furrows of the garden. It was well started already . . . peas, beans, onions, and carrots. As Mary Ann ran breathlessly up to him, he pushed the shovel into the dirt so that it stood by itself.

"What's happened now?" he asked, looking down into her tear-stained face.

Trying to hold back the tears, she burst out, "I swore . . . I just said damn . . . and Mama put cayenne pepper on my tongue."

His mouth twisted in a wry smile. "Young ladies don't say damn."

"If I'm a young lady she shouldn't treat me like a child," Mary Ann cried. "You say worse things than damn."

Tom grinned. "Not in front of Mama." He turned toward the grassy ditch bank. "Here, sit down and cool off."

Dropping down beside him in the sun-splashed shade of the poplars, she wiped the last of the tears away with her hand. No matter what she did, Tom was always her ally. She could count on him to understand, not censure or scold. Sighing, she listened to the pleasant spring sounds of bees and the murmur of water running in the ditch, the anger beginning to drain out of her. After a moment, she reached down and unbuttoned her shoes, taking them off along with the rolled-down stockings Mama wouldn't approve of either. Tucking her skirts up, she turned and dug her bare feet into the cool sandy mud of the ditch. It felt so good after those hot shoes and stockings. Some people let their children go barefoot all summer to save shoes, but not their family. They had to keep up appearances for Papa's sake, Mama said. No wonder some people thought Mama was snooty.

Tom took off his straw hat and laid it on the ground, pushing back his sweat-matted black hair. Arms folded on his knees, he watched her squishing mud between her toes.

"All Jane and Dru ever think about is getting married," she said, wiggling her toes in the cool mud, thinking with distaste of the hated quilt she must make for her unknown future husband.

Tom chuckled. "I hope you don't get married until you grow up enough to quit playing in the mud."

Relaxed and happy now in his comfortable presence, Mary Ann smiled. "It feels good." Tilting her head, she looked at him thoughtfully. "When I was little, I always planned to marry you when I grew up."

The black eyes flicked away from hers. "You can't marry your own brother."

Amused by her own childish nonsense, Mary Ann said, "You're not really my brother."

Picking up a dirt clod, Tom tossed it into the ditch, startling a frog from its hiding place under the ditch-bank grass. He laughed self-consciously. "Just the same as."

"Yes . . . I guess so," she replied idly, looking down at the clear water flowing over her pale feet. "Tom . . . are you ever sorry you were raised white . . . ever want to go and live with your own people?"

His shoulders moved in a rueful shrug, his eyes on the water staining the furrows of the garden. "Who are my 'people'? I don't even know. I wouldn't know how to be an Indian, anyway."

For the first time she realized that Tom was really not of their family, that he dwelled in a kind of strange Limbo, neither white nor Indian. He was certainly nothing like the Clara Indians who lived in such squalor and came into town begging for food. Yet, in spite of Mama thinking Tom and Brig were such good companions when they were young, Mary Ann now saw that relationship as young master and his retainer. More than once she had seen Tom finish a job Brig had left incomplete, taking it for granted Tom would do it. "I'm sorry." Her voice was contrite. "I didn't mean to hurt your feelings."

"You didn't," he answered gently, still staring at the garden. "When you can't change things, you learn to live with them."

In a silence broken only by the rippling water, Mary Ann watched his brooding face covertly. Tom was a grown man now . . . a strong and able man, for he not only looked after the house and lot, but also Papa's farm in the Tonaquint fields and his cattle herd. Why couldn't he change the things that were wrong with his life . . . just because he was an Indian? Well, she would never just learn to live with things she didn't like. It wasn't easy, being different and wanting different things. Somehow she knew her life would be lived where and how she wanted, not the way other people told her. Try as she might, she could never understand why following the rules of the Church guaranteed a place in Heaven. Some people who followed all those rules were just plain mean and dishonest outside of church, yet they were absolutely certain they would sit and rule from a golden throne in the Hereafter.

"Are you a good Mormon, Tom?" she asked, turning to look at his dark profile. He had plucked a blade of grass and chewed it reflectively.

"That's a dumb question."

"Why is it? Don't act smarty like Brig. It's just that sometimes I think I must be the only person around who doesn't believe everything the Authorities tell us to believe. I think some of their ideas are plain silly."

"I know."

"Do you believe it, Tom . . . all of it . . . the Hereafter and all?"

"No, I guess not . . . some of it, but not all." He gave her a wry grin. "After all, it says the Lamanites will become white and delightsome at the Resurrection."

Mary Ann looked up into his sardonic, shadowed face. "Why would they want to? Why is white the best color to be?"

"There's no doubt it's the best color to be in this kingdom," he replied with a sarcastic edge. His face sobered. "You're a rebellious soul, Mary Ann. I don't know what's to become of you."

"Me either." She sighed, then smiled at him. "I know I'll never be anybody's plural wife. Ugh! Those old men at meeting, squeezing your hand and making eyes."

"I sure hope you won't." Tom grinned. "You'd raise hell in a plural home."

"Tom!" Laughter bubbled between them. Mary Ann leaned to kiss his cheek. "You always make me feel better when I'm upset."

Tom stood up quickly, almost brushing off her impulsive caress. Jerking his shovel out of the dirt, he said, "We'd both better get back to work." He began shoveling a dam to divert the water to the other part of the garden.

Picking up the shoes and stockings, Mary Ann stood up beside him. "Thanks, Tom," she said softly.

He nodded without looking at her. "See if you can behave yourself the rest of the day."

I won't go back in the house, Mary Ann thought, stopping by the corral to put on shoes and stockings . . . back to Mama's accusing eyes and the gloating of Dru and Jane. She would just slip out the corral gate and go over to Regina's. Regina Blount was her best friend, off and on since Regina's allegiances were always temporary. Anything was better than going back into the house, even though sometimes she got tired of Regina. She never wanted to talk about anything except boys and getting married and what it must be like to have your husband do it to you. Mary Ann had long ago learned she could never talk to Regina the way she talked to Tom. Nothing you said was safe with her. Mama said Regina's tongue was tied in the middle and wagged at both ends.

Just last week she and Regina had slept out for the first time this summer. They made their bed on an iron cot under the cottonwoods shading the Blounts' lawn. After supper they took turns trying to dress each other's hair in the new English chignon. When that palled they braided their hair in night braids and snuggled under the quilts, looking up through cottonwood leaves at the dark, starry sky. At a pause in Regina's prattle Mary Ann got up and walked to the water barrel for a drink. The barrel stood just outside the kitchen, and through the window, in the glow of the coal-oil lamp, she could see Regina's mother and Brother Blount's younger second wife. The two women were redding up the kitchen, setting bread to rise for tomorrow. Mary Ann could not hear the words as they turned smiling toward each other. Regina's mother reached out and put her arms about her sister-wife, kissing her on the mouth in a way Mary Ann had never seen two women kiss before. Something about that kiss gave her a sick, hot feeling in the pit of her stomach. Without even lifting the lid of the water barrel, she hurried back and slipped into bed beside Regina. The scene she had witnessed continued to ferment in her mind. Strange indeed when one thought of Mama's cool dislike for Aunt Alice and Aunt Lovinia and her not-always-suppressed irritation with Aunt Nelly's doglike dependence.

At last she said, "Your Mama and your Aunt Mae seem to be fond of each other . . . not like in our family."

Regina giggled. "They care more for each other than for Papa. Some nights it's so funny the way they chase him from one bedroom to another, each one saying it's the other's turn." Unable to concern herself with anyone else for very long, Regina giggled again, "Did you see how tight Roger held me at the dance last Saturday? Mama got after me about it, but I don't care. I wish he'd get serious. I'd lots rather have a young husband."

"Me too," Mary Ann agreed, though she couldn't think of any young man she would want to marry. Oh, she liked Ben Morgan well enough, and she thought maybe he liked her though he never came to call. She guessed he knew her parents didn't approve of him because he smoked and drank. Just the same she would never be anyone's plural wife. It seemed to her plural marriage bred a sort of sickness . . . like Mama's hard inflexibility or Aunt Nelly's dependence or all the bitter jealousy she had seen in other families with the wives vying for their husband's attention; and now something else she had just seen, two women who loved each other more than their husband. Regina didn't seem to think it strange, so she guessed it must be all right.

Now Mary Ann wondered whether she could look either Sister Blount in the eyes again. Well, Regina's gossiping was better than all the criticism at home. She jumped the ditch and started down the street, the sun hot and bright on the dusty red road. Far below she could see the Temple walls rising against the hills. The plasterers were working from scaffolding, and the rough red sandstone would soon be covered by pure white plaster.

Lifting her eyes toward the cloudless sky, she saw a hawk riding the updrafts above the red sandstone cliffs. Standing very still in the middle of the street, she watched him sail the air, dipping and gliding effortlessly. The sight of that wild, free creature filled her with such a longing to be free, too; it was like wings beating inside her chest. Perhaps he had a nest and a mate somewhere high in the Vermilion Cliffs, just the two of them with no other ties. The sense of kinship was so strong she almost felt she could see the town with his eyes, spread out beneath her. Circling lazily against the intense blue of the sky, the hawk turned and winged into the distance. Something in her rose and followed him across the hills and cliffs into a great freedom beyond imagining. Someday she would truly follow. A man would come who would loose her bonds, for there was no other way for a woman to be set free. She would know him when he came, and she could wait.

Chapter 18

Standing up, Mary Ann began to clear the supper table. The glow of the coal-oil lamp lay across the clutter of dishes while outside the spring twilight deepened. A chorus of frogs thu-rumped in the distance. She smiled at her father, glad he would be in this household for two weeks now. He had always been a source of pride to her, in spite of their conflicts. As a child she had equated God with Papa and only later knew Papa had far too many faults to be God. Yet when she thought of God He still had Papa's face. The gray in Papa's hair and moustache only made him look more distinguished, but she did wish he hadn't grown so stout. Her smile faded as her eyes fell on Brig. Lucy was at her mother's, in labor with her first baby. Mary Ann thought the least Brig could do was to stay at the Gilberts' with his wife. She never would understand Brig. They had never been close. Maybe the fact that he had always been Mama's favorite had alienated him from the rest of the family. When she needed a brother there was always Tom or Isaac. They should be back tomorrow from moving Papa's cattle up to summer pasture at Pine Valley. She would far rather have gone with them than to stay and help with spring cleaning . . . but she was a girl and must do only the things females were allowed to do.

"Let me help," Nelly said, rising slowly from her chair, eyes dull in her wasted face.

"Go along to bed, Nelly," Kate ordered. "Jane, help your mother." Nelly was no longer allowed to do any work. She was sent to bed early, slept late, napped in the afternoon, and when she was up chattered guiltily about helping. No one dared say that horrifying word, *cancer*, but Mama must know the truth. Mary Ann knew her mother had taken Aunt Nelly to the doctor without Papa's knowledge. The doctor made a living, for others in town didn't cling to the doctrine of faith healing as tenaciously as Papa.

Charley had gone with Burnie to finish the chores. Drusilla set the dishpan in the dry sink and filled it with hot water. Elizabeth disappeared as she usually did when it was time to do the dishes.

Brig seemed nervous and fidgety, watching his father in a way that was almost apprehensive. At last he cleared his throat and said, "I'd like to talk to you, Papa."

Draining his glass of milk, Burns pulled his watch from the pocket of his vest and consulted it. "I have a meeting of the High Council tonight, Brig. What do you want to talk about?"

"Business," came the low reply.

Burns's eyes narrowed. Beneath the neat moustache his mouth twisted impatiently. Sighing, he rose from the table. "All right, come in the front room . . . but I have to leave in a few minutes."

The voices from the front room rose so loud no one could help overhearing. Kate's face grew pained and unhappy. Mary Ann, her hands in the soapy dishwater, wished they had shut the door.

"I don't understand you, Brig. Good Lord, that sawmill practically runs itself. You just have to be there."

No one else on earth, Mary Ann thought, could say "Good Lord" like that. Even when he was angry, Papa made it sound like a prayer. President Snow had called him down more than once for using that expression. The sin of taking the Lord's name in vain was one Papa struggled with, and he always lost in the midst of anger.

"But I've sold all the lumber to the Church, Papa," Brig replied. "And I haven't been paid. The Authorities counseled us not to sell to the Gentiles at Pioche and Silver Reef . . . to take care of our own. I've followed counsel and now I don't even have the money to pay the men."

"Why didn't you look ahead and see this was happening? You could have wired the Church office for payment." Burns's pause was eloquent. "I'll do it myself in the morning, before I leave for Mount Trumbull."

"But the men have to be paid, Papa. They've already waited two weeks."

"I'll advance the money then," Burns snapped. "I hope you've learned something. I don't care who you're dealing with . . . the Church or the mine owners . . . run that place like a business, not a charity." He grunted and jerked open the closet door. "Sometimes I think you don't have enough sense to pound sand in a rat hole."

"Yes, Papa." Brig's voice was almost inaudible.

"When's Lucy supposed to deliver?" Burns asked brusquely as he stood by the front door putting on his coat.

"Her Ma says tonight or tomorrow."

"All right," Burns said. "As soon as that's over with you get back to Pine Valley, pay the men, and take care of your business. Good Lord, women have babies all the time. They don't need a man hanging around while they do it." He vented his irritation by slamming the front door.

Without a glance at the embarrassed girls, Kate closed the cupboard on the dishes she was setting away and went into the front room. After a moment Mary Ann heard the parlor door close and grimaced to herself. There she goes again, letting Brig cry on her shoulder. Oh, Papa would be really furious if he knew. He had no patience with people who didn't do their jobs and do them well. Neither did Mama, with one exception. Everyone had thought Brig would go far, he had been so smart in school, and so handsome and devout. Now he just couldn't seem to take hold of things, as though his mind was always somewhere else. If he were like that with Lucy, their married life must be dull indeed.

Someone banged on the kitchen door. Dru jumped and gave a little squeal. Mary Ann, peering out into the darkness, saw it was Joe Gilbert, Lucy's big, rough brother. "Brig here?" he asked.

"Yes . . . we just had supper. Come on in, Joe."

"Naw . . . just tell Brig to get his ass out here. He's got a new son, and his wife is mad as hell 'cause he ain't there."

Kate laid a clean dish towel over the molded bread loaves set to rise in the morning sunlight. Wiping her hands on her apron, she turned to Mary Ann. "Would you bring in the eggs? You girls must go to the rag bee at Sister Snow's and help roll carpet rags for the Temple. I promised to bring a cake for refreshments. Might as well get it done while we have a fire." Pursing her lips, she added another stick of wood to the stove. "Guess I should take something over to Flo Gilbert. She must be worn out waiting on Lucy all day yesterday."

"All right, Mama." Mary Ann picked up the egg basket, wondering what she could do to escape being sent to the rag bee. She hated to sit all morning, cutting and rolling carpet rags, listening to the silly gossip. Regina would be there, and she thought she was the big "it" since she and Roger were getting married this fall. Because of Regina, Mary Ann guessed a little of why her mother held aloof from other women. Well, Regina could have Roger and welcome to him. The one time he had walked Mary Ann home from a dance he had mortally offended her by putting his arm around her and furtively trying to squeeze her bosom.

"Hey! Mary Ann!"

She looked up to see Charley peering down at her from the barn loft. "What're you doing?" she asked. "You're supposed to be at the field watering." Lazy thing, she thought. Here he was a full-grown man and still hanging around home. A heavy-set young man, his straw-colored hair darkened to brown, Charley's face was still strangely babyish with soft, round, almost hairless cheeks. At his age he should be out making his own living and even married. She had never liked Charley much, with his sneaky ways. He used to peek through a knothole in the outhouse to watch the girls until Drusilla told on him. Papa almost whaled the life out of him that time.

"Come up here. I wanta show you something." Charley looked down at her, his pale blue eyes gleaming. "I bet you never seen anything like it before."

Curious, in spite of her dislike for Charley, Mary Ann set the basket of eggs down and climbed the ladder. He reached down to help her step into the dim hayloft. "You're gettin' to be quite a woman, Mary Ann," he said with an odd grin. "Those are about the nicest little tits I ever did see."

"You shut up that talk, Charley." Her voice was sharp-edged with wishing she hadn't come up here. "What do you want to show me?"

"This." Quickly he unbuttoned his pants and exposed himself. "Bet you always wanted to see what a man looks like."

Caught off-guard, she stared in horrid fascination at his projecting organ. Something sour and ugly rose in her throat. "You nasty thing. I'm going to tell Mama . . ." and she started for the ladder.

"No, you ain't!" Charley grabbed her wrist so hard a pain shot up her arm. "Aw, come on, Mary Ann . . . go with me. You'll like it, I promise . . . and nobody will ever know."

"Leave me alone, you rotten pig!" Desperate, she tried to twist out of his grasp. Her breath came fast and painful from a throat suddenly clogged with fear.

Releasing her arm, Charley seized her by the shoulders, his pants fallen ludicrously around his feet. "Wildcat, ain't you? Well, the harder they fight, the better they are." He flung her backward onto the hay and fell on top of her, panting and sweaty, his face blank with lust.

Revulsion rising in a swelling tide, Mary Ann frantically scratched and kicked at him, pulling his hair, trying to squirm free. It seemed a dozen big, rough hands were everywhere, fending her off. Pinned beneath him, she gasped for breath as he tore away her skirt and clawed at her bloomers. Terror blinded her. All the air seemed to explode from her lungs. Struggling wildly against the sweaty, loathsome thing on top of her, she at last found her voice and screamed.

"Shut up, damn you!" He covered her mouth with his.

Twisting her head away from him, she spat and screamed again. The nauseating stink of him filled her nostrils. Then she heard the bloomers rip away and Charley's violent hand grabbed her bare thigh.

Suddenly the weight was gone. Dazed, she sat up, instinctively pulling her torn skirt over her bareness. Tom was standing over Charley, who had been flung halfway across the loft. Wiping the blood from his mouth, Charley staggered to his feet, trying to hold up his pants.

"You goddamn Injun," he rasped, swaying menacingly. "Mind your own business." He lunged at Tom.

The falling pants betrayed him. Tom's fist smashed into Charley's face with a sickening thud, and his knee came up hard against Charley's bare groin. With an animal cry of pain, he doubled over and fell to the floor. Instantly Tom was on top of him, his knee on Charley's chest, his fist pounding Charley's face again and again until his opponent no longer struggled to rise.

Frozen with horror, Mary Ann stared at Tom, his body taut with fury, his fists beating that bloody face as though he would not stop this side of death.

Struggling to her feet, she grabbed Tom's arm. "Stop it . . . stop it! You'll kill him!"

Tom looked up from his methodical pounding, black eyes blank with primitive rage.

"Tom, stop . . . don't kill him!"

After a moment his eyes cleared. He glanced at the bloody, unconscious Charley and stood up. Taking her shoulders in his hands he looked down at her, as gentle now as he had been brutal a moment before. "Did he hurt you?"

"No . . . no," she said, all control beginning to vanish now as the shock wore off. "He just tried . . . and then you came."

"I heard you scream." He reached to smooth the hay from her disordered hair. "You're not a screaming girl . . ."

"Oh, Tom." Trembling sped through her body, even her bones seemed to melt away. Tears of horror and relief filled her eyes.

"It's all right now," he said gently, and held her, weeping, in his arms.

Brig's head appeared in the loft opening. "What's going on?" His glance fell on the unconscious Charley. "Oh, my God . . . is he dead?" Jumping up the last step into the loft, he glanced at Mary Ann weeping in Tom's arms and at her torn bloomers lying on the hay.

"If he ain't dead, he ought to be," Tom said coldly.

"He's still breathing." Brig bent over Charley. "What shall we do?"

"Leave him here to rot," Tom replied, holding Mary Ann close.

"We'll have to tell Mama," Brig said.

"Judas Priest, Brig." Tom turned to look at him. "Don't drag her into it."

"You can't beat a man like that and think nobody will notice." Avoiding Mary Ann's furious stare, he reached down and struggled to pull up Charley's pants. "Better help me get him to the house."

"To hell with the bastard." Tom's voice was a low growl. "I'll get

Mary Ann to the house. Come on." He descended the ladder and reached up to help her down.

Vexed with herself because she could not stop crying, indignant that Brig should be so casual about what Charley had tried to do, she let herself down into Tom's arms and clung there for a moment, weeping against his shoulder.

"Don't mind Brig," he said, irony coloring his voice. "He's just embarrassed." He turned to lead her toward the house. "Embarrassed . . . for Christ's sake!"

Chapter 19

Even a blind man could tell it was peach season in St. George, for the odor lay like a miasma over the town. Almost every family held a peach cutting, the women gathering to gossip while they cut the ripe, golden fruit into slices to dry on racks covered with mosquito netting. Late summer peaches were boiled in molasses and put up in crocks to make an excellent preserve. While the peaches were on, all the peelings and the culls went into the pig trough. The droppings of pigs fed on peaches had an unholy stink to them. It even invaded Kate's bedroom where Nelly lay, the smell of her dying mingling with the stench of the pigs.

Shadows of the cottonwood leaves moved on the bedroom wall, stirred by the breeze that came, hot and dry, through the open window. The inexorable progress of cancer had swollen Nelly's stomach grotesquely on her wasted body. Mary Ann's arms ached from fanning the sallow, shrunken face lying on the white pillow. Kate insisted the girls take turns sitting with Nelly, fanning her to relieve her from the heat. It was a chore doubled by the odor of decaying flesh that filled the room.

Morning chores finished, Kate sat in a straight chair across the bed from Mary Ann. She was putting the last careful stitches in the green satin fig leaf apron for Nelly's temple clothes. Nelly had made her plans for dying and intended to be buried in those clothes.

"Will you do my temple work when the Temple is finished, Kate?" Nelly's voice was faint and halting.

Kate gave her a denying smile. "You'll be well to do it yourself," she replied with false cheerfulness.

Why lie to poor Aunt Nelly? Mary Ann thought. Only a miracle of God could make her well again, and they all knew it. Poor, suffering thing. She sympathized with Nelly's misery, but still she sighed and stole a look at the clock on the dresser, wondering when she would be relieved. Her mother frowned.

"I want to be sealed to Brother Hamilton," Nelly continued as though Kate had not answered. "We were only married for time, you know, on account of my first husband. But I've been married to Brother Hamilton for a long time. He'll have a higher place in Glory than Andy will . . . and I want all my children sealed to Brother Hamilton . . . Charley too." Nelly paused, gasping, exhausted by the effort of speech.

"Charley?" A wave of revulsion swept over Mary Ann as that hated name involuntarily escaped her. But she fell silent at her mother's frown and shake of the head.

Nelly seemed not to have heard. "Will you take care of it, Kate . . . promise me?"

"I'll see it's done, Nelly," Kate told her quietly.

Charley . . . even after all these weeks, Mary Ann couldn't hear that name without remembered horror rising sick and sharp in her throat. Thank God he was gone. Mama had sent him away as soon as he could travel, and in spite of Nelly's tears. Tom had beaten him so badly Nelly had to take him into her room and nurse him with the last of her failing strength. Papa had been at Mount Trumbull where there was trouble with the Church sawmill and knew nothing of this calamity in his household. Calling the family together, Mama gave her orders. No one was to know the reason Tom had beaten Charley. Family things were best kept in the family, and there was no need to embarrass Mary Ann. Charley would leave as soon as he was well enough, or she would have him hauled before the Bishop's Court.

Until Charley left, Tom stayed at home, his quiet presence a comfort to Mary Ann after the nightmare in the barn loft. Mama insisted Mary Ann share her bed since Papa was away. When she started awake in the nights, chilled with horror, the fear swept away at the sound of Mama's soft breathing and her warm presence.

On the advice of her friend Sister Meeks, Nelly dressed Charley's battered face with compresses of chamber lye. Isaac was beside himself with delight, whispering to Mary Ann that if anyone ever deserved to have piss on his face, it was Charley. Mary Ann heard herself laughing, the horror draining away.

"You mustn't let Mama hear you say that," she chided Isaac, knowing full well his joking was meant to ease the sick fear Charley's presence brought.

Isaac looked at her in surprise. "You think I'm dumb or something?"

Charley had written his mother that he had a job in the mines at Silver Reef. He liked it there, he said, it was better than working for his stepfather for nothing. Her son's departure seemed to have depleted the last of Nelly's will to survive, for she took to her bed soon after. Was there something about firstborn sons, Mary Ann wondered, that women seemed to dote so dearly on them? Nelly still had Burnie and Jane, who were devoted to her and treated her far better than that rotten Charley ever had. Still his heartbroken mother mourned for him. She even seemed to blame Mary Ann for what had happened, though she never said anything. Even now, three months later, Mary Ann could not enter the barn without feeling a chill run along her spine.

"I'm glad Burnie has a trade," Nelly was saying. "And Jane will be married to a good man like Brother McIntosh . . ." Her voice trailed away as though she had lost the thread of her thoughts.

Mary Ann bit her lip, not daring to look at her mother. She had not told Mama, or anyone else, that Jane had been Brother McIntosh's second choice. Papa knew, so Mama probably did too.

As far as she was concerned it was out of the clear blue sky that Brother Mac came courting last spring. She had gone by herself after supper to sit on the front porch in the long, hazy spring twilight. Beaver Dam Mountains darkened into purple as the light faded from the western sky. Fragrance of honeysuckle vines rose in the quiet air. The white walls of the Temple gleamed through the dusk, the plastering almost completed now. The building was so white and immaculate, so out of place in this barren land, it might have fallen straight from Heaven. People were still talking about the Burt boy as though it were a miracle. He had fallen from the top scaffolding on the

Temple wall, seventy feet to the ground below. They had carried him to the Big House, expecting he would live only a short time. The Elders administered to him, and in two days the boy was up and about, little the worse for his accident. Of course the ground was soft around the Temple building, but maybe God had arranged that.

" 'Evening, Mary Ann," Brother Mac said. She looked up, startled from her solitary reverie. Brother Mac was wearing his Sunday suit, his graying beard neatly combed, his shaggy eyebrows waggling at her.

"Papa's at Aunt Alice's this week," she told him.

Somewhere beneath that bushy beard he seemed to smile. Sitting down on the step beside her, he cleared his throat in an embarrassed manner. "I asked your Papa's consent to call on you."

Instantly Mary Ann's insides seemed to freeze up. Couldn't Papa ever leave her alone? Why couldn't he believe her when she said she'd never be a plural wife? Brother Mac's second wife had died, and his first wife was a huge, fat woman who ruled her household with an iron hand, while she affectionately called her husband "you old fart." There was no point in wasting time, Mary Ann thought, standing up. Anger ran along her veins, draining away her strength.

"Papa had no right to do that without asking me," she said in a shaky voice.

Brother Mac looked at her in astonishment. "Of course he had the right. He's your father."

"I'm sorry, Brother Mac," and her tart voice belied the words, "I won't marry you, and there's no use beating around the bush about it."

"Well, I'll be danged!" He rose, looking at her as though she were some strange kind of creature he had never seen before. "I'll be danged," he repeated. Shaking his head, he walked out the gate and down the road toward home.

Trembling with anger, Mary Ann ran upstairs to her bedroom. Mama had backed her refusal of Brother Berger, but would she do it again? She was so irritable and distant lately. Papa would bring all his authority to bear, and there would be no escape. Long after Drusilla slept beside her, Mary Ann stared into the darkness, filled with loathing for Brother Mac and all those eagerly marrying men . . . even Papa.

When Brother McIntosh returned the next night, again clad in his Sunday best, Mary Ann spotted him coming and escaped out the back lot gate. She ran down the street and spent an hour talking distractedly to Regina about her wedding plans. Driven by darkness and Sister Blount's meaningful frowns, Mary Ann at last dragged her footsteps home. Dru and Elizabeth were giggling in the kitchen, with Mama trying to shush them. Through the open parlor door Mary Ann saw Jane, her homely face pink as a rose, sitting on the sofa beside Brother Mac.

The marriage had been postponed because of Nelly's illness, for Jane was needed to help with her mother. Delighted with her new status, Jane was busy hemming dish towels and crocheting on pillowcases, even though she would be living with Sister McIntosh.

Where was Jane? Mary Ann wondered now. Surely it was her turn to sit with her mother.

Nelly groaned, tears gathering in her faded eyes. "I hurt so bad, Kate. Isn't there anything you can do?"

Setting aside her sewing, Kate stood up. "Go tell Jane to come take her turn," she said to Mary Ann.

Even before she left the bedroom, she saw her mother rummaging in the dresser drawer. Papa might not know about the bottle of laudanum from Johnson's drugstore, but she did. Funny how Mama defied Papa's rules behind his back and made a pretense that he ran the house. Well, the laudanum did more for Nelly than all the Elders' praying, no matter what Papa said.

Not much of a life, Mary Ann thought, sitting in the stifling meeting house, listening to the speaker praise Nelly Hamilton's exemplary life. True, Aunt Nelly had lived according to the rules of her religion, never doubting God's will even when she lost her first husband and baby, then Josie . . . even when Charley turned out so bad. They had sent word to him at Silver Reef of his mother's death, but he hadn't come.

The weather was sweltering. There was no ice to preserve the body, so the funeral had to be held the day after Nelly died. Hard to believe that it was only yesterday Nelly had requested the Elders lay hands on her head and dedicate her to the Lord. The ritual seemed to bring her peace, and she died quietly in the afternoon, filled with hope for glory in Heaven and the laudanum Kate had given her.

Much as Nelly wanted Papa to be there, he hadn't arrived until the Relief Society Sisters had come to wash Nelly's body and lay her out in her burial clothes. Mary Ann looked at her father now, sitting with bowed head on the mourners' bench in front of her. She couldn't believe Papa ever really wanted to marry Aunt Nelly. Sometimes he had just seemed to forget her existence. Even when they were in the same house, she had to remind him it was her week. Kate sat beside her husband, staring straight ahead, dry-eyed. Didn't she ever cry? Mary Ann wondered. Didn't she ever feel anything for anyone except Brig? Her mother's relationship with Nelly was beyond understanding. At the end it had almost seemed as though Nelly were Mama's child.

A good and faithful Sister, the speaker, Brother Dodge, was saying. She had dedicated her life to the service of the Lord. What good was a life of service, Mary Ann wanted to know, if it were as drab and empty as Nelly's had been? Other than her children her only joy in life had been her hope for the glory of Heaven beyond the grave. A whole lifetime spent waiting to die. Mary Ann wept for her.

Chapter 20

Disagree with him or not, Mary Ann did try to love Papa as one should love one's father. It was just that lately it seemed they could not even say hello without getting into an argument. He had never really forgiven her, she knew, for embarrassing him by turning down those two proposals of marriage. Certainly he did not approve of the curt and airy manner she assumed with any suitor who came her way.

"I don't want to get married," she told him now, staring at him across the dim, quiet parlor where he had called her for a talk.

Burns frowned, watching her narrowly. "You're almost eighteen. I'd hoped you'd be married before Drusilla. It seems only right . . . you're the oldest."

"Well, don't think my feelings are hurt because Dru is dumb enough to be Brother Whittaker's fourth wife," she replied haughtily.

"Your sister is doing God's work by marrying and living the Doctrine of Celestial Marriage. You could learn a great deal from her about how to behave."

Mary Ann looked at him in exasperation. "Papa, if you're afraid I'm worrying about what people are saying because Dru's getting married before me, you don't have to. I don't care a fig."

He walked to the window, staring out into the cold, windy spring day. Bare branches of the cottonwoods, faintly edged by the green of new leaf buds, dipped and swayed. Skiffs of dust blew down the empty street. The washing, hung out early this morning, would be coated with red sand and have to be washed all over again. Mary Ann sighed at the thought, her eyes resting on Papa's stiff, disapproving

(177)

back. She knew she had always been a trial to her family, never fitting into the pattern expected of her. Well, Papa needn't think she was as silly as Dru, giggling and fluttering around every evening when Brother Whittaker came to call. He might be almost as old as Papa, but he was still a handsome man with all that wavy gray-streaked hair, lean and tall. More to Papa's liking, he was a prosperous cattleman and could provide well for Dru. Besides that he was president of the High Council. She just didn't understand Dru. When Steve left on his mission Dru had cried as though heartbroken, promising to wait for him. Now, barely three months later, she was to marry another man. Not only that, she would be a fourth wife. Dru was so taken in by flattery and petting, and Brother Whittaker was good at that. He must have been delighted to see Steve go on a mission; certainly he had given generously to the purse made up for Steve at his farewell party.

Dru would be one of the first to have a marriage solemnized in the new St. George Temple, although people had been crowding in from all over southern Utah since the dedication in January. What had been for so long an anonymous rectangle of stone had emerged at last into a castle of gleaming white with a steeple rising from the octagonal dome at the front, its roof adorned by crenellated battlements. The snowy walls were inset with arched windows, with bull's-eye windows lighting the inside stairways. It seemed such an unlikely building there in the desert, pristine white against the desolate brown hills of Out South, the black lava runs, and the violent red sandstone.

On the day of the dedication they had all been so proud of Papa. He had been right alongside Brigham Young and Wilford Woodruff and even helped carry the ailing President Young through the sealing rooms on a chair. Everyone said how sad it was to see the Lion of the Lord wasted and gray, brought down by physical disability. But when President Young rose to speak to the congregation the old power was still there. He chastised the people for seeking after Mammon . . . for trafficking with the Gentiles at the mines. Like thunder, his words rolled across the assembly. "I never expect to be satisfied until the Devil is whipped and driven from the face of the earth!" His hickory cane smote the pulpit in emphasis. The blow had damaged the fine new wood, but the dent had since been preserved like an icon.

Papa's job in helping build the Temple would soon be finished. He and President Snow had been honored by parties and by letters of praise from the Authorities. The family was just waiting to see whether the Church would give Papa another job, or whether they would be ordinary members from now on.

"What's to become of you, daughter?" Burns's weary voice interrupted her thoughts.

"Every family needs an old maid, I guess," she replied flippantly.

Turning from the window, he frowned at her. "Perhaps you should go to the academy in Provo and learn to be a schoolteacher. If you can't find a man who suits you, then you'd better be prepared to earn your own living."

"A schoolteacher!" She wrinkled her nose in distaste. "I don't want to spend my life teaching a room full of snot-nosed kids their ABCs."

"Then what do you want to do?" he snapped, and she saw that he was thoroughly out of patience with her.

"I don't know." Mary Ann bit her lip, looking down at her hands tracing the pattern of crocheted lace on the cover of the center table. It was hard to be always in the wrong, but she was determined not to cry. "I just know I won't marry anyone who wants more than one wife."

"I've had four wives," her father reminded her in stout, resentful tones.

"I know!" she cried, staring defiantly at him. "And I won't share my husband like Mama has . . . I won't do it!"

"Mary Ann!" Kate stood in the open doorway, her chin lifted, her mouth prim and hard. "You will not speak to your father in that manner. He's simply concerned with your welfare, just as I am."

Oh, Mama, Mama, Mary Ann wanted to cry. You've suffered every day you've lived in polygamy. Don't let Papa force me into something we both hate.

Without a glance for her daughter, Kate's eyes rested on her frowning husband. That look was as cool as the wind outside. "I'm sure Mary Ann will make the right decision when the time comes. Right now, I'd appreciate five minutes of your time to help me with the guest list."

Their house was surely one of the nicest in town, Mary Ann thought. A shiny new horsehair sofa stood in the parlor on a fine States carpet. Lace curtains stirred in the breeze through the open window, bringing a welcome breath into the crowded house. Dru's wedding day, and the parlor was jammed with wedding guests, milling about, chattering, shaking hands. How Dru glowed when she was the center of attention . . . and Mary Ann tried to stifle the little twinge of envy. She should be used to it now. Dru was always the beautiful one, the daughter with more beaus than she had time for . . . yet never snotty or stuck-up, always helpful and loving. Her blonde hair was piled high, her blue eyes sparkling. The rose-colored silk wedding dress was trimmed with fine lace, its bodice limned with a million tucks Mama had laboriously stitched, the wide skirt sweeping out from Dru's slender waist.

Brother Whittaker's eyes gleamed as he watched his new young wife, though he was careful not to touch her too often. He must be circumspect in front of his other wives who, one and all, wore grim smiles upon their faces. Mary Ann frowned. That look in his eyes had nothing to do with obeying God's commands to enter into plural marriage to build up the Kingdom of God. Oh, why was Dru such a simpleton? She could have had Steve, young and handsome, if she'd waited until his mission ended. It was Papa's fault, too, encouraging Brother Whittaker and lecturing Dru on the blessings of Celestial Marriage. If only Mama had spoken out more emphatically, she could have stopped it, but she just said, "Make up your own mind, Drusilla." Mary Ann doubted Dru even knew her own mind. She'd refused to discuss it with her, just as she had never discussed her feelings for Steve. That's the way Dru was. When letters from Steve failed to arrive, Brother Whittaker was there with presents and flattery. Dru was seventeen and scared to death of being an old maid. Caught up in the excitement of wedding preparations, she seemed to have forgotten all about Steve. Then last night she suddenly started crying in the darkness of their bedroom. She refused to say why she was crying and at last went to sleep with her tear-wet face against

Mary Ann's shoulder. This morning she rode away to the Temple looking like a queen going to her coronation.

"A little more wine?" Burns asked Bishop Gardner, and filled that gentleman's glass. Kate came behind her husband, serving the wedding cake. What a lady Mama was, Mary Ann thought . . . that slim, ramrod-straight figure, her gray hair carefully combed, her head always slightly lifted, chin up. She was so queenly, almost regal in comparison with the other women present who looked mostly like dumpy peasants. Even though Mama had been only a servant girl in England, she was the wife of an important man now. She was his number-one wife and she was a formidable woman. Look at that straight, firm mouth, the piercing blue eyes. She was not a woman to cross. Yet every now and then, beneath that careful facade, one had a glimpse of hidden depths. Mary Ann sighed. Human beings were such a puzzle.

Elizabeth, full of self-importance, assisted her mother. Isaac and Burnie were probably in the kitchen stuffing themselves with cake. Brig and Lucy and the baby had come down from Pine Valley. Lucy was already plump with another child. Brig looked thin and tired. And there was Jane, clinging possessively to Brother Mac, walking with shoulders back so no one could miss the fact that she was pregnant.

If Dru had married a young man like Steve, there would have been a party at the Social Hall with dancing and supper and presents. But when you are a fourth wife, custom denied that; and anyway, Mary Ann thought, there was not much reason to celebrate.

Her eyes met Tom's across the room. He had not been invited, just happened to be down from Pine Valley today to consult Papa about selling some cattle. After all, the important people of St. George were all there: the Snows, the Gardners, the McAllisters . . . and Tom was only Papa's "Indian boy." Even though she was sure her father loved Tom almost as well as his sons and depended on him a great deal more, he was still "my Indian boy." By any standards Tom would have to be considered a handsome man . . . that strong face with high cheekbones, prominent nose, and deep-set black eyes. When those eyes met hers he started to smile. The smile quickly faded. Oh dear, she hoped no one else could see how unhappy she was for Dru. Why did Steve have to go away on a mission? It was enough to make one wonder whether Brother Whittaker had something to do with that.

Tom spoke briefly with Burns, declined a glass of wine, and went out through the kitchen. Quickly gathering up discarded cake plates, Mary Ann carried them into the kitchen where she stacked them in the dishpan. Then she slipped out the door, hurrying through the shady grape arbor toward the barn.

Tom was saddling his horse as she stepped into the dim warmth of the barn, wrinkling her nose at the ammoniac odor. "You just came down this morning," she said. "How come you're going back so soon?"

After a quick, slanting glance, he turned his attention to tightening the cinch. "Brother Cannon's buying six head of beef and I need to get them rounded up and delivered."

The center post of the barn was a huge cedar log worn smooth as glass by the rubbing sides of horses and cows. Resting her hand against it, her eyes on Tom, she caught her trembling lip in her teeth and blinked back the threatening tears. "Poor Dru," she said.

"Why poor Dru?" Tom asked, buckling the cinch strap. "She's married. Ain't that what all you girls want?"

"No!" Her voice was sharp. "Not to an old man like that . . . not when she still loves Steve . . . and she cried about it last night."

"Then why didn't she marry Steve?"

"He's gone on a mission, you know that. Brother Whittaker flattered her into thinking she wanted to marry him. Papa pushed it too . . . he thinks plural wives go straight to Heaven."

"They ought to," Tom replied mildly.

"But I feel so bad for her." Tears threatened again.

"Would you have done it?" he asked, turning to look straight at her.

"No . . . but then Brother Whittaker didn't ask for me . . . but I never would. Oh, why is Dru such a ninny?"

"Because she is," Tom replied with a wry smile, "and you can't do anything about it . . . so stop worrying."

Leaning her cheek against the smooth coolness of the post, Mary Ann sighed. "I used to see her and Steve walking home from school

. . . holding hands when they thought no one could see. I envied her so."

"Why?"

"Because she had someone who loved her. I never did."

Suddenly she was aware how still he had become. In the silence she could hear the soft murmur of the pigeons in the rafters of the barn. The horse shook its head against the flies, rattling the bridle. Tom remained immobile. Brushing away her tears, she looked up at him. One hand rested on the saddle horn, the other holding the bridle reins. The breath caught in her throat as she looked up into that dark face so filled with pain and love. Her limbs seemed to turn to water. Involuntarily she took one step toward him. "Oh, Tom!"

Instantly his face became blank and unreadable. Swinging into the saddle, he said, "Behave yourself," the words he always said instead of good-bye. His spurs touched the horse's flanks and he rode out of the barn into the brilliant sunlight.

"Oh, Tom," she said again to his retreating back, though he was already out in the road and could not hear. Standing in the open barn door, she watched until he was out of sight beyond the trees. Her heart felt like a hummingbird gone mad inside her chest. Flooded with joy so intense it was almost beyond bearing, the spirit seemed to soar out of her. At last she became aware that her mother had been calling her name for some time. The wedding guests would leave enough dirty dishes to keep her busy half the night. It didn't matter. She was drunk on the very air she breathed. The sunlight shone, pure gold, through the emerald shade of the grape vines. Everything around her seemed to come into focus, sharp and clear, as though her whole life had been aimed at this moment. She wanted to sing. Her feet hardly seemed to touch the ground. All through the busy evening she kept that look in Tom's eyes in her head, treasuring it, her knowledge a warm, bright flame in her heart.

Chapter 21

꧂ The wind stirring the dried bunch grass had a feel of autumn in it. Shadows of great cumulus clouds drifted across the sage-covered hillsides. With their passing, sunlight warmed the sagebrush, and the clean, pungent aroma rose to Mary Ann's nostrils. She liked the smell of the horse beneath her, too. Even though she hadn't run him, he was sweaty after the long ride from Brig's place. Gray, rolling sagebrush hills stretched away before her, one after another, toward the flaming sandstone of the Vermilion Cliffs on the west and the black lava flow to the south. On this side of Pine Valley mountain the luxuriant growth of pines ended and there was only the gray-green of sagebrush, interspersed by dark green juniper trees.

Although she shared her mother's love for this beautiful mountain, she didn't think Lucy was happy to have them spend a month with her and Brig. The baby, Bertie, was a year and a half old and Lucy was expecting again soon. Mama insisted Lucy needed their help, so they had brought peaches to cut and preserve when they came up two weeks ago. They had cut corn and made soap. Whether she liked it or not, Lucy followed Mama's orders, and of course Brig was always delighted to have Mama around to cater to him.

Papa was in Salt Lake where he had been called by the ailing Brigham Young. Barely a week after his departure they had heard the Tabernacle bell tolling as it never had before. People hurried through the dusty August streets to gather in the Tabernacle yard where it was announced that word had come over the telegraph: Brigham Young was dead. Even the children wept. Mary Ann wept, too; although President Young had seemed remote from her, he had been Papa's friend and mentor. Everyone had loved and leaned on their leader. Now there was fear behind the tears of sorrow. Who would lead them as well as the Lion of the Lord? she heard them ask each other. When Papa came home they would know. There would be a new President of the Church, a new Prophet of God, and Papa would have been assigned to new duties now that the Temple was finished.

Burnie was taking care of the place in town. Elizabeth had made friends with the Gardner girls and spent her days in Pine Valley at gossiping and sewing. Mama put Isaac to work cleaning up around Brig's place even though he grumbled about it. He wanted to spend his time with Tom. Feed was scarce, and the cattle had to be close-herded by late summer to keep them out of the loco weed. Tom stayed with the cattle while Isaac brought food and water to him. He had only been to the house once since they came up from St. George. It seemed to her he had avoided her all summer, ever since Dru's wedding. He hadn't been back to St. George at all. That one night in Lucy's kitchen, Mary Ann had laid her hand on his arm, and Tom jerked away as though her touch were red hot. She wondered whether he guessed how much she read in his face that day in the barn, or if he was simply afraid he might give himself away to her now. To her dismay he had managed to get away without ever spending a moment alone with her.

As the horse rounded the point of a hill, Mary Ann saw Tom watching the scattered cattle from horseback, one leg flung over the saddle horn. How alone he looked, she thought, riding toward him. He must have always been lonely, part of their family, yet never really of it. Her heart began to flutter against her ribs. Neither of them would ever be lonely again.

Waylaying Isaac, she had bribed him to let her bring the grub sack to Tom. Isaac protested so vigorously she had to promise to do the milking for a whole week, a job Isaac hated. Now he had the morning to fish down the creek with Os Snow, but he mustn't let Mama know, she told him. Mama would be furious with such unladylike behavior.

Mary Ann knew the moment Tom saw her coming by the way his back stiffened. Both feet in the stirrups now, he spurred toward her.

"Tom," she said tentatively as their horses drew abreast. A strange trembling sped along her limbs, leaving her breathless.

His face was stern. "Mary Ann, you're too old to go tomboying around like this. Folks will talk."

"What do I care?" she cried, hurt by his peremptory greeting. She had dreamed, even expected he would be happy to see her, just the way he used to be. "I made Isaac let me bring your grub." She spoke quickly to cover her feelings. It was new to her, especially with Tom, to be so light-headed and shaky. Suddenly afraid to look into his eyes, she slid down from her saddle.

Tom dismounted, dropping his horse's reins to the ground. Untying the flour sack Mama had packed with food for him, he joked, "Glad somebody remembered me. I'm so hungry my stomach and my backbone have growed together." Taking off his hat, he wiped the sweat from his forehead with his arm and took a long drag at the canteen. They sent water to him daily, because the creek down this far was tainted by the sawmills and the stock grazing above.

Standing there beside him, her head so near his shoulder, it seemed to Mary Ann she would never breathe again. A strange, lurching pain caught at her as she watched his big hands, the color of burnished copper with prominent veins over the backs and long strong fingers. Not once did he look at her as he transferred the food and water to his own saddle. His back to her as he tied the canteen to the leather thongs, he said flatly, "You can go on back now. Thanks."

A whole summer of longing rose up in her. "Oh, Tom . . . I miss you so. You're never home any more and you never talk to me when you are." When he did not turn around she flung her arms around his waist, her cheek pressed against the hard muscles of his back.

"Oh God . . . Mary Ann . . . don't!" She might have stabbed him rather than embraced him by the agony in his voice. He stood stiffened against her, his heart pounding wildly beneath her hand.

"I love you, Tom," she whispered. How many times this summer had she dreamed of hearing him say those words to her, of the words she would answer, of how he would embrace and hold her? The dream was rehearsed over and over in her head, but it never went beyond that final ecstatic embrace.

Still he would not turn to look at her. "Don't act like a silly little girl." His voice was harsh. "Go on home."

Stung by his sharpness, she dropped her arms from around him. "I'm not a silly little girl and you know it," she protested, staring at his back, willing him to turn and face her. "You're making me act shameless, but I don't care. I love you more than anything in the whole world, and you love me . . . I know it. I saw it in your face. Oh, Tom . . . please . . ." Near tears, her voice failed. When he turned around and she saw the pain in his face, the hurt and longing in his dark eyes, the tears spilled over.

Suddenly she was in his arms, held fiercely against him, her tears dampening the collar of his shirt. His mouth caressed her hair, her ear, and she lifted her face for his kiss. Even in her dreams it had not been like this, his mouth claiming hers with strength and passion, her body yielding and close against his. She had come home at last; here was the answer to all her yearnings, all her rebellions; here was sweet peace and love.

With a sound almost like a moan, Tom held her away from him. He seemed to be looking at something directly over her head. "I'm sorry, Mary. God, I'm sorry. Go home now . . . hurry!"

Reaching up, Mary Ann took his face in her hands, made him look at her, and was drenched with joy at the love in his eyes. Arms about his neck, she pressed close to him, closer when his arms came around her. "Don't, Mary," he said softly, painfully. "Please don't do this."

"But I love you," she said, reaching up to kiss his unyielding mouth.

"You can't love me!" Taking her shoulders in his hands, he held her away again. "It's impossible . . . hopeless . . ."

"But I do . . . I do love you so much," she cried. "I want to be your wife, Tom."

"Dear God!" he muttered, closing his eyes tight as though steeling himself against some excruciating pain. The hands on her shoulders tightened, bruising her flesh as he shook her roughly. His voice was angry. "Look at me, goddamn it . . . look at me! I'm not a white man. It makes a difference."

Astounded that something that mattered not at all to her should matter so much to him, she stared at his angry face. "It doesn't make a difference," she said. "Not to me."

"Listen to me," he commanded, "and use your brain this time.

I'm an Indian. Nothing's ever going to change that . . . Mormonism or anything. There are rules even you can't break."

"I don't care!"

"Oh Lord, Mary Ann," he said in exasperation. "You've always said I don't care and got yourself into all kinds of trouble. How much do you think you'd love me when your family disowned you and the neighbors wouldn't speak to you?"

"I'd still love you," she cried. Oh, what did other people matter if they loved each other. Couldn't he see?

"Listen!" His voice rose as he stared down at her, his mouth tight and angry. "I'm an Indian and you're a white girl. There's a line we can't cross."

The words were like a knife in her heart. She hadn't thought beyond the magical declaration of love. All he said was true . . . and worse, but still there had to be a way. "We could move somewhere else," she sobbed, tears streaming down her face. "We don't have to live in St. George, or even in Utah."

Tom shook his head sadly, his fingers gently wiping her tears away. "It can't happen, Mary Ann. Not ever."

Holding her as she wept her protest at the bitter truths he had flung at her, Tom bent to press his cheek against her hair. It wasn't fair, she thought, shivering as a drifting cloud obscured the sun. There were men who had taken Indian wives, mostly the early settlers, but there had never been a woman who took an Indian husband unless the Indians stole her. What difference did it make? Tom wasn't an Indian or anything else, he was simply Tom and she loved him. There had to be a way, even if they had to run away together. If he couldn't see that now, he would. She would make him see it.

"Mary," he said softly, lifting her chin in his hand. "You'd better get back. Mama will think you're lost."

Reaching up, she pressed her mouth to his and for a moment he yielded, his lips hot with longing against hers. "No more of this," he said, holding her away, unsmiling. Taking her arm he led her to the horse waiting beside a juniper tree.

"Do you love me, Tom?" Her eyes sought his.

His face was a mask, without emotion. "Sure . . . you're my little sister."

"Oh, Tom!" The words broke like a bubble of pain. "You know that's not what I mean."

"Don't mention it again . . . ever." His voice was cold as he bent and cupped his hands for her to step into the saddle.

Mounted up, she looked down into his inscrutable face. "Nothing will ever change the way I feel."

"Go home," he said brusquely, "and be nice to the next young man who comes to call on you." The corner of his mouth lifted briefly in a vain attempt at a smile. "Not the old ones, just the young ones."

Looking at the determined set of his jaw, she knew argument was futile. There would be another time, she promised herself. "I'll never love anyone but you," she said and turned the horse, urging it ahead swiftly so Tom wouldn't see she was crying again.

Mary Ann shivered, dressing hurriedly in the cold morning air, wondering whether she would dare ride out to see Tom again today. Elizabeth groaned and yawned, burying her face in the pillow. Beyond the bedroom window, Mary Ann saw for the first time a golden tinge to the aspens. They would have to go home soon. Elizabeth and Isaac had to start school, and surely Papa would be back from Salt Lake.

In the yard below she could see the rumpled quilts on the cot where Isaac had slept last night beneath the trees. Mama slept in the other upstairs bedroom, Brig and Lucy and the baby downstairs. Surely it hadn't been a dream, she thought, buttoning her dress. Sometime in the night she had heard a horse ride in and, afterward, voices . . . Tom and Isaac talking quietly. What if Tom had changed his mind? Her fingers trembled so the buttons wouldn't go right. The whine of the sawmills drifted across the valley. Mama would be after her for oversleeping again. It had been easy to oversleep this summer, lying half-awake fantasizing about Tom.

"Get up, Liz," she said, giving the girl a poke. Leaving her grumbling sister, she hurried downstairs, trying to compose herself to greet Tom if he were here.

Kate and Isaac sat at the cluttered breakfast table. Lucy was spooning mush to Bertie. Mama looked so strange, and it was not like her to sit still in such a mess of dirty dishes. Isaac's eyes were red, his bowl of mush untouched.

"What's the matter?" Mary Ann asked and was startled to see tears swimming in Kate's eyes as she looked up. Without answering, Kate handed her the sheet of paper she had been holding.

Instantly Mary Ann recognized Tom's cramped difficult handwriting. Hadn't she taught him how to write?

"Dear Mama," the brief note read. "I hope you can forgive me for going away like this. It is the best way. If you asked me to stay I could not say no and I know I have to go. I will always be grateful for all you and Papa have done for me. I love you all. God bless you. Tom."

Panic seized her. He hadn't even said where he was going. "Are you sure he's gone?" she asked, hoping to deny the words shimmering before her eyes.

Isaac fought down a sob. "He took the sorrel gelding and his saddle and all his things from the barn. I looked. He didn't say nothing last night . . . just told me I was to herd the cattle today and to go back to sleep."

"No!" she cried and flinging down the note, ran from the room, letting the screen door slam behind her. No . . . no . . . no! He couldn't desert her . . . couldn't leave her with no one in the whole world who understood and loved her. They would have found a way, there had to be a way. Stumbling, eyes blind with tears, she climbed the ladder into the hayloft where Tom usually slept and kept his things. It was empty . . . nothing but the dusty hay in the pale morning sunlight and a squawking chicken flying down into the barn at her approach. The only indication Tom had ever been there was the crushed pile of hay in the corner where he made his bed. A wave of agony washed over her. He was gone . . . like he was dead. No one knew where or if he would ever come home again. "Oh, Tom!" she cried out and flung herself down on the hay where he had once slept, lost in a black void of weeping.

It seemed long after that she returned to a sense of time and place. The loft was warm and she heard the clink of milk buckets as Isaac came into the barn to do the milking she had promised to do. Was it only yesterday? It seemed a millennium. Mary Ann lay still and quiet, drained of emotion. After a moment there were footsteps on the loft ladder.

"Mary Ann," Isaac called softly.

"Go away." Her voice was dull.

Ignoring the words, he climbed into the loft and came to sit beside her. She stared up at the cobwebs in the rafters. The hay smelled dry and sweet, and Isaac smelled of the manure on his shoes.

"He'll come back," Isaac said.

Shaking her head, Mary Ann bit her lips to stop their trembling and turned her face away. Only she knew why Tom had gone away and would never come back. If he thought he was setting her free by running away, he was wrong, for there would never be anyone else she could love.

"Stop crying, Mary Ann," Isaac's face was at once sympathetic and embarrassed. "You don't want Mama to know, do you?"

"Know what?" Her voice was sharp. The tears ceased.

"Nothing." Isaac picked up a twig of hay and studied it. "Just don't act like this. He'll be back. I know he will."

"Did he tell you that?" She rose on her elbow, flooded with hope.

"No." Isaac shook his head, but his smile was confident. "But I know it. I just know Tom will be back."

Looking into her brother's young-old face, her heart soared. Sitting up, she brushed the hay from her hair. Of course, that's why Tom had gone away . . . to find a place for them. He would come back for her and all the dreams would come true. They would be together forever and ever.

"Come on." Isaac stood up and held out his hand. "You made a deal to help me with the milking. I have to get down to the cattle herd."

Isaac was very young to be so wise, Mary Ann thought, squeezing his hand. But he knew Tom better than anyone. He had to be right, not just trying to comfort her. She would wait.

Chapter 22

For the first time since Dru's wedding the whole family was together. The long table in the kitchen had to be extended to make room for all of them. A false spring had already coaxed the almond trees into bloom, although it was only February, and the windows were open. Isaac repeated all the family jokes and led the way in reminiscing, so that the atmosphere at the table was less solemn than usual.

Brig had driven down from Pine Valley with Lucy, little Bertie, and baby Christina. Lucy sat across from Mary Ann, her hair skinned straight back in a tight knot so that her plump pink face seemed obscenely naked. She had put on weight with each of her babies, and the slender girl of three years ago had disappeared inside a mound of flesh. Discontented lines wreathed her mouth, her house was forever disorganized, and her dresses always slightly soiled across the belly and bosom. She never spoke to her husband without an edge to her voice. Brig took it in silence. Embarrassed, Mary Ann thought, watching him. He always looked pale nowadays, with shadowed eyes. Too much reading and praying couldn't be good for such a young man.

After supper they gathered in the front room. Mary Ann hurried to bring a pillow for Dru's back. Every time she looked at her sister she wanted to cry. Beautiful Drusilla was great with her first child, her once lovely skin marred by liver spots, her face thin, eyes dull and tired. She still lived with the first Sister Whittaker and would until she had children of her own. Although Dru would never admit it, Mary Ann knew that spiteful woman bullied her. It was difficult for

Dru to entertain guests, even family, in another woman's house. They seldom saw each other except for special occasions such as this. Brother Whittaker was at his ranch Out South so could not escort his young wife to her father's farewell party.

There had been farewell parties aplenty for Papa. The ward had given him a fine send-off at the Tabernacle with lots of speeches extolling Papa's work in building the Temple. The Snows had entertained him and his wives; and the High Council had a party, too. All the parties were saddened by the knowledge that the White House remained closed and shuttered. Brigham Young would never entertain there again.

A year ago Dan Jones had led a colonizing company into Arizona territory. President Young was alive then and pressing for the Church to spread out . . . to fill the empty country before the Gentiles took it over. Now the new head of the Church, John Taylor, had called Papa to lead a second company. He would be leaving tomorrow, taking Aunt Alice and Aunt Lovinia and their children. Lovinia had five now and Alice had four, two of them small. Burns Swanson and David were old enough to be of help to their father on this trek.

Persecutions were coming, Papa said. The Congress in Washington was filled with agitators for a harsh antipolygamy law. Already President Taylor had counseled the men to deed their property over to their wives so that it could not be confiscated by the United States in case of their arrest. Mama was to dispose of their property and stock. Papa would send for her when he had a home built.

Burnie, learning his trade with Brother Mansfield, the blacksmith, was courting Hannah Swenson. He sat poised in his chair, light brown hair slicked down, and Mary Ann smiled. Poor Burnie was so smitten he could hardly bear to spend this one evening away from Hannah.

Jane sat beside Brother McIntosh on the sofa, cradling her baby girl in her arms. It was funny to think that Brother Mac, with his gray hair and shaggy eyebrows, was Papa's son-in-law when he looked older than Papa.

Prissy thing, Mary Ann thought as Elizabeth settled her skirts about her. The two sisters were seldom on good terms. The vain Elizabeth always said and did the correct thing whether or not her intentions were sincere. She was continually aghast at Mary Ann's doing such things as riding astride. There seemed no common ground for the two of them. She was nearly as pretty as Dru, with the same dark blonde hair and blue eyes. But she was not truly good and warm and loving like Dru.

Shooing Isaac off the footstool, Mary Ann placed it for Dru to prop her swollen feet. Sitting down, she began gently rubbing her sister's ankles and was rewarded with a grateful smile.

Isaac dragged a chair in from the kitchen and sat down beside Burnie. He was a tall fifteen-year-old, nearly a man, and he surely did a man's work, looking after Papa's cattle and farms. His dark hair was always rumpled, his blue eyes busy and alert. All his life Isaac had found it difficult to sit still, and even when he was quiet, which was seldom, he seemed to be moving. His eyes met Mary Ann's. Quickly she looked away, thinking that only the two of them in the room would remember the person who wasn't there.

"Blood will tell," Papa had said bitterly when he came home last fall. Even when a cowboy brought a note from Tom containing money to pay for the horse and saddle he had taken, Papa had been unforgiving. He pocketed the money without a word. Mary Ann thought resentfully that Tom had earned that horse and saddle a dozen times in the years he had worked for Papa. Tom was working at the Nutter ranch out on the Buckskin, the cowboy said, his eyes moving over Mary Ann's slender figure. Burns caught that glance and dismissed the cowboy with brusque thanks.

Almost half a year now Tom had been gone, and not a word to her. Slowly and painfully she was beginning to relinquish any hope that Isaac had been right, that Tom would come back. Images haunted her. Not just the memory of the cloud-filled autumn day when she had declared her love and been rejected, but images of Tom moving through her whole lifetime. Tom, carrying her piggyback across a flooded irrigation ditch when she was small . . . long ago in Provo; Tom soberly carving a marker for the grave of her beloved kitten; Tom, squinting with effort as she led him through the pages of the McGuffey reader. His absence made a great, dismal void in her life, as though a part of herself had been lost.

Her father cleared his throat for attention, and Mary Ann looked up.

In that familiar stance, feet apart, hands clasped behind his back, Burns stood and looked about at his family. He had grown gray and heavy but was still a vigorous and commanding figure. The lamps flickered as a chill breeze signaled the end of false spring. Kate hurried to close the windows.

"It grieves me to part with you," Burns began. "But Zion is growing and colonizers are needed to maintain our foothold in Arizona territory. It would please me mightily if, when I'm settled there, all of you would join me with your families. We're warned that persecutions are coming. The United States intends to make widows and orphans of our wives and children. They wish to drive the Saints from their homes again. God will damn them to eternal hell, and those who cling to the Word of God as revealed to the Prophet Joseph shall yet see Paradise. Blessed are they who are persecuted for righteousness' sake. Amen."

"Now, my dear children . . ." He paused, took out a handkerchief, and blew his nose, wiping his eyes which had grown suddenly damp. After a moment he continued. "I'm told that the Salt River Valley is fair country and the Saints will once more make the desert blossom as the rose. We must eternally seek land the Gentiles are too weak to conquer in order to be safe and live our religion in peace. I pray you children will see fit to come along when your mother has disposed of our property here and joins me in Arizona."

Crossing the room, he placed his arm about Kate's shoulders. "In my absence," he said, "you are to obey your mother and care for her. She gave you birth and raised you up with tender love. You owe her more than you can ever repay."

Kate Hamilton stood in her husband's embrace, surrounded by her children . . . a slender, gray-haired woman. Mary Ann saw her mother's lips tremble at Burns's words, but almost immediately her mouth drew into a straight, firm line. Her head came up in that familiar regal, almost arrogant way. She did not look at Burns or return his embrace, just stared straight ahead, her eyes as cold and hard as blue glass marbles. They have been married almost thirty years, Mary

Ann thought; how can she let him go and never show a quiver of emotion? How can he leave her again, forever putting Church duties ahead of everything else?

Burns went to his children, one after another, and laid his hands upon their heads, asking the Lord to bless and care for them, to guide them in the paths of righteousness, to strengthen their testimony of the true Gospel of Jesus Christ. When his warm, strong hands lay on Mary Ann's head and his deep, resonant voice blessed her, she wept without restraint. He embraced and kissed her as he had done each of his children and she clung to him, weeping painfully, sure that never in this life would she see her father again. Burns looked around at his weeping family and wiped his own eyes. Only Kate remained dry-eyed.

"Come, children," he said, affecting a hearty tone. "We mustn't part in sorrow. Your mother has baked my favorite raisin cake. We'll have our little farewell party and pray God we'll soon be together again." He turned to Kate with a smile. "Perhaps a little tea would help us make it through this parting."

The three sisters lay in the bedroom they had shared as girls and could not talk without crying. Isaac had been sent to tell Sister Whittaker that Dru was staying the night and to bring her nightclothes. He reported it was freezing outside, there would be no almonds this year.

Now the house was quiet, the last lamp went out. Mary Ann heard her mother and father go into the big bedroom downstairs and close the door. She wondered whether they would make love tonight. Kate had sat the whole evening, her face like a graven statue, with no smile and no tears, as though she were dead inside.

"Oh!" Dru gasped. The three of them had crowded into the double bed, longing to be together, though Mary Ann and Elizabeth each had their own room now.

"What is it?" Mary Ann asked, reaching to touch her sister.

"The baby kicked," Dru answered, delight in her wavering voice.

"Let me feel." Elizabeth sat up and Dru directed her hand to her swollen belly. "That feels so funny," and she jerked her hand away.

"It means he's strong and healthy," Dru told her complacently.

"Oh, I can't wait until he's really here." Suddenly there were tears in her voice. "I can't wait to have my own baby and my own house."

"Did Brother Whittaker promise you a house?" Elizabeth asked.

"He will . . . I know he will. His other wives have their own places. Just because I'm younger . . ." Her shaky voice trailed away.

"Is he mean to you?" Mary Ann didn't like the pompous Brother Whittaker anyway and thought she might tear him apart if he hurt Dru.

"No . . . no . . . he doesn't mean . . ." Dru moved restlessly, trying to ease her heavy body. "Oh, I'm glad I'm pregnant," she burst out. "I'm glad . . . now he can't . . ." She began sobbing softly. "I used to hate to see the sun go down."

"Oh, Dru!" Mary Ann took her sister's head on her shoulder, patting the trembling arms.

"Why?" Elizabeth asked.

"Shut up, Liz . . . and go to sleep," Mary Ann told her. Polygamy was a bitter burden, she thought, holding her weeping sister. Dru had been weak in giving in, that was true, but the price she was paying was too high. It could have been so different for Dru . . . so fine, if only she'd waited for Steve. He would be home from his mission soon, handsome and self-confident. Surely it would break Dru's heart to see him.

There was a message in her sister's life, she thought sadly, a message for all of them. Long after Dru fell sobbing into sleep, and Elizabeth slept too, Mary Ann lay awake, staring at the icy winter moon gleaming through the bedroom window, listening to the coyotes howl in the distant hills. I'm not Dru, she whispered into the darkness. I can wait. Her mind flew out, across the wild and desolate country she had never seen, across the towering cliffs of Mukuntuweap to a ranch on the Buckskin. For a moment she almost felt she could see him there, hear his soft teasing voice saying, "Behave yourself, Mary Ann."

Chapter 23

ʕ۞ʔ The cast-iron stove in the middle of the store glowed red through its isinglass window, yet Mary Ann shivered. A cold October rain poured down the store windows, soaked the wooden sidewalks, turned the dirt street into a quagmire. The strange, leaden feeling she had awakened with this morning did not lighten as she stood looking out into the gloomy day. Low, dark skies, sheets of water falling seemed to obliterate everything, as though she and this store floated in a great sea with no harbors.

When Brother Judd offered her a job as clerk in the firm of Woolley, Lund and Judd it had seemed a godsend. They needed more income, what with all the spare money being sent to Papa, and Mama forever bailing Brig out of his financial troubles. In a way she was a godsend to Brother Judd too, for she was quick with figures and sometimes helped with the bookkeeping. The firm was prospering in spite of the original opposition of the Church to such private enterprise, and the partners were busy with branch stores at Silver Reef and other outlying communities.

The job kept Mary Ann busy, but the pattern of her days was a dreary one, and she often ached to be free. Mama was by turns irritable and somber, seldom good company. Elizabeth was so boy-crazy and giddy. If she and Dru had been like that Papa would have tanned their hides.

Papa had been gone four years now. Arizona was a harder country than he had guessed. He had been ill for months and unable to work. Mama had sent him what money she could scrape together, trading tithing scrip and cotton factory scrip, selling lumber and fruit and cattle to the Gentiles at Silver Reef. In spite of Brig's protests that it was against the counsel of the Authorities, Mama made him take her to that wild mining town twenty miles away. Mama negotiated the sales, proving again her good head for business against the wily merchants, and still pretending the man was in charge . . . Brig now instead of Papa.

Silver Reef had spilled its wickedness over into St. George. There were saloons on Main Street now, and often drunken miners lying in the street. A lynch mob had descended on the town two years ago, taken a miner who had killed a well-liked foreman from the jail by force, and hung him from the big cottonwood tree in front of Brother Cottams's house.

With a sigh Mary Ann turned to rearrange the bolts of cloth on the shelves. There would not be much business on a day like this. People would venture out only in desperation. Smoothing a bolt of white linen and folding it in place, she thought of the burial clothes she and Mama had made for Dru's babies from this same linen. An ache rose in her throat although it had been a year past, and tears stung her eyes. The diphtheria epidemic of 1881 would be long remembered. It had filled many small graves, and there was scarcely a house in town without reason to mourn. She missed the babies so. They had been almost like her own. The memory of their soft sweetness still made her arms ache for them.

Poor Dru. Little Tim and Mariana had been her whole life. Brother Whittaker had even promised to build her a house of her own, but when she was childless again he reneged. Mary Ann hoped he would keep that promise now that Dru was expecting again, for she knew Fanny Whittaker never missed an opportunity to be spiteful to the uncomplaining Drusilla.

Just as Papa predicted, the United States had passed a stringent antipolygamy law, the Edmunds Act. The territory of Utah seemed to be swarming with federal marshals carrying warrants for every known polygamist. Papa was wanted, and Erastus Snow, who was seldom in St. George now. The whole town was a shambles of fatherless homes, women teaching their children to lie about the identity of their fathers, men hiding in the nearby canyons and settlements when the marshals were in the vicinity. Those who weren't quick enough were arrested by Marshals Armstrong and McGeary and hustled off to District Court at Beaver City and from there to jail in Salt Lake. Still men took plural wives, never doubting they were on the side of the Lord.

Dru's husband was wanted, too, but he spent most of his time at his ranch Out South and the deputies never could catch up with him. There was even a warrant out for Dru to testify against her husband for "unlawful cohabitation" . . . an ugly phrase. When the deputies were in town Dru dared not show her face outside the house and was hidden in the homes of neighbors, shuttled from one to another.

She wondered where Dru was right now. Her time was near. Looking out into the sodden day she thought that Isaac would be wet and cold, for he had gone to drive the cattle down to winter pasture. Last spring Isaac's long-simmering rebellion boiled over and he left home, planning to be a cowboy. Within two months he was back, driven by a demanding sense of duty and by his passionate attachment for Sally Ann Parks. He had been out on the Buckskin with Tom. Five years Tom had been gone now, with only a few brief notes to Isaac or Mama. Nothing ever for herself, unless one could count "tell the girls hello" as a message. Isaac couldn't get enough of telling how well Tom had done. Having saved his money and proved up a homestead, he had his own ranch. Only a one-room cabin, but his own little herd of cattle. Tom had helped him locate some property, Isaac told them, and as soon as he was eighteen he was going to have a ranch just like Tom's. The discussion descended into a bitter quarrel between Isaac and his mother. He had a duty to her and the girls, Kate kept saying. She objected to Sally Ann, she added, only because they were both too young.

"Miss Hamilton?" The voice jerked Mary Ann back to the present. Turning, she saw an unshaven man dressed in dirty overalls and patched shirt, the brim of his Enoch hat torn and sagging. Looking around the store to make sure they were alone, he leaned across the counter and whispered. Mary Ann, bending to hear his words, almost gagged at the odor of his breath. "I got a message from Brother Whittaker for you."

Oh, dear God, she thought, a sharp pain grabbing at her chest. Something must have happened to Dru.

"Yer sister's down at my place . . . down on the Lower Clary. She's took sick and the Deps are in town. Brother Whittaker paid me to take her down there till the baby comes. My wife can do for her, but she wants you. Her old man said she was to have anything she wanted."

"Will you take me there?" she asked and at his nod went to find her boots and a slicker.

Brother Judd came out of his office. " 'Afternoon, Brother Smithers," and he nodded at the shabby man. When Mary Ann whispered to him why she must go, he patted her shoulder. "God bless you, Mary Ann. Be careful."

Rain fell, unceasing, all through the afternoon as they drove in silence toward Santa Clara. The mud made heavy going for the horses and Smithers used his whip often. He had brought a tarpaulin. Mary Ann sat beside him on the wagon seat and held it over both their heads until her arms ached. A sense of foreboding lay on her, heavier than the rain-soaked canvas.

Darkness came early, the rain still pouring as the wagon pulled up beside a low log cabin. A feeble glow from one window gilded the falling water, the light barely penetrating the night. Brother Smithers did not offer to help her. Mary Ann struggled down from the wagon, trying to hold her soaked skirts up from the mud and at the same time keep the package she had brought under her slicker. She had never helped with a birthing. Lucy had her babies at her mother's home, and there had been no babies born in their house since they came to St. George. Brother Whittaker had always insisted Dru stay at home, though Mama went to help. She did not know what to bring. Making wild guesses, she filled the package with a bolt of factory muslin, a bottle of beania oil, and a bar of Castile soap.

"Go on in," Brother Smithers shouted. "I gotta see to the horses."

The wagon drove off, and Mary Ann knocked on the plank door. It was opened by a woman even more slovenly-looking than her husband. Her dank hair had fallen from the bun on her head and hung tangled and uncombed about her skinny face. Her small, piggish eyes appraised Mary Ann. "You the sister?"

"Yes," Mary Ann replied, stepping through the doorway, thankful to be out of the drumming rain.

"Well, yer too late to be any help." The woman sniffed, turning away, scratching her behind and twitching her shapeless dress about her body. "The kid came while Pa was gone to fetch you." She bent to throw another piece of wood in the flickering fireplace. One coal-oil lamp, with a dirty chimney, illuminated the small, primitive room. Dropping her slicker on the bare earthen floor, Mary Ann hurried to the bed and stared down at her sister.

Drusilla lay with eyes closed, her face pale as death against the soiled ticking of the pillow. As she bent over the girl, Mary Ann felt a drop of water and looked up to see the roof was leaking. There was a great damp spot on the quilt covering Dru.

"Dru," she said softly. "Oh, God, my beautiful Dru." Laying her hand on the girl's forehead, she smoothed back her damp, tumbled hair, the skin hot and dry beneath her hand. With what seemed a terrible effort, Dru opened her eyes and looked up at her sister. She did not speak, but her mouth trembled and tears welled in her eyes. Mary Ann held her hands and kissed them. All the while Dru stared at her in silence, the tears flowing down her drawn face.

"Are you all right?" Mary Ann asked.

"I guess," Dru whispered, "only I hurt so bad."

"She yelled her fool head off," the woman said contemptuously, coming to stand beside the bed. "My hell, havin' babies ain't all that bad."

An almost ungovernable urge to violence filled Mary Ann. She longed to strike the woman, to beat her into a whimpering scapegoat for all Dru's suffering. Instead she clenched her fists in rage and demanded harshly, "Get some dry bedding and a pan to catch the leak. She can't lie here in a wet bed like this."

"The roof leaks," the woman sneered. "Can't be fixed while it's raining. If we can stand it, I guess you can."

Mary Ann glared at the hateful creature. "I'll be damned if we will. You were paid to take care of my sister. Now do as I say."

The woman sniffed and wiped her nose with the back of her hand. "You uppity Hamiltons . . . I guess you're no better than anybody else when the Deps are on your tail, even if your Pa is such a big bug."

"Get me a pan and some dry quilts and shut up," Mary Ann commanded.

"That's all the quilts I got." Sister Smithers pointed to a rough bunk built against the wall. "My old man'll sleep there." When she turned to take a pan from the cupboard, Mary Ann jerked the dry quilts from the bunk and exchanged them for the ones covering Dru.

"Pa won't like that," came the warning.

Ignoring her, Mary Ann rearranged the bedding, but soon saw that the roof was leaking on the other side of the bed. "You'll have to lie still and not tip over all the pans," she told Dru, trying to smile.

"I haven't seen my baby," Dru said wearily. "I guess I passed out after it came. I don't even know . . ."

"There he is." The woman pointed and went to the fireplace to stir the pot of stew she had hung there.

"Why don't you have him by the fire?" Mary Ann asked, reaching for the rough hand-built cradle which had been shoved in the dark at the other side of the bed. As she leaned over, water leaking through the roof struck the back of her neck. She felt the cold damp of the quilt covering. It was soaking wet. Her hand touched the baby's smooth skin . . it was cold as ice, unmoving . . . dead.

"You stupid, ignorant fool!" she cried and saw the woman's small eyes blaze with anger. "May God damn you to eternal hell. You've killed this baby." Dru began to weep brokenly.

"I didn't kill him . . . just a minute ago I looked. He was all right then," the woman protested.

"You're a murderer," Mary Ann screamed and began to cry. "Damn you . . . damn you!" Leaning over the bed, she held the weeping Drusilla in her arms, rocking her, trying to comfort.

"Whatsa matter?" Brother Smithers asked, stomping in, shedding wet clothes all about him.

"The baby's dead," his wife replied, looking frightened now. "He never did breathe right," she added, justifying herself.

"The Lord giveth and the Lord taketh away," Smithers answered. "Why we done had ten, and not one lived to grow up. The Lord's tried us." His face indicated neither grief nor regret as he sat down at the table and asked, "When's supper, Ma?"

Quickly his wife dished up the stew. With a minimal grace, the two of them ate noisily. Mary Ann dipped some broth from the pot and urged Dru to eat. After only a spoonful, she protested, "I'm just too tired to eat . . . let me sleep, please. Oh, my poor baby . . ." and she began to cry again.

"Won't do no good to sling snot about it," Brother Smithers said, making Dru cry harder. He made a hurried trip outside, then pulled off his boots and rolled on the bunk, grumbling about the damp quilts. He had begun to snore even before his wife finished the dishes. Unabashedly, she dragged a chamber pot from under the bed and used it. From somewhere she produced a frayed blanket and settled herself in the rocking chair with her feet propped on a low stool. "Since you think you're so much smarter than me, you take care of her," she told Mary Ann and closed her eyes.

At last Drusilla fell into a fitful slumber. She was bleeding heavily and Mary Ann was thankful she had brought the bolt of factory, though nothing else she had brought seemed of any use. When Dru was sleeping Mary Ann carried the cradle near the fire. In the flickering light she rearranged the baby's tiny limbs, wrapping him carefully in a length of muslin. Then she placed the cradle far from the fire to preserve the body. If it stopped raining, she would take Dru home tomorrow and see the baby had a decent burial.

One need not be a nurse or midwife to know Dru was suffering from more than giving birth. She had a raging fever. The damp cloths on her forehead, the careful sponging of her body did not abate it. In spite of her constant requests for water, her lips grew cracked and dry. The beautiful eyes glazed over sometimes as though she saw nothing.

I wish I could pray for you, Dru, Mary Ann thought, watching her sister's labored breathing. I wish I could ask God to help you, but tonight I hate everyone . . . even God. How could Papa do this to you? The blessings of plural marriage, he said, exaltation in Heaven as the fourth wife of the good and pious Brother Whittaker. How could Mama let him . . . and you, you could have fought him . . . waited for Steve. Oh, Dru, you were so beautiful, I guess you just weren't strong enough to fight for what you wanted. Brother Whittaker flattered and petted you, made you believe you wanted to live in Celestial Marriage, and you hated every minute of it. You even hated your husband though you wouldn't admit it.

Dru's eyelids flickered open and she stared at Mary Ann as though she had heard her thoughts. "Have you seen Steve?" she whispered hoarsely, her breath coming in little gasps. "Is he home from his mission yet?" She moved painfully and moaned. "Oh, I'd hate to have him see me like this."

Mary Ann turned her face away from Dru's questioning eyes, tasting the hot salt tears on her face. Steve will never see you again, my sweet sister, she thought . . . not on this earth.

Burning with fever, Dru drifted in and out of consciousness, her life bleeding away on the muslin cloths Mary Ann had to change so often. Sick with fear, she shook Sister Smithers awake. "She's bleeding something awful. I don't know what to do. You have to help me."

Groaning, Sister Smithers staggered to her feet. She jerked the covers off Dru, and directing Mary Ann to tear the muslin into strips, bound Dru's thighs tightly together. "She'll be all right by morning," the woman said, flopped into her chair, and was instantly asleep.

Toward morning the rain slackened off. The only sound was the drip of water running from the eaves of the cabin. Firelight flickered silently across the small room, touching Dru's face with a false glow. Mary Ann sat holding her sister's dry, burning hand, knowing her own helplessness . . . waiting.

At last Dru roused and turned her blind, glazed eyes toward Mary Ann. A smile shimmered across her haggard face. "Steve," she whispered . . . "Oh . . . Steve." Her eyes closed and after a moment she sighed . . . a deep, ragged sigh. She was so still, Mary Ann thought. The little breasts under the damp nightgown no longer rose and fell, the faint beating in her wrist gone, but somehow that last sweet smile stayed on her lips.

"I got work to do here," Brother Smithers said. "That roof . . . my late corn layin' flat in the field. Cain't be haulin' you back and forth every day."

"Then I'll hire your horses and wagon. I can drive them myself," Mary Ann told him. "You can come to St. George tomorrow for them. I'll pay you well." His avaricious little eyes gleamed. He wanted to dicker over the price, knowing he had her over a barrel, but she agreed immediately to what he asked. Drusilla's body and that of her baby were wrapped in a quilt and placed in the wagon box with a tarp covering them.

Mary Ann mounted the wagon seat, touched the whip to the horses, and did not look back. She was past tears, past any feeling at all, as dead inside as Dru herself.

She drove along the red sand dunes under a gray and leaden sky. The rounded slopes of Devil's Saddle rose before her, with the Black Ridges beyond, and the hazy blue of Pine Valley Mountain. Far beyond that were the lavender cliffs of Mukuntuweap.

Two horsemen appeared. Dull-eyed, she watched them ride toward her under the dreary sky. One of the men rode up and arrogantly pulled the team to a halt. McGeary and Armstrong, the federal deputies . . . one of them a fat frog of a man, the other a skinny vulture.

"We're federal marshals," said the frog, riding up beside the wagon. "Whatcha got in the wagon, Sister?"

"Tryin' ta sneak some cohab back into St. George," the other snorted, riding to the back of the wagon.

"It's my sister," she told them in an exhausted voice, as the deputy threw back the canvas. "She's dead."

"Well." The Dep looked embarrassed. "Poor critter," and he lay the canvas back over Dru's body.

"Who's wife are you?" the vulture asked with a leer, his horse moving nervously close to the wagon.

"Nobody's!" Her voice was harsh and her hand tightened on the whip handle, ready to use it if he came any closer. "I'm not anybody's wife . . . and by God, I never will be."

Chapter 24

An icy gust of wind blew the gate shut behind Mary Ann. It rattled the bare branches of the orchard trees and slammed at the barn door. Drawing her shawl closer around her shoulders, she hurried toward the house. The store had been busy today with people getting ready for Christmas. She was tired, constantly tired, it seemed, since Dru died. Dying was right only when you were old and weary, with your life all lived. Dru had never had a real chance at life. Oh, why did nothing turn out happily? She had thought she would have Dru's babies to love if she had nothing else. Dear as Dru had been to her, she had never been able to cry . . . as though she hurt too much for tears. And Mama, she had locked her bedroom door and wept alone.

Now they had all the trouble about Isaac's marriage. He was only eighteen. Mama wanted him to go on a mission and grow up some more. That was not for Isaac, so they had quarreled about it, quarreled cruelly. Mama had even sent for Brig to come talk to Isaac. If one of her sons had made a bad marriage, she told Mary Ann, the other could well learn from that mistake. Yet it was Brig who walked out of the parlor from his private interview with Isaac, his eyes gleaming damply, his face a tragic mask. A glowering Isaac followed and stomped from the house without a word. No doubt Brig had told Mama what took place, but no one else would ever know for Isaac refused to discuss it.

Just a month ago, Isaac and his adored Sally had been married by her ward bishop at her parents' home. Mama stood by, looking resigned, while Sister Parks wept noisily. Mary Ann knew everyone suspected it was a case of "have to." What did it matter if they had, as the Elders said, "taken the fruit before it was ripe"? Isaac seemed ridiculously happy, even though they were living with the Parkses and he had no way to earn a living except to work for Mama.

Just as Mary Ann reached the back porch, Elizabeth opened the kitchen door, letting warmth and light stream out into the windy darkness.

"Oh, Mary . . . look!" she cried, holding up the bolt of blue silk she was carrying. "Isn't it beautiful? I'm going to have it for my wedding dress and I have to show it to Clarissa right now." She dashed up the path, heading for her friend's house in the next block.

Puzzled, Mary Ann stepped into the kitchen, laying her shawl over a chair back. Mama wasn't busy at the stove as she usually was this time of the evening, but there were voices in the front room.

"Tom's here," Kate said, looking up from the bolts of dress goods lying on the round oak table. She smiled. "He's brought all of us new dresses."

Mary Ann stood in the doorway, the breath gone from her lungs, her heart stopped. The edges of memory had grown dull. She wouldn't have believed it could hurt so much to see him again. "It's been a long time," she managed to say and could hardly hear her own voice for the thundering of her heart. How handsome he was, taller than she remembered, standing there smiling at her. He wore denim waist overalls with a silver-studded belt, a new white store-bought shirt, and high-heeled boots. There seemed a new dimension to him, a self-confidence he had not possessed before.

"I'll get supper on," Kate said quickly, before Tom could speak. "Brother Parsons brought over the backstrap from the hog he killed yesterday. Would you like that, Tom?"

"Sounds good, Mama."

As Kate left the room, she inexplicably closed the door behind her. For a long moment they silently avoided each other's eyes. The memory of that cloud-filled day on the slopes of Pine Valley Mountain was so strong Mary Ann could almost smell the sagebrush.

With a vain attempt at nonchalance, Tom said, "I thought sure you'd be married by now."

Her mouth twisted wryly. "I'm the old maid of the family."

There was a brief embarrassed silence while Tom looked down at the dress goods piled on the table. "I helped drive a herd of cattle to Denver last fall," he said. "I wanted to bring all of you a present. This is the best I could think of. You can take your choice."

"Tom!" He met her eyes at last and pain stabbed through her when she saw how much he cared. "Why did you stay away all these years? Didn't you know I needed you . . . that I'd wait forever?"

His mouth tightened, and he turned to stare out the dark window, standing in a way so reminiscent of Papa, feet apart, hands clasped behind his back. After a moment he spoke, so quietly she had to strain to hear the words. "It can't be, Mary Ann. I've accepted that. If you would, maybe you'd be content."

Looking at his tall, straight back, the thick, black hair trimmed short about his ears, a slow pulsing ache spread through her body, like a rising fever. "Are you content, Tom?" she asked. He lowered his head and did not reply. In the silence the pain of his rejection rose bitter as bile in her mouth and with it a terrible desire to hurt him back in some way.

"Dru's dead!" The words were harsh and angry. "Did you know that?"

Tom nodded, turning to look at her with dark somber eyes. "I heard."

"The fourth wife of a man she didn't even like, and dead because of him." The words tumbled out of her. Reaching out, she gripped a chair back, trying to stifle the longing to be held in his arms and comforted.

"I'm sorry," he said softly.

"Oh, Tom," she cried. "Isn't anyone on this earth happy?"

"Mary Ann . . ." he began, shaking his head.

"Poor Dru," she interrupted. "I think she was glad to die and be out of her misery. And Mama . . . ever since Papa left we have to send him every cent we can scrape together to help support Alice and Lovinia. Do you think she likes that?" She paused, breathless, knowing she was talking compulsively, remembering all the times he had listened and understood. "Now she's trying to run Isaac's life."

"Your mother is a good woman," Tom said.

"She's a miserable one," Mary Ann retorted. "We all are . . . Brig . . . he's so strange now . . . fasting and praying all the time. Hating himself for not being pure as Jesus Christ."

"I'll go see him before I leave."

"It won't do any good . . . he won't listen to you, or anyone but Mama. Oh, Tom . . . sometimes I sit in church and listen to the Elders preach about living the Gospel to avoid the everlasting fires of hell. It's all a lie . . . we're in hell now. This earth is a hell, and we're all suffering for the sins we committed in another life." The tears she had been unable to shed for so long burst through. She held out her arms. "Oh, Tom . . . hold me . . . just for a minute . . . please."

Two long strides across the room and his arms were around her, his cheek touching her hair as she wept against his shoulder. All the lonely days and nights, all the pent-up sorrow for Dru flooded out in those tears. Even when the torrent subsided she stayed there, clinging to him.

"Take me with you, Tom," she whispered. "Please. There's never a day I don't long for you."

"Mary . . . Mary," he murmured. "Don't . . . you mustn't." But he continued to hold her, smoothing her hair.

Drawing away, she looked up at him. "I love you, Tom. I'll love you till I die."

"Oh God, Mary . . . don't!" His arms tightened convulsively about her.

There was a sharp rap on the door and Kate's voice called, "Supper's ready, children."

Tom stepped away from Mary Ann as though the touch of her burned him.

The table that had once held so many Hamiltons was set for four. Sliding into the chair next to Tom, Mary Ann wondered how much her mother guessed. It was not like Kate to close doors. When Elizabeth's beaus came to call doors were left ostentatiously open.

"Can't remember when anything tasted so good," Tom said, pouring sop gravy, made from drippings of the fried pork tenderloin, over a thick slice of light bread. "Better than all the fancy restaurants in Denver."

"We're glad to have you home." Kate smiled at him. Was she? Mary Ann wondered. Unlike Papa, Mama had never uttered a word of blame for Tom, but neither had she expressed any sorrow at losing him. One could never be really sure how Mama felt about anything.

"Clarissa was just green," Elizabeth crowed. "I'll have the most beautiful wedding dress St. George ever saw." She turned to Tom. "John and I are getting married in the spring. He's coming to pick me up for Drama Club practice in a little while so you can see how adorable he is."

Tom grinned and Mary Ann winced at the description of gangly, awkward John as adorable.

"How's Brig doing?" Tom asked.

"Fine . . . just fine," Kate said, too quickly. "Doing well . . . four children now." Mary Ann could not look at her mother, knowing how she denied herself and went without to make up for the poor way Brig ran his business.

"And Isaac?" Something in the way Tom said the words made her heart sink. He had come here for Isaac's sake, not hers.

Kate's mouth thinned, her eyes cool. "He has some grand ideas for an eighteen-year-old," she said dryly.

"Well . . ." Tom drawled the word out in a way that seemed to disagree with her. "That range me and him staked out on the Strip would make him a good living if he had a few cows to start with. He's a hard worker and what he doesn't know I could teach him." Ignoring Kate's silence, he continued, "Kanab's growing into a nice little town. Isaac and his wife could live there."

Kate's face relaxed into thoughtful lines. Rarely enough Mary Ann could guess what her mother was thinking. This time it was only because there had been so much discussion about Isaac's marriage. If Sally was going to have a baby too soon, better she have it in Kanab than St. George.

"Maybe we could work something out," Kate said. "I guess I could lease the farm." She gave Tom a piercing look. "I wish you'd stay for Christmas. Tell me, are you doing well?"

"I get by." With a shy smile, he added, "I like that country. Why, from my place you can see a hundred miles . . . clear from the Vermilion Cliffs to the rim of the Grand Canyon."

Elizabeth stopped eating long enough to eye Tom curiously. "You're so far from everything out there. Don't you get lonesome?"

Of course he did, Mary Ann thought, moving her leg under the table so that her knee pressed against Tom's. She felt him stiffen, but he smiled at Elizabeth. "I have a gift Mary Ann gave me . . . I can read. A book and a cigarette can fill a lot of lonely hours."

Kate frowned. "I thought I smelled tobacco on you, Tom. I'd never countenance a boy of mine breaking the Word of Wisdom. It's the Devil's weed and makes slaves of its users. I'll pray you find strength to give it up."

Mary Ann sighed impatiently. Mama was so pious since President Taylor had the revelation that the Word of Wisdom should be a law, she had even made them give up their tea. It was a comfort they all missed. Mama too, she was sure. A stiff silence fell. The warm glow of the coal-oil lamp reflected dully on the oil-cloth table cover. Outside the trumpet vines rattled in the wind. Looking sideways, Mary Ann could see the pulse beating in Tom's throat rising smooth and dark against the white shirt. A familiar ache rose in her, so heavy and painful it almost made her ill. In her mind she could see him on the long evenings out on the desolate Strip with only a book and a cigarette for company. He could have her there, she thought miserably, if only he would listen and not care what other people thought.

Moonlight through her window made a silvery pathway across the room. Mary Ann moved restlessly in her bed, thinking of Tom sleeping down the hall in the boys' room, Elizabeth next door in her own bedroom, and Kate downstairs. This was a big house for three women . . . and soon only two of them. She moved her hand so that the moonlight gleamed from the ring on her fingers. After family prayers Tom had slipped a small box into her hand. His warning look told her it was a secret between them. Alone in her room, she opened the box and her eyes filled with tears at the beauty of the multicolored stone with its pierced gold setting. The ring on her finger had no magic to still the clamor in her body. The vague, painful yearnings, so long denied, perhaps never to be fulfilled, seemed now too much to bear. The memory of Tom's arms about her, his mouth against hers, stabbed through her and she sat up, unable to lie there any longer. The winter air was cold. Mary Ann shivered as her bare feet touched the icy floor. Without thought, as though driven, she moved silently down the hall and softly turned the doorknob of the boys' room. Tom came instantly awake and sat up as she closed the door behind her.

When she turned so he could see her face in the moonlight, he spoke, low and sharp. "Get back to your room, Mary Ann . . . right now. You got no business in here."

Ignoring his words, she sat down on the edge of the bed. Tom lay back with a groan, rigid and resisting. "I opened the package," she said, holding out her hand. "The ring is beautiful, Tom. What kind of stone is it?"

"You can thank me in the morning," he said gruffly. "It's an opal, and you shouldn't be in here."

"I never saw one before." She laid her hand on his bare chest to let the moonlight catch the fire from the ring on her finger. Almost involuntarily her hand moved across the smooth muscles of his chest and felt his heart pounding against her touch.

"For God's sake, Mary Ann!" He sounded as though he were speaking through clenched teeth. "Do you know what you're doing? Get out of here."

A breeze stirred the muslin curtains. Mary Ann shivered. "It's cold," she whispered. In one swift movement, she lifted the covers and slipped into bed beside him.

Tom stiffened and tried to move away from her on the narrow bed. "Don't do this to me, Mary. You don't know . . . oh, God!"

Mary Ann rose on her elbow, laying the palm of her hand gently against his agonized face. "Tom, I love you so. I've never stopped loving you." Bending, she pressed her mouth against his. Slowly, as though against his will, his arms came around her . . . then tighter and tighter until her breasts bruised against his ribs.

"You mustn't fight me when I'm trying to do right." His breath came hot and fast against her cheek, his hands on her shoulders pushing her away. "For God's sake, Mary, don't tempt me like this. Now go back to your room. Hurry!"

She sat up and heard him sigh with relief. Instead of getting up she pulled the nightdress off over her head and lay down again, her naked body pressed against his. With a groan of surrender, Tom seized her in his arms, kissing her mouth, her throat, her breasts, until she was filled with an almost unbearable longing. His hand moved over her body, touching all the secret places no one had ever touched before. His body covered hers. A twinge of pain and he was part of her, moving against her, filling her with strange and wonderful sensations. With an agonized moan, he lunged against her and then lay still, breathing hard. There was something more, she knew, something just beyond this that they would find together. But for now it was enough to be part of this man she had loved all her life . . . united body and soul.

Tom held her to him, kissing her over and over. Returning his kisses, she knew they had passed over some kind of threshold, that life would be different forever after. Her eyes would see the world in a new way, her body initiated now into the ageless mystery.

"Oh, Mary . . . I'm sorry . . . I'm sorry," Tom murmured against her throat. His voice broke. "God, I love you so much."

"Don't be sorry," she whispered, a sweet glowing contentment spreading through her. "We love each other and I'm your wife now . . . more truly than if the Elders said the words over us. Here . . ." Taking the ring from her finger, she pressed it into his hand.

"What?" In the moonlight she could see his puzzled frown.

"Put the ring on my finger," she told him softly, "and say the words with me. With this ring I make thee my wife, to love and cherish through all eternity."

The words said, he slipped the ring on her third finger, left hand, and kissed it in place. Then he kissed her mouth and they lay close together, arms about each other. "Are you happy, Tom?" she asked. "I've never been so happy."

"We're playing games, Mary . . . dangerous games." Cruel words, but his voice was gentle.

Tears stung her eyes. Did he always have to be so honest? "I know it," she replied, "but I'm so happy. Please, Tom, let's have this one night out of all our lives . . . even if this is all . . . and just be together, not think about tomorrow, or anything. Please."

Tom sighed, his mouth warm against her forehead. "All right, sweetheart . . . tonight." Holding her close, he kissed her eyelids. "Sleep now and I'll wake you before sunup."

Gray light of predawn filled the bedroom when Mary Ann awakened and looked into Tom's sleeping face. That face, always so rigidly controlled in the daytime, was relaxed in sleep, the straight, firm mouth curled at the corners, almost in a smile. Love for him filled her, almost suffocating, and something else she could now call by its real name . . . desire. Her hand moved over the dark smooth skin of his chest and hesitantly downward. Tom's eyelids flickered and his hand caught hers. "Don't, Mary," he said sleepily. But she took the hand, placing it over her breast. With a soft moan, he stirred and drew her into his arms.

Perhaps it was better every time, she thought afterward, lying breathless and spent in Tom's arms, her heart pounding against his. This morning they had crossed another threshold where she had seemed to drown in a wild, blind rapture that still tingled through her body.

A rooster crowed in anticipation of dawn and was echoed by rival roosters all across the town. Sparrows in the bare cottonwoods began to chatter. Above the black volcanic ridge, the sky took on the pink tinge of sunrise. This night had ended that she wished might last forever.

"You'd better go." Tom gently brushed back her rumpled hair.

"I wish I never had to leave you," she whispered.

"Dearest girl, so do I . . . but you must."

Startled by the sound of Kate shaking the ashes down in the cook stove, Mary Ann sat up and pulled her nightdress on over her head. Leaning across, she kissed Tom hard on the mouth. "My husband . . . my love," she said, looking into his sad dark eyes, and turned to hurry silently down the hallway to her bedroom.

Sitting at the breakfast table, Mary Ann wondered whether anyone could tell. Washed and dressed, she had stood before the mirror in her bedroom, trying to detect some outward difference that might give her away. There in the reflection was the same shining coronet of brown braids, the same slender brown-eyed woman who had lived one dreary day after another these past years. Now it was over . . . now . . . Oh, she wished they were married already and alone, a hundred miles from anyone, without all the trouble and business in between. She didn't dare look at him. If their eyes met, surely something in her would explode like a skyrocket on the Fourth of July.

"I have to help decorate the Ward Hall for the Mutual dance tonight," Elizabeth said, gulping her cornmeal mush. "Are you going, Mary Ann?"

"I might," she replied, carefully buttering a biscuit, "if Tom will stay and go with me. He should stay for Christmas anyway and not be in such a rush."

"Tom?" Elizabeth was aghast.

That single word, with all its implications, fell like a stone in water, silence widening in circles from its impact. At last Tom said lightly, "You're right, Liz. I'm too old for that nonsense." Pushing his chair back from the table, he rose and turned to Kate, who was packing dried fruit in a clean sack. "That ready, Mama?" Tightlipped, she nodded. He took the sack from her. "I'd better get my mule packed and get home. Probably got cattle scattered from Paria to Pa's Pocket by now."

As soon as the door closed behind him Mary Ann whirled on her sister. "You little snot! After all Tom's done for you . . . even bought your wedding dress." Her breath came out in a fierce explosion. "I'd like to slap your face."

"But Tom's an Indian. He'd be out of place," Elizabeth replied, her blue eyes wide and guileless.

"Indian!" Mary Ann exploded. "He's been like your brother and you have the nerve to sit there and make him sound like one of those dirty Clara Indians who come in every year to be baptized and get a new shirt. Oh . . . damn you!" Shaking with anger, she rushed out the door.

The wind came straight from the snows of Pine Valley Mountain. It picked at the bare branches of the grape vine and whistled through the barn loft. The animals, even the chickens, huddled indoors out of the cold blue day. Tom was saddling his horse when she came into the barn. Quickly she went up behind him and put her arms about his waist. "I love you," she said, pressing her cheek hard against his back.

"Mary . . . Mary." He turned to look at her with a wry smile, one big hand reaching to smooth back her windblown hair. "You're the only person in this world who's totally color-blind."

"Oh, I could kill Liz." With a sob she moved into the warm circle of his embrace.

His mouth touched her forehead. "Never mind," he said. "She's right. There's no place for me here and she sees it better than you or me." Tom's arms tightened about her, his voice was bleak. "No place anywhere for the two of us."

The opal ring gleamed on her finger as Mary Ann moved back to look up at him. "After last night I . . . I just knew you'd change your mind . . ." The words faltered and fell away at the anguish in his face. Releasing her, he turned back to adjust the saddle.

"Last night was wrong," he said hoarsely. "I had no right . . ."

"It wasn't wrong!" The opal caught the fire of the morning sun as she covered his hand with hers. "I'm your wife, Tom."

He jerked his hand away. "Oh God! Mary . . . don't play any more games."

"It's true . . . before God, I'll never marry anyone else. Tell me you won't . . . because if you did, I'd die."

Dark eyes moist, a muscle working in his jaw, Tom turned to look at her. "Never anyone else," he said, as though swearing an oath.

She was in his arms then, held fiercely against him, his mouth searching for hers, sealing his promise. Clinging to him while he kissed her eyes, her face, her throat, she whispered breathlessly, "I wouldn't trade last night for all God's kingdoms."

He let her go so quickly she almost stumbled. His voice was harsh. "It won't happen again. I promise you."

"No. I don't want you to promise that."

"Oh Lord, Mary . . . what if I've . . ." He seemed to choke on the words.

"What if you've given me a baby?" she finished for him, filled with a sudden soaring joy at the thought. Pray it was true . . . that she already carried his child inside her. "Then we'd get married . . . you'd have to." Embracing him, she looked into his unhappy eyes. "I'd lay in your arms every night for the rest of our lives and love you . . . and have your babies. Oh Tom, it could be so anyway, don't you see? . . . Please, Tom."

Reaching up, he clasped her wrists and took her arms from around his neck. Joy plunged into despair, a sob caught in her throat, for she had never seen such misery in a human face. "Go into the house now," he said, each word an effort. "If you need me send word by Isaac. I'll always do right by you . . . always."

Tears spilled from her eyes, streaking hot down her face. His hands held her arms, keeping her away from him. "I love you, Tom," she said brokenly.

"I know." His mouth was stern, her own agony reflected in the black eyes staring down at her.

"And you love me?"

"Yes." His jaw tightened. "Let me go, Mary . . . please, just let me go." When he released her wrists she flung herself into his arms. For a brief moment he held her as though he would absorb her into his own body. His mouth found hers in a long yearning kiss. Gently he pushed her away. "Go into the house now . . . quickly."

Half-blind with tears, she turned and fled.

Chapter 25

The back lot gate squeaked open. Mary Ann looked up from shelling peas to watch her father walking toward the house. Burns and Erastus Snow had arrived yesterday morning, waiting outside town until they were sure the federal deputies were away at court in Beaver. Min Snow came with her husband, sharing his travels, as enduring as the basalt cliffs. An ache rose in her throat as Mary Ann watched her father come toward her. His hair and moustache were almost white now, with only a few streaks of brown. He had always been so strong and vigorous, so seldom ill that he took even a head cold as a personal affront. Five hard years and the long illness in Arizona had taken a toll. Although he walked with the same air of self-confidence, the old vigor was gone. His broad shoulders were just slightly stooped, the lines in his face many and deep.

Beside her on the back porch a hummingbird ravished one trumpet blossom after another. Tiny green grapes hung from the grape arbor, soaking up the warmth of the early summer sun. The apricot trees were a froth of chartreuse lace. Plymouth Rock hens in the chicken run scratched and clucked to their ugly adolescent chicks.

"Ah, Mary Ann," Burns said, sitting down beside her, removing his hat. "Fresh peas. I hope there'll be new potatoes to go with them."

"Of course." Mary Ann smiled at him. "And fried chicken too. Your favorite meal . . . we remembered." If only he would stay here and never go away again. He had always had to spread himself in so many places they had never had enough of his company.

Reaching into the bowl on Mary Ann's lap, he took a few shelled peas to eat. Her thumb cracking open the pods and slipping along the spine to set the peas free, she watched her father's thoughtful face. He looked different, his face changed in some subtle way. It was only after she saw him cleaning his false teeth this morning that she realized this was the reason.

"I've worried about your not marrying, daughter," he said. "But when I see what a help and comfort you are to your mother, I feel perhaps it was God's will."

Not God, she thought with an old familiar pain. Not God's will, but the inflexible will of Thomas Hamilton, tied and bound by what he thought were unbreakable rules.

"What would you think of coming to Mexico with your mother?" Burns asked. "Surely that job in the store isn't enough to keep you here?"

"What's it like in Mexico, Papa?" She had avoided answering his question.

"It's fine country me and President Snow are buying for the Church. Fine country . . . with water and timber. I can be a lumberman again. The Saints can irrigate and raise crops and be safe from the persecutions of the United States. The sacred law of plural marriage can be practiced without fear."

A sigh escaped his lips, and Mary Ann thought how weary he looked. It was wrong of the Church to send a man of Papa's age colonizing again. Arizona had almost killed him. She wondered whether he could survive this move to a foreign land to start all over again taming a wild and unsettled country.

"I'm sorry to miss seeing Isaac," Burns continued. "He was such a harum-scarum it's a relief to hear he's doing well, though it wasn't right of Mother to give him all those cattle."

"Isaac's paying Mama back," Mary Ann replied, resenting the fact that Mama hadn't told him. Kate was still embarrassed by Isaac and Sally's seven-month baby boy who had weighed ten pounds at birth. The baby had been born in Kanab where Isaac lived now, but word filtered back and was repeated by all the St. George gossips. Dear as Isaac was to her, Mary Ann had been almost glad when they moved. She couldn't help envying their happiness . . . the secret looks and touches revealing their private joy.

"Your mother's a good manager," Burns went on. "I have no reservations about leaving my property in her hands." He shook his head thoughtfully. "Though I'd have thought she'd have disposed of some of it by now."

"No one can afford to buy property," Mary Ann told him. "With most of the men on the Underground, hiding from the Deps, people can't even manage the property they have. Nobody has any money except those who work at the mines or sell goods there."

Burns's lips drew into a straight, intolerant line. "Well, I pray your mother has followed counsel and stayed away from those Gentiles and their holes in the ground."

Finishing the peas, Mary Ann set them aside. No use telling Papa that the money he had lived on in Arizona came from the produce, beef, and lumber they had sold at Silver Reef. Without the mines they would have all starved to death.

"I'd like to sell the farm," Burns continued reflectively, looking out across the town. "Burnie is no farmer, and it's hard to find a good renter."

"Farms are the hardest to sell," she said. "Maybe John would run it."

"No." Burns sighed again. "He has his father's place now, and that's almost too much." He seemed to sigh a lot, as though he were too weary ever to catch his breath completely. "God will open a way," he said, standing up.

"Give these to Mama." Mary Ann held the bowl out to him, gathering the pods in her apron. "I'll put the pods in the swill barrel."

Returning to the house, she had one foot on the back porch when she heard her father, inside the kitchen, say, "This house and lot are in a prime location. I should have no trouble selling them." Mary Ann's heart sank. This house was Mama's pride and joy and for her it was all the home she had. She could never go to Mexico . . . that much farther away from Tom . . . not ever.

"This house is not for sale!" Kate's voice was shrill. "It's my home and I intend to stay here among my children." Mama had acted sulky and odd at breakfast . . . and now, talking like a fishwife. Even when she quarreled with Papa or Isaac she did it in a soft voice. Mama must have guessed this was coming, Mary Ann thought, remembering her mother's eyes this morning . . . bleak and empty as though something in her had died.

Burns spoke in that old pedantic preachy way. "It's a woman's duty to go where her husband tells her to go. His priesthood is her guide to salvation. A woman alone is nothing."

"What need do you have of me?" Kate returned bitterly. Mary Ann stood with one hand on the porch pillar, too embarrassed to enter the kitchen and afraid to run away for fear they would hear her.

"You're my wife," Burns said in surprise.

"I'm old," Kate cried in a strangled voice. "Beyond childbearing . . . and you . . . you can't even bring yourself to love me."

Burns cleared his throat and replied in a low, embarrassed voice. "My dear, sexual congress is only for the purpose of begetting children, not for man's pleasure."

"Oh, shit!" Kate snapped. Mary Ann gasped. She had never heard her mother use such a word before. Less refined women used that expletive all the time . . . after all it was not taking the name of the Lord in vain. Was it possible that even at Mama's age a woman could still know the loneliness of unfulfilled desire? Despair clotted her throat and the empty years stretched endlessly ahead.

There was a long silence in the kitchen as Mary Ann wondered uneasily what she should do. She could hear her mother banging pans on the stove as she often did when she was upset.

"I'm surprised at you, Kate," Burns said stiffly. "You've fallen from the paths of righteousness if you can use that kind of language."

Kate's reply came in a strange, almost tearful voice. "Oh, Burns, Burns, is it only my language that concerns you?"

"I don't understand you any more," he replied. "You've changed."

"Some of us change because we have to," she said in a low, weary tone.

"Oh, Papa!" It was Hannah, come in the front door without so much as a knock. "Burnie had to take the water, but I brought the baby to show you."

When Mary Ann stepped into the kitchen, Kate was busy at the stove. Burns sat in a kitchen chair, dandling Burnie and Hannah's baby boy on his knee.

They were all there after supper. Jane and Brother McIntosh and their two little children, for Brother Mac was making a visit to his wives while the Deps were gone. Burnie and Hannah with their baby and Elizabeth and John, still calf-eyed newlyweds. Word had been sent to Brig, and his family would no doubt arrive tomorrow. Mary Ann moved among them, filling lemonade glasses, dispensing cake. She could see herself, grown old, still doing the same things. The old maid aunt . . . the one who could help out when the babies were sick, or their mother bedded in childbirth . . . the one who could lend a few dollars when things were tight . . . who could be depended on for birthdays and Christmas. Aunt Mary . . . all alone. Escape . . . escape, she sometimes thought the night wind whispered. But how escape when there was never enough money and the only place she wanted to go was to Tom.

"You got nobody to blame but yourself for being an old maid," Regina had said. "You could have married Joe."

Joe Gilbert, Lucy's brother, suddenly widowed and left with five children his mother wasn't eager to raise. Mary Ann winced, remembering how he came courting within the month after his wife's burial; courting without bothering to shave or take a bath. Standing on the front porch, thumbs hooked through the galluses of his bib overalls, he had looked down at Mary Ann with a confident grin. "I sure need a wife, Mary Ann," he said, "both me and the kids. I reckon you need a husband, too. Ain't much to be said for being an old maid."

Too stunned to speak, Mary Ann stared at him, almost overcome with revulsion at the thought of sharing his bed. Recovering, she answered crisply, "No thanks, Joe."

Astonishment flooded his face, as though he could not believe she meant to turn him down. "By gad, Mary Ann," he said. "You're gettin' a little long in the tooth. You ain't gonna have too many chances to get a man."

"I can do without a man," she replied sharply, holding in her fury. How dared he . . . how could he ever think she would be so hard up as to marry the likes of him? She would go to her grave and whatever Limbo awaited unmarried women on the other side before she would marry trash like Joe Gilbert. Or anyone but Tom, she thought, suddenly wanting to cry. "You'll have to look somewhere else," she said, her voice shaking. "Good night, Joe," and she closed the door in his face.

Alone in her room, she wept angry tears that her life had come down to this . . . that people thought anything, any trashy man, was better than being an old maid. There was no place in this society for a single woman; even in the Gospel they were less than fallen angels. "I don't care," she sobbed aloud, then wept fresh tears remembering Tom teasing her for those words.

Burns sat at the round table in the front room, his business papers spread out before him. He had sold Lovinia's house and made the deed over to Brother Crandall. The stock in Canaan Cattle Company had been easy to sell. The company was prospering and some years paid dividends of 30 percent. But he had been unable to find a buyer for Alice's house or the farm, and no one in town could afford to purchase his business property on Main Street. Now he was making up a sale contract for the sawmill for Brig to sign. Even in the family, Burns kept things on a businesslike basis. Everything must be finished up today, for he and President Snow were leaving in the morning. They had both spoken at church today, greeted with affection and honor by the congregation.

"Sign this, Brig," Burns said, "and you'll be owner of the sawmill. Your mother will know where I am and can send the payments on to me."

More likely she'll make them herself, Mary Ann thought, watching Brig bend to sign the agreement. Mama had sold all the lumber that had gone to Silver Reef the past few years. Brig had no get up and go to him. His family would have starved without Mama's managing.

Lucy sat on the sofa, nursing her baby, watching Brig with hostile eyes. The way she nagged at him all the time made it an embarrassment to be around them. He hardly ever answered her back. Maybe if he had been man enough to tell her to shut up, she would have quit.

"There's Brother Warren now," Burns said, and he went to the door to greet his visitor.

Through the open door they could hear the shouts of Brig's children playing on the lawn. I should probably go out and watch them, Mary Ann thought. Mama would have a fit if they trampled her flowers.

" 'Evening, Sister Hamilton," stout Brother Warren said, shaking hands with Burns and Brig, nodding to Lucy.

"Nice to see you," Kate acknowledged. "What brings you out this evening?" Her face was pleasant and smiling, but there was a pinched, suspicious expression around her eyes.

"I've always fancied this house and lot," Brother Warren said, looking about with a proprietary air. "When Burns told me it was for sale I jumped at the chance."

"It's not for sale," Kate said, her voice like ice.

"What?" Brother Warren asked. Both men looked at her as though not quite sure what they had heard.

"This house is in my name." Kate stared at him, her slender figure taut with anger. "It's not for sale."

"Well, I . . ." Brother Warren turned to Burns who was staring at his wife in disbelief.

"Now, my dear," Burns began in a placating voice. "Surely you understand that we must sell everything we can. You and Mary Ann can live in Alice's house until I send for you to come to Mexico."

"This house is not for sale," she repeated, her voice rising, edged with violence.

"Kate!" Burns almost shouted the word.

"It's my house." Kate looked at him with hatred. "The deed is in my name and I am the only one who can sell it."

"Well, I certainly didn't expect this." Brother Warren looked about nervously. "Maybe you and your wife . . ."

"I'm sorry, Bill." Burns put his arm about Brother Warren's shoulder and led him toward the door, giving Kate a furious look. "Come outside and we'll talk."

Kate burst into tears and ran into the kitchen, hands covering her face. Immediately Brig rose to follow her. Through the doorway Mary Ann could see him holding his weeping mother in his arms, patting her back, whispering words of comfort.

Lucy seemed to have forgotten the baby she held, her bitter eyes staring at the scene in the kitchen. Tugging futilely at his mother's breast, the baby began to cry.

Chapter 26

Carefully Mary Ann counted the eggs from Sister Primm's basket and wrote a receipt for two dozen. "Do you want anything today?" she asked.

The old lady pushed back her homemade calico sunbonnet, her shoe-button eyes darting about the store. "Jest some thread, I guess."

Mary Ann opened the drawer of the thread cabinet. Sister Primm was a lonely widow; she had nothing else to do. Let her take her time with this tiny decision. While the old lady rooted through the drawer, Mary Ann's eyes wandered to the bright spring day outside. Another spring. They seemed to come faster now, swiftly lost in the whirl of the years. They heard of Tom only through Isaac. There were letters from Papa demanding that Mama sell their property and come to Mexico. Mama had stopped reading or answering them. Mary Ann sighed, bending to straighten the spools Sister Primm had left awry.

At the sound of the door closing, she looked up and her heart seemed to leap from her chest. It was almost two years. She had despaired of ever seeing him again. Now he stood just inside the doorway, watching her in the same old grave, quiet way.

"Tom!" she cried and was embarrassed by Sister Primm's curious glance.

"Hello, Mary Ann."

Sister Primm looked from one of them to the other, handing Mary Ann the thread with a sly glance. Hands shaking, Mary Ann wrote out a charge slip for the thread and handed it to the old woman.

"Ain't that yer Pa's Indian boy?" Sister Primm asked.

Mary Ann turned her back and finished rearranging the thread drawer, refusing to answer, wishing the old lady gone, wondering whether she could possibly conceal the storm sweeping through her.

"I'll take a ball of crotchey thread, too," Sister Primm decided and Mary Ann violently wished her dead. She handed over a ball of white before there was a chance to debate the color and began writing it down.

"Good-bye, Sister Primm," she said decisively. Tom took off his wide-brimmed Stetson hat and nodded to the old lady, holding the door open for her reluctant exit.

"Oh, Tom!" As the door closed Mary Ann let the mask go, not caring that he could see how she longed for him. It would never change, she knew that now. This time, she would make him see it, too.

"Mama thought you'd be about ready to come home for dinner," he said, giving her a carefully guarded smile. "She said I'd better buy a new shirt." He turned to show her the ragged elbows of the blue cotton shirt he wore.

"Those ready-made shirts aren't much good," she said. They were in a public place, Brother Judd in the back room working the telegraph, and customers in and out the door all the time. This was no place for declarations of love. "If you'll be here a while I'll get some material and make some shirts for you."

"No." Reaching behind the counter, he took two shirts from the shelf. "I have to go right on."

"Where?" Her heart plunged in fear that he would leave now . . . this minute, before she had time to convince him that he could never again go away without her.

"I'm on a cattle-buying trip," he said, handing her the shirts and digging in his pants pocket for money. "Cattle business is booming in Wyoming. I figure on swinging through all the southern Utah settlements, buying cows . . . hire help as I need it. Then I'll put the herd together with the cows me and Isaac are selling and drive them north into Wyoming." He grinned at her across the cash register. "I might be a rich man next time you see me . . . if prices hold and the cows don't drown crossing Green River."

"Isaac said you're doing well, Tom." She handed him the change, almost losing her composure as their hands touched.

"Need any help, Mary Ann?" Brother Judd peered out from the back room. He did not approve of cowboys, considering them a bunch of ruffians. Since Tom was dressed like one and apparently was not recognized, he came on into the store.

"Don't you remember Tom?" she asked quickly.

"Why yes . . . of course." His voice was hearty, although it was obvious he had not remembered. "Mary Ann tells me you're doing well . . . got a place of your own now. Just goes to show what can be done with a little ambition."

She knew that wry twist to Tom's mouth if Brother Judd did not. A kindly gentleman, he probably did not even realize he sounded condescending.

"Is it all right if I go to eat now?" she asked, eager to get away, to be alone with Tom.

"Sure . . . go ahead." He shook Tom's hand. "Good to see you."

The dusty streets gleamed in the brilliant spring sunshine. Green filaree still colored the hills, and the immaculate white of the Temple rose from a splendor of blossoming fruit trees. Scented with blossoms, the warm air touched her face like a caressing hand. As they crossed the street and started toward home, Mary Ann reached over and slipped her hand into Tom's. Immediately he tried to pull away, but she interlaced her fingers with his and held on tight.

"Mary Ann!" His voice was low. "Somebody will see you."

"I don't care." The inner trembling made her voice tremulous.

"You haven't changed," he said, in a vain attempt at the old teasing way. "You still say I don't care."

"No, I haven't changed." She said it softly, although the street was deserted and no one could have heard. "I still love you. I will always love you."

His jaw tightened. He looked straight ahead . . . silent.

"Do you still love me, Tom?" If he said no, she thought she would surely die.

"For two years I've tried to stop." His voice was careful and quiet. "I guess I can't. I guess I never will."

"Oh, Tom!" Tension drained out of her. All the longing of the past two years welled up inside so that it required a conscious effort to hold herself back from him. Releasing her hand, Tom opened the gate of the back lot. The apple trees were covered with white and pink nosegays among burgeoning pale green leaves, filled with the drone of bees. The warm perfumed air was like an aphrodisiac and her desire was so strong she ached with it. Pausing under the trees, she looked up at him.

"How long will you stay?"

"I'm going on today," he said, refusing to meet her eyes. "I have to look at some cows upriver."

"That isn't the real reason," she challenged.

"No, I guess not," he admitted, then sighed. "Nothing's changed, Mary Ann. Nothing."

"You're going to be rich." She smiled at him.

Tom chuckled. "Maybe that's just a dream, too."

"You'll do all right . . . I know it," she said. "Have you told Mama?" When he shook his head, watching her pensively, she rushed on. "Mama will be disappointed if you don't at least stay overnight. She misses you, and you should go see Burnie and Jane and Liz. Please, Tom." Holding her breath, she waited. Guile was so foreign to her nature, she could not tell whether her ruse would succeed. Mama didn't care whether Tom stayed . . . or Burnie, or anyone except herself.

His smile was wistful. "Well . . . all right. I guess I'd just like to sit and look at you for a while. But promise you won't . . ." The words trailed away.

With an enigmatic smile, Mary Ann reached up and picked a sprig of apple blossom, smelled it, and held it to Tom's nose. He looked at her with shadowed eyes. As they walked toward the house she slipped her hand back into his.

Kate was delighted Tom had decided to stay. There were so many things needing fixing around the place and Tom was so handy. The hired man came to do the plowing and the heavy work, but he had his own farm and their work came last. Burnie and John never seemed to find the time to help out. When Mary Ann left after dinner to go back to the store Tom already had the tools out, fixing the broken step on the front porch.

A long, hazy spring twilight filled the valley. Feathered wisps of coral pink cloud glowed against the cobalt west, now darkening into magenta and gray with the sky fading until it was as translucent as clear water. Kate rocked slowly on the front porch, her never idle hands busy with the knitting that required no light. Tom sat on the step, his back propped against the railing of the porch. She mustn't sit near him, Mary Ann thought as she sat down on the opposite side of the step. The longing to touch him was so intense she could hardly contain herself. Watching his profile silhouetted against the darkening sky, the arched prominent nose, the strong line of his jaw, she hoped it was dark enough so no one could read the desire in her face. Against a chorus of crickets and spring frogs, Tom talked idly of his visit to the Indian country last fall.

Suddenly stunned with jealousy, Mary Ann looked down at her hands. "I hear the Navajo women are very pretty." In spite of herself her voice was tart.

"Like all women," he said with a smile. "Some good, some bad."

Glancing covertly at him she wondered, had he had other women? Jealousy rose like a sickness. Still, they said men had to have a woman. Oh damn, she thought miserably, if he has to, it's going to be me . . . and all the time.

"I'd better set the bread to rise," Kate said abruptly. Mary Ann watched the screen door close behind her mother, feeling time drain away like water in the sand. Tom had visited briefly with the other members of the family this afternoon. Early tomorrow morning he would be on his way again.

"Can't you stay longer, Tom?"

"Not if I expect to make any money this year," he said wryly.

"Then take me with you." There . . . she had said it.

Tom's eyes flicked toward the house where they could hear Kate bustling about in the kitchen. "Don't!" The word was a command.

"Guess I'll go up through Pine Valley and Pinto on my way," he said, obviously making conversation. "Stop and see Brig and Lucy."

Mary Ann remained silent, too hurt to speak, wondering why Tom would bother. Brig had always taken Tom for granted when they were young . . . like master and servant. Tom was too loyal. Brig would be cold with him now, just as he was with everyone.

"Mama didn't have much to say about Brig," he continued. "Just that he isn't well. What's the trouble?"

"I wish I knew," she answered, simmering with resentment at this reminder of all her mother did for Brig. "He has spells where he just sits and stares . . . won't even talk. And he looks awful . . . so much older than he really is. It's scary. He can't seem to manage anything right. The sawmill's always broken down . . . or his help steals him blind. Mama's always bailing him out of his money troubles and selling his lumber for him."

"How's Lucy and the kids?"

"Oh, Tom," she sighed. "It's turned out so bad. Lucy whines and nags all the time, and her house is the dirtiest in the country."

Tom shook his head, looking down at his hands. "He had everything I never had," he said in a strange, quiet voice. "How could it go so wrong?"

"I guess it all started on his mission."

"Oh, hell," he said impatiently. "Everybody makes mistakes. You have to go on from there and make your life right again. It's crazy to spend your life brooding about one mistake."

"I know," she replied, shivering. "Crazy . . ."

The screen door slammed and Kate took her seat in the rocker once more. "My goodness," she said after a moment's awkward silence. "It's gotten chilly out here. We'd better go in."

How quiet the town was under the dark, starry sky . . . only the music of crickets and frogs . . . all the lights out . . . still and silent and perfumed with apple blossoms. Mary Ann's bare feet took the pathway through the grape arbor, barely visible in the starlight. Tom's cigarette was a faint red spark beneath the apple trees. He had refused to sleep in the house, saying he was used to sleeping outdoors, insisted, in fact, over Kate's protests. Mary Ann had kept silent, knowing his reasons all too well. He didn't know that by now her mother was used to her nightly prowling about the house. There had been few nights she had slept through in the past two years, rising to walk until her yearnings lost themselves in fatigue.

Holding her wrapper about her, she stopped beside him. "I didn't promise."

"No." He sighed and ground the cigarette out in the grass where he sat beneath the apple tree. "I knew you'd come and I know how weak I am. Mary . . . I want everything good for you, and I don't ever want to do wrong by you."

She dropped down beside him, sitting close, leaning to kiss the edge of his jaw, the pulse at the base of his throat. Tom's arm encircled her shoulders, his hand moving gently on her neck. The smooth skin of his chest was warm to her touch. "I still wear your ring," she whispered. "I'm still your wife." Her voice broke. "Oh, Tom . . . love me. I need so much to be loved."

When she opened her eyes to the jeweled sky, she thought she was drowning in stars. The scent of apple blossoms mingled with the stale odor of Tom's bedroll. She had slept . . . that deep, delicious sleep that follows loving. Memory flooded back and her body trembled, the waves of rapture still receding in a slow tide. Turning her head she saw the gleam of Tom's eyes watching her.

"Sweet Mary," he said, and drew her close to kiss her mouth. His fingers touched her face gently. "It's wrong . . . I know it is, but I think of you no matter where I am, and want you like this."

"How could anything so wonderful be wrong?" she whispered and pressed close to him. "Take me with you, Tom . . . please." A sense of urgency seized her. "I don't even care if you marry me . . . just so I can be with you."

Tom shook his head, his voice weary. "We've talked all this out before, sweetheart. It's no use. Maybe . . . maybe if there wasn't anyone but us to consider . . . not your mother or your family . . . or . . ." His voice faltered.

"Or the babies," she finished in a trembling voice. "Do you think I wouldn't be proud to have your babies?"

"They'd be half-breeds," he said sadly. "Have you thought of that . . . and what it means?"

Her eyes flooded with tears. "We'd love them so much it wouldn't matter." Silent, Tom held her close as she wept against his shoulder.

Suddenly he stiffened at the sound of footsteps. "Oh God!" Holding her tight, he pulled the quilt over her head. Lifting a corner of the covering, she peeked out to see the light of a lantern swinging down the middle of the street and the moving silhouette of a man carrying a shovel. The thonk-thonk of his gum boots echoed in the silent night. A dog began to bark.

"It's Brother Cottam," she whispered, "going to take his night water turn." They clung together and watched the lantern-shine recede down the road.

Sighing, Tom kissed her. "You'd best go in before light."

"That's a long time."

"Not really . . . see the Big Dipper up there." He pointed, then explained how the cowboys told time by the Big Dipper moving around the North Star. Smiling, sunk in contentment, Mary Ann listened, thinking how wonderful it would be if they could spend every night of their lives together like this . . . loving, talking, sharing.

"Take me with you," she asked once more.

One big hand gently smoothed her hair. "It's a rough trip, Mary. I'll be on the trail nearly six months."

"And you'll make a lot of money?"

He chuckled softly. "I hope so."

Rising on her elbow, she looked down into his face barely visible in the darkness. "Maybe I could marry you for your money?"

"You're crazy." He grinned, pulling her down into his embrace. After a moment he said reflectively, "Money buys more than just things, doesn't it?"

Mary Ann lay silent for a long moment, seeing her way clearly now, marshalling her arguments. "It buys a lot of respect," she began. "Look at the mine owners and the big ranchers who aren't even Mormons. Why, people around here kowtow to them all the time, just because they're rich. It seems like it doesn't matter who or what you are, if you have plenty of money. You've seen that, haven't you?"

The answer was a noncommittal grunt, and she rushed on. "I'm twenty-six, Tom . . . a woman, not a silly little girl. I could have married, but I won't . . . not ever, unless it's you." She held him in a fierce embrace. "Oh, Tom, can't you believe I'm strong enough to stand with you no matter what other people say? How could I have loved you all these years . . ." She paused as tears neared the surface again.

For a moment, she was afraid he would never answer. Then he moved restlessly. "Damnit, Mary, don't you think I want to believe what you say? You know how much I want you. Then I think you'd end up hating me . . . when people snub you . . . and all the misery your kids are bound to go through."

"When did I ever care what people say?" she demanded. "Don't get me mixed up with Mama. I don't need anyone else . . . only you. We'd even have enough money to send our kids away to school if we wanted to."

He was silent, as though he had run out of arguments. "I'd be away a lot . . ." he began tentatively.

"And I'd be waiting when you came home," she said, pressing against him, her hand moving urgently down his hard-muscled body. "And I'd love you . . . I'd love you until you begged for mercy."

Tom made a strange sound, half-groan, half-laugh, and drew her close. Their mouths met hungrily and there were no more words.

Limbs still entwined, they lay together in the sweet, languorous afterglow, and Mary Ann knew she had won. She knew it even before he kissed her and said, "I'll be back to get you at Christmas time."

Chapter 27

The early August heat was sweltering, even in the shade of the porch. Mary Ann sat down in one of the two rocking chairs her mother kept on the porch in the summertime, fanning herself with the copy of *The Women's Exponent* that had come in the mail. The air was heavy and still, the trees motionless, their leaves the deep, ripe green of midsummer. Down the street she could hear the choir practicing in the Tabernacle, the voices strong and resolute: "The spirit of God like a fire is burning . . ." The music rose in a flowing curve of sound. A mockingbird returned his serenade from the gatepost, suddenly leaping into the air as though he could not contain his joy. She almost laughed aloud, knowing exactly how he felt. There had been a small package in the mail, addressed in Tom's handwriting, and she turned it in her hands, savoring the anticipation before opening.

Looking down at her name written in Tom's awkward handwriting, she was shaken by the memory of his last morning here. She had come into the kitchen, washed and dressed, feeling so extraordinarily well she wanted to sing. Tom was already sitting at the breakfast table, but he did not look up. At last, when Kate went into the pantry for something he did look at her . . . a look of such blazing passion she thought she would melt, like a dish of butter on a hot summer day. When Kate came back into the room, he turned away, leaving Mary Ann so shaken she could not eat breakfast at all.

With a quick peck on the cheek, Kate made her good-byes to Tom at the kitchen door. Ignoring her mother's inquiring glance, Mary Ann walked with Tom toward the barn. His horse was saddled, the mule packed and waiting, tied to a corral rail. Without a word to each other they stepped inside the barn and she was in his arms. He kissed her so that her mouth felt bruised; held her so close her ribs hurt, and she did not care.

"Oh, Mary," he said at last, taking a long, shuddering breath. "My sweet Mary."

Through misty eyes, she looked up at him. "If I didn't know you'd be back I couldn't stand to let you go."

"I'll be back." His fingers gently traced the outline of her cheek. "You could always make me do what you wanted."

"Not so," she protested. "Or we wouldn't have wasted all these years."

"They weren't wasted." His eyes were tender. "Now I can give you all the things you deserve . . . a nice home . . . money."

Sighing, she pressed her head into the hollow of his shoulder. "Unimportant things."

"No," he said and his voice took on that familiar stubborn ring. "I wouldn't do it without the money."

Lifting her face, she kissed the strong line of his jaw. "You've promised now," she said with a smile.

"Mary . . ." Embarrassment stamped his strong features. She wanted to laugh. He was always so afraid to talk about getting babies. "I'll write so you'll know where I am if . . . if . . ."

Mary Ann regarded him tenderly. "If I'm pregnant?"

"Yes." Tom cleared his throat. "Go to Isaac and he'll see you get to me. Promise?"

"I promise." It had been ordained, she thought. All their lives they had been meant only for each other. The months of waiting stretching before her seemed interminable.

"Mary," he whispered, his face against her hair. "I want this so much. Tell me again it'll be all right."

"It will be the rightest thing in the whole world, Tom."

At the corner of the street he reined up his horse and turned for one last look. Mary Ann, leaning across the gate, blew him a kiss, uncaring of the neighbors' eyes watching.

"What's the package?" Kate asked, closing the screen door and settling herself in the rocker on the shady porch, her mending basket in her lap.

MARY ANN

Mary Ann bit her lip in disappointment. All summer she had managed to pick up the mail herself, so that when the two letters from Tom came she did not need to share them. Not that he ever wrote anything revealing. The letters were short, stilted, and misspelled and they were not love letters beyond being signed, Love, Tom. Still they were hers alone to read over and treasure. "It's a package from Tom," she replied, making her voice calm and easy as she took her mother's sewing scissors to cut the string. "From Green River. What a funny place to buy a present."

Beneath the crumpled newspaper lay a small ornate bottle labeled "Eau de Cologne" and a slip of paper on which Tom had written, "This reminded me of you." She managed to conceal the note and lifted the bottle to show Kate.

"Toilet water." Kate looked disapproving. "He must have bought it from some traveling peddler. I surely thought I'd taught him better than to spend his money on such folderol."

Mary Ann scarcely heard the words, for she had worked the stopper loose and held it to her nose. Suddenly she was once more drowned in stars, the scent of apple blossoms, and the miracle of loving. With the sweet imitation odor of the cologne, Tom had reached out across the miles and touched her. He remembered! He remembered as exquisitely as she did, and she was almost sick with wanting him.

"Well, it just goes to show," Kate continued, tight-lipped, a touch of envy in the sharp eyes peering over her glasses. "You can't make a silk purse out of a sow's ear. Never was an Indian had any sense about money."

For one stark, terrible moment Mary Ann thought she might strike her mother. Dazedly she rose and walked into the house, upstairs to her bedroom. Closing the door, she burst into tears.

That hateful tongue of Mama's! How could she ruin the joy in Tom's small gift? How could she talk that way about a man who had been like a son . . . who had done more for her than her flesh-and-blood sons? Tom had acquired all he owned beginning with nothing, and look how Brig had failed with all the help in the world.

All the years Mama had lived in this town and she still had no close friends, never visiting back and forth as other women did. Oh, she did her duty, helped lay out the dead, sat up with the sick, brought food to the bereaved and ill, made her Relief Society visits like clockwork with her partner, pert, chipper Sister Pritchett . . . but it was surely done as a duty, not with love. What had happened to change her down the years from the brisk and busy Mama of her childhood who always had time for a hug or a word of comfort? She would not even open Papa's letters now, or mention his name except as one might speak of the dead. Last time President Snow had been in town he asked Kate at meeting what she had heard from Burns. Kate had replied coldly that she never expected to hear from Burns Hamilton again until the morning of the Resurrection. President Snow looked shocked and Mary Ann had been thankful someone interrupted the conversation or he might have raked Mama over the coals for such talk.

Wiping her tears on the pillowcase, Mary Ann read Tom's words again. She stroked the cologne bottle lovingly. His hands had touched it and she pressed it against her mouth. If only she could share with someone . . . with her mother . . . this wonderful, painful thing of loving. But the woman downstairs was all alone behind a wall of her own building. Now that Papa was gone she cared only for Brig. Well, when Tom came back she would have no qualms about leaving her mother.

Beneath her hand the summer grass was soft as fur and smelled sweet and damp. On a quilt spread in the deep shade of the cottonwoods, Isaac's baby slept. Parks lay with arms outflung, fists clenched softly, lost in slumber. Mary Ann sat beside him, fanning him to keep away the flies. She wished he would wake up so she could hold him, kissing his chubby neck until he squealed with joy.

"This has been a wonderful day," Kate said, looking with pride at her children. Isaac had brought chairs from the kitchen to the front lawn for Kate and Elizabeth, and for Sally who was pregnant again. John lay sprawled asleep in the shade, snoring gently. Elizabeth rocked her tiny baby. "Now all my children have been through the Temple," Kate continued. "I couldn't ask the Lord for a better day than this."

"Glad you're happy, Mama." Isaac stood with his hand resting on his wife's shoulder. He winked at Mary Ann. They had attended the

MARY ANN

morning session at the Temple where Isaac and Sally had been married for time and eternity. He had given up his chewing tobacco in order to get a recommend to the Temple and gone through the ceremonies only to please his adored wife. Mama could have talked until kingdom come, Mary Ann thought, and never have convinced him to go to the Temple. Sally had only to ask.

Kate had insisted Mary Ann go through the Temple with them and receive her Endowments. It wasn't something she wanted to do; for one thing she would forever after be obliged to wear garments, the ugly underwear, marked with cabalistic signs, which the Mormons thought kept one from harm. Some people never took their garments off completely for fear of the Devil, keeping one foot in their underwear while they bathed. She had finally agreed to go out of sheer weariness with her mother's arguments. The ceremonies were long, boring, and occasionally ludicrous. How could words spoken by mere human beings bind God to a commitment to save this man and damn another, she wondered. Surely a powerful Being who could create this earth had more important things to do than write down who went through the Temple and who did not.

Once the ceremonies were over it was a happy day, with so many of the family there for dinner. Jane came with her two toddlers, although she had to leave early to help Sister McIntosh with the chores since their husband was still on the dodge. Burnie and Hannah came with their babies, and Sally's parents. They had gone home now. Isaac and Sally would spend the night with the Parkses, leaving for Kanab in the morning. It was a good, comfortable feeling, lazing away the pleasant summer afternoon with the family.

John had brought a block of ice from the Atkins storehouse, and Mary Ann made pitcher after pitcher of lemonade. Isaac refilled his wife's glass and handed it to her. His big, rough hand smoothed her hair, his eyes adoring. Sally reached to squeeze his hand, giving him a melting look. She was a plain girl, with a long face and large teeth, blue eyes and light brown hair, but then Isaac was no beauty either. Somehow the family looks had come out wrong in Isaac. No matter, Mary Ann thought, regarding her brother fondly, physical beauty did not always make beautiful people. Enviously she watched her brother and his wife loving each other with their eyes. Being married to

(239)

someone you loved must be so wonderful. There seemed to be few such lucky ones. Look at Regina and Roger, bickering constantly . . . and Brig and Lucy. I'll be one of the lucky ones, she thought, longing to leap across the time between now and Christmas.

Isaac refilled his own lemonade glass and came to sit on his heels beside Mary Ann. She suspected he was guzzling lemonade because he missed his tobacco. It wouldn't surprise her if he started chewing again as soon as he and Sally drove out of town.

He grinned at her. "Tom's well on his way to Wyoming now."

The name sent needles pricking along her limbs. If only she could share this joy with all of them, but no one would understand, no one . . . except maybe Isaac. Surely he had guessed it all that long-ago day Tom had left Pine Valley forever.

Looking into her brother's crinkled blue eyes, she knew he knew. "Yes . . . he'll be back before Christmas, he said." For me . . . for me . . . her mind echoed.

"I'm glad, Mary." Isaac looked at her intently.

Tears pricked at her eyes. "Isaac, you're the only one . . ."

"What's that you said about Tom?" Kate interrupted, leaning toward them.

Isaac unfolded his long body easily, standing up, grinning down at Mary Ann. "I said he'll make a lot of money on this cattle deal. He's got a good head on his shoulders." He turned to look coolly at his mother. "Nobody ever gave him credit for that."

"Well, I did," Kate protested, pursing her lips and frowning. "I always said he had unusual qualities for an Indian."

"Crap," Isaac said under his breath and went to pick up the empty lemonade pitcher sitting on the grass beside Sally's chair.

Mary Ann concentrated her attention on the baby who was just beginning to stir. She had promised herself she would not be angry with Mama today, no matter what happened. Parks's eyes fluttered open and focused on her after a moment. His mouth spread in a toothless grin. Immediately she picked him up, holding him close against her, inhaling the sweet baby smell of him. Did she love him best of her nieces and nephews because he belonged to Isaac . . . just as she had loved Dru's babies best? She couldn't wait to have her own baby. Little Parks almost made her wish she had caught a baby last spring. It would have been awkward, though, chasing Tom around the country to get married in time. Besides, they would have all winter together, alone in his cabin out on the Strip . . . all winter to make beautiful, black-eyed babies.

"I wish you'd seen Brig," Kate said.

"Yeah." The voice was noncommittal as Isaac stared into the empty pitcher in his hand. Didn't Mama guess at the unbridgeable chasm she had created between her sons when she insisted Brig try to talk Isaac out of marrying Sally?

"Lucy wrote that he'd had a bad spell and shouldn't travel," Kate went on. "You know he hasn't been well."

"What's wrong with him . . . besides an overdose of religion?" Isaac asked.

"Isaac!" Elizabeth gave him a reproving look.

Isaac had never repeated what passed between him and Brig during their interview before Sally and Isaac were married, but watching him now, Mary Ann guessed Brig had hurt him more than anyone knew.

"A little more religion wouldn't hurt you," his mother said coldly, her eyes shadowed, her face tightly under control.

Sally bit her lip, her eyes moist. Shrugging, Isaac started toward the house, carrying the empty lemonade pitcher.

Now you've really lost him, Mama, Mary Ann thought, her mouth pressed softly against Parks's fat cheek. Just because Isaac jokes about things doesn't mean he isn't sensitive. He can be hurt as easily as Brig . . . but you don't care, not for anyone but Brig. Oh, Isaac will be dutiful toward you, that's his way. I guess we all will. Burnie and Jane because you were good to their mother and to them since she's been gone. The rest of us because we were brought up to respect you, but I hope Brig loves you enough to make up for all of us.

Lucy's small kitchen was warm and filled with the strong sweet odor of peaches cooking in molasses. Mary Ann shoved the huge preserving kettle aside and lifted the lid to put more wood in the stove. The inside of her arms itched from the peach fuzz, her fingertips were shriveled and stained from cutting fruit. She was so tired of peaches after all those she had cut on shares for Sister Dodge.

Her share would make a winter's supply of dried peaches to take when she went with Tom. Stepping outside the kitchen door she caught a whiff of pine-scented air and longed to escape. Not today. This batch would finish the preserves, with a few choice fruits left to serve with sugar and cream for supper. Filling her pan with fruit from the basket sitting by the door, she returned to sit beside Lucy.

Silently Lucy peeled and pitted peaches from the bowl in her stout lap. Mary Ann sighed. She had always found it difficult to talk to Lucy and she did not relish the prospect of a month in Lucy's company. Mama and Brig had left in the buggy this morning. They would drive to Milford and take the train to Salt Lake City where Brig would see the doctors. Mama worried and fussed so over Brig, but even to Mary Ann it had become obvious that something must be done about a young man who seemed constantly fatigued and immersed in melancholia. Mary Ann was to stay with Lucy while they were gone since she was no longer working at the store full-time. The sawmill was shut down, seemed to be shut down half the time. Brig couldn't get help, or couldn't pay them, or the machinery was broken . . . always something. And the lumber market was bad now that the mines were playing out at Silver Reef. Lucy had wanted to go to Salt Lake, too. She had never been there. But Mama was paying all the expenses, and she had made it clear that Lucy should stay home and take care of her children. Mama had friends in Salt Lake where she and Brig could stay while Brig saw the doctors. As long as they were there it would be nice to stay on for October Conference. She could have taken Lucy and left the children with me, Mary Ann thought, but apparently Mama hadn't even considered that.

Why couldn't Mama admit that Brig was weak and incompetent, not sick? She never liked to bring things out in the open . . . wouldn't admit that Dru's husband had neglected and killed her . . . that Isaac chewed tobacco and cussed . . . or that she and Papa were really separated. Mama thought it was better to pretend everything was fine, as though pretending would make it so, and convince the neighbors.

One after another, Mary Ann cut, pitted, and peeled the peaches, slicing them into a kettle for the next batch of preserves. She didn't want to think of Mama and Brig any more, and she turned her mind

to Tom. Time had dragged this summer, but the months were passing and he would be here . . . soon . . . soon. Longing went
through her body like a flashing pain. Mustn't think of that, she told
herself. Think about the quilt she must finish so Lucy could help her
tie it off. She and Tom would lie under that quilt . . . Mary Ann
hardly noticed the itchy discomfort of the peach fuzz, the hot
kitchen, and the sweat running down her back. After a time she became aware that Lucy was weeping silently into the bowl of peaches
on her lap. Had she wanted to go to Salt Lake that badly? Mama
really had Lucy buffaloed. She wouldn't dare ask to go. Mary Ann
didn't know what to do. Perhaps if she ignored it Lucy would control
herself in a minute.

Lucy's weeping became audible, strangled by her efforts to suppress
the sound. "You mustn't cry," Mary Ann said at last, searching for
words to comfort her sister-in-law. "When Brig is well the two of you
can go to Salt Lake. That will be nicer . . . just the two of you . . .
like a real honeymoon."

"No," Lucy sobbed, wiping her nose on her peach-stained apron.
"He'll never take me. I know it. Sometimes I think he's ashamed I'm
his wife."

"That's not true, Lucy," Mary Ann protested, struck with shame at
her inconsiderate brother. Lucy had grown grossly fat since her
babies came, but she could still be an attractive woman if she would
take the time. True, her housekeeping and her personal hygiene left
much to be desired, but somehow she should get herself together and
improve. Her nagging was enough to put any man off, but then Brig
couldn't be much of a joy to live with . . . his head always in a book
. . . always consulting Mama about his business and his life. Brig
certainly was no help around the house and yard. Fortunately, the
boys were big enough to milk and care for the animals now. This
morning all four children had gone to take their turn watching the
town cow herd and wouldn't be back until evening.

"I'll tell you what we'll do" she said, hoping to cheer Lucy up.
"While he's gone we'll make you some new clothes. I'll show you a
new way to do your hair. You're a real pretty woman when you're
dressed up, Lucy. Why, Brig will fall in love with you all over
again."

Tears drying on her face, her mouth drawn down in a bitter line, Lucy stared at the bowl of peaches. "He never did love me, Mary."

Shocked, Mary Ann turned to stare at her sister-in-law. "Of course he loves you. He married you."

"Oh, for heaven's sake, Mary Ann." Lucy's voice was sharp. "You're old enough to know you don't have to love someone to marry them." She pushed back a strand of lank brown hair with her arm. Shoulders sagging, she continued in a dull voice. "He just married me because I wanted him so bad . . . and he was so down about being in disgrace and all that."

"But you had babies together . . ." Mary Ann began.

An anguished sob escaped Lucy's lips. "Oh dear God, Mary Ann. How would you like to go to bed with a man you loved and know that in the dark he was pretending you were another woman?"

"Lucy! You can't mean that!"

"It's true." Lucy's face writhed painfully. "Sometimes he even called me Monica . . . at first."

"Oh, Lucy!" Mary Ann wanted to weep. Kate had never thought Lucy good enough for Brig, even though in the beginning there had been no doubt that she loved him devotedly. They had all blamed Lucy for her whining and nagging. Poor creature. The hell she must have gone through, suffering it alone until now when she could no longer hold back.

"Oh, I thought he'd get over it . . . prayed he'd forget her and love me. I don't know . . . I just don't know. Maybe it's God's punishment for loving a man too much." Lucy began to cry again, plump shoulders shaking. She set the bowl of peaches on the stained floor and covered her face with her apron. After a few moments she wiped her tears on the apron and stared, empty-eyed, at Mary Ann. "He'll never love me. He hasn't even touched me since Joey was born."

"Four years?" Mary Ann looked into Lucy's desolate face, remembering all the aching nights she had walked the house wanting Tom, needing to be loved. Dear God . . . four years in the same house with a man you loved. Poor Lucy. What could she say? Brig was an unsolvable puzzle . . . she didn't understand him . . . never had understood him. Lucy was weeping into her apron again. Mary Ann watched her, sympathy for this woman she had never liked hot and painful in her throat. How little we know of the agonies of another human being's soul. How little we ever guess of what makes people behave as they do.

"Now listen to me, Lucy," she said gently. "Mama's right. Brig's sick. That has to be why he's acted this way. It's not natural for a man to behave like that." Standing up, she dumped the peach peelings into the slops bucket. False confidence in her voice, she faced Lucy. "That doctor in Salt Lake will fix Brig up like new. Everything will be different when he's well again. I just know God will answer your prayers."

Lowering her apron, Lucy lifted her tear-streaked face, hope beginning to rise in her eyes. "Do you really think so?"

"Of course," Mary Ann lied bravely.

"Oh Mary Ann!" Lucy stood up and embraced her. "You're the best friend I've got in the whole world." Lucy wiped her tears and managed a shaky smile. "I do think you're right. Why, we'll do all the things you said . . . make me some new dresses and fix my hair and fix up the house." An earnest, hopeful glow brightened her eyes. "Oh, Mary Ann . . . I just know everything's going to turn out fine."

Patting her arm, Mary Ann turned quickly to the stove to take off the kettle of preserves, ready now to be skimmed and poured into the clean crocks. She wanted to cry for Lucy, couldn't look at her or she might burst into tears. Maybe she had been wrong, and even cruel, to offer Lucy hope when deep in her own heart she felt that nothing would change. Life had set poor Lucy on a hard trail, and Mary Ann could not believe God had any intention of rescuing her.

Chapter 28

Bleak and barren hills faded in the early winter dusk. The night wind whistled, cold and lonely, through the bare branches of the trees. Beyond the western mountains the last light was dying as Mary Ann hurried toward home, hugging her shawl about her. Almost New Year's, and a faint apprehension vibrated along her nerves like a vague headache. It was not just the long, wearying day taking inventory at the store. Tension lay like a lead ball in the pit of her stomach. All day long she had flinched at every opening of the door. Tom had promised to come for her at Christmas time. The last part of waiting had been so hard, until it seemed that Christmas was the pinnacle of an enormous mountain she was climbing. When he didn't come for Christmas she told herself she knew it was all right . . . the kind of life he led . . . the far places he had been . . . you couldn't expect him to name a day he would return. But beneath her attempts to reassure herself the questions tumbled: Was he lying hurt somewhere? . . . Had he changed his mind? . . . Trying to keep busy, she had gone to the Christmas programs and parties with Mama. People expected them as a twosome now . . . Kate Hamilton and her old maid daughter. Then Christmas was over and the days dragged, as leaden as the weather. She had waited so long that now she thought she couldn't bear to wait another day. A hundred times she had gone through her things to make sure everything was ready. A hundred miles she had walked back and forth in her room, driven by an inner urgency, sleeping only in exhaustion, awakening in the cloudy morning light hovering between hope and despair.

A big roan horse stuck his head over the corral pole and whinnied at her as she came down the path through the back lot. Her heart leaped and began to pound so wildly for a moment she was afraid she might faint with relief. Isaac loved that ugly animal, swore it was the best cow horse in the country. If Isaac was here . . . then Tom was here, too, though she couldn't see his horse in the gathering darkness. She began to run. Now she wouldn't care who knew . . . she could hold him and kiss him in front of all of them and not care. Someone else would have to finish the inventory, she thought, almost laughing as she sped through the dark grape arbor toward the kitchen lights. Tom was here and it would take her no more than an hour to be ready to go. She hoped Mama wouldn't be mean, but it didn't matter . . . nothing could stop them. They would be married in Kanab. It didn't matter where . . . only that now they would be together forever and ever.

The kitchen door banged shut behind her and she paused, breathless. The room was warm and deathly still. Kate sat at the kitchen table, and inexplicably, Mary Ann wondered why she hadn't started supper. Isaac turned to look at her, unsmiling, one hand on his mother's shoulder. It always amazed Mary Ann that this big, horny-handed man in cowboy clothes was her little brother Isaac.

"Where's Tom?" she asked, breathless from running, and watched in horror as her brother's sun-weathered young face crumpled and tears filled his eyes. Slowly, as in a dream, her mother turned to look at her and Mary Ann saw that she wept too.

"Where's Tom?" she repeated, aware of the sharp rising edge in her voice, feeling the same helpless terror she had once felt as a child, standing on the banks of the Virgin River while the swift-running water pulled the sand from beneath her feet.

Isaac seemed unable to speak, mopping his eyes with a crumpled handkerchief. It was Kate who spoke, her voice quick and cutting, as though to say it swiftly would be merciful. "He's dead, Mary Ann."

Time stopped. No matter that the shelf clock went on ticking loudly. Time was at an end. She stared at her mother, numb just as a wound is numb at first, the body sending out its own anesthesia against the insult to its flesh. Life seemed to drain from her, dripping out her boneless fingertips, her eyes blank and empty as though she had suddenly died herself. "No!" she cried, as the blessed numbness wore off and pain ripped through her. "No!"

Isaac's arm went around her. With the other hand he pulled a chair back from the table. "Lord, Mary, sit down. You look like you're going to faint." Stuffing his handkerchief in his pocket, he wiped his eyes on his shirt sleeve.

Mary Ann looked at the ice cold hands lying before her on the table as though they were the hands of some stranger's corpse. Isaac touched her shoulder, but his words seemed to come from far away.

"When he didn't come in for Christmas I got worried. He knew Sally and me were expecting him. He'd been in to settle up with me for the cattle. Bought a load of lumber to fix up his cabin and . . . and a feather bed from Sister Hamblin." Again Isaac fished in his pocket for his handkerchief and blew his nose loudly. "Me and Joe Johnson rode out that way right after Christmas . . . to Tom's cabin . . ." His voice faltered. "He'd been shot . . . the place torn apart. Feathers . . ." Isaac choked on the word. ". . . feathers all over everything."

Kate drew in a long, shuddering sigh. "Why, Isaac . . . why?"

"Tom made a lot of money on that cattle drive and folks knew it. There was lots of talk around town about it. Me and Joe figure somebody came to rob him and had to shoot him . . . Oh, Judas Priest!" Isaac turned and went outside the kitchen door, having chewed his tobacco so nervously and incautiously he needed to spit.

Stunned and dry-eyed, Mary Ann stared at the pale hands lying before her on the green and white printed oilcloth. Pain had held her immobile, but now the ache was growing . . . rising . . . rising toward a bursting point.

"Did you bring him here?" She whirled on Isaac, feeling hysteria mount inside her. "I want him here . . . buried in St. George."

"My God, Mary Ann," Isaac protested. "He'd been dead three . . . four days. We had to bury him in a hurry as it was."

Nausea filled her throat at the hideous picture of him lying dead and alone, uncared for, brutally and senselessly dead. "Oh, Tom!" she cried and the words seemed torn from the depths of her being, tumbling from her lips like a painful hemorrhage. "Oh, my God . . . Tom!" Dropping her head on her arms, she let the flood of tears come. There was no reality of world or time . . . only this pain so intense death itself could not hurt more. If she could die too she would gladly go from this empty world where there was no longer any hope for happiness. All these years, no matter how seldom she saw him, she could always know that he was there . . . somewhere out across the desolate hills. Sometimes at night, lying in bed, she almost felt she could reach out and touch him . . . that he was thinking of her at that moment, their minds reaching out to each other across the miles. Now he was gone, forever beyond reach.

Kate rose and stood beside her. The starched, clean smell that had always meant Mama brought an unexpected flash of memory. Long ago, when she lay ill with pneumonia, that fragrance had meant the comfort of Mama's presence. Gently, Kate smoothed her daughter's hair. The tenderness in that unusual gesture reinforced the memory: a gentle hand on her burning forehead, and all through the hazy night her mother's pale face watching over her like a guardian angel. That cool hand lay against her cheek now, comforting. Impulsively, Mary Ann covered her mother's hand with her own, turning to kiss the scarred palm lying against her face. With a strangled sob, Kate reached out and lifted Mary Ann into her embrace. The two women stood together lost in a paroxysm of grief. Son and lover gone beyond recall. Such a display of emotion from her undemonstrative mother opened further floodgates until Mary Ann knew she was weeping hysterically, and yet she could not stop.

Isaac's hands were tight on her shoulders. His voice had a frantic note. "What will we do with her, Mama? I didn't think she'd take it so hard."

Still held in her mother's embrace, Mary Ann could feel Kate stiffen into self-control once more. "She's lost . . ." The words were almost drowned in the sob rising in Kate's throat. ". . . lost Tom." Sighing, she patted Mary Ann's back. "Get the laudanum from the top of the cupboard, Isaac. Then you can help me put her to bed."

How could the sun shine this morning? Mary Ann wondered, opening her eyes reluctantly. The world should look as empty and gray as her life. Full knowledge struck her, and the pain was like a knife run the length of her body. Tom was dead . . . dead. That meant forever. Never again to lie in his arms, never hear his laugh or see the tenderness in his black eyes. All these years she had waited, she thought, staring out the window at the leafless cottonwood branches gleaming in the morning sun . . . all these years, knowing there would never be another man for her. Tears scalded her eyes. God would not have snatched him from her just at the brink of fulfillment. She could not believe in such a cruel God, Tom's death was acceptable only if there was no God . . . only if life was chaos and disorder and emptiness. There would be no golden Eternity where she and Tom would meet again. Even if that Celestial Kingdom she had heard pictured so many times existed, there would be no place in it for the two of them. Tom was gone forever, and her life was dust and ashes. If only she could be dead, too, lying beside him under a pile of rocks out on the desolate Strip. Mary Ann turned her face into the pillow and wept great racking sobs. The laudanum last night, bitter in a glass of water, had sent her weeping into a drugged sleep. All that pain she should have wept out last night rose now through the hazy remnant of the drug.

"Mary Ann, dear." Kate opened the door quietly. "Would you like a little something to eat?"

Torn with weeping, she could not answer. "Oh, Mary Ann . . . Mary Ann . . ." Kate sounded distracted. "You mustn't behave like this. Tom's at peace now. Please believe he dwells in Paradise with God this very day."

Mary Ann turned her face from the pillow to stare at her mother's somber eyes. "There is no God!" she cried wildly.

"You mustn't say that," Kate gasped, her eyes flicking around the room as though afraid God might have overheard. "If we don't have faith in God and the Gospel, then we have nothing."

Dimly, through her grief, Mary Ann watched her mother, astounded at the fear in her eyes, seeing that she believed not from love or any overwhelming testimony to the truth, only from fear of an everlasting darkness.

Sitting down on the bed, Kate took Mary Ann's hand. "I'll have Tom's temple work done. Then we can all be together on the other side." For a moment her composure shattered and her voice broke. "If I didn't have faith in the immortality of man I couldn't bear it."

"God wouldn't have taken Tom," Mary Ann sobbed. "Not just when we were going to be married."

Kate bit her lip, looking down at her hands, gently rubbing the angry scars. "We can't question God's reasons, Mary Ann." Her voice was wavering and damp with unshed tears. "Tom was my son. I raised him and I loved him." She seemed to choke on unsaid words. "All these years . . ." Her head came up in that familiar arrogant way. "God is not kind," she said with finality.

For one brief, electric moment there flashed between them a sense of sharing that loneliest of emotions, grief. But the habit of reticence was too strong. Kate stood up with a brisk movement, retreating once more behind the wall that had for so many years hidden her private agonies. "I'll fix some custard for you." Quickly she went out the door as though afraid she had revealed too much of her self.

Mary Ann had wept to the point of exhaustion and now lay staring, dry-eyed, at the clouds shifting and rolling above Pine Valley Mountain. A winter storm was coming down from the north, already blotting out the pale sunshine. The door opened and she turned to meet Isaac's melancholy eyes.

"Mary Ann . . . Mary . . ." he said, sitting gingerly on the edge of the bed.

"Oh, Isaac!" she cried and sitting up, flung herself into his arms, taken by a new storm of weeping.

"There . . . there . . ." He patted her back awkwardly. "It's going to be all right."

"Nothing will ever be all right for me . . . not without Tom," she sobbed and looked into her brother's face. "I loved him so, Isaac. I loved him more than all the world."

"I know." Isaac tried to wipe her tears with his big calloused hand. "I know he loved you, too. Oh, God, Mary Ann . . . I'm sorry." Tears slid down Isaac's cheeks. "Don't you know I'll miss him too? He was the best friend I ever had."

Releasing her, Isaac searched for his handkerchief and blew his nose. "You have to get hold of yourself. Brother Ivins came by this morning with Tom's will." Clearing his throat he looked directly at her. "He left everything to you . . . his ranch, cattle. Those robbers couldn't have got much. All his money is in the bank in Salt Lake . . . and it's yours now."

"Oh, damn the money!" The words were an anguished cry. "He wanted it for me, and he was killed for it. Damn the money! I don't want it."

Isaac studied his hands, then her face. "Tom wanted you to have it. He arranged it in case anything happened to him. You would have been his wife . . ."

"I was his wife," she said dully and lay back against the pillow, turning the opal ring around and around on her finger. From the window she could see the orchard, the trees bare now, the grass beneath brown and dead. Only last spring she had been wife to him there beneath the apple trees, and she thought she could never bear to see them bloom again. She flung the words at Isaac's surprised face. "I was his wife and I'll never be wife to any other man."

He looked away, embarrassed. Staring out the window, still overwhelmed by the enormity of her loss, she did not care what he thought.

Sighing, Isaac reached to smooth her hair back from her forehead. "Do you want to get up?" he asked, as though speaking to a sick person. "Or can I bring you something? Something to eat or . . . or some more laudanum?"

"No." The compassion in his rough young face only intensified her pain. "You're a good brother, Isaac." She patted his hand, her mouth trembling. "Will you do something for me? Promise you will?"

Isaac swallowed hard. "Guess I'd do most anything for you, Mary."

"Bring Tom home in the spring. Promise me you'll bring him home, so I'll have him close to me."

"Oh, Mary . . . Judas Priest!" His face worked painfully.

"Please, Isaac. If I could just have his grave here . . . close. I know it's a hard thing to ask . . . but please do it for me when the snow's gone."

"All right, Mary," Isaac said, his voice low and strangled. "I'll bring Tom home in the spring."

BOOK THREE

Mother and Daughter

For if they fall, the one will lift up his fellow;
but woe to him that is alone when he falleth;
for he hath not another to help him up.

Ecclesiastes 4:10

Chapter 29

I don't see why Tom left everything to Mary Ann," Elizabeth said, cradling her second son in her arms as he tugged at her breast. She sat in the kitchen rocker, her two-year-old Johnny at her feet, scattering blocks on his grandmother's kitchen linoleum.

Kate carefully folded the pillowcase she had just ironed and returned the sadiron to the hot stove, replacing it with a heated one. In passing, she glanced out the kitchen window at the garden where Mary Ann, face hidden by her sunbonnet, was hoeing weeds. "She was his favorite," Kate replied quietly.

"Well!" Elizabeth sniffed. "John and I could have used some of that money."

Kate spread a dampened pillowcase on the ironing table. Her voice was cool. "Do you and John need money? I could make you a loan if you do." She knew very well they didn't. John was an ambitious young man. With his farm and his driving freight from California in the winter time, they were doing fine.

"No . . . it isn't that." Elizabeth said resentfully, shifting the baby to her other breast. "It's just that it's so unfair."

Raising her head from the ironing, Kate looked out the window. Summer light blazed from the bare backyard. The trumpet vine stirred, and hollyhocks blew in the hot wind. Along the green rows of the garden, Mary Ann's hoe moved rhythmically. "Life is unfair, Elizabeth," Kate said flatly. "Didn't you know that?"

Annoyed, Kate watched the hot iron smooth the wrinkles from the white cotton, steam rising to bead her forehead and upper lip. She hadn't meant to be ironing so late in the heat of the day, but this past year her scarred hand had become troublesome and it took longer to do her work. The ironing must be finished so she and Mary Ann could leave for Pine Valley tomorrow morning. Every year they went the last part of August to escape the miserable heat in St. George and to take Brig and Lucy their winter supply of peaches and sorghum. Sighing, she assessed the bushel basket with its tightly rolled burden of dampened clothes. Half empty now, and the figure in the garden caught her eye again. Dear Lord, Mary Ann looked like the wrath of God. She must have lost twenty pounds this year. Her clothes hung on her and she refused to alter them, the loose dresses making her hollow-eyed face even more wraithlike. Maybe the mountain air would give her an appetite. Kate wished she knew how to give comfort, for she too knew what it was to love someone beyond anything else on earth. But there had never been a rapport between her and Mary Ann such as she had with Brig. Then, too, it had been a town scandal and she hated a scandal. The circumstances of Tom's death and his will had kept the gossips' tongues wagging. Long ago she had learned to meet sly innuendos with a blank, cold stare, never revealing the hurt beneath. She supposed there would have been a scandal to face either way . . . with Tom alive and married to Mary Ann, or Tom dead and being buried by Mary Ann.

When Isaac brought Tom's body home, Kate had gone to the Bishop to make funeral arrangements, only to find Mary Ann had been there before her. Shamed, she rushed home to confront her daughter. All her protestations were shut out by that cold face and those empty eyes. Just the family went to the graveyard to see the pine box lowered into the grave. Burnie and his wife were there; Jane, alone with her babies, for her husband was still hiding out; Elizabeth and John. There was no time for Brig and Lucy to come down from Pine Valley. Mary Ann didn't want any outsiders, although Kate was aware of eyes watching as they stood in the cemetery on that cold spring day with the dusty green plumes of the tamarack bushes waving mournfully in the chill wind. The Bishop came to say the prayers dedicating Tom's grave. All the time he prayed Mary Ann stood dry-eyed and haggard, staring Out South toward the place where Tom had been killed. Now that she no longer worked at the store, she found time every day to walk to the cemetery and stand by

Tom's grave. If there were flowers in bloom she took them. Why, she had almost stripped the apple trees of blossoms to lay on Tom's grave.

Endure, Kate wanted to tell her unconfiding daughter and could not. When you have lost your love only time grows scars so thick no pain comes through. She seldom thought of Burns now, and the children were diffident about mentioning him in her presence. He no longer attempted to communicate with her, although he corresponded with Mary Ann. When her reply was written, Mary Ann would always lay both letters out to be read. Kate read them as though they were the correspondence of two strangers and never made a comment.

Still, sometimes in the night she awakened, stark and clear in her mind the memory of a young Englishwoman with her first prayed-for son and her beloved husband, safe at last in Zion with a glorious future before them. Time, Kate thought, suddenly aware that the sadiron had grown cool and must be exchanged for a hot one . . . time is a robber of dreams and the thief of love. When she thought how far she had come from England it seemed to her she had lived forever. Burns could never hurt her again. They would meet at last in the glory of the Celestial Kingdom, and he would be once more her young and loving husband. Then she would know happiness eternal, earthly jealousy and rejection no longer there to cause her pain. She had borne the trials God sent: Burns's other wives, the loss of her baby boys, and Dru's tragic death. Now she would be content with what she had. She had Brigham and the other children, her home, an income. If she had only neighbors and acquaintances, not friends, that did not make her unhappy. A private person such as she had no need of other people.

"I suppose I should get on home," Elizabeth said, wiping her breast and tucking it back into her bodice. "John will be wanting supper." One pat on the baby's back brought forth a loud burp. The women laughed and the baby responded with a toothless grin.

"I wrote down our water turns for him," Kate said, taking a piece of paper from the clock shelf and handing it to Elizabeth. "He always takes good care of the place for me."

"Are you going to stay a month this time?" Elizabeth asked, gathering scattered baby things into her basket.

"It depends . . ." Kate's eyes wandered once more to the lonely figure in the garden. Mary Ann had never enjoyed Pine Valley since Tom went away, but at least it would be a change. When they came home she would try to get Mary Ann more involved in their business, keeping records and collecting rents . . . anything to keep her mind occupied. Mary Ann would not forget Tom, she knew that, they had loved each other too many years, but eventually the pain would ease. Perhaps it was better to have lost your love that way than as she had, a little at a time, smothered by duty, desiccated by neglect. Even now she remembered how it had frightened her when she first became aware of the depth of feeling between those two, for she knew there would never be anything but hurt for both of them. Such a relationship was unseemly, it was wrong, it was simply not done. She had even hoped the passion would fade with Tom so far away. But it had not, and now never would for the heart is as unreasonable, it seemed to her, as the whims of God.

"What did you bring me, Grandma?" Christina jumped up and down, blonde sausage curls bouncing against her shoulders, blue eyes eager. The boys, Bert and Frank, were unloading the peaches Kate had brought, the tins of sorghum and sacks of sugar and flour. Five-year-old Joey clung to his mother's skirts.

"Shush, Tina," Lucy said, frowning at her daughter. "Don't be asking Grandma for things." Mary Ann's effort to rehabilitate Lucy had gone down to failure. Lucy's dress was soiled across the bosom, her graying hair, dark with oil, pulled into a tight, unbecoming knot.

Kate tried to avoid looking at her daughter-in-law, knowing her disapproval would show. The Gilberts had spoiled their only daughter, or she wouldn't have turned into such a slatternly nag. Now she was spoiling Christina, too . . . spending all that time with a curling iron on the girl's hair, time she might better have spent washing her own hair. Brig had always been so fastidious, it must be offensive to him the way Lucy kept the house and herself. Still, he never complained, even when Kate gently prompted him to confide in her.

"I brought some material for school dresses," she told her granddaughter. When Tina's face fell, Kate gave her a stern look. "We have to be practical in these hard times."

Everywhere she turned to look at this beloved mountain valley, lush greenery met her eyes. The aroma of pine hung in the cool air. Aspens glittered, trembling, in the late afternoon sun. The lawn grass lay over, grown tall in the deep shade around the house, and never mowed. Kate took a breath of scented air. How she loved this place. If only she didn't have so many business interests in St. George she would consider moving up here. Even the severe winters wouldn't bother her, although perhaps her blood had grown thin from the hot climate down below.

"I brought a special present for your Papa," Kate told Tina. Brig was still at the sawmill. What a wonderful surprise it would be to have the pictures hung when he came home. The portraits had arrived at last two weeks ago. They had been taken when she and Brig were in Salt Lake almost a year ago. That photographer had no conscience at all. She had to write him several times before he finally finished the pictures, framed, and shipped them. They had been carefully wrapped in quilts for the trip to Pine Valley. Now she helped Lucy and Mary Ann lift the heavy gilt frame from the wagon. Smiling, she held Brig's portrait to show them, leaning it against the wagon.

"Do you like it?" she asked, ignoring Mary Ann's veiled expression. "It's so natural, I think . . . so handsome . . . just like Brig. He felt so much better while he was in Salt Lake."

Lucy's mouth writhed in a strange way, her eyes hard and bitter. "Very handsome. But I can't see that all the doctor's pills and medicines have improved him since then." She picked up the portrait in her plump, strong arms to carry it into the house, Tina skipping behind her.

"We'll hang them in the front room," Kate called after Lucy. Reaching into the wagon, she removed the wrappings from the other portrait. Mary Ann took it from her to carry into the house. "Hang it next to Brig's," Kate told her, following her inside.

Hammer and nail ready, Lucy was standing on a chair by the east wall. "Wait, Lucy," Kate said. "There are two pictures."

Slowly Lucy turned to stare at the portrait of her mother-in-law that Mary Ann held. Her face grew sick and pale. The hammer fell from her limp hand, banging on the chair and then on the floor.

"Well, let Mary Ann do it then," Kate's voice was sharp. "She's handy at everything." What a stupid ninny Lucy was, standing and staring, probably mad because it wasn't her picture. The portraits were a gift for Brig and none of Lucy's business.

As though in a trance, Lucy stepped down from the chair and walked into the kitchen.

All evening Lucy was strangely quiet, not even snapping at the children or nagging at Brig as she usually did. Her attitude vexed Kate. Poor Brig, Lucy seemed destined to spend her life spoiling things for him. He had loved the pictures, hugged her and said over and over what a beautiful mother he had. But as Kate watched him across the supper table she felt a growing sense of unease. Lucy was right about one thing. Brig was no better than he had been a year ago. The doctor had said Brig was suffering from a blood disorder and added confidently that the prescribed tonics would soon clear it up. Obviously, they had not. These past few months, she realized now, he had withdrawn from her, too . . . little by little, so that now he had no one in whom he could confide. The melancholia had deepened; his handsome face was thin and shadowed. He seldom even spoke to his children. Maybe she should move to Pine Valley, Kate thought. Brig needed someone to talk to, someone to lean on, and Lucy would never be the one. He had too much time to himself. The sawmill only ran one or two days a week. Since the mines had closed down, the lumber market was poor. She knew that the days he was not at the mill were spent reading the Bible or the Book of Mormon, or walking by himself. A solitary man, and she was aware people had begun to make fun of him for such peculiar ways. Something had to be done, Kate told herself now as she searched his brown-gold eyes lost in shadows cast by the coal-oil lamp. Whether Lucy liked it or not she was going to take Brig to Salt Lake again. They would try another doctor. Their visit in Salt Lake last year had been so enjoyable . . . going to Conference . . . visiting her old friends. Brig had seemed a different person, like the old Brig of long ago.

After supper he went into the front room and began to read his Bible. Lem, the hired man, was courting a widow down in Diamond Valley, and he departed on horseback as soon as he had eaten. The three women cleaned up the kitchen, Kate wincing at the grubby state of the room. Tomorrow there were peaches to be done. The children were sent to bed, the three boys sleeping outside in the summertime when their grandmother was in residence. Mary Ann slept with Tina, although Kate knew she hated it, for Tina still wet the bed.

Taking her knitting, Kate went into the front room to sit near the lighted lamp. Mary Ann followed with a book she had brought. She never seemed to sew any more since Isaac had brought Tom's books to her.

Lucy seemed distracted and accomplished little on the basket of mending in her lap. Her eyes kept straying to the portraits hanging on the wall: the handsome dark-haired young man with a full moustache and deep-set dark eyes; the gray-haired aristocratic woman, her chin lifted regally, her mouth firm and strong. Kate sighed. It was not a happy beginning to the month she meant for her and Mary Ann to spend here in the mountains. Lucy would surely get over it. After the peaches were done she and Mary Ann would clean house and do school sewing for Tina and the boys. Instead of being so sulky, Lucy should be glad she had so much help.

Tension hung in the silent room. Perhaps a night's sleep would help erase the problem. "I guess the trip tired me more than I thought," Kate said, folding up her knitting. "I'll just go along to bed now. Are you sleeping with Tina, Mary Ann?"

"Is that right, Lucy?" Mary Ann managed to suppress her grimace. Lucy only nodded, her mouth a taut line in her plump pink face. She really is in a snit, Kate thought as she bent to kiss Brigham good night.

Tired as she was, Kate could not sleep. Outside the pine trees sighed sadly in a wind that had an edge to it. Autumn came early here. Through the open door of her bedroom at the head of the stairs she could see the light from the lamp in the front room and hear the creak of Lucy's rocking chair.

"I suppose you're awful proud of those pictures." Lucy's voice was caustic.

"Mama bought them," Brig replied quietly.

"Of course she did," Lucy sneered. "Anything for her little boy."

"Now, Lucy . . ."

"Look at the two of you hanging together on the wall . . . and where is your wife? Out in the cold like she's always been. Nobody cares about Lucy. Why, I guess you'd be ashamed to have my picture hung by yours."

"Lucy, don't. Mama might hear you."

"I don't care if the old bitch does hear me." Lucy's voice rose.

Stunned, Kate pulled the pillow around her ears . . . longing to not hear the words, unable to stop listening.

Something crashed to the floor and Lucy's footsteps moved back and forth in the front room. "You never loved me, Brig," Lucy continued relentlessly. "Never . . . the cruelest thing you ever did was to marry me." There was no answer from Brig. Lucy's shadow moved back and forth on the stair wall, her hands wringing each other. "Oh, I was a fool, too. I thought I could make you forget that girl back east . . . the one . . ." She spit the words out. ". . . the one you committed adultery with . . . the one you were disgraced for."

"Oh, my God, Lucy . . . don't!"

"I was wrong, wasn't I, Brig." The voice was cold and vicious. "It wasn't the girl who was my rival . . . not ever. It was your own mother."

"Lucy! You don't know what you're saying!"

"I know . . . dear God, how well I know after this many years. It's always been your mother. You love her too much, Brig . . . too much for me to compete with . . . too much to be natural."

"Lucy!" The word was an anguished cry.

The foul torrent issuing from Lucy's mouth flowed on. "You couldn't love me . . . couldn't even be man enough to be a husband to me, because all the time you wanted your mother . . . wanted her for a wife . . . not me!"

"Shut up, Lucy!" Brig's voice was a horror-stricken croak. "Shut your filthy mouth or I'll kill you!"

Lucy burst into tears. "God help me," she moaned. "God help us all. Brig . . . where are you going? Come back here!"

The front door slammed in reply, and Lucy dissolved into bitter sobbing.

Kate stared at the dark ceiling of the bedroom. Tears streamed from her eyes and wave after wave of nausea rolled over her.

MOTHER AND DAUGHTER

A good thing she hadn't had time to unpack yesterday, Kate thought, dressing quickly in the cool morning air. It would be that much easier to get ready to leave for Salt Lake. She hadn't slept all night, even after Lucy dragged herself off to bed. By daylight she had made her plans. They would leave for Salt Lake this very day. Brig could see a doctor. There would have to be a divorce. Disgraceful as a divorce might be, she would not have her son imprisoned in a marriage to that filthy-minded Lucy. Oh, poor Brig, hadn't he suffered enough without this? As soon as they could get ready they would leave for Milford to catch the train. Mary Ann could take care of things until they came back, and Lucy . . . Lucy could go to hell where she deserved to go.

He was not in the kitchen where Lucy was starting the breakfast fire. In answer to her question Lucy replied sullenly, "How should I know where he is? He never tells me anything."

Brig must have spent the night in the barn, Kate thought, to get away from that harridan. The early morning sun hung in a sky of cloudless blue. Beneath the rippling shade of the cottonwoods the air was crisp with a promise of coming winter, and Kate shivered. As she hurried toward the barn she saw Lem come out the side door.

"Don't go in there, Sister Hamilton," Lem said, standing squarely in her path, his face contorted. "For God's sake, don't go in there!"

Suddenly cold as ice, Kate brushed past him into the barn. Sunlight slanted through the opening in the loft, and a shadow fell against the far wall. Sickness rose in her, growing until it seemed her brain would burst from the bony case of her skull. The shadow, like a limp rag doll on a string, moved slightly in the breeze from the open door.

Chapter 30

Just as the round edge of the sun disappeared behind Beaver Dam Mountains an evening wind broke the heat, picking up skiffs of dust as it swept through the graveyard. Mary Ann straightened up from laying the roses on Tom's grave, steadying herself with a hand on the top of his tombstone. The last light caught the opal ring on her finger, and it gleamed against gray granite. Thomas Hamilton, the headstone read, died 1884; and next to it, Brigham Young Hamilton, died 1885. Mama had ordered the markers from Salt Lake, and they stood side by side as though the two who lay there were twins. Almost a year now since Brig had joined Tom here. If only the hired man hadn't found him, people might have believed her mother's lies about his death and never known Brig killed himself. The word *suicide* was never mentioned in the family, a conspiracy of silence to protect the children and themselves.

Aunt Nelly and her daughter Josie lay nearby and all Aunt Alice's stillborn babies, with Dru and her babies across the way in the Whittaker lot. Papa had bought a full lot, room for all of them to lie here in the dusty cemetery with the white trumpets of Jimson weed drooping on their graves.

Tamarack plumes dipped and swayed in the gathering twilight. Scattered wisps of coral pink cloud faded into gray, and the sky grew clear and translucent in this final moment before darkness. A cadence of crickets began. That sound, the quality of the light, brought back a spring evening long ago. She saw clearly Tom's profile against the glowing west, smelled the scent of honeysuckle on the front porch. "My love . . ." She almost cried the words aloud. As though

(264)

he were there, she heard his voice echo back from that half-forgotten evening.

". . . Start from here and make your life right again . . ." He had been speaking of Brig then, but it seemed now the words were for her. How can I, she wanted to cry, when I will love you all my life?

He might have been truly there, not dust and bones in the ground, so clearly could she hear him say, "Love me, but you cannot grieve forever. Go free now and make your life right again."

Mary Ann wept then, as though some inner growth filled with festering poison had burst and poured out in her tears. Somehow, when it was over the loneliness and the desperate longing for him had eased. Here in the cemetery she had always felt close to him. Now she could sense his presence. "I will love you all my life," she said into the deepening twilight, and waited. There was no answer.

With a flick of the whip Mary Ann forced the horse into a trot. Dolly was a handsome sorrel, her flanks shining now in the midday sun. She was one of Tom's horses, and Isaac had trained her for the buggy. Oh Tom! The name quivered along her nerves, momentarily possessing her as he had once possessed her. A meadowlark called from the fields, and unaccountably her spirits rose with its rising song. Even without Tom her own life went on. Just as she had last night, she could watch the light fade beyond the western hills, endure the darkness, and watch the morning blossom above the lava ridges, every day a replica of the day before. But perhaps, from within her innermost self, she could somehow change what the morning brought. Life had a way of exacting payments you never anticipated. You learned to accept it as it was, not as you wished it to be. It was a hard lesson. Only now could she begin to guess how difficult it had been for her mother to learn that lesson.

A scorching day. Mary Ann felt the perspiration gather under her arms and breasts, her navy blue delaine skirts smothering about her legs and thighs. A sidelong glance at her black-clad mother's grim face squelched any comment on the weather. Silence was the general rule when they rode together unless they were discussing business. This had been a business day and they had left the house early.

Luke, the hired boy, had hitched the horse to the buggy, listening to Kate's long list of duties for the day. Luke came from a poor and enormous family in the Pig Patch south of town. They had been glad to hire their boy out for board and room and were even more grateful when Kate bought his clothing and paid him a little wage.

Caring for the property filled their time, for Mama was not one to let anything go unsupervised. Her attitude had been a sore trial to Papa. He begged for understanding in the letters Kate ignored and Mary Ann must answer as best she could. When President Snow was last in St. George, he had been to Mexico and seen Papa. He was well, President Snow said, and prospering. "But," he had sighed, "growing old like all of us." It was a good thing Papa was prospering, for he would never again get anything out of Mama. She said unequivocally that the property was hers and what she did with it was none of Burns's business. Chances were, he would never come back now, for antipolygamy laws were being enforced ever more vigorously.

This morning they had collected rents at the building they owned on Main Street: the drugstore, the shoe shop, and the milliner, and the lawyer's office upstairs. Besides the rents there were regular dividends from their stock in ZCMI and the Walker Bank. Alice's house had been turned over to Lucy, the house in Pine Valley sold. Kate had leased the sawmill and saw that Lucy was provided for from that income, since Lucy was totally helpless at finances. The cattle Tom had left to Mary Ann had been turned out with Isaac's herd and he received every third calf for caring for them. By St. George standards they were well fixed, but Kate never let down. After the rents were collected she stopped to pay her tithing at the T.O., then insisted they must drive to the fields to check out the farm she had leased on shares. Brother Ives was not at the farm, but it was obvious he had been and often. There was a good stand of Chinese cane for molasses, and corn and wheat. The lucerne had been cut and stacked to dry. Its sweet, clean smell drifted up to them through the still summer air.

"He's a good worker," Kate said, pleased by the thrifty appearance of the farm.

The sun was at its meridian and blazing hot by the time Kate agreed they should head the buggy toward home. As they passed the green oasis of fields on both sides of the road, blackbirds chattered from the hedgerow of goldenrod along the ditch banks. Sunflowers lifted brown and yellow faces toward the hot sky. Below the fields the river was hidden by a tangle of cottonwood and black willow. When they drove up from the fields into the rock-strewn hills the aromatic odor of mesquite rose in the burning air. Swords of the oose plant thrust upward among the brush where an occasional cactus bloom flashed brilliant color in the brown desolation. A lizard skittered across the dusty road. This was not a land where human beings could ever feel comfortably at home. It fought them constantly, depleted their fortitude, drained their energies. Only a people as stubborn and driven as the Mormons could have made any inroads toward subduing it for their purposes.

Mama had always hated this country, always remembered the beautiful Utah Valley with longing. Pine Valley had been the place where she found respite from the demands of the desert. Now that was ruined for her. They had not been back since Brig's death. Mary Ann still wondered how Mama could ever forgive Lucy for the things she had said in that last hideous quarrel with Brig. Still awake, she had listened in horror, thankful that Tina was asleep. Mama never mentioned it. She saw that Lucy had money to live on, and she was kind to Brig's children, even though the boys were wild and Tina was a spoiled little brat. Brig had been strange, but Mary Ann couldn't believe what Lucy said was true . . . that he wanted Mama that way. It made her sick when she thought about it, just as it had made her sick that night, the taste of bile hot and stinging in her mouth. Sometimes she wondered how Mama lived with it, for she must have heard too. Well, she knew now that we must all live with our own private devils. At least Isaac was happy, and Elizabeth and Burnie, and Jane, too, now that her husband's first wife had died and he was home to stay.

Watching the horse pick its neat-footed way along the rough road, Mary Ann thought hell must look something like this . . . hot and desolate. The brown, barren hills, the black ridges of the lava flows, and beyond them, the red sandstone cliffs. Like hell, too, the inaccessible towering blue of Pine Valley Mountain, forever beyond reach now. It seemed to her, not just Pine Valley, but life, was inaccessible. The two of them, side by side, yet all alone. Glancing at her mother's closed and silent face, she realized that she was totally ignorant of her mother's inner life. Surely she and Papa must have loved each other deeply long ago. Mama had lived a lifetime her daughter knew nothing about and could not understand. Yet she had lived a life before her mother's very eyes that would remain an enigma to Kate.

Only the two of them now, alone and separate from each other even though they shared every day. Make your life right again, Tom had said. One of them must begin and it would not be Mama. She had closed herself in a shell for so many years, and it had only hardened since Brig's death. No one really stands alone, Mary Ann thought now. If we don't reach out and live together, we shall merely die together. Taking a deep breath she almost forced the words out.

"I think we should go to Kanab and visit Isaac next week. I'd like to see the new baby." She was surprised how firm her voice sounded, although she had not been able to say the baby's name . . . Thomas.

Kate's glance was questioning, the blue eyes puzzled. Did her mother guess, Mary Ann wondered, what that trip would cost her in pain, seeing Isaac and Sally's overflowing love for each other and their little family . . . all that she and Tom might have had?

"We'll take a load of peaches to peddle," Kate said, sounding almost cheerful. "Folks in Kanab are always glad to get some fruit. We could make enough to pay our way to October Conference in Salt Lake." Her voice fell. "That is, if you'd like to go to Conference."

Mary Ann smiled. Trust Mama. They could well afford to go without selling fruit, but that was the way Mama thought now, always business. She had nearly doubled the value of everything Papa had left behind.

"I think we should go," Mary Ann answered with decision, then added recklessly, "Maybe we could even take the train to California."

Shocked out of her customary impassiveness, Kate stared at her daughter. Then her lips curved upward and a faint light gleamed in her eyes. "We'll think about it," she said with a nod of her head.

Silence fell. Kate's proud face resumed its accustomed lines, mouth tight, all feeling repressed. Mary Ann sighed, feeling their aloneness again. Perhaps, though, they had made a beginning at sharing. And she retreated into her own thoughts.

They went to all the Church meetings together, she and Mama. Sunday School and Sacrament Meeting, Fast Meeting and Relief Society. There was little else to do in St. George. Mary Ann took no part, she was merely there, lost and empty, and the words falling on her ears had less meaning than the sound of raindrops. She remained an alien, as she had always been. She wanted, as she had always wanted, the impossible . . . freedom in a place where there could be no real freedom. One was forever tied to the demanding land, to family, to the Church. Still she went to meeting, hoping one day a word would be spoken and point the way toward the ultimate truth. More than ever now she longed for that elusive thing called faith, but no matter how much she wished for the comforts given a true believer like Mama, it seemed they were not to be hers.

"Do you want to go by the cemetery?" Kate asked abruptly.

The pain behind Mary Ann's eyes was almost unbearable. Not yet, she could not share what she had found just yet. Nor could she now bring herself to say to her mother that one must not grieve forever.

The reins flicked Dolly's rump and she stepped out smartly. "No, Mama," Mary Ann said. "Dolly's tired. We'd better get home."

The hot silence was like a weight, the only sounds the scrape of buggy wheels on the rocky road and the ring of the horse's metal shoes. Dust lay in a thin layer on her clothes and skin. Rivulets of sweat streaked her face and trickled down her back. The oppressive heat was like a living enemy. For one irrational moment Mary Ann thought this drive might never end. She and that proud and bitter woman beside her would be driving on forever like this . . . through all eternity, in a kind of hell built of black volcanic rock and stinking mesquite.

"She's overheated. Rub her down good while she's cooling off," Mary Ann told Luke. "If anything happens to her I'll have your hide."

"Yes, Ma-am." The boy ducked his head and led the mare into the barn.

With a weary sigh, Mary Ann turned to walk toward the house. Luke was scared of her . . . that mean old maid. Well, maybe she could learn to soften a little. Mama, too, even though she knew the whole town considered them odd.

Intense sunlight blazed from the bare back yard. She stepped into the grape arbor walk from the barn to the house, grateful for the shade, although it was heavy with the scent of fermenting unpicked grapes and the damn sour swill barrel. A black cloud of flies rose from the barrel as she passed. Mama ought to give up keeping pigs and get rid of that thing. Sheep were cleaner, but Mama had always hated mutton.

Dear God, she was tired, the heat wore her down. She needed to change clothes and lie down in the cool house. Mounting the back steps, she let her hand touch the smooth firmness of a blossom on the trumpet vine cascading from the porch. A hummingbird darted among the blooms, its iridescent wings blurring in the air. Filled with life and purpose, it sought the nectar in one bright blossom after another. Why should a hummingbird gathering sweets from the trumpet vine make her want to cry?

Mary Ann paused with her hand on the screen door. On the kitchen table sat the Lowestoft teapot and two cups. They had been so long set away in the top of the cupboard that the pink roses were almost lost in dust. How many years since they had shared a cup of tea?

Brisk and efficient as always, Kate had kindled a fire and set the tea kettle to heat. She turned from the cook stove, picking up a dish towel to wipe the dust from the teapot. For one brief moment her face crumpled into an expression of such anguished regret Mary Ann could hardly bear to watch. At the sound of the screen door opening, Kate straightened quickly. The gray head came up in that familiar arrogant way. Without looking at Mary Ann, she reached into the top of the cupboard for the dusty tea canister, the tremor of her scarred hand barely perceptible.

"Would you like a little tea?" she asked.

Mary Ann felt her throat constrict, but she managed a thin, shaky smile and answered gently. "Yes, I would, Mama. It will help me through the day."